Praise for Ka

'Lots of twists and turns in this gripping story, wealthy family in swanky Monaco. Perfect literary entertainment for the summer season' *Heat*

'For escapism slathered with lashings of sultry glamour, *Saints v Sinners* is the ideal way to while away an afternoon . . . Set against the decadent backdrop of Monaco, Agnews's pitch-perfect eye for detail will keep you captivated page after page' *Sunday Herald*

'A delectable tale of husbands, lovers and how far a woman will go to find happiness' *Daily Express*

'Expect to see this tale of sex and scandal entertaining women on beaches and beside pools all summer long'
Daily Record

'Exciting and surprising . . . it's unputdownable. 5 stars'
Closer

'A grown-up novel that excites from the off: Agnew has a keen eye on the dark side of the high life as well as its shallowness, and her writing is as lively as her plotting' *Metro*

Katie Agnew was born in Edinburgh and spent her childhood in Scotland. She worked as a journalist for many years, writing for *Marie Claire*, *Cosmopolitan*, *Red* and the *Daily Mail* amongst other publications. Kate now lives in Bath with her family.

By Katie Agnew

Drop Dead Gorgeous
Before We Were Thirty
Wives v Girlfriends
Saints v Sinners

Saints v Sinners

Katie Agnew

An Orion paperback

First published in Great Britain in 2010
by Orion
This paperback published in 2010
by Orion Books Ltd,
Orion House, 5 Upper Saint Martin's Lane
London WC2H 9EA

An Hachette UK company

1 3 5 7 9 10 8 6 4 2

A CIP catalogue record for this book is
available from the British Library.

ISBN 978-1-4091-1821-3

Typeset by Deltatype Ltd, Birkenhead, Merseyside

Printed in Great Britain by Clays Ltd, St Ives plc

The Orion Publishing Group's policy is to use papers that are natural,
renewable and recyclable products and made from wood grown in
sustainable forests. The logging and manufacturing processes are expected
to conform to the environmental regulations of the country of origin.

www.orionbooks.co.uk

For my children, Olivia and Charlie

Acknowledgements

Thank you to my brilliant agent, Lizzy Kremer at David Higham Associates, always there with a shoulder to cry on, or a kick up the backside; whichever I needed most. Lizzy, I'd never have done it without you. Thank you, too, to the lovely team at Orion, especially my very talented and patient editor, Genevieve Pegg, for her unwavering support and encouragement, even in times of crisis.

To my wonderful family, thanks for putting up with me, supporting me, lending me your spare rooms and taking over babysitting duties. Thanks to my fabulous friends for inspiring me, cheering me up, reading my drafts and for being good (and occasionally bad) influences on me when I was on deadline. I hope you all spot the cameo roles and private jokes I've included for your amusement!

To Victoria Fulljames and Pegeen Rowley, thanks so much for coming to Monaco with me. I'd never have done such extensive research without you gorgeous girls there to share the champagne, plot ideas and extortionate taxi fares.

And finally, a huge thank you to the expert who kept me straight on fast cars, superyachts, the Grand Prix and male grooming habits.

Without the help of all these people this book would never have been finished. Believe me! It was a turbulent time, but Nice was a ray of sunshine.

Prologue

It was just like Fatty to choose the hottest day of the year to be buried. In life he'd revelled in making people feel uncomfortable and in death he was doing exactly the same thing. Yes, he would have loved this, thought Francesca, wiping a droplet of perspiration from her forehead, two hundred people sweating in their finest designer funeral wear under the scorching Mediterranean sun. It was late September but now, in the throes of an Indian summer, the Cimetière de Monaco felt hotter than the fires of hell.

The mourners were all wearing black. The men in sharp, slim-fitting suits, white shirts offsetting their deep tans, tearless eyes hidden behind black or gold Ray-Bans, fine Italian leather shoes so highly polished that their owners could glance down and admire their own impeccable appearance whenever they felt the urge. The women wore chic black shift dresses by Chanel, Valentino or Dior, their glossy manes, blonde or black, accessorised with elaborate headpieces – feathers, lace, net, pearls. Their sunglasses were so huge and their cheek and collarbones so sharp that it was hard for Francesca to make out one passing acquaintance from the next.

Press helicopters buzzed overhead with more persistence than the wasps that buzzed around the mourners, attracted by the clouds of perfume and cologne. Of course that was why they were all here: the billionaires, oligarchs, racing drivers, actresses, models and movie stars. They didn't give a damn about Fatty's demise but his funeral was a great chance to grab some tabloid attention now that the summer season was over. And wasn't it convenient timing with the Monaco Yacht Show kicking off this weekend? thought Francesca cynically. Everything about the scene was reminiscent of a movie. The beautiful setting, the dazzling cast, the brilliant blue sky. It was so fake that Francesca had to fight the urge to walk off set.

The priest, Padre Gabriele Fontana, had been flown in from Palermo, as requested by Fatty in his will. He was a tall, charismatic, silver-haired fox of a man, who looked more like an extra from *The Godfather* than a man of the Lord. Even he wore black sunglasses. He towered above the grave, with the cemetery falling behind him in terraces towards the sea, perfectly framed by the midday sun. Francesca listened patiently as the priest lamented the tragic and untimely passing of his second cousin and close personal friend, Giancarlo Roberto LaFata, in lyrical, heavily accented English.

Francesca's younger brother, Giancarlo Junior, took a half step closer to her and whispered, 'Who the fuck is he talking about?' into her ear.

'Ssh!' she scolded, but Carlo did have a point. The brave, bold, upstanding man of the people that the priest spoke about bore little resemblance to the lovable rogue being buried there that day.

Yes, Fatty had had his good points. He'd been larger than life and not just because of his six-foot, twenty-five-stone frame. Nobody's voice had boomed louder, nobody's laugh had reverberated around a room in quite the same way. For the first time that day, Francesca felt a tear prickle in the corner of her eye. She remembered him dancing the tarantella at her birthday party last year, eyes flashing, cheeks flushed with champagne, ridiculously light on his feet for such a huge man. She remembered him dressed as Father Christmas when she was a little girl, his breath hot and smelling of brandy, promising presents that always materialised even when he was broke. She remembered him making 'Frankie' pizza in the tiny kitchen of the family restaurant her parents had run when she was a child. Pepperoni and red peppers arranged into a smiley face with mozzarella hair. She'd never forget the bear hugs that had left her gasping for air, or the diamond earrings he'd given her for her sixteenth birthday, the same pair she wore today. Her fingers touched her ears automatically, just to check they were still there, everything so much more precious now he was gone.

But Francesca was under no illusions. The man had been no saint. She also remembered the furious temper, the threats, the accusations. The women whose hearts he'd broken, the innocent employees he'd sacked on a whim, the plates he'd smashed, the birthdays he'd missed, the cars he'd crashed, the lives he'd ruined ... She brushed the single stray tear from her cheek and tried to regain her composure.

'Frankie,' Carlo nudged her back into the present.

The priest was quiet now and the congregation stared expectantly at Francesca. They looked sombre and respectful but no more tears were being shed for Giancarlo LaFata. Francesca stepped forward and stood at the edge of the grave, staring down at the large mahogany coffin below.

She threw a single white rose into the grave. A rose for the man who'd always claimed to come up smelling of roses. Well now he would go down smelling of roses too.

'Bye, Dad,' she said simply. There was nothing left to say.

3

The rest of the family followed suit, throwing in their own flowers and saying their own goodbyes, and then the crowd began to wander off towards their waiting Bentleys, Range Rovers and Ferraris, heading to the lavish wake Francesca had organised at the Hotel de Paris.

The close family lingered by the grave a little longer, each lost in their own thoughts, until finally Carlo said, 'Come on, this show's over. Let's get drunk.'

He glanced at the grave one last time, undid the top button of his shirt, loosened his tie, tossed his thick black hair off his face and lit a cigarette. He was handsome as hell and he knew it. Every move he made was careful, considered and probably practised in front of a mirror. Carlo lived for an audience. He sauntered off, without a backward glance, all long, loose limbs and nonchalance, looking every inch the cool, *GQ* model. But he couldn't fool Francesca. She knew he was hurting inside. Carlo might have inherited his mother's vanity and his father's pride but as she watched her brother go, all Francesca saw was a little boy who'd just lost his daddy.

The others followed Carlo, but Francesca stayed put, her feet cemented to the earth, her eyes fixed on the coffin. Her heart felt heavy but not broken. She felt ... what did she feel exactly? Regret? Remorse? Well, yes, both of those things but there was something else too. More than anything, what Francesca felt was relief. Yes, that was it. Relief. Finally, it was over.

But where had it all begun? In the dusty back streets of Sicily in 1946 when Giancarlo LaFata was born? In Edinburgh in 1970 when the immigrant son opened his first pizza parlour and started the 'Fatty's' brand? In 1988, when the millionaire entrepreneur moved his family to Monaco

4

as a tax exile? Perhaps. But that's not where it started for Francesca. She could pinpoint the exact moment where it had all started to go so horribly wrong …

Chapter One

Four months earlier ...

Francesca woke with a jolt from a disturbing dream that vanished the minute she opened her eyes. She'd had a lot of those recently. She could never remember what had happened but she was left in a cold sweat, with a racing heart and a slight panic in her chest. The room came into focus slowly, muted by the half-light of dawn. Her bed sheets were damp and cold and she shivered in her flimsy cotton nightdress. The air conditioning must be set too high again, she thought. It wasn't midsummer yet. She'd have to have a word with the housekeeper about that later. She pressed the bell on the wall above the bed, signalling to the kitchen that she was awake and ready for her morning coffee.

She rolled onto the dry side of the bed and pulled the sheet up to her chin. William wasn't there, of course. He had taken to sleeping in another room. It had started with him 'working late' and 'not wanting to disturb you, darling' but it had gradually become the norm. Francesca was torn by her husband's decision to leave the marital bed. On the one hand she enjoyed her own space. William was a big man and for eight years she'd had to put up with his snoring, his mumbling and, worst of all, his midnight fumbling. Her husband had his good points but he wasn't the most pleasant bedtime companion. And she certainly didn't miss

6

the sex. Francesca was a good wife, but the truth was, she was relieved to have given up that particular spousal arrangement. She shuddered at the memory.

The last time they'd made love … No! That was silly. Not made love. In hindsight they'd never actually *made love*. That was what people did in films. No, their sex life had never exactly been, well, sexy. The last time they'd had *sex* was six months earlier. She remembered, with a slightly queasy feeling, the way he'd rolled his middle-aged body onto her and kissed her very briefly, before burying his face in her hair and getting on with the job in hand. There was no foreplay. Just a kind of unspoken mutual understanding that this was a ritual they went through once a fortnight because that's what married people did. She'd stared over his shoulder, thinking about work, and the children, feeling, well, nothing much really, other than a vague longing for something better. But their efforts never lasted very long and the performance was short-lived. He'd grunted, lain there heavily for a few minutes, panting into her ear, and then rolled over to his side of the bed.

'Thank you, darling,' he'd said politely, as if she'd cooked him a nice meal. 'Goodnight.'

And then he'd fallen asleep.

Francesca hadn't been able to sleep though. She'd lain awake for hours that night, trying to ignore the nagging voice in her head that kept telling her, over and over, 'There must be something better than this.'

Did she love William any more? God, had she ever loved him properly? Had she been so hell-bent on finding stability that she'd made a terrible mistake? And did he still love her? Sometimes when he looked at her his expression scared her. He looked cold, hard almost. No, she was being paranoid, she told herself. William was a good man. He was just a bit, well, set in his ways. And she was just a bit bored. Marriage was like that, wasn't it? It got monotonous after almost a decade. And anyway, what was the alternative? Divorce? That was unthinkable. Francesca was not the sort of woman to leave her husband. Besides, it would destroy the children. And what about the business? The LaFata empire, LaFata International, was publicly headed by her father Giancarlo 'Fatty' LaFata. But it was Francesca who ran the day-to-day business. And it was William who ran the financial side of things. William and Francesca were not only husband and wife, they were business partners. Their lives were so irreversibly linked that there was no way Francesca could ever unravel herself from him. No, she'd made her bed, she'd thought, glancing at William's snoring bulk beside her, and now she was very definitely having to lie in it.

Francesca didn't know if it was coincidence, or if William had somehow read her mind that night, but for some reason he had decided to move to his own room the very next day. And, now, although she didn't miss the sex one bit, she did have a niggling feeling of failure that he'd chosen to move out of their bedroom. What sort of wife drives her husband to the spare room? Was their relationship such a disaster? Was she *that* unsexy? Did he even care about her any more?

But then William wasn't exactly a passionate man. He didn't get fired up about football, or Formula One, or gardening or books, nor politics or history. And certainly not sex. He was completely addicted to checking the stock markets online but that didn't really count as a passion, did it? She'd dated a string of handsome bastards before William came along, and all they'd taught her was that love hurts. William had seemed delightfully easy in comparison.

8

He wasn't a handsome man. He wasn't particularly tall. His shoulders drooped forward slightly. But it wasn't his looks that had attracted Francesca to him in the first place. His steady, level manner appealed to her and although she'd never fancied him, she had respected his calm approach and had gradually begun to feel a fondness for him that, on a good day, felt a little like love. He was ultra-reliable, never late, he was true to his word, he didn't flirt with her friends, or letch at women on the street. They rarely argued, even now. And most importantly, he never hurt her. He was safe. A little dull, maybe, but safe. And Francesca had had enough turbulence in her life already.

She'd watched her father break women's hearts all her life, she'd witnessed the pain he'd caused her poor mother first hand, and she'd vowed at a young age that she was never going to fall for a philanderer like Fatty. But now she knew that by avoiding the bad parts of a passionate relationship, she'd also sacrificed the good bits. Francesca never felt butterflies in her stomach, she never had wild, clothes-ripping sex, she didn't get serenaded or have poetry written for her. Christ, she didn't even get flowers or chocolates. William just wasn't like that. He didn't really 'do' emotion. He did 'respectable' very well. He was a dab hand at 'reliable'. And he positively shone at 'responsible'. But 'emotional'? No. That wasn't his forte. The few emotions he did have were hidden so deeply that Francesca had only ever caught glimpses of them. She remembered spotting the hint of a tear in the corner of his eye when Luca was born. But by the time Benito had come along two years later, William had felt that a hedge-fund meeting in Frankfurt should take precedence. Here was a man who put his father-in-law's investment portfolio before the birth of his son. He chose head over heart every time. And sometimes Francesca found herself fantasising about men who drove too fast and drank too much, who cried out when they were hurt, and shouted when they were angry, and who made mad passionate love in the middle of the afternoon when they should have been in the office.

Maybe she was just having some sort of early mid-life crisis, she told herself. Craving a romantic fantasy that didn't even exist, just because she was a bit fed up with the routine of her marriage. It wasn't as if she would ever actually have an affair or anything. And it wasn't about sex. Not really. She'd never really been that into it. Maybe that's why she'd said yes to William, the most sexless man who ever lived. Francesca had never experienced that urgent, got-to-have-you-right-now sexual attraction that she read about in books. And, truth be told, she suspected it might be a bit of a myth. And as for romantic love? She wasn't really convinced by that either. Her little sister Angelica fell madly in love at least once a month and it never caused her anything but heartbreak, disappointment and another stint in rehab. No, Francesca didn't need a new man. She had her kids and her career. And, for all his faults, she had William. Francesca sighed a little forlornly at the thought.

There had been one man who'd stirred her. But it wasn't as if she was ever going to see him again. And that was probably for the best. He was just another one of those good-looking bastards she'd sworn to steer clear of all those years ago. Dangerous. And to be avoided at all costs.

Chapter Two

Her gold Cartier Tank Française told her it was only five thirty a.m., but Francesca was wide awake and there was no point in trying to get back to sleep. The business was playing heavily on her mind and if she got up now she could get an hour or two's work done before the children woke up. The credit crunch had finally begun to hit LaFata International. A hotel complex in Dubai had been abandoned half built because the building contractors had gone bust, half the family investments had been wiped out by the falling interest rates, the restaurant chain back in the UK was foundering as people tightened their belts and ate at home instead, and even the Formula One team the family sponsored was in trouble as their new supercar failed to win a single race. Not that that could be blamed on the credit crunch. That was entirely the fault of the German car designer (who Daddy had just sacked).

Her dad kept telling her that everything would be OK, that he had it under control. He'd survived the last recession, he boasted, and he sure as hell would survive this one. Hell, he was going to come out of it smelling of roses. Just like he always did. What was it he always said?

'The bigger the risk, the bigger the reward, Frankie!'

And Fatty had always been a gambling man. How else had he become a billionaire by forty-five? No, he insisted, he had so much money that nothing could touch him now.

Francesca knew this was absolute rubbish. She was more in 'the bigger they are, the harder they fall' school of thought, but there was no telling her dad that. He wouldn't listen. The only thing bigger than Fatty's waistline was his ego. That man was never wrong. You could hold a Jack of Spades in front of him and he would swear blind it was the King of Hearts until you started to doubt yourself.

And so Fatty kept throwing money at new projects and buying up failing companies, shops, restaurants and hotels at what he called bargain-basement prices. He was behaving more like a bankrupt shopaholic, who kept buying shoes on a credit card, than an astute billionaire businessman. It was the one thing Francesca and William agreed on – Fatty seemed to be losing the plot. And so they quietly tried to tighten the family belt behind his back – laying off staff, moving investments and closing down some of the smaller restaurants and hotels in the hope he wouldn't notice. So far they'd got away with it. But their efforts were useless while Fatty kept spending. It was like trying to bail out the *Titanic* with a teaspoon.

Francesca slipped out of bed and opened the white wooden shutters on the floor-to-ceiling windows. The world was caught in that romantic hazy light between night and day. It was magical. The sun was just beginning to rise but the lights of Monte Carlo still twinkled below. She stepped out onto the Juliet balcony and breathed in the cool spring air. There were no clouds in the sky. Later it would be warm, and the tourists would brave the beaches, much to the locals' amusement. It's May, not August, they'd tut as they pulled their jackets around them. But for now, it was decidedly nippy. Francesca heard the door open behind her and Audrey, the pretty, young maid her dad had just employed (they were always pretty but at least this one could make a good cappuccino), appeared with her morning coffee. She thanked the girl and accepted the coffee gratefully, warming her hands on the fine china cup as she shivered on the balcony.

She loved this view from high up on the hill, above the modern apartment blocks, villas, hotels and shops of Monaco. The LaFata mansion, Le Grand Bleu, was a rare gem in the principality, a grand and beautifully restored 200-year-old Italianate house, in its own grounds, tucked away off the cliff road to Italy. It had twelve huge shuttered windows facing the sea, an elaborate frieze running around the roofline and the most exquisite dovecote imaginable perched on the roof. To Francesca the building had always looked like an enormous dolls' house. It was almost too pretty to be real.

More and more apartment blocks had sprung up between the house and the ocean over the years but miraculously, from Francesca's balcony, there was still a clear, unobstructed view of the Mediterranean below. It was as if the place had been blessed. Or perhaps her father had bribed the developers to move their buildings a few metres to the left or right according to how their location would obscure his view. It was the sort of thing Fatty would do. Francesca smiled at the thought.

She remembered when her father had the house painted bright azure blue, back in 1988 when they'd first arrived in Monaco, flush with success and new-found wealth. She'd loved how their home had stood out on the hill, screaming their arrival. Look, it seemed to shout, the LaFatas are here!

'We're a-loud, we're a-brash and we're going to a-make a splash!' her father would chant in his booming Scottish-Italian accent as he floored his Aston Martin up the winding road to the house. You couldn't miss Fatty, with his brand-new French film-star girlfriend, his flash sports car and his bright blue house on the hill.

Francesca had been fourteen then and torn between two worlds. She'd left her old life behind in Edinburgh. It had been a wrench to leave the sturdy family home in Corstorphine, that had once seemed so grand but now looked decidedly modest compared to the palace in Monaco. But she did miss her pale pink bedroom with the flowery Laura Ashley wallpaper, her ponies, Smudge and Fudge, her best friend, Heather, from school. And worst of all her mum, Maggie.

'It's your choice,' her father had told her. 'Come to Monaco with me or stay here with that bitch.'

Her poor mum was anything but a bitch. Her only crime had been to finally divorce her pathologically unfaithful husband. But even at fourteen Francesca had known there was no such thing as choice when it came to Fatty's wishes. He'd narrowed his eyes and added coldly, 'But if you stay, I will disown you, you hear me? You will be as dead to me as your mother. Your choice, Francesca, my darling, your choice.'

Fatty spoke with such venom about his ex-wife that it had made Francesca shudder. Poor Maggie, she'd got rid of her husband but she'd lost her only child in the process. Only now, as a mother herself, could Francesca fully understand what a tough decision that must have been to make. Not that Maggie had had much of a choice. In the end, Fatty's affair with the French tart, Sandrine de la Plage (or Sandy Beach as Francesca and her mum always called her) had been plastered all over the papers and by the time Maggie had filed for divorce, Sandrine was already pregnant. How could Maggie have stayed with Fatty like that, with everyone knowing he'd got another woman pregnant?

14

Maggie was way too proud to put up with that sort of public humiliation and, to be fair, she'd been incredibly tolerant of Fatty's behaviour over the years. And the poor woman had had bigger issues to deal with besides ...

'Do I have to go?' Francesca had asked her mum, tearfully. 'I love Dad but I think I'd rather stay with you.'

Maggie had hugged her daughter tight. 'I know, sweetheart,' she'd said tenderly. 'But this is a great opportunity for you. You're growing up. It's an exciting adventure. You go out there and you shine. But just remember that I'm always thinking about you and whatever happens, I'm always here for you. OK?'

Francesca had nodded, bravely, but the truth was she'd been a bit upset by how easily her mum had let her go.

'And please, Frankie,' Maggie had added gravely, 'don't let him hurt you.'

'Dad would never hurt me,' Francesca had said, feeling annoyed now, sick of constantly having to defend one parent against the other. 'He loves me just as much as you do. He would never hurt me. He's never even smacked me. Just because you don't love him any more doesn't mean you can turn me against him, Mum.'

'I know that, sweetheart,' Maggie had said with a heavy sigh. 'And I don't want to turn you against your dad. Believe it or not I do still love him. I always will, in a way. But he's a difficult man, Frankie. Selfish, self-obsessed and stubborn as hell. His ambition and drive can be frightening sometimes. He'll never let anyone get in the way of his dreams. Even you.'

'But Daddy loves me more than anyone else in the world,' Francesca had declared proudly. He was always telling her that, loudly and publicly, for everyone to hear.

'Yes,' Maggie had replied calmly. 'That's true. Your dad loves you more than anyone else in the world *except himself*! And that's what you have to remember, Frankie. In a fire, Giancarlo LaFata would save himself first and leave the rest of us to burn. If you remember that, you'll be OK.'

She had then kissed her daughter's long, brown hair and whispered, 'I love you' so quietly that Francesca could only just make out the words. Her mum had never been big on sweeping statements of love – she was as strong and proud as her father was, but that's where the similarity ended. While Fatty was passionate, loud, temperamental and emotional, Maggie was quiet, reserved and private. Her love for Francesca simmered silently behind her steely grey-blue eyes, while Fatty shouted his love from the rooftops. Fatty showed his love for Frankie with ponies and Tiffany charm bracelets, while Maggie showed hers with plasters on scraped knees, perfectly ironed school uniforms and the odd home-made chocolate brownie hidden in a packed lunch box. And so Francesca had been torn. Torn between her mum and dad. Torn between Scotland and Monaco. Torn between her old life of middle-class comfort and her new life of high-class glamour on the Riviera. Of course she'd gone with Fatty. Everybody always did.

It had quickly become clear to Francesca why her mum had handed her over to her dad so freely. She was being selfless. Maggie must have known, as she'd hugged her daughter goodbye at the airport, that she would never see her only child again. But she'd stayed strong. Francesca's last memory of her mother was of her smiling warmly and encouragingly, waving her bon voyage as she left on a flight to Nice. In hindsight she had looked very thin, and a little pale. God, how long had Maggie known about the cancer? Francesca would never know. All she knew was that within three months of her arrival in Monaco, her mother was dead. The call from the Edinburgh Royal Infirmary, informing her of her mother's passing, was the first Francesca knew of her illness. Fatty had clearly had no idea either. He'd crumbled to the floor like a giant rag doll and sobbed at the news. Mumbling, 'Maggie, my Maggie, no. No. No …' And then he had never mentioned her again. He'd locked his ex-wife's memory in a vault called 'The Past' and soldiered on.

The next couple of months were a blur of tears and pain. But gradually Francesca had let in the warm Mediterranean sunshine. There was nothing left for her in Edinburgh with Maggie gone. And so the big blue house on the hill had become home. Now she couldn't imagine living anywhere else. Her younger half-siblings had moved down to luxury apartments on the waterfront the minute the ink had dried on their eighteenth birthday cards, but not Francesca. When she'd married William, eight years ago, he'd wanted them to get a place of their own, but Francesca had made it clear that she would never leave her father's house. Just as she'd made it clear that she would never give up her father's name. And so Francesca LaFata she'd remained. Francesca LaFata from Le Grand Bleu. Her name, her home.

Over the years the paint had faded to the colour of the sky and Francesca loved it that way. Whenever her father threatened to have the house repainted, as he did every spring, she would beg him not to. Le Grand Bleu had toned down and merged comfortably into the landscape over the years and Francesca liked to think she'd done the same thing too. She'd arrived in Monaco a brash, naive, gauche teenager, and gradually acclimatised herself to her new surroundings until she'd become as much a part of polite Monégasque society as the Grimaldis themselves. She was proud of what she'd become. She was a shrewd businesswoman, a proud mother, a fine hostess, a loyal daughter, a good wife. Well, maybe not such a good wife but everyone was allowed one failure.

Francesca shivered. Every time she thought about the situation with William, she felt her chest tighten. Maybe she should talk it through with her father? Had her dad noticed they were now in separate rooms? Would he have any wise words of advice? God, it was at times like these that Francesca missed her mother most. No, Fatty wasn't the one to discuss this with. He had enough on his plate with the business, he didn't need to worry about the state of Francesca's marriage. Anyway, he would just tell her to leave. He'd never been a huge fan of William. Fatty was a complete inverted snob. Having come from nothing himself, he had a deeply held belief that those born into money were just lazy, stuck-up slobs, who sailed through life by talking 'proper' and making the right connections at school. It was true that William had been born into privilege in leafy Surrey. He'd gone to Eton and then studied economics at Cambridge. Yes, he came from wealthy stock but William really was quite brilliant when it came to anything financial. He'd already made a name for himself as a director of a city bank by the time Francesca had met him when he was just thirty-three.

They'd gone out together for two years before William had thrown in his job and offered to work for Fatty. Francesca had been so impressed by his commitment to her family that she'd felt she had no choice but to say yes when he'd asked her to marry him. Even then, as she'd prepared for her wedding, she'd worried that she'd made a mistake. William was clever and he was nice. But was *nice* good enough for happily ever after? Deep down, even as she was walking down the aisle, Francesca had known she was sacrificing passion for stability – but decided it was a fair price to pay. William would never let her down and he would never break her heart. How could he, when he'd never really had it to begin with? Besides, William had shown enormous loyalty to her dad in taking over the financial division of LaFata International. He deserved some reward. He certainly never got any thanks from Fatty who, even now, insisted on calling his son-in-law, the financial whizz, his 'accountant'. No, her dad would definitely just tell her to walk.

Besides, he was on his fourth wife now. For a Catholic, he had very little respect for the sanctity of marriage. He seemed to be working on the basis that one wife per decade was a pretty good arrangement. But it was different for Fatty. Men like Fatty were expected to have affairs and trade their wives in for younger, more glamorous models every few years. It just added to their reputation. And as for her brother Carlo, well he changed his women more often than he changed his Calvins. Francesca had to read the British tabloids to keep up with which nubile, blonde model/actress/pop star/'it' girl her brother was bedding at any given time. But she had always presented herself as the serious, trustworthy, respectable LaFata. She was proud of her reputation. OK, so maybe she didn't like it when her younger sister, Angelica, called her the 'boring one', but to Angel, anyone who hadn't freebased heroin was a square.

Francesca could not be seen to up and leave her husband. Women like her just didn't do things like that. She would stay, at least until her youngest son, Benito, turned eighteen. Then she would re-evaluate the situation. She had another thirteen years to wait. Until then, she might as well try to make the most of things. She and William had become virtual strangers lately. Nodding politely to each other at the breakfast table, discussing spreadsheets like work colleagues, air-kissing each other hello and goodbye in public, keeping up appearances in case anyone noticed that their marriage was cracking faster than a dropped vase. Francesca couldn't let things get any worse. She was quite happy to let their sex life go, that she could happily live without, but their friendship? Because there had once been a very good friendship. That she had to reclaim somehow. Maybe she should take him out to lunch this week, just the two of them. It wasn't exactly a grand romantic gesture, but it would be a start.

Friendship would be enough to get her through. After all, nobody could have it all. And Francesca knew she had a lot in her life to be thankful for – her boys, her family, her wealth, her status, her career, her health. She had led a blessed life in lots of ways. Her mum had always made sure she'd understood that.

'Don't become spoilt, Frankie,' she'd warned, over and over, as the family fortune grew, and they'd moved from the council flat in Leith, to the semi-detached new-build in Joppa, and then to the grand Victorian villa in Corstorphine. She'd said it again on the day Francesca had started at Mary Erskine's when she was eleven. 'Just because you're at a private girls' school now doesn't make you better than your old friends,' her mother had reminded her. 'Never forget where you come from, sweetheart. We're not better than anyone else, we've just been lucky.'

'Lucky?!' Fatty had bellowed, overhearing the conversation. 'Lucky?! Don't talk nonsense, woman. It has nothing to do with luck. I did this,' he declared proudly, sweeping his arms around the plush drawing room. '*Mio dio*! When I was a boy in Sicily we were a so poor that I—'

'—had to walk to school with no shoes,' Francesca had interrupted, giggling. She'd heard the story a thousand times before.

'You scoff, young lady,' Fatty had continued. 'But I left school at twelve. Twelve! You hear me? Just six months older than you are now. Top of the class I was but my family, they needed me to work, to bring in the dough. My father he was a useless donkey. Lazy. Mama, she needed me to help, or my brothers and sisters, they would have starved to death without me.'

Francesca and Maggie had shared a 'here he goes again' look and listened patiently as Fatty continued his monologue.

'Then when I was barely fifteen years old, fifteen, you hear?! My father he die and I was the man of the family. But I was brave. A gambler. I took a chance. I left Sicily without a bean in my pocket and I come to Scotland. I couldn't speak a word of English. I make pizza for Uncle Enzo in his restaurant in Glasgow. You remember Uncle Enzo? He die when you were three. Anyways, he pay me nothing. He just let me sleep on his sofa for a year and I eat the scraps from the restaurant. But I wanted more and I persuade him to let me manage his new restaurant in Edinburgh. He say yes because I am family and he knows he can trust me but also because I am cheap and I will live in the dirty room behind the kitchen. That's where I meet your mother. In the restaurant, not the dirty room behind the kitchen, although later she comes there a lot, hee, hee, hee. Anyways, she is a student, she comes in with her hoity-toity student friends. They all think they are too good for Fatty but I teach them different soon enough. Don't I, Maggie? I teach those posh girls that Fatty is a loving machine. Hee, hee, hee. Isn't that so, Maggie?'

It wasn't a question and Fatty hadn't waited for a response, but even at that age Francesca had seen a look in her mother's eye of love mixed with hurt. She'd overheard them arguing loads of times about other women. And even at eleven Francesca had understood that her father had other lovers besides her mum. She'd even seen him with them sometimes in his restaurants; waitresses who stood too close, customers who came in too frequently, and even one of her mum's friends who popped round to visit when Maggie wasn't there. Francesca had always been a bright girl, she wasn't easily deceived.

'By the time Enzo has his third heart attack I have turned the restaurant into the little gold mine. I have made the old man rich and so, when he dies, he leaves me the restaurant in his will. I change the name from LaFata's to Fatty's, change the decorations to something more bright, more *moderno* and *opla*! Suddenly it is the most popular restaurant in town. His son, my cousin, Enzo Junior, he never forgive me. To this day that man will not speak my name. He hates that I make Fatty's such a success. Ah, but jealousy, she is a terrible emotion. Isn't she, Maggie?'

He'd glanced at his wife with a smirk on his face and then carried on. 'Anyways, by the time you are five year old, my darling, I am wealthy man. I buy us a house and another restaurant. And then I buy three more restaurants and a half a hotel with my second cousin Tony. Then I buy us this beautiful big house, another hotel, and this summer I open restaurants in Birmingham, Newcastle, Manchester and London. Soon there will be a Fatty's on every high street in the country. And now today, my *bambino*, she go to Mary Erskine School for Girls and I am a proud, proud Papa, because *mia figlia*, she will never have to walk to school with no shoes on!'

And then her dad had whisked her out of the house and into his shiny green Bentley (registration number Fatty1) which Francesca had always been rather embarrassed about, preferring the relative anonymity of her mum's BMW. But her dad had always loved his flash toys. And who could blame him? As he so often said himself, he was the shoeless immigrant boy without a penny to his name – who could begrudge him the trappings of wealth that his hard work had earned him?

Francesca stared down the hill, over the rooftops of the apartment blocks, the shops, the casino, the Hotel de Paris, and east towards the harbour at Port Hercule. She was so familiar with the yachts that she could spot her friends' and families' even from up here. There was Carlo's brand-new 120-foot boy-toy. It was sleek, black and menacing, and Francesca thought it looked as if it should belong to a Bond villain. The name on the stern read *Pulling Power*, but Carlo always referred to the yacht as the 'Pussy Magnet'. Angelica's yacht was much prettier, hell, everything about Angelica was pretty! It was just a modest, white wood eighty-footer. Fatty had bought it for her twenty-first birthday and called it *Daddy's Money*, which made him laugh and Angelica blush. William and Francesca owned a sturdy 150-foot yacht called *The Conqueror* (as in William the Conqueror, which always made Francesca cringe) but even that looked like a minnow compared to Fatty's beast, the 240-foot *Vigorosa III*.

'Ooh, couldn't you have called it "Lady Jade"?' Fatty's latest wife had whined when he'd first taken the family to see his new toy.

Fatty had laughed heartily and patted his young wife's pert bottom. 'Don't be silly, my darling. I might sell you to an Arab prince but I am keeping this beauty for ever!'

Francesca squinted and frowned. The early morning light was still not good but she could tell something wasn't quite right. *Vigorosa III* wasn't moored neatly between *Pulling Power* and *The Conqueror* as usual. In fact, from up here it looked as if *Vigorosa III* was heading towards the mouth of the harbour. Why would her dad be taking the yacht out at this time of day? Surely he was asleep downstairs in his room? He rarely let the fifteen-man crew take her out without him. Not without a good reason. Sometimes they picked up friends or business associates from Cannes, Antibes or St Tropez but never without warning and Francesca would have known if he'd had a visit scheduled. She knew every date in her dad's diary. Anyway, it was Saturday. Her dad never worked on Saturdays. Francesca chewed a broken nail nervously. Something didn't feel right. What if the yacht had been stolen? Pirates? You read about things like that happening in the Caribbean – crews being murdered in their cabins and yachts being taken in the dead of night – but not here, in Monaco. Maybe Carlo had set the yacht adrift as a drunken practical joke? But no, surely not even Carlo would do something that stupid. And the crew would have stopped him! Francesca rubbed her temples. This was all wrong.

She went back inside and paced her bedroom for a while, then she went back out onto the balcony and checked that she wasn't hallucinating. No, *Vigorosa III* was definitely out of her mooring. Oh rats! She was going to have to do something about this. She ran down the sweeping spiral staircase to the first floor where her dad's bedroom was. She knocked loudly on his door. Silence. She knocked louder. Nothing.

'Dad?' she called. 'Dad? Are you there?'

Francesca would never normally enter her father's bedroom, especially now that Jade had moved in. But there was something so odd about seeing the *Vigorosa III* floating adrift in the harbour that she knew she had to do *something*.

She opened the door quietly and peered in. Her father's was the largest bedroom in the house; it had dark wooden panelled walls, an enormous, ornate marble fireplace, two huge balconied windows and a giant, oak, hand-carved antique four-poster bed, swathed in dove-grey, velvet curtains. In the middle of this huge bed lay a tiny blonde girl. She was fast asleep on top of crisp sheets, in a blue silk negligee, her pale blonde curls falling around her oh-so-pretty face in clouds. Her full lips pouted as she murmured in her sleep and her right thumb hovered by her mouth as if she was about to suck it. She had the face of an angel and the body of a Playboy Bunny. The negligee had ridden up to reveal curvy, toned, tanned legs, and the girl's enhanced left breast had escaped altogether. This was Francesca's latest 'stepmother', 26-year-old Jade LaFata. A stepmother who was nine years younger than her. How ridiculous was that?!

'Jade,' whispered Francesca from the door. 'Jade, wake up.'

Jade murmured a little more loudly, stretched out her brown legs and then turned onto her stomach and continued to sleep. Francesca tiptoed into the bedroom and stood by the bed.

'Jade,' she called a bit more loudly this time. 'Wake up.'

But Jade didn't move. Francesca leaned over and gently prodded the girl's shoulder. Jade stirred, muttered something that sounded vaguely rude and then lay there in silence again.

'Jade!' Francesca shouted this time, about three inches from her stepmother's face. 'Wake up!'

'Hmm?' Jade turned onto her back slowly and opened her enormous blue eyes. She stared at Francesca for a few moments, looking bewildered, as if she'd never seen the woman before, and then she rubbed her eyes and said, 'Frankie? What the …? It's the middle of the night. What's wrong?'

'It's nearly six o'clock,' said Francesca.

'Exactly,' said Jade. 'The middle of the night.'

'Jade,' said Francesca patiently, knowing now wasn't the time to start a debate about exactly when night finishes and day begins. 'Where's my dad?'

Jade looked at the empty half of the bed beside her and then peered around the rest of the room. She looked confused. But then Jade often looked confused. She was a sweet girl, kind and undoubtedly pretty, but she was never going to be invited to join MENSA, that was for sure.

'Um ...' Jade sat up and tucked herself back into her nightie. 'Um ...' She looked around the bedroom some more. 'I don't know where Fatty is.'

'Did he come home last night?' asked Francesca, patiently. Talking to Jade was a bit like talking to a three-year-old.

Jade thought for a minute, clearly trying to remember the events of the previous evening and then she frowned. 'No,' she said with a little pout. 'He called me at around eleven and said he was going to be late, that he'd bumped into an old friend, and that I should go to bed without him.'

That wasn't unusual. Fatty led a very independent life. Although he'd banned Jade from partying with her friends the moment they'd become engaged, he himself continued to gamble, drink and party with his old cronies almost every night. Jade seemed to spend most of her evenings watching TV on her own. Francesca almost felt sorry for her. Almost.

'He said he'd see me in the morning,' remembered Jade. 'But he's not here.'

'No,' agreed Francesca. 'He's not here. Look, you go back to sleep, Jade. I'll call him. He's probably at some all-night poker game.'

'Why?' asked Jade with wide eyes. 'What's wrong?'

'Nothing for you to worry about,' said Francesca softly. 'There's just a little problem with Dad's yacht, that's all. You sleep. I'll see you later.'

'Oh, OK, Frankie,' said Jade obediently. 'Night night.'

'It's the bloody morning,' Francesca muttered to herself as she shut the bedroom door behind her.

She grabbed the nearest phone, on the table on the landing, and pressed 1, which went straight through to Fatty's mobile number. The phone was dead. 'This number is currently unavailable,' a robotic voice told her. 'Please try later.'

'What?!' Fatty's phone was never switched off. Francesca tried again immediately. And then she tried again, and again and ... The same thing happened every time.

Francesca took a deep breath. There had to be a logical explanation for all this. She dialled 6, the direct line to the satellite phone on her dad's yacht. It rang and rang and rang but nobody answered.

'What the hell is going on?' she muttered to herself, as she hit the next number. James would know what was happening. He was the captain of *Vigorosa III*. A strapping, blond, ruddy-cheeked Canadian in his late forties, he'd worked for Fatty for ten years. If anyone knew what was going on it would be him.

'James?!' said Francesca frantically when he finally answered, sounding groggy. It was obvious she'd woken him up but this was an emergency. 'At last! It's Francesca here. Sorry if this is none of my business but what's happening with *Vigorosa*? Where are you taking her?'

There was a long silence before James replied. 'Francesca, I'm onshore with the rest of the crew. Your dad gave us the night off. He came on board last night and practically threw us off the yacht.'

'What? I don't understand ...'

'Neither did we,' said James a little indignantly. 'He said he just wanted some peace. I thought maybe he'd had an argument with Jade or something. Not my place to question him. He's the boss. Um, why? Is there a problem?'

'James, please just get to the harbour. Either Dad's taken *Vigorosa* out on his own or she's adrift.'

'Holy shit,' said James. 'Fatty never takes her out on his own. What's he playing at?'

'I don't know,' replied Francesca, panic rising in her chest. 'Please, James, just go and find out what's happening. I'll meet you at the harbour in fifteen minutes.'

She ran back upstairs, two at a time and burst into William's room without knocking. William was sitting at his desk in his checked pyjamas with his glasses perched on the end of his nose, his laptop open in front of him. He jumped, and snapped the computer shut in a hurry. There was a hint of a blush in his cheeks. Francesca wondered briefly if he had something to hide from her, maybe he was looking at porn? She quickly banished the thought from her head.

'Don't we have an agreement that we knock these days?' he asked. He sounded almost angry but now wasn't the time to worry about that.

'No,' said Francesca breathlessly. 'Not when Dad's phone's switched off, the *Vigorosa* is out of its berth and James is onshore with the rest of the crew.'

'Oh,' said William, the colour draining from his face. He walked to his window and opened the shutters. 'Oh,' he said again, peering down the hill to the harbour where the yacht continued to drift towards the harbour mouth. 'That's not right, is it?'

He picked up his mobile from the desk and rang Fatty. Francesca rolled her eyes.

'Don't you think I've tried that?' she asked impatiently.

'Well, there's no harm in trying again, is there,' he said in a patronising tone.

She watched as William shook his head. 'Dead,' he said. 'He never switches his phone off.'

'I know,' said Francesca. 'I thought the same thing. That's why this is all so worrying. And nobody's answering the phone on board either.'

'Should we call the police?' asked William, still pressing redial on his phone. 'Do you think it might be theft? That's over a hundred million euros' worth of yacht down there and we have absolutely no idea who's controlling her.'

Trust William to think about money at a time like this, thought Francesca, but she kept it to herself. Now was not the time to start a petty argument.

'The thought did cross my mind, but no, let's not involve the police yet, there might be a perfectly reasonable explanation,' she said instead, trying to convince herself more than William. 'Let's just get down there. I've told James we'll meet him at the harbour. I'll throw some clothes on and see you out front in five minutes.'

William nodded gravely. He looked serious but not panicked. If Francesca had one good thing to say about William it was that he was incredibly cool in a crisis. By the time she'd thrown on a pair of white jeans and a blue cashmere sweater and run downstairs, he was waiting in the passenger seat of her white Range Rover Sport. He preferred to be driven. He was a nervous driver and, besides, his eyesight wasn't very good. William had always been happy to let Francesca take the driving seat.

Chapter Three

Carlo LaFata winced at the sound of his phone ringing. He automatically threw his hand in the general direction of the bedside table, knocking over a half-drunk bottle of Cristal as he did so.

'Bollocks,' he muttered as the room filled with the smell of stale champagne.

He flailed around in the dark, trying to find the offending bottle. The cowhide rug beside the bed was soaked now and the bottle empty. His phone stopped ringing. Who the hell was calling him at this time? And what the fuck time was it anyway? It had to be the middle of the night. He felt like he'd only had about two minutes' sleep. Carlo felt around for his iPhone. He eventually found it under a damp tissue, which he threw on the rug beside the empty bottle. He squinted at the phone. 6.27 a.m. Missed call. Frankie. Well, she could wait. Just because his perky, do-good big sister was up at this ungodly hour didn't mean he had to be. And it was a Saturday, for Christ's sake! What was she thinking? Nothing could be important enough to wake him up at half bloody six. She knew he never went to bed until at least three on Friday.

He flopped back down on his pillow. The world spun around him for a moment and a wave of nausea hit him. He had *the* hangover from hell. Again. What time had he got to bed? *How* had he got to bed? Carlo had absolutely no clue.

He tried to piece together the events of the night before but there was nothing – just a big, fat, gaping black hole where his memory should have been. Urgh! What did it matter? Right now all he needed was some more sleep. The spilled champagne could wait and Frankie could definitely wait. He closed his eyes. Immediately, the phone started ringing again.

'Oh, for Christ's sake …' He picked up the phone again. It was Frankie again.

'Fuck. Off,' said Carlo, pressing the reject button and turning the phone off.

What was with her this morning? He'd probably forgotten someone's birthday or something, and Little Miss Efficiency was calling to remind him. Sleep. Now he would go back to sleep. Whatever Frankie wanted could wait. Carlo lay in the pitch black and waited for sleep to come. But now his head was pounding and his mouth was disgustingly dry and it tasted of stale champagne and, oh God, he felt queasy. The room was spinning in the dark. And something else was wrong. Something he couldn't quite put his finger on. Carlo felt strangely claustrophobic.

The apartment was in total darkness thanks to the black-out blinds on the windows. He had great panoramic views of the beach and the sea from his fifth-floor penthouse but those early morning sunrises were a killer for a party boy like him. And it should have been deadly quiet thanks to the triple glazing he'd had installed. Carlo loved the sea, he could stare at the waves for hours, but the noise of them destroyed his lie-ins. He'd had the sea silenced. So what the hell was that gentle, snuffling noise coming from somewhere near his left ear? He lay there and listened for a while to the soft rise and fall of the snuffling. It sounded almost like a kitten purring. But of course he didn't have a kitten.

A kitten would need to be fed and watered and loved. And that would be far too much of a commitment for him. He groaned inwardly. Oh God, not again ...

Carlo couldn't see a thing but he had a niggling feeling that perhaps he wasn't exactly alone in his apartment. He walked his fingers tentatively along the sheets, under the duvet, until he touched something warm, soft and undeniably human. Shit! He pulled his hand back as if he'd been electrocuted. There was definitely someone there, in his bed. His heart sank. Why did he keep doing this? He'd made a pact with himself that he would never, *ever*, invite a woman to stay the night again. It always got so messy and awkward in the morning, with her asking when she could see him again, and insisting he took her number, when all he wanted her to do was disappear.

Carlo did not want a relationship. What was so wrong with that? He loved women, loved sex, but he was only twenty-three and he sure as hell was not ready for the whole boring, monogamy thing that girls seemed so keen on. They just didn't get it. OK, so he bought them drinks, danced with them, kissed them, told them they were beautiful, took them home to bed, showed them a good time and then, bam, in the morning they thought it was true love. What part of One-Night Stand did these girls not understand? They watched too many cheesy movies and read too many trashy novels. Got silly ideas into their pretty little heads about romantic walks along the beach and diamond engagement rings. No, Carlo was not supposed to be in this situation. It was the drink! A few glasses of bubbly and his dick started to overrule his brain. And so here he was again, lying beside some unknown woman, with no idea who she was, how she'd got there in the first place, or how he was going to get rid of her.

The snuffling got louder, turned into a mumble and then the mystery houseguest rolled towards him. Carlo jumped out of bed and stepped in the puddle of champagne. Something cold and sticky stuck to his bare foot. How gross! It was a used condom. He kicked it off his foot in disgust. The fact that he'd had safe sex was of little consolation right at this moment.

He stumbled his way towards the en-suite bathroom in the dark. He felt for the door handle and the light switch, ducked inside and locked the door behind him. He blinked under the spotlights and had to steady himself on the limestone sink. His head was killing him and his reflection was swimming in front of his bleary eyes in the mirror. He was damned if he could remember a thing about last night. He stared at his reflection. 'Who the hell is in my bed?' he asked himself. But the tall, dark, dishevelled young man in the mirror, with the bloodshot eyes, had no answers. Carlo splashed his face with cold water and then slapped his cheeks hard, trying to knock some sense into himself. OK, so he'd gone to Stars'n'Bars for a bite to eat with the guys – burgers and beers. Then he and Christian had gone on to Jimmy'z nightclub. Christian was his best mate. The heir to a Swedish frozen foods empire, and as blond as Carlo was dark, they were quite a double act. The ladies didn't stand a chance with those two in the room. During the drive to Jimmy'z they'd picked up a couple of young English students, on a day trip from Nice, just for the ego boost. It was so easy to pull girls in his Lamborghini Gallardo Spyder. Christian had a black one, but Carlo preferred his red model. That baby never failed, it was almost as much of a pussy magnet as his yacht. The girls had been cute enough, but their grating accents had put Carlo off, and he didn't remember talking to them again once he'd paid for them to get into the club and bought them their first drinks.

Jimmy'z had been full of the usual crowd – friends from way back, whose dads were mates with his dad, the Casiraghis were there, Lewis Hamilton and his Pussycat Doll, and lots of tanned men in white shirts gyrating on the dance floor with tall, skinny, blonde girls, who looked like models, but were probably just expensive Russian hookers. It was sometimes hard to tell the difference between an oligarch's daughter and a prostitute in Monaco. Especially with your beer goggles on.

They'd necked a few bottles of Cristal, celebrating some business deal of Christian's that he'd just signed over lunch in Paris.

'What was the deal?' Carlo had asked him.

But Christian had just shrugged, casually, and said, 'I dunno. Something to do with prawns.'

And then the two young men had laughed hysterically because, well, prawns were just funny, weren't they? Christian didn't exactly have a head for business. He was a director of the company on paper. But in reality he just went to the odd meeting with his dad, looked the part in his Savile Row suit, and signed whatever document was waved under his nose with his Mont Blanc pen. He was the first to admit that he didn't really get what was going on, but he did love having his own PA (who was quite tasty) and a helicopter at his disposal. Christian was well built, energetic, eager to please, loyal and enthusiastic, kind of like a Golden Retriever, Carlo had always thought. He was one of the few people Carlo genuinely loved and trusted. It was a cliché, and a bit soft, but Christian was like the brother Carlo had never had.

Much to his father Sven's regret, Christian had inherited

both his good looks and his limited intellect from his mother, Inga, a singer from Norway who'd enjoyed a couple of minor hits in the eighties with her hilariously cheesy brand of Euro pop. The irony was that Christian's younger sister, Ingrid, was the spitting image of her dad – mousy, scrawny, bespectacled and knock-kneed – but she was at Harvard Business School and everybody knew that she was the one who would take over the family business when she graduated. And when that happened Christian would be the first to congratulate her. He didn't seem to have an envious molecule in his body.

Carlo sometimes wished he could be more like his friend – easy-going, laid-back and generous of spirit. Carlo wasn't tight. He parted with his money (well, his dad's money) freely. Wasn't he the first to pay for a table at the Amber Lounge – even during Grand Prix week when it costs £24,000? But when it came to his emotions Carlo knew he could be a bit, well, mean really. He didn't like to show his feelings. It wasn't that he didn't have feelings. But if you showed how you felt you could get hurt. And who wanted to get hurt? And as for envy? Christ, he was riddled with the stuff, especially when it came to his sisters ...

Unlike Carlo, who prided himself on the fact he'd never fallen in love and never been dumped, Christian fell in love easily and got dumped often. Right now, flavour of the month was an American heiress called Sasha Constantine, a sexy brunette with a fiery temper and way too much attitude for her own good. She was undeniably hot, like seriously, achingly, orgasmically hot, but Carlo didn't like her one bit. Partly because she was mouthy, opinionated and argued with everything Carlo said, and partly because she'd been monopolising his best friend's time since before Christmas. But mostly he didn't like her because she so obviously couldn't stand him. And Carlo had no time for people who didn't like him.

In fact, come to think of it, Sasha had turned up last night. Carlo remembered now. She'd arrived with her annoying little friend, Teri, the daughter of a Texan oil baron who Carlo had accidentally laid one drunken night last summer and who now seemed to think it was her right to climb onto his knee every time they bumped into each other. She'd done that last night and he'd pushed her off. She'd fallen on the floor in a heap and then run off to the Ladies in floods of tears. Silly girl. Carlo smirked at himself in the mirror. It had been quite funny really. Oh God, that was it though. Now he remembered! Sasha had had a go at him about the way he'd treated Teri. And then she'd had a go at him about the way he treated women in general. And then she'd shouted something about him being a pathetic piece of Euro trash, told him she hoped he had the clap and thrown a shot of tequila in his face. Bitch!

Then what? Carlo screwed his face up and willed the events of the night before to come back to him. But it was no good. The fight with Sasha was blurry at best, and anything that happened after that was a total blank. He sighed and wrapped a fluffy white towel around his naked waist. So who the hell was that in his bed? Please, God, don't let it be Teri.

He crept back into the bedroom, leaving the bathroom door ajar and the light on so that he could see. His eyes acclimatised to the half-light and he could now clearly make out the shape of a body in his bed. She was curled up in the foetal position, duvet pulled up to her chin, with a mass of dark hair covering her face. A brunette? Well, that made a change. And it ruled Teri out at least. Phew! Carlo was intrigued now. He didn't normally *do* brunettes. He stepped closer to the bed and leant towards the girl. She smelled of oranges and vanilla. It was a vaguely familiar scent but Carlo couldn't place where he'd smelled it before. The girl was still snuffling and purring in her sleep. Carlo nervously tried to push a few strands of hair off her face so that he could see what she looked like, but it was so thick and long that it was impossible to uncover anything except a glimpse of full, quivering, half-open lips. The only bit of flesh he could see was an inch of shoulder poking out from the top of the duvet. It was tanned and smooth. Carlo wanted to see more. He peeled the duvet back as gently and slowly as he could until the girl was naked to the waist.

Whoah! The boy had done good! The naked body in front of him was supremely hot. Slim, curvy, toned and utterly gorgeous. Carlo felt himself getting hard as he let his eyes feast on her full, round breasts, her toned arms, the curve of her waist and her tight brown stomach. He let the towel slip from his waist as he watched her tits rise and fall as she breathed. He didn't know who she was and he couldn't see her face and somehow that made her all the sexier. Maybe last night hadn't been such a mistake after all.

He spotted a pair of lacy black knickers on the floor at his feet. He picked them up and checked the size. Petite. That was good. He wasn't into big butts. And then he couldn't help himself ...

'Carlo, you fucking pervert! What the hell are you doing?!' shrieked a voice.

He dropped the knickers and felt his hard-on subside as he stared in horror at the girl in his bed. She was sitting bolt upright and pushing her wild mane of hair off her face.

'Holy fuck, what am I *doing* here?!' she continued ranting. 'Why am I naked? Why are *you* naked? What were you doing with my panties and, oh my God, you were playing with yourself, you disgusting, perverted, fucking bastard!'

'Sasha!' Carlo couldn't have been more shocked or appalled if he'd found a headless horse in his bed. 'It's you …'

Chapter Four

James Sanderson had spent his entire adult life on the water. For almost thirty years, yachts of all shapes and sizes had been his livelihood and his home. He'd survived storms off the Cape of Good Hope, icebergs off Nova Scotia and a shark attack off New South Wales. And he had never, *ever*, lost a vessel. Until now ...

He was proud of his one hundred per cent safety record. He was middle-aged now and his years of high adrenalin were over, so he'd made himself a comfortable life here in Monaco, working for Fatty LaFata. He liked his boss well enough. Granted, the guy was full of bullshit, and had an ego larger than his bank balance, but he sure did make James laugh. Fatty was also generous, paying a third more than the going rate for the captain of a superyacht, and he pretty much let James get on with running *Vigorosa III* without sticking his nose in. In fact, James thought of *Vigorosa* as his own. He was the one who knew her inside out. OK, so he didn't use the cinema room, the retractable helipad or the miniature infinity pool (even though Fatty had told him to help himself), but he was the one who could turn that beauty on a halfpenny, outrun the paparazzi during the Cannes Film Festival, or park her in a tight spot during the upcoming Grand Prix weekend. The truth was James loved that yacht more than he'd ever loved any woman. And now she was floating adrift in the harbour. At best it was embarrassing. At worst it would lose him his job. And his beloved *Vigorosa*.

'Monsieur Sanderson?' asked the policeman. 'You are the captain?'

'Yes, sir,' said James, shaking the guy's hand firmly.

James had taken it upon himself to contact the Maritime Police. Francesca LaFata had said she'd meet him at the harbour but screw that. This was an emergency. James could tell no one was at the helm. Christ, any idiot could see that her motor wasn't running. He also knew the tides better than anyone and if they didn't get on board the *Vigorosa* in the next twenty minutes she was going to crash straight into Roman Abramovich's yacht, and that would be a humiliation James would never live down.

'We will take our boat,' said the policeman, briskly.

'Sure thing,' James replied and followed the guy down the steps to the red police boat, nodding politely at the skipper as he did so.

'My colleague will ensure no other vessels are in danger from *Vigorosa III* while we go aboard,' explained the policeman. 'And then you will take her back to her mooring promptly.'

They chugged between the moored yachts and superyachts, then across the harbour towards *Vigorosa III*. As they pulled up beside the giant yacht, James felt a wave of nausea wash over him. Thirty years at sea and this was the closest he'd ever felt to seasickness. Something in his bones told him that today was a day that would change his life. And not in a good way. James was not a nervous man. He thrived on challenges and rarely felt fear, even when he knew his life was in danger, but as he followed the policeman up the ladder to the first deck of *Vigorosa III*, James's heart was in his mouth.

'*Allô!*' called the policeman as he climbed on board the lowest deck. 'Monsieur LaFata!'

'He won't be on this deck, sir,' said James. 'This is the crew's quarters. Mr LaFata has never been down here. Follow me.'

James led the policeman to the glass lift that would take them to the higher decks. *Vigorosa* was eerily quiet. James was used to hearing the crew chatting on deck, music playing through the Bang and Olufsen sound system, the LaFata family and their friends laughing upstairs, the sound of wine glasses clinking, caterers carrying plates, Fatty's grandsons running barefoot on the wooden decks. But now there was nothing but the sound of the waves below and the shrieks of the seagulls overhead.

They checked Fatty's suite first. James held his breath as he opened the heavy oak door, half expecting to find Fatty laid out on his enormous bed, dead from a heart attack. He wasn't one for drama, but James had been worrying about the boss's health for some time. The guy was well into his sixties, obese and his eating habits were terrible, even by Italian standards. And as for the amount of alcohol the guy consumed … jeez, it was beyond belief. Wine, champagne, brandy, cognac, whisky, beer, whatever he could get his hands on as long as it was liquor. James had never seen a drop of water pass the guy's lips. Lately Fatty's breath had become shorter and his determined stride had become more of a slow waddle. James had found himself worrying that his boss might not be around for much longer. He didn't worry about his job, whoever took over *Vigorosa III* would almost certainly keep him on. No, he worried about Fatty because he would miss the guy if he was gone.

James was hugely relieved to find the master suite empty. He checked the dressing room, the en-suite and the private lounge. Everything was as it had been left the night before. The bed made, cushions plumped, flowers in their vases, *The Economist* (Fatty's) and the latest issue of *Hello!* (Jade's) laid out neatly on the glass coffee table, just so. They checked the other four bedrooms but they too were empty and untouched. And then they took the lift up to the top deck.

James had always thought *Vigorosa III* was like a boutique hotel on water, not that he'd ever stayed at a boutique hotel, but he'd flicked through Jade's magazines often enough to know what one looked like. The yacht had been built just down the coast in Cannes and the interior styled by some fancy lady designer from Paris. James and the policeman wandered into the lounge looking for signs of life.

'And you say Monsieur LaFata was on board last night?' asked the policeman, eyeing the expensive white leather Italian sofas, the goatskin armchairs, the enormous plasma TV and the state-of-the-art, remote-control fire. The guy seemed unimpressed by the lavish surroundings. He saw yachts like these every day in his job, James guessed.

'Sure was,' replied James. 'He came on board at about eleven-thirty p.m. and told us to go ashore. He gave me a bundle of cash and said I should show the guys a good time.'

'Was this normal?' asked the policeman.

'Hell no!' replied James. 'He's never done that before in the ten years I've been working for him.'

There was no sign of Fatty having been in the lounge. The boss wasn't known for clearing up after himself. His huge arse would have left a dent in the sofa and a cigar butt or two would be lingering in the ashtray. James fingered the sterling silver ashtray on the walnut coffee table almost fondly. He'd always hated the stench of the guy's cigars but now he wished the room was filled with the smell of stale tobacco. Any sign of life would have been a relief.

'Please do not touch anything, Monsieur Sanderson,' said the policeman, curtly. 'We may be dealing with a crime scene.'

'Uh, yeah, sure,' said James, pulling his hand away. A crime scene? Shit! He hadn't thought of it like that.

'And how was Monsieur LaFata?' asked the policeman as he headed through the open French doors and out into the outdoor seating area.

James followed him. 'He was in good spirits,' he remembered. 'Jolly, I would say.'

'Under the influence?' asked the policeman, curtly. It wasn't such a rude question. Fatty was one of the most public characters in Monaco and everybody knew the guy enjoyed a drink.

' Well, I wouldn't say he was drunk exactly,' replied James, carefully. 'But he'd certainly had a few ...'

The two men eyed the teak sofas and steamer chairs on deck. Nothing looked as if it had been breathed on, let alone sat on by a 350-pound butt.

'And he was alone?' continued the policeman, examining the infinity pool and hot tub.

'Yes,' said James, peering into the swimming pool, relieved to see the water was still and clear. There was no body lurking beneath the surface.

'What's through here?' asked the policeman, gesturing towards a set of double doors.

'The formal dining room,' replied James. 'Well, it's more of a ballroom to be honest, it's where the LaFatas host dinners and dances. But it's only ever used for parties so it's probably locked ...'

But the dining room wasn't locked and the policeman was

already entering. He found the light switch and the grand hall was immediately lit up by a giant glass chandelier.

'*Mon dieu!*' exclaimed the policeman.

This was the fanciest room on the yacht by far. While the rest of the décor was modern, sleek and very Manhattan bachelor pad, the dining room was pure indulgence and fantasy. It had been Jade's project. It was a circular room with a domed ceiling, painted in frescoes of angels, mermaids and nymphs, with the faces of Fatty's children and grandchildren. And of course there was a life-size painting of a naked Jade, which always made James blush. The walls were swathed in red velvet and the wooden floor was so highly polished that waitresses were constantly slipping over and dropping plates and glasses during dinner parties. In the centre of the room was a thirty-foot mahogany table, surrounded by twenty dining chairs. When Fatty was entertaining the table would be laden with fancy cloths and napkins, silver cutlery, floral displays and ice sculptures. But now it was empty. Or at least it was empty except for a bottle of brandy and two crystal glasses at the far end.

The policeman's footsteps echoed in James's ears as he strode purposefully down the room. He stopped by the bottle, peered closely at it and took a sharp intake of breath.

'Hennessy, Beauté de Siècle,' he stated. 'A hundred thousand euros a bottle.'

He shook his head and tutted as if he found the whole idea distasteful. James had got used to the outrageous spending habits of the super-wealthy over the years but even by Fatty's lavish standards that seemed a hell of a lot to pay for a bottle of brandy. He must have been celebrating something. But what? And with whom?

'And two glasses ...' mused the officer. 'So, it seems, he was not alone after all.'

The heavy carving chair, which should have been at the head of the table, lay on its back on the floor a few feet from its usual place. It looked to James as if it had been pushed back in a hurry. Fatty's favourite navy blazer lay on the floor beneath the chair, as if it had been thrown over the back before it toppled over.

'We must leave,' stated the officer suddenly.

James nodded and looked at his watch. He needed to move *Vigorosa* pronto anyway. Or he'd have Mr Abramovich to answer to.

'Shall I start her up and take her back to her mooring?' he asked the policeman.

'Yes, if you would, Monsieur Sanderson. But please do not touch anything.'

James left the officer in the dining room talking hurriedly into his radio in French. The feeling of seasickness was still there. He felt every ebb and flow of the waves beneath him. James was a creature of habit. He liked routine. That's why a life on the sea had suited him so well. Nothing could change the tides. They were absolute. He knew where he stood with the ocean. James woke at six thirty every morning and went to sleep at midnight every night. He drank three mugs of coffee in the morning, two glasses of red wine in the evening, and a litre and half of Evian in between. He had many rituals. He called his mother in Vancouver every Sunday, he did a hundred push-ups before bed at night, he ate steak at the same back-street restaurant in Nice on his day off, he bought the same pair of Sebago deck shoes in tan leather twice a year, every year, he only ever read crime thrillers. James had never needed a house, or a city, or even a country to call his own, all he needed was his routine. That kept him grounded and sane. But last night, when Fatty had come on board and sent the crew onshore, something had shifted, his world had lurched, his routine had been broken. And now what? Chaos? As he steered the yacht back towards her mooring he felt sure that he was steering straight into the eye of a storm.

Chapter Five

Sasha glared at Carlo with wild, flashing, green eyes, rimmed with smudged black eye make-up from the night before. She looked like a woman possessed. Demonic. Scary. Her tangled mane of dark hair fell round her face like Medusa's snakes. She looked kind of like a witch, but a seriously sexy little witch. She leapt out of bed and started grabbing her clothes from the floor, all the time swearing and lecturing Carlo about what a no-good, filthy, low-life pervert he was.

Carlo watched his best friend's girlfriend with a mixture of amusement and horror. There was no doubt the hot-headed American heiress was an entertaining house guest but she was also Christian's chick and that made this situation so damn wrong! Sasha was struggling into those lacy black knickers now, hopping on one foot, and then the other, her pert tits bouncing up and down as she did so. Carlo couldn't help but notice that her perfect nipples were erect. It crossed his mind that it might be nice to take them in his mouth and suck them.

'I can't believe you took advantage of me like that, Carlo. Wait till Christian hears about this ...' she was shouting.

Carlo raised a quizzical eyebrow at her.

'And you're going to explain this to Christian how, exactly?' he asked, teasing her.

'Oh God, I dunno!' Sasha looked up at him in disgust. 'I

can't even remember where I lost him last night. Can you?'

Carlo shook his head and handed Sasha her black cocktail dress. She snatched it without thanking him and wriggled her hot little body into the tight Versace strapless number.

'Make yourself useful and do me up,' she ordered, turning her bare brown back towards him.

Carlo zipped the dress up slowly, taking in the cleft of her bum, the curve of her spine and the tiny scar on her left shoulder blade.

'Hurry up,' she snapped. 'I gotta get outta here! But I need coffee first. Make me a coffee. Black, no sugar.'

No sugar? Jesus, if anyone needed sweetening up it was Sasha. Carlo did as he was told though and made her a fresh espresso from his machine.

'So, are you going to tell Christian what happened?' he asked as he handed her the coffee.

He sure as hell hoped not. He didn't have many real friends in this world and he couldn't afford to go losing Christian. Besides, Christian was a big boy, a punch from him would break Carlo's nose. And he rather liked his nose the way it was.

Sasha narrowed her eyes. 'Tell him what? I don't even remember what happened. Do you?'

Carlo shrugged and shook his head. 'It's all a blank,' he said. 'Which is a shame because I'm sure we had fun last night.'

'Oh, purlease, Carlo, do not flatter yourself. I wouldn't sleep with you if you were the last guy standing after a nuclear bomb hit. I bet we just ended up back here for ...' She thought for a moment and then shrugged. 'Well, for whatever reason, and then we just crashed out.'

Carlo looked round the room and spotted the used condom he'd trodden on earlier. It was now stuck to the marble base of his arc floor lamp. He picked it up and swung it in front of Sasha's face, triumphantly, as she sipped her coffee.

'I don't think so, Sasha,' he grinned, pointing at the evidence. 'We definitely did the business.'

Sasha's green eyes followed his gaze. Her top lip curled and she placed her free hand firmly on her hip.

'Hmmph,' she snorted. 'What does that prove? You probably fucked yourself, Carlo. Everybody knows you get hard just looking at yourself in the mirror. You are the most narcissistic, egotistical bastard I have ever come across. And d'you know what? You're not even all that!'

She eyed his naked body with a sneer, her eyes resting on his cock. 'And if we did do it last night I can see why you didn't make much of an impact,' she quipped. 'That's nothing to be proud of.'

Carlo felt his cock shrivel. She couldn't have hurt him more if she'd stabbed him in the heart. Girls always said he had a huge cock! A glorious, beautiful, magnificent cock! And he had regular crack-and-sack waxes to keep himself smooth and neat for the ladies. Sasha was a lying bitch!

'No one else has ever complained,' he heard himself saying. He knew he sounded a bit pathetic but it was true. How dare she say that!

'Women lie, Carlo,' said Sasha with a smirk. 'All the damn time. Oh, darling that's soo good. Oh please, honey, just there, that's amazing. Wow, that's the biggest I've ever seen. Oh yeah, baby, I'm coming, I'm coming, I'm coming ...'

She grinned smugly at him, finished her coffee in one gulp and handed the empty cup back to him. 'Oh, you have a lot to learn, Carlo baby,' she said, half patting, half slapping him on the cheek. 'Where's the washroom?'

Carlo pointed towards the en-suite. Sasha sashayed towards the bathroom, barefoot, carrying her snakeskin Chanel clutch bag. Carlo followed her and watched from the door as she brushed her long hair, tidied up her eye make-up and reapplied her lipgloss. She was so beautiful. Why did she hate him so much? It bothered him. Girls always fell for him. *Always*. What was wrong with Sasha?

'Why do you hate me so much?' he found himself asking. He cringed the minute the words escaped his lips. He sounded like a schmuck!

'Jeez, Carlo, you are so whack!' laughed Sasha, catching his eye in the mirror. 'I don't hate you. I don't care enough to hate you. I'd say indifferent was more like it.'

She sprayed herself with L'Occitane perfume – aha, that was the familiar smell of oranges and vanilla – and admired her reflection for a moment. She seemed pleased with what she saw and completely unashamed of her vanity. Christ, maybe he'd finally met his match. This one didn't seem to have any of the usual hang-ups or insecurities. But this one was also his best friend's girlfriend, he reminded himself. Which made her totally off limits. Which in turn made her all the more desirable.

'Excuse me,' she said curtly, squeezing past him.

Carlo felt his cock stir again as her bottom brushed past his still naked skin. Shit, he fancied the pants off the little tease. The more he willed his penis to calm down, the more it stood to attention.

'You really are disgusting,' said Sasha, looking disinterestedly at his hard-on. 'You probably spiked my drink last night just to get your pathetic little rocks off.'

'You know I wouldn't do that, Sasha,' said Carlo. 'I don't know why you've got such a low opinion of me. I'm quite a good guy, really. Ask Christian.'

She laughed in his face. 'Ask Christian? Yeah, like Christian would think you were a *really* good guy if he could see you now ...'

Carlo felt humiliated. She was quick. Quicker than him. 'Well, I certainly don't need to spike girls' drinks to get laid, OK?' he added, weakly.

He was beginning to feel very small, like a child who'd been told off by his favourite teacher and now desperately wanted to get back in her good books.

'Hmm, maybe not,' she mused, taking a step towards him. 'Have I offended the poor little sensitive baby?'

She brushed his dick ever so lightly with her fingertips. Carlo wasn't sure if she'd meant to do it or not.

'Are you trying to tell me you're all front, Carlo?' she teased. 'That you're not really the Big I Am after all? Have I misunderstood you, baby?'

She was about five foot five in her bare feet and Carlo, at six foot three, towered above her. She looked up at him with those wild green eyes and took another step towards him, until she was pressed against him. Fuck, he wanted her. He wanted her more than he'd ever wanted any woman before. Did she want him? Christ! What was she playing at? He was supposed to be the player here, so why did he feel as though he was being played? She tilted her head back with her full lips parted. Her tongue licked her teeth provocatively. Her eyes bored into his for a moment and if Carlo could have read minds he was sure hers was saying, 'Fuck me, Carlo. Please.' But then she pushed him away and spun on her heels.

'Where the hell did I put my Jimmy Choos?' she muttered, throwing the duvet off the bed and the cushions off the chaise longue.

'Your rug's soaking wet,' she told him briskly. 'And it's all sticky.'

'I spilled a bottle of champagne,' he explained.

'I don't really like champagne,' said Sasha, getting down on all fours and fishing around under the bed for her missing shoes. 'I prefer hard liquor.'

'Figures,' said Carlo, watching her short dress ride up to her hips.

'*Voilà!*' she said, surfacing from under the bed with two strappy, spiky-heeled black sandals. 'Right, I'm outta here.'

Carlo was disappointed. He didn't want her to go. She was rude and obnoxious and she treated him with complete disdain, but Christ she was something else.

'Oh, baby,' she said in her most sarcastic tone. 'Don't look so sad. You gonna miss me when I'm gone?'

'Why are you so nasty, Sasha?' snapped Carlo.

'Oh, I dunno,' she quipped. 'Maybe because you're my boyfriend's best buddy and I woke up butt naked in your bed this morning, to the sight of you holding my panties and jerking off. I think I've got the right to be a little pissed with you, don't I?'

She was standing too close to him again with her short dress up around her hips and that 'fuck me' look in her eyes. Carlo took a gamble. He put his hand on her bare thigh. She didn't flinch. He stroked his fingers up until he brushed against the lace of her knickers. Still she didn't move. Her flesh felt warm and inviting. Carlo let out an involuntary groan. She smirked again. And then his fingers were wriggling underneath the lace and touching her hot, damp pussy.

'If you hate me so much, why are you so turned on?' he asked her breathlessly.

'Don't flatter yourself, Carlo,' she said evenly. 'I'm always horny in the morning. You're just in the right place at the right time, that's all. Anyway, I told you. I don't hate you. I'm indifferent.'

And then she grabbed the back of his neck and pulled his mouth to hers. She tasted of toothpaste and coffee. Her lips were plump, soft and warm. Her tongue pushed into his mouth as his fingers pushed deeper into her pussy and then suddenly she was pushing him down onto the cold marble floor, peeling off her knickers, straddling him, still wearing her little black cocktail dress. It was an awesome sight, Sasha Constantine, astride him.

'You are so fucking sexy,' he told her breathlessly.

Sasha just smiled, knowingly, as she rubbed the tip of his rock-hard cock against her. And then she was on him, sliding him deep inside her, and she was fucking him hard, rhythmically, totally in control, totally in charge. Which was more than Carlo was. Christ, he was going to come any minute. She lifted her dress up so he could watch, and she touched herself as she rode him. She closed her eyes and threw her head back, rubbing her clit faster and faster, harder and harder, until she groaned and let out a cry of pleasure. But still she didn't look at him. Carlo had never been with a woman who was so confident with her body and so unfazed by sex.

He tried to think about something unsexy, anything to stop him coming too soon and looking like an amateur in front of Sasha, who was clearly anything but. He thought about his dog dying when he was twelve, and about the Porsche he'd written off last summer, but it was no good. All he could see was this amazing, sexy girl, on top of him, screwing his brains out.

'I'm going to come, Sasha,' he blurted out, not a minute too soon.

'Oh my God,' he gasped. 'Oh my God. That is amazing, Sasha. I'm still coming. I'm still coming.' Carlo thought he'd died and gone to heaven. Never in his life had he met a woman who seemed to enjoy sex so much.

'Right,' said Sasha, standing up and climbing into her knickers for the second time that morning. 'Now, I really *must* get outta here!'

Carlo scrambled to his feet.

'Um, do you want my number?' he asked her. He never offered girls his number, but Sasha was different. Sasha was something else.

She frowned at him. 'No, Carlo. Don't be silly. Why would I want your number?' she asked.

Carlo blushed and shrugged and kicked the cowhide rug with his feet.

'No reason, I just thought maybe ...' he mumbled, embarrassed.

'Carlo, this was a one-off.' She stated matter-of-factly. 'I told you, I get horny in the mornings. I would normally have got my Rabbit out but since you were here ...'

He wanted the ground to open up and swallow him. Now he knew how girls felt when he refused to give them his number.

Sasha leant her hand on his arm to steady herself as she put on a sandal.

'Oh, by the way,' she said suddenly, standing up and waving the other spike-heeled shoe in his face. 'If you ever, *ever* tell Christian about this, I will cut that itty bitty cock of yours off with a blunt bread knife, *comprenez?*'

Carlo nodded. He didn't know what to say. Then she wriggled into her second sandal, pulled her dress down over her bum, walked out into the hall and opened the apartment door.

'See ya!' she called, as she strutted off down the hall towards the lift.

He watched her perfect little arse wiggling away from him, out of reach. He watched her all the way to the lift. He watched her press the button and readjust her dress while she waited. He watched her fish her phone out of her bag and check for messages. He watched her reapply her lipgloss. He watched her all the time it took for the lift to arrive, willing her to turn round and smile, or wave, or anything. But Sasha never looked back. When the lift arrived, she stepped in, the doors closed behind her and then she was gone. Carlo had no idea when he would see her again. And the thought killed him.

Back in the bedroom, he picked up the duvet off the floor where Sasha had discarded it and got back under the covers. He could smell her perfume. It wasn't even eight o'clock yet. He normally slept until lunchtime on a Saturday. What else was there to do? But now he was wide awake and his mind was racing. Should he call Christian? He had no idea how Sasha had ended up back at his place. Where had Christian got to? What the hell had happened last night?

He reached for his phone and switched it on. It immediately beeped and told him he had three new messages. Oh God, was it Christian? Did he already know where Sasha had stayed last night? Had Carlo made a move on her in front of Christian? He wished he could remember something about the night before. Anything! He listened nervously to his messages, dreading hearing his friend's voice. But the messages weren't from Christian. They were all from Francesca. And his normally unflappable big sister sounded in a terrible state. As he listened to the final message, Carlo felt the colour drain from his face and suddenly all thoughts of Sasha and Christian were forgotten.

Chapter Six

Francesca paced the harbourside for what felt like the millionth time. She didn't know what else to do, except to keep walking, moving, doing something, *anything*, however futile, to pass the time while the police searched the boat with their sniffer dogs. Her heels clipped the paving stones as James's words rang in her ears: 'It's like the *Marie Celeste* in there,' he'd said. 'It's as if Fatty's vanished into thin air.' The yacht's tender, a mini hovercraft, was still in its garage in *Vigorosa III*'s stern, alongside two jet skis, a banana float and the diving and water-skiing equipment. The only way that Fatty could have got back to shore was to swim. And Francesca knew better than anyone that Fatty couldn't swim. 'Is not natural,' he'd always scoffed. 'If God had wanted us to swim he would have given us webbed feet.' It had always made Francesca laugh when he'd said that, but suddenly it didn't seem so funny.

Everything was happening so fast but time was passing painfully slowly. There was a forensic team on board now. They'd arrived about ten minutes ago, three men and a woman, wearing white overalls and serious expressions. Nobody had told Francesca what was going on but she knew perfectly well that the police divers who'd just disappeared into the blue-green water in the harbour were looking for a body. Her dad's body. How could that be? It was all so horribly unreal.

She'd last seen him yesterday afternoon at the office. He'd arrived in high spirits, even louder and more full of himself than usual. But his good mood hadn't lasted long. She'd asked him about a deal he'd been discussing with some Italian businessmen. He kept popping along the coast for meetings in San Remo but refused to put names or company details in the diary. It was frustrating. Francesca liked to research new associates before getting involved with them but her father had told her it was nothing for her to concern herself with. She'd been annoyed. Really bloody annoyed. She felt pushed out, and worried that he was throwing more money down the drain. He'd reminded her, his famous temper rising, that this was still his business and told her in no uncertain terms that she worked for him. Fatty would answer to himself only, not to anyone else, and certainly not to his daughter. *Capisci*? He'd put her in her place and she hadn't liked it one bit.

'This business would disintegrate around your ears if I didn't do all this,' Francesca had told him, sweeping her arms around the office at the perfectly programmed computers and neat files of paperwork. Every shelf was lined with leather-bound files in chronological and alphabetical order. She was proud of the well-oiled machine she ran.

Her father had laughed at her. 'Oh, Francesca, *la mia bella*. You have much to learn still. You think you control all this? I have let you *think* you control all this. But believe me, *bambino*, you only see what I let you see. You have no idea what goes on beneath the surface.'

'Don't patronise me, Dad,' she'd retorted, crossly. 'And don't keep secrets from me either. This is a family business. It works because we trust each other and we'd never lie to each other. You're the one who told me that. You drummed that into me over the years. So why are you keeping things from me now? Who are these Italians? What's the deal?'

'*Basta!*' he'd shouted, the colour rising in his florid cheeks and the vein in his right temple pulsing as it always did when she pushed things too far. Then his shoulders had dropped, he'd sighed and looked at her with his head on one side.

'Do you remember what I used to tell you when you were a little girl, Frankie? When you caught me eating biscuits before dinner?' he'd asked, looking serious now. 'Don't do as I do, do as I say. You remember? Well, that is the way it still works. I am the father, and I am the boss. You are a bright girl, but you do not know everything.'

'I know a hell of a lot more than you give me credit for,' she'd snapped.

'No,' Fatty had stated flatly, shaking his head as he walked out the door. '*Si è ancora ingenuo, bambino!*'

You are still naive, child. The words rung in her ears now. Would those be the last words he ever said to her?

William appeared with a steaming mug of coffee for her. 'From Wally,' he said. Wally Johnson was the skipper of Carlo's yacht.

'Thanks,' said Francesca. 'Any news from Carlo?'

William nodded. 'I've just spoken to him. He's on his way.'

'And Angelica?' Francesca bit her lip. How was she going to explain this to Angel? The youngest and most vulnerable LaFata. She was only twenty-one, still the baby. And always Daddy's girl.

William shook his head. 'She's been shooting swimwear in Miami. She's on an overnight flight back to London at the moment. She's not due to land for a few hours yet. But that's a good thing. Perhaps we'll have some positive news by the time she touches down. Who knows, Fatty could turn up any minute, laughing at all this fuss he's caused.'

He smiled at Francesca weakly, but he didn't look convinced. He stepped forward and hugged her awkwardly; his arms were round her shoulders but his body remained a few inches away from hers. It was the first physical contact they'd had in months. William wasn't a naturally tactile man. He'd never been into hugs, or hand holding, or kissing just for the sake of it, even when they'd been happy, well happy-*ish*, in those early days. He was equally distant with his sons, so Francesca made up for it by lavishing her boys with endless cuddles and kisses. He was trying to offer her comfort now, but his awkward, stilted attempt at affection only made her feel more alone. His heart wasn't in it, that was obvious, but he was trying to do the right thing. But what Francesca needed right now was *real* love. She wished Carlo would hurry up and get here. Her brother was unreliable, self-centred and spoilt but at least he was family. And family, as Fatty had always told them, was everything in this world.

Carlo floored his Lamborghini round the hairpin bend at the Monaco Grand Hotel as fast as any F1 driver taking the same bend during the Grand Prix. He'd had barely any sleep but he felt more wide awake and wired than ever before. He had the roof down and the wind whipped his hair round his face, half-blinding him every time he turned a bend. He needed to get to Port Hercule and he needed to get there fast. What a morning. Christ! What a weird, mind-bending morning it had been. First he wakes up with Sasha, his best mate's girlfriend, in his bed, then she screws with his head, then she screws him for real, and then he finds out that his dad is missing. Vanished from *Vigorosa III*,

William had said. What the hell was going on? None of it made any sense.

As he sped into the district of La Condamine and towards the harbour he could already see that his dad's disappearance had caused a stir. There were police everywhere, some with dogs, and the entire western end of the harbour had been cordoned off with tape. A large group of onlookers had already gathered on the pavement above the harbour. Being a Saturday, hundreds of tourists were on day trips to Monte Carlo from their hotels in Nice, or their cruise ships, docked just down the coast at Villefranche. The day-trippers were spilling out of the train station and scurrying straight down to the port like ants. 'Fucking parasites!' he shouted, making no attempt to slow down as a bunch of Japanese kids crossed the road in front of him. They ran for their lives and Carlo knew it was more by luck than judgement that he missed their toes. He glared at them from behind his gold Ray-Bans as they held up their phones to take pictures of his car.

Carlo flew towards the police tape and screeched to a halt inches from the officer who was manning the entrance to the scene.

'I'm Giancarlo LaFata Junior,' he stated grandly. 'I believe my father is missing.'

The policeman ushered him through the cordon and Carlo parked up beside Frankie's Range Rover Sport. He could see his sister standing by the water's edge, head on one side, nodding, listening intently to what a senior police officer was telling her. She looked anxious but in control. Just the way she likes it, thought Carlo, a little bitterly. The first-born. The chosen one. The boss.

'Carlo!' she called. 'Carlo, darling, thank God you're here.'

She hugged him with real warmth and Carlo felt immediately guilty for being so jealous of her. He loved his sister and even admired her, albeit grudgingly. She was a smart cookie. Straight as a die. Trustworthy, solid, fair, responsible and a proper grown-up. She was twelve years older than him, the daughter of his dad's first marriage. But it wasn't just the age difference that drove a wedge between them. It was more the fact that their father trusted her implicitly. When Fatty looked at Francesca his eyes filled with pride, when Carlo looked in his father's eyes all he saw was disappointment.

'You are a waste of the space, Giancarlo! When are you going to do something with your life? Become a man, huh? You should be more like your sister Francesca!'

How often had he heard those words from his dad? Often enough for them to sink in and fester, that was for sure. Yup, Frankie was everything Carlo wasn't and part of him hated her for it. Or maybe he hated himself for not being more like her. He wasn't quite sure, sometimes, where the sibling rivalry ended and the self-loathing began.

'This is my brother, Carlo,' she told the officer. 'He might know more than I do.'

Frankie turned to him, her pale grey-blue eyes full of questions. Her eyes were always a surprise in such a dark, olive-skinned face. She'd inherited them, along with her long, coltish legs, from her mum, Maggie. The rest was pure LaFata. Even at thirty-five, Frankie remained a real Italian beauty. Sophia Loren with blue eyes.

'When was the last time you saw Dad?' asked Frankie, hopefully.

The policeman took out his notebook and said, 'Thank you, Ms LaFata, that will be all. I shall speak with your brother now. In private.'

'Oh, yes, right, of course,' said Frankie.

She patted Carlo's arm affectionately and walked off to join William.

'Did you see your father last night?' asked the officer.

'Yes,' replied Carlo. 'At Stars'n'Bars. I had a meal there with some friends. He popped over to say hello.'

'What time was this?'

Carlo shrugged. 'Not sure, really. About ten maybe? Ish ...'

The policeman sighed. He too seemed disappointed in Carlo and he had only been in his company for a minute.

'Could anyone give me a more specific time?' he continued, patiently.

'Well, my friends were pretty hammered to be honest, but the waitress might remember. We're regulars and she's our favourite. Dominique, she's the cute black girl with legs up to her armpits, you can't miss her.'

The policeman tutted and wrote something in his notebook but Carlo doubted it was 'legs up to her armpits'.

'And he was alone, your father?'

Carlo nodded. 'Yup, but he said he was going to meet a friend. He only stayed five minutes. Didn't even have a drink, which is most unlike him. Paid our tab on the way out though, come to think of it. I'll have to thank him for that when I see him ...'

His voice trailed off. What if he never got the chance to thank him?

'Did he say who this friend was?'

Carlo shook his head. 'Dad's got lots of friends. He's a popular chap. Very well known in Monaco but then I guess you're aware of that already.'

The policeman shrugged, obviously unimpressed by Fatty's standing in society. 'It does not matter to me who your father is, only that we find him safe and well,' he replied.

Carlo felt himself bristle. Giancarlo LaFata was one of the wealthiest and most charismatic men in the principality. The guy was a legend! He couldn't stand it when people didn't treat his father with the deference he deserved. It was OK for Carlo to get pissed off with him. He was his *dad*. But not some jumped-up harbour cop who thought he was the big man because he had a few stripes on his shoulders.

'And your father, what was his mood?'

'He was happy,' said Carlo, remembering his dad slapping him and Christian on the back, jovially. 'He's been pretty grumpy lately but last night he seemed better, more relaxed.'

'Do you know why he has been, erm, how you put it? Grumpy recently?' asked the officer.

Carlo shrugged. 'Business, I guess. The credit crunch. You'd have to ask Frankie, um, I mean Francesca, about that though. She's the brains of the operation. I don't get involved in the business side of things. I'm better at spending money than making it.'

He laughed to show he was joking but the policeman eyed him with distaste, his top lip curling, as if he had just tasted a particularly offensive cheap wine. The guy was really beginning to piss Carlo off now.

'That will be all,' said the officer briskly. 'I suggest you and your family go home now and let us get on with our job here. I see quite a crowd has gathered. It will be just a matter of time before the press arrive and your presence will only encourage them.'

'I just want to know where my father is,' said Carlo, aware that he sounded desperate. 'I want to be here if anything' – he glanced at *Vigorosa III*, still crawling with police, dogs and forensic experts – 'if anything happens.'

'We will be in touch with any news and a senior detective

will be interviewing you all at length later. In the meantime, do not leave Monaco please, sir. *Comprenez?*'

'Understood,' replied Carlo coldly.

He lit a cigarette and glared at the policeman's retreating back. Where was the compassion? He bet the guy hadn't spoken to Frankie like that. Men never liked him. He was young, good-looking, rich and, well, kind of famous these days. Carlo guessed that men found him intimidating. Hmph. Do not leave Monaco indeed! What the hell was that all about? Did the police think the family might have something to do with Fatty's disappearance? As if! Didn't he know who they were? The LaFatas practically *owned* Monaco for God's sake! And you couldn't meet a closer family. They were rock solid. They had no secrets from one another.

Wait until his dad heard about this treatment. Fatty was good friends with the chief of police and he'd have something to say about this when he ... When he what? Turned up? Carlo looked again at his father's yacht and his heart fell into the pit of his stomach. Maybe his dad wasn't going to turn up? What if Fatty had gone for good? Carlo felt tears well up and he thought that his knees were going to buckle beneath him. He crouched down and put his hand over his eyes, shielding his tears. Big boys didn't cry. What would his dad say if he could see him now, crying like a baby, eh? He would say, 'Don't be such a girl, Giancarlo. Stand up. Be a man. You are embarrassing me, my son.'

'You OK, Carlo?' asked Frankie, placing her hand on his shoulder.

Carlo nodded but didn't look up at his sister.

'Hungover,' he mumbled. 'And I just got smoke in my eye.'

He threw his cigarette butt into the water and wiped his eyes. Then he stood up and forced a smile.

'What the hell has the old man got up to this time, eh?' he said, trying to sound cheerful.

Frankie smiled at him but her eyes were sad and full of pain.

'Come here, baby brother,' she said softly, just as she'd done when she was fifteen and he was three, and he'd been told off by his daddy.

And then she pulled him towards her and let him bury his head in her soft black hair as he sobbed.

'Everything will be OK,' she whispered into his ear. 'Just you wait and see, Carlo. Daddy will be fine. He always comes up smelling of roses, remember?'

Christian ran all the way from his apartment block in Fontvieille to Port Hercule when he heard the news. He could see from his balcony that the traffic was gridlocked, so he left the car in its garage and ran, as fast as his legs would carry him, bumping into tourists, stepping on small dogs and saying, 'Sorry, sorry, uh, erm, sorry,' all the way.

Last night he'd been pissed off with Carlo. He'd seen the way his best friend had looked at his girlfriend and he hadn't liked it one bit. Sasha pretended to hate Carlo but Christian wasn't stupid. No woman hated Carlo, however much she might want to. It was that whole 'every girl loves a bastard' thing. Oh, they banged on about equality and feminism, but most girls he knew still seemed to want a caveman who'd bash her over the head, drag her back to his cave and then leave her there while he fucked the cave-woman next door. And Sasha, for all her bravado and front, was no different.

It made no sense to Christian, who'd always treated

65

girls with respect. Carlo really didn't seem to give a toss about women's feelings. And yet it was Carlo who got the girls. Carlo, who never gave out his number. Carlo, who didn't do second dates. Carlo, who called every girl he met 'sugar' or 'honey', or 'babe', because he couldn't be bothered to remember her name. It wasn't right and it wasn't fair. But it was life. And usually Christian watched his friend's behaviour with bemusement rather than jealousy. But last night, Carlo had almost crossed the line. When he'd danced with Sasha, Christian had seen the way his friend's hand had slid down her waist and onto her bum. He'd also noted that Sasha hadn't moved Carlo's hand. Christian had felt stupid, hurt and disrespected. But he wasn't one for confrontation. It was just drunken flirting and it wouldn't go anywhere. Carlo would never do that to him, Christian was sure of that fact. It just wasn't easy to watch. And so, instead of putting himself through it, he had sloped off quietly and gone home to bed.

Carlo wasn't popular with most men. He was cocky, vain, rich and good-looking. Not a great combination when it came to bonding with the guys. He didn't do anything, career-wise, that other guys respected. Living off your dad's earnings wasn't seen as a respectable lifestyle choice even in Monaco. And then, of course, there was his popularity with the ladies. It was all down to jealousy really.

But Christian saw beyond Carlo's sharp suits and smooth talk, to the man underneath, and he knew his friend was a good guy. It couldn't have been easy growing up in Fatty's shadow and Carlo had just developed a front to cope with life the best way he knew how. And when push came to shove, Carlo would always be there for Christian.

He remembered one time, when they were teenagers, Christian had been set on by a couple of older lads. The boys had been on the beach together during the school summer holidays with Christian's parents. But, being thirteen, they'd taken themselves off down the beach away from the grown-ups. Carlo had gone off to buy drinks and while he was gone, two thugs of about sixteen had come over to Christian and started teasing him about his mum, saying she was sexy, and that they wanted to fuck her. Christian didn't usually have a temper, but these boys were saying some really disgusting things and he'd flipped, shouted at them to piss off, and then kicked sand in their faces. The next thing he knew he was face down on the beach, with a mouth full of sand and a fist in his kidneys.

Carlo had always been tall and even at that young age he'd towered over the older boys. Christian remembered seeing his attacker flying through the air and landing several metres away with a thump. Then Carlo had grabbed hold of the other boy by the balls and told him that he was Fatty LaFata's son and didn't he know how well connected the LaFatas were? He said if they so much as looked at Christian's mother again, he would order a Mafia hitman to shoot them dead. That got rid of them. As Christian watched the older boys flee, Carlo had flopped back down on his towel and said, 'Your mum is pretty sexy, mind you.' For some reason it was OK for Carlo to say that. For some reason, whatever Carlo did or said, it was OK by Christian.

But now his friend needed his help. As Christian pushed his way through the crowds he spotted Carlo and Francesca, standing on the quay, with their arms round each other. They both looked exhausted and distressed. And worse, they were playing out this nightmare scene in front of hundreds of people. Being a LaFata must be like living in a goldfish bowl, thought Christian, as he shoved a couple of journalists out of the way and got to the front of the police cordon.

'I'm a family friend,' Christian told the police officer.

The policeman laughed and said, 'Everyone here is a family friend, today. Go on, off you go.'

'No, really, I am,' insisted Christian.

'Of course you are,' replied the officer sarcastically. 'And I am Prince Albert's long-lost twin brother.'

Luckily, Francesca looked up at just that moment and spotted Christian. She came rushing over and explained to the policeman that he was 'with the family'. Christian smiled smugly at the embarrassed officer and hugged Francesca warmly.

'I'm so sorry about all this,' he said, not really sure how else to put it.

What the hell did you say to a woman whose father had just disappeared from his yacht? Francesca nodded, said thank you, and forced a weak smile.

'We have no idea what's going on, Christian,' she added. 'But I'm sure the police will get to the bottom of it quickly. You know Dad. Anything could have happened ...'

Her voice trailed off and she glanced over at a police diver who'd just got out of the water. Christian had no idea what was going on either but it didn't look good. He noticed that Carlo was hanging back, pretending not to have seen him. Was he feeling awkward about flirting with Sasha last night? Silly sod! What did that matter at a time like this? Christian walked boldly up to his best friend and threw his arms around him.

'Sorry, mate,' he said. 'This must be really difficult for you. I came as soon as I heard. Let me help. What can I do?'

Christian meant it. He would do anything to help the LaFatas. He loved them all.

'Thanks, Chris,' said Carlo gratefully. His eyes were red and it looked like he'd been crying. Christian was shocked. He'd never seen his friend cry before.

'It's just a waiting game at the moment,' he continued, running his hands through his hair like he always did when he was nervous. 'A nightmare, to be honest. I don't know how I'm going to tell Angel ...'

'Where is Angelica?' asked Christian, worrying suddenly about the youngest LaFata.

'On her way back from Miami,' said Carlo. He put his hands over his mouth and sighed deeply. 'Oh fuck, Chris, what am I going to do about Angel? She's going to arrive in London to this madness.' He nodded his head towards the group of journalists and TV crews that had just arrived and set up camp at the harbour.

'When does her flight get in?' asked Christian. 'And where?'

'One o'clock,' said Carlo. 'Gatwick.'

Christian glanced at his watch.

'Fine,' he said. 'Well, that's one thing sorted. I'm going to take the jet to London and collect her. She needs to see a friendly face when she arrives.'

'Really?' said Carlo. 'You'd do that?'

'Just try stopping me,' said Christian emphatically.

Carlo squeezed Christian's shoulder hard.

'You're a good friend, Christian,' he said. 'You know Angel needs the kid-glove treatment but she trusts you. It'll put my mind at rest knowing you'll be there to meet her.'

The truth was, Christian would have run barefoot over hot coals to get to Angelica LaFata. He'd been in love with her for as long as he could remember. Most people grow out of their first crush but Christian's had just grown into full-blown infatuation. Unfortunately it was a rather one-sided affair. Angelica seemed to like him well enough but he was just her big brother's dependable friend. Always there to carry her home when she collapsed in a bar, or mop up her tears when some bastard broke her heart. She had no idea how Christian felt about her.

And thankfully neither did Carlo. He would have flipped if he'd known that Christian went to sleep thinking about Angel most nights. Carlo might treat most women like dog shit on his best Gucci loafers, but with Angelica he was different. When it came to his baby sister, Carlo could be very protective indeed. A bit rich from the guy who thought it was OK to refer to Christian's mum as 'The Milf' but understandable all the same. Carlo's little sister was one of the highest-paid models in the world, and every man on the planet wanted to have her. It did Carlo's head in. Christian had lost count of the times he'd heard Carlo threaten to punch some guy for just looking at 'his Angel' in the wrong way. No, best to keep his feelings for Angelica to himself.

It wasn't as if Christian thought he actually stood a chance with Angelica. She was way out of his league. So he carried on seeing other girls and trying desperately to fall in love with them instead. But it was no good. He liked Sasha. She was beautiful and smart. A bit scary maybe, but he didn't mind a woman with her own opinions. But he didn't love her and if Angelica LaFata ever showed him even the slightest hint of interest, he would drop Sasha in an instant.

'Right,' he said to Carlo now, patting him on the arm. 'I'll get off then. If I get a helicopter to the airport, I can be at Gatwick before Angelica.'

Chapter Seven

'Holy fuck, Robbie. I think I've got one you're going to like here!' shouted Bernie Ferguson, the chief sub, from his desk across the office. He sounded very pleased with himself. 'Just come in on AFP.'

Robbie looked up from his computer and smiled patiently at Bernie, humouring him, pretending to be interested. Bernie didn't have a great nose for news, which was why he was a sub, not a reporter. Besides, AFP, or Agence France Press, was the French news agency. Most of the big stories came in on the Reuters or Press Association wire. Bernie was a bit of a dinosaur in newspaper terms and stubbornly old school in his views. He abhorred today's celebrity culture and was constantly lamenting the demise of political awareness in Scotland.

'It used to be,' he would often reminisce to his younger colleagues over a pint or two in the Waverley Tavern, 'that your average man on the street, and I mean Leith Walk not Heriot Row, would have an opinion on everything, from nuclear submarines on the Holy Loch, to the rightful home of the Stone of Destiny. Which is a fake anyway, of course. But these days, all folk care about is whether Jennifer Aniston has finally found a man, or what that Cheryl Cole lassie wore on *X Factor* on Saturday night. It beggars belief, it really does.'

The others laughed at Bernie behind his back, but Robbie

was genuinely fond of the guy. He'd worked for the paper for so long that he talked about the miners' strike as if it was recent news. But he was a good bloke and bloody brilliant at his job, the best headline writer on any paper in the country in Robbie's opinion, so he always humoured him.

'Yeah, what's the story, Bernie?' asked Robbie jovially. 'Alex Ferguson's won the Nobel Peace prize? Gordon Brown's had Botox?'

'Better than that,' said Bernie excitedly. 'Fatty LaFata's done a Robert Maxwell.'

'You what?!' Robbie nearly choked on his mid-morning Kit-Kat. 'What d'you mean?'

'Your pet project, and Edinburgh's most famous pizza maker, has gone missing off the side of his yacht in Monte Bloody Carlo, hasn't he?' exclaimed Bernie, his eyes popping behind the lenses of his glasses. 'They've got police divers searching the harbour for his body and wait, it's all over the internet already. I've got pictures here of that nancy boy son of his, blubbing like a bairn.'

Robbie leapt out of his chair and ran over to Bernie's desk. It was Saturday, the paper was on skeleton staff, and the two men had the vast open-plan office to themselves. Robbie's heart was pounding in his chest. Giancarlo LaFata was more of an obsession than a pet project and he couldn't quite believe what he was hearing. He peered over Bernie's shoulder and scanned the words and photos on screen. Finally, it had happened. The big one. The story he'd been waiting for!

'I've got to get over there, Bernie,' said Robbie. 'ASAP.'

'You'll be lucky,' guffawed the older man. 'There's no way the boss is going to let you go swanning off to Monaco again in a hurry. Not after the last time. You nearly got sacked over that expenses claim.'

'I'll pay for it myself if I have to,' replied Robbie. 'Anyway, I had to go to the casinos and the clubs to get a proper taste of the place. It was work. Not my fault a beer cost twenty-five euros.'

'I think it was the helicopter transfer from the airport that the boss objected to most, if I remember rightly,' laughed Bernie. 'You've got ideas above your station, Robbie McLean. And I mean that in the nicest possible way.'

Robbie stood up and tucked his shirt back into his jeans. The boss hated jeans. He wished he'd worn his suit today of all days.

'Where are you off to?' asked Bernie.

'To get the green light from the boss for my Monaco trip,' he replied confidently.

Bernie almost toppled backwards off his swivel chair, he was laughing so hard. 'You've got a brass neck, Rob. The boss is going to hit the roof when he hears this idea.'

'Nah, he'll see it's a great opportunity. How often does Scotland's richest man go missing at sea? There's a huge story here. And I think I know what it's all about, Bernie. Nobody knows the LaFata story like I do. I'm the world's expert on the guy and I'm telling you, like I've been telling you all for months, he's a crook. He's in it up to his neck. And I'm the one who's going to tell the world.'

'You're so modest! That's what I love about you, Robbie.' Bernie was still laughing. 'Oh well, good luck. I'll put my earplugs in now, though, because you are going to get such a bollocking for even suggesting this ...'

But Robbie wasn't big-headed, he was just confident of his abilities. He knew he was one of the best crime reporters in the country. Hadn't he been headhunted by every national tabloid over the years? If it wasn't for his girls, he'd have been in London years ago, making a name for himself and a hell of a lot more money than he was making by staying here. But every time he got offered a job it was the same story. His head said yes, but his heart said no way, José. He saw little enough of Grace and Ruby as it was since the divorce – one night a week and every second weekend, that was all Lady Heather (as his mum called his ex-wife) and her new husband, Lord Fuckwit, allowed. He wasn't about to up sticks and move four hundred miles away from them, however good the job offer was. Only see his beloved girls during the school holidays and for special occasions? No way. Over his dead body! Robbie loved his daughters more than life itself. He lived for those gorgeous girls and would die for them gladly. And so Robbie stayed in Edinburgh.

Heather and Fuckwit, or Fraser Magnuson, as the rest of the world called him, were always trying to encourage him to leave, of course. They'd love that. To see the back of him so they could get on with their perfect family life without the complication of an annoying ex-husband hanging around. But luckily, Robbie always had the kids on his side. They loved their dad. And he loved them. Nothing was ever going to get in their way.

Fraser always made a big deal out of inviting Robbie into the enormous hall of his enormous house in Morningside, whenever he arrived to collect the kids. He pretended to be hospitable, but Robbie saw right through him. What he really wanted to do was show Robbie how obscenely wealthy he was, to make the point that Heather and the girls were so much better off now that they were living here, with him, than they'd ever been in the modest little terrace in Trinity with him. He'd done it again last weekend.

'I hear you won another award, Robert,' Fraser had wittered. 'Good stuff. Jolly good stuff. Pleased to hear it. Jolly pleased to hear it.'

74

He always did that. Said everything twice, like a particularly pompous parrot. Ruby did a great impersonation of her stepfather that always made Robbie howl with laughter. Stepfather. Ouch! It still killed him to think of his girls having any other father than him.

'I'm surprised a man of your talents isn't in London,' Fraser had continued, oblivious to Ruby sticking her tongue out at him from halfway up the stairs. 'A man of your talents belongs in London ...'

Robbie had half listened. He'd been busy frowning at Ruby, warning her to stop being cheeky, while trying to stifle a laugh at the same time. That was the thing with kids, they were often at their funniest when they were at their naughtiest. Besides, he'd heard it all before.

'Och, I'm not going anywhere, Fraser,' Robbie had interrupted finally, as the girls had run down the stairs with their overnight bags. They'd glued themselves to his side and he'd wrapped an arm around each of their blonde heads, protectively. 'Not unless these two come with me.'

Heather had appeared from the landing just in time to hear his comment. She was so tall, blonde and ethereally beautiful that, even now, after all the pain she'd caused him, he still had to catch his breath when he saw her. She'd frowned at her ex-husband as she'd wafted down the stairs.

'Don't listen to him, we all know that's never going to happen, Fraser,' she'd retorted, entwining herself in his arms. 'So let's not have any more silly talk, shall we?' She'd glared at Robbie with icy blue eyes.

Robbie had squeezed the girls in closer to him, engaging in some juvenile hug-off with his ex-wife. See, you might have *him*, he was telling her, but I still have *them*. It had been three years since Heather had left him for Fuckwit, the owner of the events management company she worked for. But it still felt all wrong to see her there, wrapped in another man's arms. Because she used to be his Heather. And although he barely recognised the woman she'd become – so frosty, expensively dressed and well groomed – somewhere under the make-up and the designer clothes the girl he'd fallen in love with still lurked.

'Well, perhaps Fraser would stop suggesting I move away then?' Robbie had replied.

Fraser had sucked in his breath, and shared a 'look' with Heather.

'Robbie, Robbie, Robbie,' Fraser had sighed. 'I was merely taking an interest in your career. There's no need to be so—'

'Bloody childish!' Heather had interjected. And then she'd turned to Fraser and said, 'Don't waste your breath, darling. Robbie has always been nothing but a big kid and there's no way he's going to change now. Just ignore him. I do.'

And she did. That was exactly what she did, in front of the children, at parents' evening at school, at ballet shows and gymnastics competitions. She just acted as if he wasn't there. And it hurt. It bloody well hurt. After six years of marriage and two children, she couldn't even bring herself to talk to him. If belittling had been an Olympic event, Heather would have been a gold medal winner.

'And girls,' Heather had called as Robbie had ushered the kids out of the door, 'make sure you brush your teeth, don't stay up too late and do not let your father feed you junk food!'

He'd got Heather pregnant during the last year of her law degree at Edinburgh University. He was twenty-five at the time, and had just started as a junior reporter on the paper. She had just turned twenty-three. Heather wore white to the wedding despite her bump. Then she'd finished her law degree before she had the baby. But she'd never got round to practising law. Instead she'd found herself trapped in a world of nappies, breastfeeding and NCT coffee mornings with women ten years her senior. She'd hated it. And then just as Grace had turned from baby to toddler, Heather had got pregnant again. Another accident! She'd threatened to have an abortion this time but Robbie had begged and pleaded with her to keep their child. Didn't Grace deserve a sibling? She'd given in eventually, and resentfully, but she'd never let go of her resentment. She'd felt she'd sacrificed herself on the altar of motherhood. And she'd blamed Robbie.

He'd tried to support her, to tell her that he was there for her, that he admired her, that she was doing a brilliant job of raising their babies and that her time would come. She could get a job when Ruby was at school. She was still young. She had her whole life in front of her. But Robbie had been wrong. By the time their youngest started primary school it had been too late. He'd watched Heather send out CV after CV to every law firm in Edinburgh. Most never even got back to her. Those who did explained that she just didn't have the relevant experience they required. Robbie had watched his wife's resentment and frustration grow like a cancer, as her love for him evaporated into thin air. And then, out of desperation, she'd taken the job at the events management company, organising charity balls, music events and business conventions. It wasn't her dream job, and at first she'd hated it, but gradually she'd seemed happier, back out there in the adult world, making her own money. For about six months Robbie had hoped that their marriage was on the mend but then Heather had dropped the bombshell – she'd fallen in love with her boss – and within a week she'd moved herself and the children out of the family home and into Fraser's enormous townhouse. And the rest, as they say, is history.

Maybe it had been doomed from the start. The young couple had only been together for a few months when Heather fell pregnant. She was so beautiful that Robbie couldn't believe his luck. Why would a girl like Heather want to settle down with a guy like him? And what's more, she was posh – a public school girl who'd been brought up in a big house, with a dad who went to work in a suit, carrying a briefcase, and a mum who played the piano and spoke fluent French. By contrast, Robbie had been brought up in a council flat in Wester Hailes by his mum, Brenda, who worked at the Co-op stacking shelves. He hadn't seen his dad since he'd pissed off to Ireland with his new girlfriend in 1979. And he hadn't missed the useless bastard either. His mum was a grafter, and she kept her three kids clean, tidy and well fed. She made sure they went to school and did their homework but Robbie's academic success took even Brenda by surprise.

'I dinna ken where you got they brains fae,' his mum would laugh throatily from behind her Lambert and Butler when his glowing school reports came home. 'It wisnae fae me, that's for sure. But good on ye, son. I'm proud as punch.'

From a very young age Robbie had been bright, quick-witted and hell-bent on getting out of the sink estate he'd been brought up on. He worked hard at school and the teachers, relieved to have at least one attentive pupil in their class, gave him all the attention and support he needed.

He was in awe of the private school boys he saw in town. While his mates shouted abuse at them, Robbie just wished he could talk nicely like they did, and play rugby, and go to university. Those boys had it made. Their futures would be full of nice houses, fast cars and, best of all, posh girls with great legs, high cheekbones and long, shiny, rich-girl hair. Robbie had always been popular with the lassies but he doubted he'd ever get a girl like that. But that's what he wanted – a nice, respectable, middle-class life with a nice respectable middle-class girl. It was the type of life he saw on the telly, in those sit-coms set down south, where nobody seemed to be on the dole, or on the game, or sniffing glue, or injecting smack.

Robbie got good grades and announced that he wanted to be a journalist. His mum nearly wet herself laughing at the idea of him, a McLean, working for a newspaper. To Brenda McLean, newspapers were something you found wrapped around your fish supper on a Friday night. But he'd never relied on his family's support, financial or emotional. Robbie had always been a self-contained soul. He believed in himself and that was enough. He worked late nights in a bar on Rose Street to support himself through his journalism course at Napier College and then, when he graduated top of his year, he walked straight into a job as junior reporter on a local paper in West Lothian.

By the time he met Heather, in a café in genteel Stockbridge, he was already working for Scotland's best-selling national newspaper. But he had no intention of staying there. It was a springboard to a job in London and then, who knew? New York maybe? Robbie had big ideas and back then he'd had no doubts that he would achieve every goal he set himself.

Heather blew him away. Tall, leggy and a natural blonde, she oozed breeding and class. She spoke in a lovely, clipped Edinburgh accent, like one of Miss Jean Brodie's girls, and Robbie thought she was the crème de la bloody crème! She flicked her long hair from side to side as she spoke, enthusiastically, about everything from indie music to devolution. She had the kind of self-confidence that only money could buy. It turned out her flat was just round the corner from Robbie's and they started meeting regularly at the café. He'd walk her home, hand in hand, through the cobbled streets in the rain, the proudest man in Scotland to have such a beauty on his arm. Then they'd share coffee-flavoured kisses and chat on her sofa for hours. He loved listening to her voice. She told Robbie that when she finished her law degree she would move to London and work in the City. She said that Edinburgh was too small a town for her and that she wanted to get out and see the world, achieve things. He hung on every perfectly articulated word and thought he'd met his soulmate. Robbie sighed, sadly, at the memory. He was still baffled about where the hell that girl had gone.

And so now he lived alone most of the time, in the modest little house that used to be his family's home. He'd got used to being without Heather but he could never quite get used to waking up and finding the girls' bedroom empty and silent. The truth was Robbie was lonely. There had been a handful of girlfriends since Heather's departure. But none of them filled the gaping hole left by the break-up of his marriage and he'd always let them go, gently, before things had got too serious, scared of hurting, and of being hurt, and of making another mistake. Only one other woman had really stirred him. The truth was she'd totally bowled him over! But she was *way* out of his league. He'd always kind of suspected that Heather was too classy for him even before she'd left him. And Christ, if Heather was from a different class, this one was from a totally different planet! No, best not to pursue that one. It would only end in tears. His!

And so Robbie threw himself into his career, working

evenings and weekends, winning awards, chasing the dirty crime stories that no one else would touch for fear of re-criminations. He knew his editor, Ed Patterson, rated him, but Bernie was right about the Monaco trip. He was pushing it there. His expenses had come to almost three grand last time and he'd only been there for two days. To make matters worse the story about Giancarlo 'Fatty' LaFata had never actually been published because the newspaper's lawyers were too nervous to run it. But he'd made good contacts when he'd been out there and now there was a story. Fatty was missing, presumed drowned, and Robbie had to get out there. He pushed his sandy blond hair back off his face and took a deep breath before knocking on Patterson's office door. He needed this to go the right way. He had to go to Monaco today.

'Come in, Robbie,' called Patterson impatiently from behind his closed office door.

How the hell did he do that? Robbie was always amazed at his editor's ability to see through doors, round corners and into the future. You could never pull the wool over his eyes because he had some kind of sixth sense about what was really going on.

Robbie opened the door and walked in. Patterson made him nervous. He rubbed his slightly sweaty palms on the back pockets of his jeans and cleared his throat to speak.

'The answer is yes, no, no and yes,' said Patterson bluntly.

'Pardon?' said Robbie. Ed Patterson had a way of making him feel stupid, even though he knew he was anything but.

Patterson sighed as if it was Robbie being obtuse.

'Yes, you can go to Monaco. No, you can't have another helicopter ride. No, you can't charter yourself a yacht. And yes, I do think that LaFata is dead.'

'Seriously?' Robbie hasn't expected it to be that easy. 'Ye-es!' He punched the air with his fist.

'Seriously,' said Patterson, rolling his eyes at Robbie's enthusiasm. 'But this time make it stick, Robbie. I need cold, hard facts about what LaFata has been up to. Is he dead? If so, is it suicide or murder? I'm relying on you, Robbie. I want the story behind the mystery. I want the scoop.'

'You've got it,' said Robbie, grinning. 'You won't regret this, boss.'

'I'd better not,' replied Patterson flatly. 'Now go home and grab a bag. I want you on the scene as quickly as possible.'

Then, as Robbie was walking out the door, Patterson added, 'But do not bankrupt the paper this time, McLean. D'you hear me? Hire a car, not a bloody helicopter. That's an order!'

Chapter Eight

The tourists scuttle like rats around the harbour, pushing and shoving, treading and climbing on each other to get a better view. When watched from a distance, it is clear that human beings are basically selfish creatures.

The police scuttle too, with an over-inflated sense of self-importance. It is a strange man who wishes to spend his life in a uniform giving and receiving orders. There is a theory that the desire to become a police officer should ban you from ever becoming one. The police shout at the tourists to stay back, and shoo them away like pigeons, but they too are enjoying the circus at Port Hercule today. Monaco is tiny, just under two square kilometres, only the Vatican City is smaller, but it is also the most heavily policed country in the world. And the crime rate is low. So, the truth is, the police are bored stupid most of the time. But today, Giancarlo 'Fatty' LaFata has given them something to do. For that they must be truly grateful.

A small group of journalists and television crews have already set up camp beside the Monaco Yacht Club. And the first press helicopters have begun to swarm in like wasps around a picnic. They hover so low that they threaten to clip the masts of the superyachts in the harbour. Now that would be an unexpected and highly amusing twist to today's events – a helicopter crash. Yes, that would certainly add to the day's carnival atmosphere.

The family have left now and are driving back up the hill towards their home. The two older children, Francesca and

Giancarlo Junior, were here earlier, talking to the police, looking anxious and upset. Carlo wept, something he hasn't done since he was a boy. Meanwhile, the youngest daughter, Angelica, will be landing in London from Miami right about now. She will be greeted by a family friend, who will tell her the dreadful news about her father's disappearance. The girl will fall to pieces. She is her daddy's favourite. It's a great shame that the poor child has to go through the ordeal but life is cruel. She has to learn.

No one has thought to tell LaFata's wife, Jade, that her husband is missing yet. She will be an afterthought. Francesca will feel guilty when she realises the oversight she's made but Carlo will not care. He is a self-centred boy who only worries about himself. As a child, he was horribly spoilt by his mother, and his father did not discipline him often enough. It is always the fault of the parents.

The children do not consider Jade to be part of the family. They do not consider her at all. They think she is stupid and dull and hope that their father will soon become bored with her. Perhaps they are right. Perhaps they are wrong. Perhaps now they will never know.

Police divers continue to search the water for a body but they won't find what they are looking for today. The sniffer dogs on Vigorosa III are also searching in vain. LaFata's body does not lurk on board.

The police have failed to spot LaFata's Rolls-Royce Phantom parked two streets back from the harbour. They are unaware that in the early hours of the morning, long before Francesca awoke and spotted the yacht drifting in the harbour, a smartly dressed young man, with a scar on his right cheek, opened the boot of the Phantom and retrieved a black briefcase from inside. He took the briefcase, and hailed a cab to the Monte Carlo Casino, where his red Ferrari had been valet-parked the night before. He tipped the valet generously and threw the briefcase on the back seat.

84

Then he drove back across the Italian border before the sun had risen and met a private jet at San Remo airport. The briefcase was then flown to Palermo and finally its precious contents arrived safely back in Sicily where it belonged.

Meanwhile, the young man with the scar and the smart suit drove back to Monaco, checked into the Hotel de Paris, showered, changed, and enjoyed a breakfast of croissants and fresh coffee on his private balcony overlooking the sea. And then he got back to work. He is down there now, amongst the scuttling tourists, watching the police and the press helicopters from behind his dark sunglasses with a hint of a smile on his handsome face. He is the only one who has any idea what is going on at Port Hercule today. But he won't be telling anybody what he knows. Not if he values his life.

Chapter Nine

Angelica LaFata adjusted her enormous Oliver Peoples sunglasses onto the top of her head, pulled her skin-tight, body-con dress down an inch or two to protect her modesty, and tossed her mane of honey-blonde hair over her shoulders. She wobbled slightly on her new Louboutins as she juggled her purple Hermès Birkin bag with her Louis Vuitton suitcase, but she soon found her balance. She was used to walking in high heels. She'd started wearing her mum's stilettos when she was eighteen months old and there were plenty of home movies to prove it!

There, she was ready for her close-up. If there were any paparazzi lurking in the arrivals hall, she would be ready for them. The truth was, Angelica was hoping that she would get snapped. Actually, she was *dying* to be papped. She looked good, she knew she did. A couple of pounds heavier than last year, maybe, but she had a glow in her cheeks and a sparkle in her eye that had been missing for far too long. Now, when she looked in the mirror, she liked the girl who smiled back at her. And not just her appearance either, she liked who that girl had become. As her therapist kept telling her, she was growing into a well-adjusted young woman. 'I am amazing. I am amazing. I am amazing.' Her therapist's mantra. Finally Angelica's head was sorted.

She also loved the positive attention she was getting suddenly. Her photo had appeared in *Grazia* magazine last week (they admired the way she teamed her Burberry trench coat with bare legs and chunky ankle boots apparently), and she'd been in a couple of the tabloids the week before, snapped leaving Nobu after a meal with friends. One caption had simply read, 'Fashionista Angelica LaFata', while the other had said, 'Fatty's pizza heiress, Angelica LaFata, samples some upmarket cuisine. What would Daddy say?' As if she would actually eat that carb-loaded junk they served in her family's chain of restaurants! And as if Daddy would want her to! Purlease! But, hey ho, *what-ever*, compared to the press she used to get, it was all good, clean fun.

Fashionista, she liked that. Angelica had always adored clothes but lately she'd begun to develop her own style, mixing modern designer pieces with her mother's vintage Pucci and Ozzie Clarke. Today she was in Herve Leger. She loved the way his dresses clung to her new curves. Suddenly, Angelica had boobs and a bum and she was buggered if she was going to hide them! She hadn't travelled in this outfit of course. She wasn't crazy. A transatlantic flight in a bandage dress and six-inch platform shoe boots was just plain ridiculous. No, she'd done the usual celebrity trick of boarding the aeroplane in her glad rags and then immediately changing into her cashmere hoody, leggings and Uggs for the flight. A year ago, a long-haul flight would have involved a couple of bottles of champagne, a few neat vodkas, and several trips to the toilet to snort coke. But last night she'd taken off her make-up, applied a thick layer of Crème de la Mer, popped a sleeping pill and snuggled down in her bed in Upper Class, under a soft blanket and a satin eye mask. She'd slept like a baby for a full eight hours and woken up feeling surprisingly refreshed. Half an hour before touchdown she'd changed back into her Herve Leger dress and reapplied her make-up – not an easy job in an airline toilet but, as a model, Angelica was used to getting changed in tight spots – and *voilà*, as her mum would say, *magnifique*!

Angelica's star was rising. Her modelling career had really taken off lately, with high-profile campaigns for Gucci and L'Oréal, not to mention the Melissa Odabash swimwear shoot she'd just done in Miami. And she'd even presented a couple of segments about her native Cote d'Azur for MTV. They'd lined her up for more work next weekend when the Monaco Grand Prix was on. She couldn't wait!

Angelica felt fit, healthy, happy and positive. Her whole life was spread in front of her like the blank pages of an unwritten novel, ready to be filled with a glittering career, fabulous parties, exquisite dresses and hot young guys. Long gone were those dark days of drinking and drug-taking that had her in and out of rehab more often than Amy Winehouse. And no more breaking her heart, and messing up her head, over no-good loser men either. No, thanks to her sister Francesca's dogged determination (or bullying as she'd seen it at the time), a long stint in a hard-core rehab centre in Arizona had finally cured her of her demons and for the past nine months she'd been clean. Clean of drink, clean of drugs and clean of toxic men.

As far as the press were concerned, she still teetered some-where between fame and infamy, but she felt as though she was finally being recognised for something positive. No more headlines about the 'Junkie Heiress', or their favourite, 'Fallen Angel', which was always plastered across a picture of her falling out of a nightclub at four a.m. with somebody else's husband. Fallen Angel. Ha, bloody, ha! No, these days Angelica could hold her head up high. And she was such a good girl that she practically had a halo.

She strutted through the gate, as best she could while

pulling a suitcase on wheels, with her shoulders back and her new boobs thrust forward, hoping that a photographer or two might be waiting for her. Then she'd jump in a cab to Sloane Square and meet up with a couple of girlfriends for lunch and shopping on the King's Road. Angelica shared her time between her beachfront apartment in Monaco and her mews house in Chelsea. Daddy had bought her the sweet little mews as a 'well-done' present when she first got signed to a modelling agency at seventeen and it really was a godsend now her career had picked up again. She had another shoot in London on Tuesday so there was no point in going back to the Riviera this weekend. She'd fly back on Wednesday, just in time to catch the biggest parties at the Cannes Film Festival, which was happening this week.

She took a deep breath and turned on her winning smile as the door swung open. It froze on her face. Nothing could have prepared Angelica for the sight she found as the automatic doors opened into the arrivals hall. Not just one or two paparazzi were waiting, but dozens of them. What the hell was going on? What had she done now? Angelica racked her brain for something, anything, she'd done lately that would cause such a stir, but there was nothing. She hadn't even snogged any of her friends' boyfriends recently. She really was a reformed character. A swarm of photographers jostled with each other, their cameras flashing in her face, and they were all shouting at her. They kept asking about her dad. She heard their questions but the words didn't make any sense.

'Angel! Angel! How do you feel?'

'What do you think has happened to your dad?'

'Did he jump or was he pushed?'

'Are you going back to Monaco now?'

Angelica felt paralysed for a moment, her feet glued

to the spot, her eyes blinking against the flashbulbs, their words swimming in her ears. She was a rabbit caught in the headlights, all she could see was a wall of cameras and unfamiliar faces. Suddenly Angelica felt scared. Her new-found confidence evaporated into the air as the paparazzi surged towards her like an attacking army. Her head began to spin and her knees felt weak. She dropped her Birkin bag and watched helplessly as her phone, make-up and purse fell onto the floor and all the time the cameras kept flashing. As she dropped to her knees and began shakily collecting her belongings, she heard a familiar, deep, male voice.

'Let me through, you leeches,' the voice ordered. 'Let me help the lady.'

And then suddenly Christian was there beside her, his kind, handsome face smiling at her, swiftly shoving her belongings back into her bag, taking her suitcase, shoving the photographers out of the way, herding Angelica hurriedly through the airport with a gentle but firm hand on the small of her back, towards the door and into a waiting black Mercedes with blacked-out windows.

Christian was her brother Carlo's best friend and he was a total sweetie. He was the kind of guy you could throw up in front of and he would stand there patiently, rubbing your back and holding your hair off your face. He was good-looking too, in a hunky, blond, Scandinavian kind of way. Not Angel's type, of course. She preferred her men skinny, dark and fronting up a rock band, but she did adore him. It was like having two big brothers – a crazy, wild, party-animal one in Carlo, and a warm, kind, huggable one in Christian. And Angel was certainly relieved to see Christian now. Something seriously weird was going on.

'What's happening, Chris?' she asked shakily, scared of the answer but desperate to know the truth. Photographers were running alongside the car now, slamming their hands against the side, thrusting their cameras right up to the blacked-out windows, still trying to get a shot.

'We're going back to Monaco, Angel,' said Christian, taking her hand and squeezing it. 'My plane's waiting for us on the runway. I'm afraid I've got some bad news to tell you about your dad.'

The LaFata family waited in pained silence in the first-floor drawing room of Le Grand Bleu. Every now and then the sound of Benito and Luca's high-pitched laughter wafted up through the open window from the garden below. The boys were playing with their nanny, blissfully unaware of the drama unfolding all around them. Francesca wished she could be with them, playing hide and seek between the palms and pine trees. God, she longed to hold her boys close, feel their plump arms round her neck and their damp, sticky kisses on her cheeks. But if they looked at her now, they would know something was wrong, and Francesca had no way of explaining. She had no answers for them. Hell, *she* didn't understand a damn thing about what was going on, how could she explain to a five and a seven-year-old that their beloved grandpa had vanished into thin air?

Jade sat facing the window on a piano stool with her back to the others, staring out to sea with her head slightly bowed and her shoulders slumped forward. Even her back looked sad. She was in a real state about Fatty's disappearance but she was also angry with Francesca and Carlo. Not that Francesca could blame her. What a stupid mistake, forgetting to call Jade straight away. The poor girl had to hear the news from the maid, who'd heard what had happened on the radio. She'd been frantic by the time Francesca, William and Carlo got back to the house. Francesca had apologised until she was blue in the face, and she'd tried to explain that in the confusion, and the hurry, she'd just forgotten to call. She felt genuinely awful about what she'd done. Or, at least, what she *hadn't* done. It wasn't like Francesca to mess up. She was normally super-organised, but then she'd never been in this situation before.

Thankfully, Jade wasn't one for arguments. She was more of a huffer than a shouter. Maybe that's what Fatty liked about her so much. She didn't answer back. She either did what she was told, or huffed quietly in her room when she didn't get her own way. She never raised her voice. In fact, she was pretty quiet most of the time. Sometimes Francesca forgot that she even lived in the house. Which was probably why she'd forgotten to ring her this morning. Once Jade had calmed down and stopped crying, she'd grudgingly accepted Francesca's apology. But she hadn't said a word since and it was obvious from her body language that she was still sulking.

Carlo lounged on a chair in the corner, staring blankly into space, humming some unrecognisable dance tune over and over. Every couple of minutes he would check his Rolex, tut, and then start humming again. He was getting on Francesca's nerves but she didn't have the heart to tell him to shut up. Francesca herself sat on the edge of the sofa, clutching her phone and waiting for something to happen. Anything. A call from the police or a visit from a detective. Anything would be better than this unbearable limbo. Suddenly her phone beeped in her hand. Francesca jumped, Carlo stopped humming and Jade swung round in her stool.

'It's Christian. He's got Angelica. They're on the runway,' said Francesca. 'They'll be here in a couple of hours.'

'Poor Angel,' said Carlo, sitting up. 'It's great that

Christian's with her but I bet she's taken this hard. Fuck, this is the last thing she needs. We've only just got her back on the rails.'

'We?' asked Francesca. Well, he had a bloody cheek! '*We've* got her back on the rails, have we? I seem to remember you were usually the one falling out of nightclubs with her in the middle of the night.'

Carlo glowered at his sister. 'Yeah, maybe, but I was just looking after my baby sister. Anyway, you know I don't do drugs. Never have.'

'Nah, just hard drink, fast cars and loose women for you, Saint Giancarlo ...' retorted Francesca.

Carlo frowned at her moodily from behind his long, thick, black eyelashes. He was trying his best to look pissed off, but his brown eyes were still tinged with red from crying and he was biting his bottom lip to stop it from wobbling. Oh God, she was being unfair on him. Carlo was no angel but he was her kid brother, and the last thing he needed right now was a lecture from Francesca. She was taking her frustration and anxiety out on him and it wasn't right. He was hurting just as badly as she was.

'Sorry,' she said quietly. 'It's the stress.'

'We're all under stress, Francesca,' muttered Carlo. 'It doesn't give you the right to behave like a complete bitch.'

'Oh, just shut up, both of you,' snapped Jade. Her sudden outburst was so out of character that it made Francesca jump. 'Think about poor Fatty and stop feeling sorry for yourselves. Stop acting like spoilt brats.'

Francesca and Carlo shared a guilty look. Jade was right. But Francesca found thinking about her dad was horrible. Where was he? She'd been through every possibility but she always came up with the same answer. As far as she could see, the only logical explanation was that he'd drowned. The thought of her father's huge body, floating, lost somewhere in the Mediterranean, made her shudder with horror.

A phrase popped into her head suddenly – sleeping with the fishes. It was how all Dad's stories about Sicily had ended. When she was a little girl he used to sit on her bed at night and tell these mad, unbelievable tales about long-lost great-uncles who'd upset the Cosa Nostra back in the old country. Sometimes Uncle Alfonso had seduced the beautiful teenage daughter of a priest, or Uncle Federico had beaten the local Mafia chief at cards, or Uncle Guido had refused to carry out a murder for a crime lord. The names and the plots changed slightly each time but the stories were basically the same. The fearless LaFata hero would go on the run and survive on his wits, through earthquakes, wars, famines and assassination attempts. And the ending was always identical.

'What happened to him, Daddy?' Francesca would ask, eyes like saucers, hoping in vain for a happy ending.

'Ah, *molto triste*,' Fatty would sigh, shrugging his vast shoulders and shaking his head forlornly. 'He ended up sleeping with the fishes.'

Had Fatty ended up sleeping with the fishes? Francesca felt sick. She hadn't eaten a thing all day and she'd had so much coffee that her hands were shaking. Or maybe that was the shock.

The heavy wooden door creaked open and William appeared in the room, looking grim and ashen-faced. Francesca stared at him, willing him to say something that would make the pain go away, but knowing already, from the look on his face, that he had bad news.

'They've found Fatty's phone,' he said gravely.

'Where?' asked Francesca, Carlo and Jade in unison.

They'd all kept trying his number but the line was still dead.

'I'm afraid a police diver found it at the bottom of the harbour,' he replied.

His words hung over the silent room like a toxic gas. Francesca felt as if she couldn't breathe properly. No one said anything for a long time.

'Well that's that then,' said Carlo, finally breaking the silence. 'He's gone.'

Jade flew off her stool, sending it flying across the room, and fled out of the door, sobbing.

'Carlo, please!' scolded Francesca. 'There was no need to say that.'

'Yes there was,' said Carlo angrily. 'The stupid old fool's drunk a hundred grand's worth of brandy and fallen overboard, hasn't he? What other explanation is there?'

'I don't know, Carlo,' said Francesca, desperately trying to think of something. 'I really don't know. But it's not over until …'

'Until what, Frankie?' Carlo stood up and ran his fingers through his hair in despair. 'Until the fat lady sings? Or until the fat man's body gets washed up at Cap Ferrat?'

Chapter Ten

Padre Gabriele Fontana sat on his sun-soaked terrace, admiring his view of the Bay of Palermo and sipping a delicious glass of Chianti. He stared straight over the head of his companion and only half listened as the man babbled on about his trip. He had not offered his visitor a drink. He would not be staying long.

'Do you like my home, Marco?' asked Fontana, suddenly, bored with the younger man's conversation.

Marco nodded enthusiastically. 'It is very beautiful, Padre,' he said. 'And I am honoured to be here.'

Fontana nodded. Of course this stupid young man was impressed by his home. It was a magnificent building, medieval, built into the mountainside above Palermo with panoramic views of the city and the sea beyond. Who would not be impressed by such beauty?

'And so down to business,' said Fontana, suddenly keen to get the matter over and done with and for this Marco character to be gone. 'You have the briefcase?'

'I do,' said Marco proudly.

He lifted the briefcase carefully onto the table and laid it down gently before the priest.

'I was told it was very precious, Padre. I have looked after it with my life,' said Marco proudly.

'I would expect nothing less,' replied Fontana.

The young man stared expectantly at the case, clearly

willing Fontana to open it now. He was naive and unfamiliar with how these things worked. That was why he had been chosen for the job. Marco had no idea what he was involved in. Besides, his eyes were set too far apart, Fontana decided. He didn't care to look at him any longer. He felt irritated now by this intrusion into his day. There was no way the case would be opened until this Marco character was gone. Not that it mattered whether the young idiot saw the contents, of course. Fontana simply did not want to give him the satisfaction.

'You have been paid?' asked Fontana abruptly.

Marco nodded. 'Very generously, yes, thank you, Padre.'

'Well, you may go now, Marco.' Fontana dismissed the younger man impatiently. 'Go on. Shoo!'

Marco's face fell with disappointment but even he knew better than to loiter once he had been told to leave. He stood up, a little reluctantly, and half-bowed to the priest.

'It has been an honour to have served you, sir,' he stated grandly.

Fontana laughed at Marco's stupidity.

'I am a priest, not a god,' he scoffed. 'There is no need to grovel, my son. My maid will see you to the door. *Addio*.'

'*Arrivederci*, Padre,' said Marco, still bowing and tripping over himself as he retreated backwards towards the house, where Fontana's maid Karina waited. She was large and robust for a woman of her age and she took Marco firmly by the elbow as she led him inside the house. Finally he was gone and Fontana had some peace. He sat a little longer, enjoying his wine and the view. It was late afternoon and the sun was getting low in the sky. Soon it would be sunset, Fontana's favourite time of day.

Marco had been gone for half an hour before Fontana opened the briefcase. He did so slowly and methodically, savouring the moment, as if he were unwrapping a much longed-for gift. And then finally his eyes fell on the prize. At last. It was just as he remembered it. The precious contents of the briefcase were back in Sicily where they belonged. Fontana had been waiting years for this moment and now, finally, thanks to Giancarlo LaFata, a dream had been fulfilled. Fontana smiled to himself, poured another glass of Chianti and sat back to watch the sunset over the bay. He raised his glass in the air and shouted, '*Salute*, Fatty!' His voice echoed against the rocks. 'Fatty, Fatty, Fatty …'

Padre Gabriele Fontana couldn't remember a time when he had felt quite so content. He only wished his distant cousin and good friend Giancarlo Roberto LaFata could be here to celebrate with him now.

Marco steered his Vespa through the winding back streets of Palermo, his heart racing and his head spinning. Five thousand euros! For one day's work! It was crazy. If he hurried he could get to the jewellers before it shut. He imagined Gabriella's face when he gave her the ring. She would be so happy, so proud, so surprised! He had seen her gaze at those rings so many times as she walked past the shop on her way to work at the hairdresser's on the corner. It was the sapphires she loved best, blue like the sea, and Marco was going to get her the biggest sapphire engagement ring five thousand euros could buy.

He couldn't believe it when his cousin had told him about the job. All he'd had to do was meet a smartly dressed man in a café near the airport, pick up the briefcase and drive it up into the mountains to Padre Gabriele Fontana's home. To be honest the guy in the café had been a bit scary. But Marco had only had to spend five minutes with him. And now he had enough money to buy his beautiful Gabriella a ring and tonight, over dinner in a fancy restaurant, he would ask her to be his wife. Perhaps Padre Fontana would agree to marry them. Now wouldn't that be the icing on the wedding cake?

Marco sped round the corner so fast that he almost crashed into the stationary Fiat in front. He slammed on his brakes and beeped his horn three times. He was in a hurry! He had a ring to buy! The car didn't move. It was a narrow lane and there was no room for Marco to get past. Perhaps the car had broken down. Normally Marco would have offered his help but this evening there was no time to spare. He would turn around and go another route. Just as he began to reverse, a second car came whizzing in behind him and slammed on its brakes. *Mio dio*! Now he was trapped. This wasn't going according to plan.

'Come on. Move, move!' Marco shouted impatiently, flapping his arms at the car behind. 'Reverse!'

But the second car didn't budge either. And now the doors were opening and a man was getting out. He was smartly dressed in a black suit and Marco recognised him instantly as the guy from the café earlier that day. The one who'd given him the briefcase.

'Is something wrong?' asked Marco, suddenly feeling nervous as the man walked towards him. 'I've given Padre Fontana the briefcase, just as you said.'

'Give me the money,' said the man coldly. He was a few inches taller than Marco, and several inches wider. 'The five thousand euros. Give me it now.'

'No,' said Marco. 'I did what I was asked to do. Why should I give you my money?'

Marco was not a particularly brave man but he had a strong sense of right and wrong. And this was definitely wrong. He was not going to part with his money easily, not when it was going to buy Gabriella an engagement ring. But the tall man pulled a knife from his waist and held the glistening blade to Marco's neck. 'Just give me the money, you little maggot,' he spat.

Marco could feel the cold steel of the blade against his skin. The blood drained from his face, his knees buckled beneath him and he felt his bladder give way. He opened his mouth to speak but it was so dry that he couldn't find the words. The larger man threw him to the ground and Marco felt his brow bone crack on the cobbled paving stones. And then the brute was standing on his back as he bent down to frisk him. Marco's wallet was easy to find in the back pocket of his jeans. Over his shoulder he could see the man help himself to the notes, count them and then toss the wallet across the street. He bundled the money into his breast pocket then grabbed Marco by the shoulders and hauled him back to his feet. Marco could feel blood trickling down his face. He thought about his mother, and Gabriella, and prayed to God that the ordeal would soon be over. The man still held the knife in his hand.

Finally Marco found his voice. 'What would Padre Fontana say about this?' he asked, hoping to stir the thief's conscience.

'Ha!' The man threw his head back and laughed. 'Padre Fontana said he did not like your face. He said your eyes were too far apart.'

Marco stared at the man, confused and disorientated. It felt as if the world was shifting beneath his feet. What was he saying? What did he mean? All his life he had been a good Catholic. Devout. He had never missed Mass. He went to confession regularly and he idolised the priests, just as his mother had taught him to do. Could such a famous and well-known priest as Padre Fontana have something to do with this crime? No. The man was lying. Playing with Marco's mind. He was nothing but a common thief and a damned liar!

As he opened his mouth to tell his attacker what he thought, Marco saw a flash of metal and felt the thump of a punch against his throat. There were no words, just a gurgle and a strangled, choking noise as the blood filled his mouth. The last thought Marco had as he crumpled to the ground was that poor Gabriella would never get her sapphire now.

Chapter Eleven

It was a smooth flight. The skies were clear and Robbie celebrated the start of his trip with a cold beer. He hadn't been surprised to see a couple of journalists from rival papers on the same plane. This story was huge and the world's press were already covering it. But it amused him to see the different papers' take on the LaFata scandal. The tabloid had sent their celebrity writer, while the broadsheet had sent their financial reporter. Robbie was chief crime writer and he felt sure that Fatty LaFata's disappearance had far more to do with his specialist subject than it had to do with economics or·fame.

The three journalists had chatted in the departure lounge, worked out they were staying in neighbouring hotels and arranged to meet for a drink in Monte Carlo later that evening. Simon Featherstone-Waugh and Dan Donovan were good guys. Just because they worked for rival publications, and they were coming at the story from different angles, didn't mean they couldn't have a bit of fun on their trip. It needn't be all work and no play, after all. It was Heather's weekend with the girls. And a couple of days in Monaco sure as hell beat another lonely weekend in an empty house.

'Monaco?' Heather had said icily, when he'd called to tell her he might not be back to have the girls on Tuesday night and could he please have them another night instead.

'Again? I seem to remember you let the children down last time you went to Monte Carlo?'

It was the only time she spoke to him directly. On the phone. And even then, everything she said sounded as if it was directed at an audience. Her responses never seemed to be for his benefit, but rather to reinforce to some third party how right she had been to leave this useless man. Robbie found himself wondering, not for the first time, whether Heather put him on speakerphone and talked to him in front of Fuckwit. Yes, he'd bet that was it. He could just see them, sitting on the sofa in their grand drawing room, with their knees touching, exchanging their smug little 'looks'.

'Heather,' Robbie had responded patiently, 'it's work. I would never let the girls down intentionally. You know that. But my job's unpredictable. I can't control when a story breaks. It's not as if I'm going off on holiday. I haven't packed my trunks and my suntan lotion. This is my job. The job that pays the girls' maintenance.'

Robbie had flinched as he'd listened to Heather laugh condescendingly. 'Robbie,' she'd sneered, 'the pittance you pay towards Grace and Ruby's upkeep barely pays for their piano and horse riding lessons.'

'I pay as much as I can,' Robbie had replied, trying to stay calm and keep the anger out of his voice. This was so unfair. He paid her almost half his bloody salary and still it wasn't enough!

'I know you do, Robbie.' That patronising laugh again. 'I'm aware that you don't earn much. Thankfully, Fraser is in a position to pay for the girls' school fees ...'

'Yeah well, you know what I think about that subject,' he'd replied, finally losing his temper. 'I never wanted them going to that poncy school in the first place. They were doing perfectly well at the local primary. And a state education never did me any harm.'

'No, Robbie,' Heather had said sarcastically. 'You're such a success story. Pushing forty, single, living in a cramped little terraced house and working for a provincial rag. Well, do forgive me, but I want more than that for my girls.'

'Our girls,' Robbie had snapped back.

'I'm not going to rearrange the girls' schedules around your jolly to Monte Carlo, Robbie. You won't be able to see them this week. You can wait until next Saturday.'

'God, you are such a bitch, Heather,' Robbie heard himself saying and then immediately kicked himself for letting her get to him. He felt sure Fraser was listening, which only made her treatment of him even more humiliating.

Heather was silent for a long time and then she sniffed, loudly, and said, 'I will not be spoken to like that, Robbie. Goodbye.'

Robbie had slammed down the phone, run upstairs and thrown the contents of his wardrobe onto the bed. Everything was creased and there was no time to hunt down the iron, so Robbie had stuffed his suit, his best (of a bad bunch) jeans and his two best white shirts into a battered old holdall with a couple of clean pairs of pants and some socks that smelled as if they'd only been worn once. His wardrobe was definitely more Midlothian than Monte Carlo but now wasn't the time to worry about that, the taxi was already waiting outside.

The flight gave Robbie a chance to reflect on the case. He was already several steps ahead of any other reporter, because Giancarlo LaFata had long since been an obsession of his. Every journalist had a story that got under his skin and festered, and this was Robbie's. He could barely remember a time when he hadn't known who LaFata was. Everybody in

Edinburgh knew about him when Robbie was a kid because he was seen as a kind of local hero. He was always sponsoring sports teams and raising money for charity. Pictures of his big, round, jolly face were always grinning from the front pages of the local papers. By the time Robbie was a teenager in the eighties, Fatty's restaurants were *the* places to go for a meal. Oh, they weren't posh. Far from it. And they weren't expensive either. It was where Brenda had always taken the kids for their birthday meals and the McLeans were hardly flush! But the pizzas were fantastic and the ice cream was to die for. Sometimes Robbie had seen Fatty driving around town in his green Bentley and he'd always been impressed that this man, who'd come from nothing, had done so well for himself. As a poor teenager himself, Robbie had felt inspired by the stories he'd heard about the penniless immigrant who'd come to Scotland and made his fortune.

And then, of course, Fatty had left Edinburgh. Just when he was at the peak of his popularity, he'd jumped ship, divorced his good, solid Scottish wife and run off to Monaco as a tax exile with his new French film-star girlfriend, Sandrine de la Plage. Within weeks of his departure, Maggie LaFata was dead. And even though the post-mortem had stated breast cancer, the Scottish press had implied she'd died of a broken heart after Fatty took her daughter from her. There was a collective feeling in Scotland that Fatty, their adopted National Treasure, had let them down.

Robbie hadn't forgotten about LaFata over the years. There were always stories in the press about his marriages and divorces, his increasingly outlandish spending habits and, in more recent years, about the wayward behaviour of his children. But it had been a conversation in his local about a year ago that had flicked Robbie's switch. An old chap called Rick, who habitually propped up the bar in the

Waverley Tavern, had been blethering away as usual about this, that and the next thing, when suddenly he'd mentioned a fatal fire that had happened in Edinburgh when Robbie was a kid. Robbie had remembered the incident because he'd happened to walk past the scene on Lothian Road the next day, just as the coroner was bringing out the charred remains of the victim. It was something you didn't forget. The burned-out building had been an Italian restaurant called Giuseppe's and the unfortunate owner, Giuseppe Romano, had been inside when the blaze took hold.

'I do remember that,' Robbie had said to Rick. 'It was a faulty oven, wasn't it?'

'Nah!' Rick had scoffed, downing his whisky in one. 'It was Fatty LaFata who did that.'

'What?' Robbie had almost choked on his pint. 'Don't be daft, Rick. Are you seriously suggesting that Giancarlo LaFata set fire to that place?'

'Aye,' Rick had nodded. 'Well, he maybe didnae light the match, but he certainly paid whoever did. Giuseppe's was his main competition in those days. And then, whoosh, overnight the problem was solved. Very neat. It was after Giuseppe's burned down that Fatty's really took off.'

As a crime reporter, Robbie was used to hearing conspiracy theories and he'd been about to write the story off as just another piece of drunken fantasy when Rick had added, 'Actually, I heard that story in here, from Pete Wallace.'

Pete Wallace had been the chief crime reporter at the paper when Robbie was just a junior reporter. Robbie had always looked up to Pete, and he'd been gutted when the poor bloke got killed in a car crash in the Borders a few years back.

'Are you sure about that, Rick?' Robbie had asked.

'Aye, quite sure.' Rick had nodded emphatically. 'That was definitely what Pete telt me.'

Back at the office, Robbie had searched through the archives, but there was no record of any link ever being made to Giancarlo LaFata and the Giuseppe's fire.

'What happened to Pete Wallace's files when he died?' he'd asked Bernie.

'Well, anything he was working on at the time would be handed over to other members of staff,' Bernie had said. 'But I seem to remember there were a few notebooks that weren't much use to anybody. Pete's shorthand was self-taught, you see. Only he could read it.'

Bernie had smiled at the memory. He and Pete had been good friends.

'I remember I didn't want to throw them out, though,' Bernie had continued. 'It seemed wrong to just bin his hard work so I think I ...'

Bernie had got out of his chair and taken a set of keys from his top drawer. Then he'd hurried across the office to an old metal filing cabinet, gathering dust in the corner by the water cooler.

'I think I put them in here,' he'd said as he unlocked the bottom drawer and started rooting around. 'Aye, here they are.' Bernie had stood up and dusted off a couple of old A4 notepads.

It had taken Robbie weeks to work out Pete's shorthand system. He couldn't spend his time at the office deciphering the notebooks so he'd taken them home and spent evenings and weekends poring over them.

Finally, Pete's scribbles and scrawls had begun to make sense. To Robbie, the notebooks were as valuable as gold bullion. Pete had been on to Giancarlo LaFata. He'd been doing some serious sniffing around before he died and he'd uncovered some pretty dodgy dealings – money laundering, fraud, embezzlement and, of course, the suspicious fire at Giuseppe's. But it had all been hearsay, mainly gossip from petty criminals, and Pete had obviously died before he'd had a chance to corroborate any of his stories. Robbie was more fired up about this than he'd ever been about any other story in his career. What's more, he felt it was his duty to take over Pete's hunch and finally get to the bottom of things. What better way would there be to honour Pete Wallace's memory?

But most of the Edinburgh stuff was too old. Witnesses had died, records had been lost or destroyed and people's memories had faded over the years. What Robbie needed to do was go to Monaco and dredge up some more recent history. It had taken weeks of begging and pleading with Patterson before he'd got the go-ahead but, finally, last October, he was told he could go for one weekend only. It had been an insightful trip in lots of ways. And now he was going back to reap the rewards of all his hard work.

Robbie stared out of the window of the plane. It was getting dark outside but he could make out the ghostly peaks of the Alps below him. It wouldn't be long before they were landing. He was excited about the trip. He felt sure that all the research he'd done into LaFata in the past would start to make sense in the wake of his disappearance. Now people would begin to talk. He just had to make sure that it was Robbie McLean they spoke to and not one of the hundred other journalists who were crawling all over the story.

It wasn't that he hadn't uncovered some pretty juicy dirt on the guy during the last trip, it was just that he hadn't been able to make any of it stick. Giancarlo LaFata always seemed to be just one step away from trouble. In Dubai, his hotel complex was part-funded by a sheikh whose brother had previously been linked with international arms dealers. His Russian business associates were rumoured to have once been in partnership with a man who was now languishing in a Washington jail, awaiting trial on money-laundering charges amounting to seven billion dollars. And then there were the ex-employees who'd mysteriously disappeared and the ex-wife who'd committed suicide – all within days of being dumped by Giancarlo LaFata.

But, despite all this, Giancarlo LaFata was one of the most popular men in Monaco. Nobody had a bad word to say about the guy. The words jolly, funny, generous and charismatic were bandied about by everyone from the landlord of his favourite bar, to the skipper of his yacht, to the woman who did his dry-cleaning. It sounded as if they were describing Santa Bloody Claus. Everyone liked Fatty. Or at least everyone *had* liked Fatty. Because it looked increasingly likely now, twelve hours after his disappearance, that LaFata was dead. What Robbie wanted to know was how and why. A tragic accident? The guy couldn't swim so could he have fallen overboard and drowned? Robbie hoped not. It seemed such a lame way to go. Suicide? Had the credit crunch hit the LaFata empire so hard that Fatty couldn't take the strain? It seemed unlikely. The man had umpteen business ventures on the go, not to mention his yachts, private jets and houses all over the world. Surely he could just have sold some of his assets if he'd been feeling the pinch. And besides, for all his faults, Robbie felt sure that Giancarlo LaFata was no coward. So that left murder. Maybe Fatty hadn't been quite so well liked by everyone after all.

Suddenly Robbie could see the lights of the Riviera below him, twinkling neon stars in a sky of black sea. From up here the entire coast looked like a giant theme park. Which in a way, Robbie guessed, it was. The playground of the rich and famous – beaches, restaurants, bars, casinos, nightclubs. It all stretched out before him. As the plane banked sharply over the Mediterranean and made its descent towards Nice Airport, Robbie felt butterflies of excitement rise in his stomach.

Chapter Twelve

The detectives had been and gone. Carlo stood on the balcony, dragged hard on his cigarette and then watched as the smoke rings he blew drifted into the night, disintegrated and disappeared. He tried to make sense of what the police had told him. They'd found two glasses on the table on *Vigorosa III*, but only one person's fingerprints and DNA. They were working on the assumption that the samples belonged to his dad but it would be a few days before they had the results. They'd all had to give samples of their DNA. It was nothing personal, the lady detective had explained, as she'd thrust a swab into Carlo's mouth, anyone who'd been on board the yacht in the last few days was being swabbed – family, friends, business associates and crew – for elimination purposes. The whole thing seemed so unreal that Carlo felt as if he was watching himself in an episode of *CSI*.

It turned out there had been a couple of witnesses. The yacht had still been in its berth at one a.m., when Wally, the captain of Carlo's yacht *Pulling Power*, had gone to bed. Fatty must have been there then, with whoever he'd been sharing the brandy with, but Wally hadn't noticed any sign of life on board. At four a.m., a cleaner in an office block across the road from the harbour had noticed that *Vigorosa III* seemed to be out of her mooring, but the woman wasn't an expert on luxury superyachts, so she'd just assumed that the owner knew what they were doing. She hadn't seen anybody on deck either.

And then came the really scary part. Forensic detectives had found evidence that his dad had fallen overboard. A tiny piece of white cotton had been found caught on the wooden railings surrounding the top deck, a single shirt button had been found on the floor and fresh fingerprints had been taken from the handrail. Carlo had been able to confirm to the detectives that his dad had indeed been wearing a white shirt the night before. Beige slacks, white shirt, navy blazer, all in a size XXL. It was his favourite outfit. The phone company had confirmed that his dad's mobile had stopped working at 2.47 a.m. The police said they were very sorry, but they were now working on the assumption that Giancarlo LaFata had drowned and they would be putting all their efforts into locating his body. Then, once they had a body, they would be able to piece together exactly how he had died.

Carlo still suspected that his father had been drunk and fallen overboard by accident. Or perhaps he'd had a heart attack while he'd been leaning over the handrail, enjoying the view and smoking a cigar. How many times had Carlo seen him do exactly that? Yes, that would make sense. Dad's health certainly hadn't been good lately.

Carlo's relationship with his father had never been easy. He'd always felt like a bit of a spare part in the family and he'd wondered sometimes if his dad would even notice if he wasn't there. The girls had their roles. Francesca had always been the brains of the operation and, being twelve years older than Carlo, she'd already established herself as second-in-command at LaFata International before he'd even finished school. So, there was no vacancy there. And Angel, God bless her, had been born so cute and blonde and perfect that she'd always been the one who'd had Daddy's heart in her pocket. Carlo remembered when they were kids, whenever their dad came home from work, the three LaFata children would run out into the drive to greet him. First he would scoop Angel up in his arms and kiss her pretty little face, then he would bend down and kiss Francesca's cheek and ask her about her studies, or her opinion on whatever was in the news that day and then, finally, he would ruffle Carlo's hair half-heartedly and say, 'OK, son?' But he would never wait for a reply. By the time Carlo opened his mouth to answer, his dad would be halfway to the house, still carrying Angel and hanging on Francesca's every word. Carlo would be left behind, standing by the car, watching Daddy's girls from afar. It was then that he learned how much love could hurt. When you cared about someone, they had the power to cause you pain. Better to switch off your feelings and protect your heart.

While Angel went to a private girls' school in Monaco, Carlo had been sent to boarding school in England at the age of eight. He knew his dad was sending him away because he was too much trouble. He'd heard his mum and dad arguing about it. Mum had wanted him to stay at home but Dad had insisted that he went. Mind you, his parents had argued about everything by then. They split up during his first term at boarding school.

It turned out that school wasn't so bad. Christian was there too and the boys already knew each other from Monaco where their mums were friends. Carlo was popular with the other boys back then, and he was good at sport, but he'd never really seen the point in working hard to get good grades. His dad had so much money that it wasn't as if he was ever going to actually have to get a job or anything boring like that. Nah, Carlo had put all his energy into having fun. Much to his teachers' frustration! By the time he was in his early teens, he'd worked out that the more trouble he got into at school, the more attention he got from his father. OK, so the bollocking he'd got the time Dad had had to fly over for an emergency meeting with the headmaster had been terrifying. All he'd done was set fire to the playing fields. What did it matter if the Firsts couldn't play rugby that weekend? It wasn't as if anyone had been hurt.

'You are a disgrace, Giancarlo!' his dad had bellowed, cheeks on fire, veins pulsing. 'I am a busy man. You think I no have more important things to do than sit and be lectured about my son's behaviour by some, how you say it? Some humped-up teacher!'

'Jumped up,' Carlo had corrected him, trying to stifle a giggle.

'They are this close to expelling you, my boy! This close!'

Fatty had held his chubby thumb and forefinger very close together. 'Now I have had to offer to pay for new sports field and, as a gesture of good will, a new swimming pool, just so they will not expel you. You have cost me time and you have cost me money. I am no happy with you, Giancarlo. I am no happy with you at all. You bring shame to the family. Your sisters, they are never trouble. But you? With you it is always one thing after the next thing.'

It wasn't that Carlo enjoyed being shouted at by his father but it sure beat being ignored. In recent years it had been Angelica who had taken over as the most troublesome child, with her addiction problems, her breakdowns and her stints in rehab. But still it was Carlo who got the blame. Carlo had watched as his father broke his heart over Angel, doing everything in his power to help her. But not once had Fatty got angry with Angel, he just made endless excuses for her and picked her up every time she fell off the pedestal he'd built for her.

'Is not her fault,' he would say. 'Angel is very fragile. She is easily led. I blame these friends of hers. Is your job to keep her away from them, Carlo, you hear me? She is your sister, you must protect her. If anything bad happens to my Angel I will blame you, OK?'

But it wasn't OK. How could Carlo keep control of Angelica's behaviour when her modelling career took her to London, New York, Paris and Milan? How could he stop her from hanging out with junky rock stars, or having affairs with married actors?

Meanwhile, Fatty took little or no notice of Carlo's life. He paid an allowance into his son's bank account every month and pretty much just let him get on with things. Every now and then he would give Carlo advice on women.

'You are too young to settle down, my son,' he would say. 'Play the field, sow your wild oaties. You are lucky to live here, in Monaco. Here is where you will find the most beautiful women in the world. You are a good-looking boy. Just like your father. Ha ha! You have the choice of many, many girls. Women are like cars, a new one is fun for a while, but soon you will be bored of her and will want to trade her in for a new model.'

Carlo's mind wandered to Sasha briefly. Fuck, was that just this morning? It seemed like weeks ago. She was something else, that girl. Unfinished business. But she would have to wait.

Angelica spotted Carlo through the open balcony doors.

'Can I have a ciggie please, Carlo?' she asked.

'Course you can, gorgeous,' replied Carlo, trying to force a smile. But Angelica could see he'd been crying.

'You OK?' she asked him, even though she knew it was a stupid question.

Carlo shrugged. 'Kind of,' he said unconvincingly. 'You?'

Angelica shook her head. No, she wasn't OK. She wasn't even on the same page as OK. They'd all told her that Daddy was probably dead but she couldn't bring herself to believe it. Not Daddy. He would never leave her. She shivered, even though the evening was mild. Carlo handed her a lit Marlboro Light.

'I don't think he's dead,' she told Carlo defiantly. 'If he was dead they'd have found his body by now.'

Carlo eyed her warily. She could tell he was thinking hard about his response before he opened his mouth. They all thought she was so bloody breakable that they were scared to say what they really felt.

'Sometimes it takes weeks for a body to wash up on shore,' said Carlo gently. 'James says it depends on the tides. But maybe you're right. Maybe Dad's still alive.'

Angelica could see in his eyes that he was lying. He didn't believe for a moment that Fatty was still alive. He was just saying that to make her feel better. She looked across the floodlit garden and down to the lights of Monte Carlo below. It all looked exactly the same as it had done when she'd left for Miami three days ago. How could her world have changed so dramatically and yet look exactly the same? She felt sure that she would know if her dad had died. They were so close. How could he have stopped breathing without Angelica knowing about it? No, he couldn't be dead. That wouldn't be fair!

'Well, I'm not going to start grieving,' Angelica told her brother, feeling almost angry at the rest of them for believing the worst. 'I won't. I can't give up hope just because

116

nobody's seen him all day. That's ridiculous. I mean, I know it looks suspicious. And I heard what the police said about the shirt and the phone and everything but ...'

She took a drag of her cigarette and sighed. 'But Daddy wouldn't just leave me like this. So, I'm going to keep waiting and hoping and that will keep me sane.'

Carlo flicked his cigarette butt over the balcony and put his arms gently around Angelica's shoulders.

'We just have to stick together,' he said. 'Whatever happens. As long as we're there for each other, we'll be OK. That's what Dad would want.'

Angelica nodded. Carlo was right. Dad had drilled the importance of family into them from birth. Friends were all well and good but the only people you could really trust were your family.

'Just let me know if there's anything I can do to help, Angel,' said Carlo.

Angelica thought for a moment. There was something she knew would help. Something that would take the edge off this horrible, hollow, ache she felt inside.

'Well, there is one thing, Carlo,' she said, smiling sweetly up at her big brother. 'I do kind of feel like going out tonight. It's like a morgue in there. Frankie's on the phone the whole time to the police and the lawyers. William's surgically attached to his computer and Jade's been given Valium by the doctor and is zonked out in bed. I mean, I don't know why she's so upset. She's only known Daddy for about five minutes. We've known him all our lives.'

Carlo managed a weak smile. 'It is a bit depressing in there, I must admit,' he said. 'But I thought you weren't drinking?'

'I'm not.' Angelica flashed him her best good-girl eyes. 'I just want to get out of the house for a while.'

Angelica had learned at a tender age that no man could resist her when she flashed those baby blues.

Francesca couldn't believe it when Carlo and Angelica announced they were going out.

'Are you two mad?' she demanded, staring in disbelief at her siblings, dressed to kill and ready to hit the town. 'Dad's missing, presumed dead, there are about five thousand photographers camped out at the gates, we're all in pieces and you two want to go out?! Jesus Christ, I've heard it all now.'

'But, Frankie,' said Angel, widening her eyes, 'we can't bear all this waiting. It's too painful. We just need to do something.'

'And what? Going out and getting smashed is going to make you feel better is it?' she demanded. 'I thought you were clean now, Angel. You promised me you wouldn't drink again. How can you even think about going out at a time like this?'

'I'm not going out for a drink,' replied Angel. 'I'm just going out to keep Carlo company. Isn't that right, Carlo?'

But Francesca didn't miss a trick. She knew her little sister inside out and she saw Angel jab Carlo in the ribs. She also didn't miss the slightly shocked look on his face as his sister gave him the blame. Although why Carlo was surprised was a mystery. He'd been taking the blame for Angelica ever since the day she was born.

'Um, er, yes, it was my idea. Angel just offered to come with me, that's all,' he mumbled.

God, why were all men such idiots around Angelica, wondered Francesca. Even Carlo, who never normally put anyone before himself, would willingly throw himself off a cliff if that was what Angel wanted him to do. The problem with Angel was she had no boundaries. Nobody had ever said no to her, so she'd pushed and pushed, and discovered that whatever she did and however badly she behaved, there were no consequences. Everybody always forgave her. Worse! They told her it wasn't her fault. Francesca had been as bad, always making excuses for her, clearing up her mess and picking up the pieces when she fell apart, but no more. Francesca had just lost her dad and she wasn't about to let another member of her family out of her grasp.

'You're not going out, young lady,' Francesca ordered. 'You will stay here with your family and show your poor missing father some respect.'

'Who the hell do you think you are, Frankie?' Angelica shouted, stamping her stiletto-clad foot. 'You're only my sister. I'm twenty-one. An adult. You don't tell me what to do, understand? You're not my mother!'

'No, but maybe if your mother had done a better job of raising you, you wouldn't have turned out to be such a spoilt, messed-up little cow!' Francesca found herself screaming back.

The minute the words were out of her mouth, she regretted saying them, but it was too late, they were out there, floating about the room and she had no way of taking them back.

'I'm sorry, Angel,' she apologised immediately. 'It's been a stressful day and I know you're upset, darling, but I just don't think that going out is the answer for you.'

'Oh, go to hell, Francesca,' spat Angel, spinning on her heels. 'Come on, Carlo, let's get out of this madhouse.'

Carlo threw Francesca a sheepish look, muttered something about having to go to look after Angel and then they were gone. Francesca collapsed onto the nearest chair and for the first time that day, burst into tears. She felt horribly alone. Scared, unloved, frightened and alone.

'I want my daddy,' she sobbed, uncontrollably. 'I just want my daddy.'

Chapter Thirteen

Near Palermo, Sicily, September 1961

The cousins have grown tired of laying the traps and poison for the rats. The older boy's father has ordered them to get rid of the vermin from the ramshackle old barn on his smallholding because they are destroying the olive harvest. But it is a hot, airless day and there is no breeze here in the village. They decide to head for the beach to cool off.

They scramble down the rocks from the village road to the beach below. The younger cousin finds a dead squid in the sand. He picks it up and flicks it in the older boy's face, and then the two boys are running, laughing, playing chase. They run into a cave at the far end of the beach, breathless with laughter. The tide is out and the cave stretches before them like a tunnel.

The older boy, who has recently started stealing his father's cigarettes, has a box of matches in his pocket. He lights a match, shields it with his hand, and signals for his cousin to follow him. They step cautiously deeper and deeper into the cave, laughing nervously from time to time, their voices echoing against the damp stone walls. The cave smells bad. Really bad. Worse than the abattoir in the village. The match fizzles out and the older boy fumbles in his pocket for the box.

In the darkness, his foot hits something soft on the ground. He trips and falls to his knees. When he strikes the match the cave becomes light again and the two boys stare in amazement at the sight in front of them. It is a man. Or at least, it had once been a man. Now he is a decomposing body, bloated by the sea. The younger boy gags and then throws up violently.

'I want to go home,' he tells his cousin. 'I don't like this. I'm scared.'

But the older boy is fascinated. The body is dressed in a black pinstripe suit with wide lapels, a white shirt and a black tie. The men in the village do not dress in this way. Their clothes are old and tatty, faded from working the land in the sun. The body has lost a shoe, but the remaining one is still shiny, black and smart. His hat has somehow stayed firmly wedged on his head, and just below its rim the boy can clearly make out the perfect round mark of a bullet hole.

'Cosa Nostra!' says the boy, in awe.

'Please, I want to go home. I'm scared,' cries the boy's cousin again.

'One minute,' orders the older boy.

He is the boss. Always has been, always will be. His cousin sobs quietly beside him and waits. The boy can see a red cloth bag tucked into the waistband of the dead man's trousers. He tugs at the bag until it comes loose and then he lays it down on the sand and opens it. Inside he finds a heavy gold cross, bearing the figure of Christ. It is intricately engraved with some strange words and set with red jewels.

'Padre celeste,' mutters the younger boy, crossing himself frantically.

The older boy stuffs the cross back into the red cloth bag and pokes his cousin in the ribs.

'Come on!' he orders. 'Let's go. Quick!'

The boys stumble and trip their way back out of the cave, along the beach and up the steep cliff face to the road. Back at the older boy's home, they hide in the barn and look more closely at their find.

'Do you think it's worth something?' asks the younger boy.

The older boy nods confidently. 'It's solid gold. And it belonged to ...'

Suddenly, a shadow falls over them and the older boy's father appears.

'Show me what you have there, boys,' he orders.

He is drunk, as usual, and stumbling. The older boy grabs his treasure and holds it tight to his chest.

'No, it is ours. We found it on the beach.'

But his father is a giant bully of a man and he soon overpowers his son, pushing him to the floor of the barn and snatching the cross.

'Mio dio!' he exclaims. 'I don't believe my eyes. Do you know what this is?'

The boys shake their heads.

'This is the cross of Saint Nicasius,' he says breathlessly. 'My mother used to take me to pray to it when I was a boy. It is a relic! It was in a special locked case but then, one night, it was stolen. It was a huge scandal, a terrible crime, and the search for it went on for years. And now, now, I have it in my hand!'

A greedy smile breaks over the father's face. 'And I will be a very rich man because I am the one who retrieved it! The Church, they will pay me grandly for this.'

The older boy is incensed. 'But you did not find it, Father,' he argues. 'We found it. If there is a reward, it should be ours.'

His father pushes him back to the ground, gathers up the cross, puts it back in the red cloth bag and turns to leave the barn.

'And who will believe your word over mine?' he laughs. 'No, I found the cross of Saint Nicasius. Not you.'

Suddenly there is a loud thwacking noise as the younger cousin hits his uncle over the head with a rake. The older boy stares in wonder as his father stumbles backwards and then falls into the baskets of ripe black olives.

'What do we do now?' asks the younger cousin, shaking in disbelief at what he has just done.

The older boy's father groans and holds his head. He is hurt but still conscious.

'Pass me the rat poison,' orders the older boy. 'Quickly!'

The younger boy does as he is told and then watches in amazement as his cousin pours rat poison down his father's throat. The old man's eyes are very wide open and he starts to make a gargled, choking noise. Then finally, he lies still.

'Is he dead?' the younger boy asks his cousin.

'Yes,' says the older boy, matter-of-factly. 'He was a no-good donkey anyway. Good riddance, I say.'

The boys clear up the spilled poison and drag the heavy body back into the house where they slump him onto his favourite chair. The older boy's mother will be home soon with his younger brothers and sisters and they need to work fast.

'Now, we must go,' says the older cousin. 'And pretend we have been far away from here this afternoon.'

'What about the cross?' asks the younger boy.

'I will keep it safe for now. We cannot let anybody know we have found it until the time is right. But I promise you that it is as much yours as it is mine. We're in this together. Cousins. Blood brothers. Give me your hand.'

The older boy takes a penknife out of his pocket and makes a small cut on his cousin's thumb. Then he does the same on his own and holds his bleeding skin against the younger boy's.

'This will be our secret, for ever,' says the older boy gravely.

'For ever,' nods the younger boy.

And the two boys run as fast as they can, out of the smallholding, through the olive groves and up the hill behind the village. They keep running for a very long time.

Chapter Fourteen

Jade LaFata listened to the shouting downstairs and shook her head. Stupid, spoilt brats. They didn't know they were born. They'd had everything handed to them on a plate and they still argued and whined and complained. They were all acting so upset about Fatty's disappearance but they were probably just wondering who was going to be their meal ticket now.

Jade couldn't stand any of them. Francesca acted like she was a fucking saint but Jade had her number. That marriage to William was a joke for starters, they didn't even sleep with each other, let alone love each other. Francesca thought no one had noticed William moving out. But Jade was always watching. That was the beauty of her set-up here in Le Grand Bleu. No one noticed her but she noticed everything. And it was all up here, in her pretty little head, just waiting to be used to her advantage whenever she needed it. And she had a feeling she'd be needing it pretty soon.

Carlo was the best of a bad bunch, Jade decided grudgingly. He was a big-headed bastard and he dressed like a twat in all those James Bond suits and designer shades. He was pretty cheesy really. But at least he was something nice to look at in this horrible old house. If Jade could tape up that big mouth of his and strip him naked he might be worth a fuck. She wondered if he'd enjoy that. Probably.

His dad certainly enjoyed the dominatrix treatment. Filthy old tosser. God rest his soul.

And then there was Angelica. Daddy's little Angel. Urgh! She was the worst. Prancing around in those ridiculous designer clothes, with her bouncy, flouncy hair and her skinny legs like a show pony! The girl made Jade want to throw up. It wasn't natural for a girl and her father to be that close. It was sick. Angelica still sat on Fatty's knee and she still wrapped him round her little finger whenever she wanted anything. Which was all the bloody time. At least, she *used* to wrap him round her finger. Past tense. Quite what 'Angel' was going to do now Fatty was gone was a mystery. Ha! The thought made Jade smile.

She watched Carlo and Angelica get into Carlo's Lamborghini and drive off. They got caught for a few minutes at the gates, trying to get past the group of photographers who were waiting there. Oh, how they must have loved that! Jade had never met such attention-grabbing desperadoes in her life. Carlo and Angelica were both so 'Look at me! Look at me!' that they failed to look at anything else. Neither of them had a clue what was going on under their noses. Which only worked to Jade's advantage.

Suddenly Jade heard a floorboard creak outside her room. She threw herself on the bed, closed her eyes and pretended to sleep. She heard a soft knock, which she ignored, and then the squeak of the door opening and footsteps by the bed. It would be Saint Francesca, checking up on 'poor, little Jade'. She heard Francesca sniff. Oh, what a shame. The poor love had been crying. Jade had to bite her pillow to stifle a giggle. They all thought she was distraught too, so upset in fact that the doctor had had to give her Valium. That was a joke. Jade wanted to throw a party. Fatty was dead and she was free! The footsteps walked off and the door closed behind them.

Jade was a good actress and she'd done a great job of playing the grieving wife today. She'd also done a great job of acting the devoted wife for the past few months. Jade had met Fatty on the internet. He'd tracked her down after seeing one of her adult movies. Jade, or Madame Jaja, as she was known in the trade, was a dominatrix, specialising in punishment, pain and humiliation. It was just what powerful men like Fatty craved in the bedroom after all that back-slapping and adulation they got in the boardroom. Fatty loved nothing more than to be chained up and whipped by Jade in her rubber fetish suit. It was an arrangement that suited them both fine. There had never been any love between them but there was a mutual respect. Fatty got what he needed sexually, while still enjoying his freedom, and Jade got to lounge around in this mansion watching her favourite soaps, or mooch around Monte Carlo spending her husband's money in Hermès, Versace or Chanel. Madame Juju always wore her mask in her movies, so there was no chance of anyone recognising her, and she'd reverted to her old name. No, it was a good deal for a girl like Jade.

And besides, Fatty had already been old and unhealthy when she'd married him. She'd never thought the arrangement would last very long. She was always hoping he'd have a fatal heart attack and leave her a very wealthy widow. And now things had taken this happy, if unexpected turn, and Jade couldn't have been more delighted.

Well, Patterson had said to hire a car, Robbie told himself. He was only following orders. OK, so he hadn't actually said to hire a brand-new, shiny, silver Audi R8 convertible, at two thousand euros a week, but Robbie had to look the part, didn't he? And he couldn't exactly go driving around Monte Carlo in a Fiat Punto. As he sped along the winding coast road from Nice he felt freer and more alive than he had in years. He turned the radio up full blast and put his foot down on the accelerator. He was in his element – a flash car, a great story to chase, a hotel booked in Monte Carlo and perhaps another meeting with the woman of his dreams?

His hotel was halfway between the casino and the Med. Like the car, it was a bit over budget, OK, *well* over budget, but it had been difficult to find a room with all the journalists flooding into Monaco to cover the LaFata story. And beggars couldn't be choosers, could they? So, this particular beggar was slumming it in the five-star Fairmont Monte Carlo (a snip at 450 euros a night). It's a hard life, thought Robbie with a grin, as he unpacked his clothes into the vast wardrobe. His shirts and suit looked a bit sad in their new luxury surroundings. And his shoes were just a fucking disgrace! He'd travelled in his jeans and Converse All Stars, which looked kind of cool on the school run in Edinburgh, but now looked woefully tatty in Monaco. Ah well, not to worry. Who was he trying to impress?

Robbie met up with Simon and Dan at a bar on Place du Casino, the main square in the glittering hub of Monte Carlo, and sat themselves opposite the entrance to the casino. They sat at a table on the pavement, watched the mad, mad world of Monte Carlo go by and got slowly tanked, despite the extortionate cost of a beer. They started off discussing the LaFata case. Tomorrow, when they made their own enquiries, they'd keep their secrets to themselves, but tonight it was open season. Rumours were spreading round Monte Carlo faster than chlamydia on an 18–30 holiday.

'The old pisshead probably just fell in, let's face it,' said Dan. 'But let's just pretend for a moment that we know it was murder. Who's in the frame?'

Dan Donovan was the youngest of the three. He was in his late twenties, a cocky Glaswegian, short but reasonably good-looking in a low-rent boyband kind of way. He talked a lot but he was funny and always full of gossip, just like a showbiz reporter should be.

'Well, you always have to look at the family first,' said Simon Featherstone-Waugh, warming to the game.

Simon was older, pushing fifty, and Robbie had always written him off as a bit of a nerd until now. He usually came across as stiff and antisocial. He was a financial journalist who got his kicks from stock market crashes and interest rate cuts, so he was hardly rock'n'roll. But now, after a few beers, he was beginning to relax and Robbie found himself enjoying the guy's company.

'OK, so this is what we know,' said Dan, his eyes gleaming, enjoying himself. 'Angelica LaFata ... sex on legs, that girl. Anyway, that little honey was shooting swimwear in Miami so she's out of the picture. Carlo, the international playboy, was allegedly in bed with his best mate's girlfriend. You heard it here first! So he's in the clear too ...'

'And Francesca and Jade LaFata were tucked up in bed at the family mansion up there,' added Simon, pointing up the hill behind them.

'What about that William Hillier character?' asked Robbie. 'The son-in-law. Francesca's husband. He's in charge of the money at LaFata International. He's got to have a motive.'

'In bed with his wife, by all accounts,' said Dan.

'Nah,' Robbie shook his head. 'Separate bedrooms those two.'

'How would you know that?' asked Dan, laughing.

Robbie tapped the side of his nose and grinned. 'I have my sources, young man. I've been here before, remember.'

'Right, well, that changes things,' said Simon. He was taking the game rather more seriously than the others. 'That means that Francesca, William and Jade don't really have alibis. If the daughter and her husband are in separate rooms they can't vouch for each other and if LaFata was on board the yacht, then his wife must have been alone in her bed.'

'Ah, curiouser and curiouser ...' said Dan with a grin. 'What about motive?'

'Oh, that's easy,' said Robbie, enjoying himself now. 'It's always the wife. She's only been married to him for a few months, she's almost forty years younger than him and she stands to inherit a small fortune.'

'You're wrong there,' said Simon, shaking his head. 'There's a pre-nup, she only gets a few million when the old man dies. It's the children who get the billions.'

'Which leads us to the lovely Francesca,' grinned Dan.

Robbie felt himself flinch. 'Nah,' he said. 'I can't see that. She seems pretty straight to me.'

'Ah, but it's always the quiet ones,' laughed Dan. 'Mind you, you're right, the son-in-law's got motive. I heard that Fatty couldn't stand the guy, and he is in charge of all that Monopoly money, and if things are shaky with the wife ...'

'Probably suicide,' interjected Simon with a hiccup. 'LaFata International has lost millions in the last quarter alone. Who knows what's going on behind closed bank vaults. But I intend to find out.'

'Hmm, well let's hope it's something juicy,' said Dan.

'It'll be sooo fucking dull if he just got pissed and drowned. Another beer, boys?'

Robbie nodded. Another beer was definitely in order.

Jade waited until the house was quiet before getting the suitcase out from under the bed. She unlocked a drawer in the wardrobe and started packing the case with its contents. Handcuffs, whips, chains, ropes, vibrators, lubricant, rubber suits, spiky heels, studded collars, gimp masks … The police would be sniffing around tomorrow. She had to get rid of the evidence. Not for Fatty's sake. She was sure her husband was dead. What use was a good reputation to him now? But for her own sake she had to lose this stuff. She'd come this far unscathed and she wasn't about to ruin it all now. Not when she was so close to the prize.

She sent her lover a text message, telling him she was on her way. He would help her. He always did. And then she sneaked, barefooted, slowly and silently down the stairs, carrying the suitcase and her shoes. She called the two guard dogs in from the garden and let them through the back door into the laundry room. She rubbed their heads affectionately. Jade had always been good with animals. Then she shut them in with a couple of fillet steaks. She stepped out into the garden and slipped her ballet pumps on. She was more of a heels girl normally but these were flat, comfortable and rubber-soled.

She hurried along the side of the house, ducking behind bushes and statues to avoid the security cameras. She knew exactly where the black spots were. It wasn't the first time she'd sneaked out of Le Grand Bleu in the dead of night. And then she sprinted as fast as she could, while carrying the heavy case, across the lawn, as the sprinklers showered her with water. She hauled the case up and wedged it between two branches of a cedar tree, then scrambled up behind it. From her perch she managed to throw the case over the back wall of the garden and onto the lane below. Then Jade pulled herself up on the wall, clambered over and hung there for a few moments before she found the nerve to let go. It was a long drop but Jade had been a gymnast as a girl and she landed lightly on bended knees. She picked up the slightly bashed suitcase, crossed the lane and made her way through the woods opposite until she got to the main road. The car pulled up with its lights off. Jade threw the suitcase in the boot, opened the door and jumped in beside her lover with a satisfied grin.

'That's my girl,' he said proudly.

'I am indeed your girl,' she agreed happily, leaning over and giving him a long, lingering kiss. 'And don't you forget it!'

'So, Robbie, you reckon they're all hookers?' asked Simon, his eyes widening.

'Yup,' nodded Robbie with confidence. 'Each and every one of them.'

'What?' said Dan. 'Even that one there?'

He pointed at a strikingly beautiful young woman, who looked very classy indeed in a knee-length white dress. Her long, jet-black hair swung over her shoulders as she slinked past on the arm of a pot-bellied man in his mid-sixties.

'Especially that one there,' replied Robbie. 'There's no way that old boy could pull a girl like that if he wasn't paying for her.'

He was talking bullshit of course. He had absolutely no idea if the woman was a prostitute, she could quite easily be the daughter of a Russian oligarch, but it was his line for the evening, and he was sticking to it. And it was true, there were a lot of escort girls in Monaco.

'What I don't understand,' said Dan, his voice a little slurred, 'is why all the men dress exactly the bloody same.'

It was true, every bloke who walked past, regardless of age or build, wore an identical uniform – smart, narrow-legged dark denim jeans, a crisp white shirt with a big collar, a black or navy blazer, and smooth black or brown Italian shoes.

'Smart casual, I think you call it,' mused Simon.

'Didn't have you down as a fashion expert, Si,' Dan spluttered on his sixth beer.

Robbie found himself laughing too. Simon, bless him, was wearing worn old cords, a checked shirt, a tweed jacket and tan brogues.

'At least I'm making an effort to look smart,' retorted Simon. 'Not like you, Robbie. You still dress like a teenager. You're how old? Pushing forty?'

'No way! I'm thirty-six,' said Robbie, offended. 'And I'm only just thirty-six.'

'Yes, so, nearly forty,' Simon continued. 'And yet you still wear baggy jeans, T-shirts and trainers. I'm not a fashion expert, no. But even I know that that look went out with Blur and Oasis.'

Robbie laughed because it would look childish to be offended by jokey comments about his dress sense, but deep down he was a bit miffed. Simon did have a point. Robbie had been dressing exactly the same way for fifteen years now.

'Yeah, you need a serious makeover, mate,' Dan joined in. 'Always thought that about you – you're a good-looking bugger but your clothes are a disgrace!'

Robbie was just opening his mouth to defend himself

when Dan suddenly shouted, 'Whoah! Look at this beauty!'

The men's heads swivelled in unison. They'd been watching the cars arriving at the casino all night. Robbie had noticed two things in particular. 1) That almost all cars in Monaco were black (except for Ferraris, they had to be red), and 2) there was a very strict hierarchy when it came to valet parking outside the casino. The journalists had watched in amazement as a black Audi RS6, which would have been the envy of the neighbourhood back home, got parked round the back with the 'also rans'. Only the really flash motors were parked out the front. One obviously couldn't have anything worth less than 250,000 euros lowering the tone of the neighbourhood.

'What is that?' asked Simon, scratching his head.

'It's a Bugatti Veyron,' said Dan excitedly. 'And if you wanted one of those babies you wouldn't get much change out of a million.'

'This place is something else,' said Simon in awe. 'I feel like I've stepped through the looking glass.'

'D'you know how much money you need in your bank account to become a resident here?' asked Dan.

Robbie and Simon shook their heads.

'Me neither,' giggled Dan. 'But I bet he does!'

He pointed at the Bugatti driver.

'Money, money, money,' Simon started singing suddenly, in a deep and surprisingly tuneful voice. 'Must be funny …'

'In a rich man's world!' Dan and Robbie joined in, laughing.

'Money, money, money,' Simon continued. 'Always sunny …'

'In a rich man's world. Aha-ahaaa!!!'

'So I must leave, I have to go …'

'To Las Vegas or MONACO!'

Suddenly a bright red Lamborghini came flying round the square, followed by a pack of photographers on motorbikes and mopeds. The Lamborghini screeched to a halt outside the casino and a valet opened the driver's door. A tall, chiselled young man in a sharp black suit got out, ran his fingers through his floppy dark hair and walked round to open the passenger door. A pair of incredibly long slim legs appeared from the car, wearing bright red, patent stilettos, which matched the car perfectly. And then in a swish of long blonde hair, a breathtakingly beautiful girl took the young man's hand and stepped out of the car.

'I don't believe it,' said Dan. 'It's the LaFata kids.'

'Well, they certainly know how to grieve in style!' added Simon.

And then all hell broke loose. The paparazzi were shouting out, 'Carlo! Angelica!' Journalists and photographers were running through the square towards the casino, some clambering over the fountain in the middle in an attempt to get there first. Curious onlookers stood up from their tables in bars and restaurants and made their way towards the scene. It was practically a stampede.

'Come on!' shouted Robbie. 'Let's get a closer look. Hurry!'

He didn't wait for the others. His journalistic instinct kicked in and he was up and running towards the LaFatas before his friends were out of their seats. He pushed his way as close to the front of the throng as he could manage, his heart pounding in his chest, adrenalin pulsing through his veins. He got to the steps of the casino just in time to see Carlo and Angelica reach the revolving doors. The girl turned her head and looked back at the crowd for a moment. She was beautiful, there was no doubt about that, but the glazed look in her eyes made Robbie's heart sink. He'd met enough junkies in his life to know the signs. Angelica LaFata was young and gorgeous. She had everything to live for. But her eyes were dead.

By the time Dan caught up with him the LaFatas had vanished into the casino. He stood panting at Robbie's shoulder, trying to get his breath back.

'Did you see that?' asked Robbie, shaking his head sadly.

'See what?' asked Dan.

'Angelica LaFata,' he replied.

'Only from a distance. What a stunner, eh? And even better in the flesh,' grinned Dan.

Robbie shook his head. 'No,' he said. 'She wasn't stunning. She was out of it. Her eyes … She was high, Dan. Out of her daft little head.'

'Back to rehab for Angel, then, I'm guessing,' shrugged Dan. 'Ah well, it sells papers.'

Robbie smiled weakly at his friend but the gloss had come off his night. 'Think I'll hit the sack,' he said, suddenly realising how tired he was. 'Big day tomorrow. Work to do, people to see, places to go …'

'Are you mad?' asked Dan incredulously. 'I'm staying here to see what happens next. I'm not going to bed while those LaFata kids are still out on the tiles.'

Finally, Simon arrived. 'You boys owe me a hundred euros each,' he said breathlessly.

'A hundred euros?!' shouted Dan. 'For six beers? Are you having a laugh?'

'Welcome to Monte Carlo,' said Simon.

Chapter Fifteen

'No, Audrey, I'm sorry, I don't know where Chef's steaks are,' said Francesca patiently to the maid.

Like she needed this right now. So a couple of fillet steaks were missing from the fridge? Big deal! With her dad missing at sea, it hardly seemed important.

'I really don't think any of us are very hungry today anyway,' she added. 'Tell Chef we'll have salad for lunch. Tell him Carlo's not here and Angelica's not very well so they won't be eating. Thank you, Audrey. That's all.'

Fatty had been missing for almost thirty-six hours now and Francesca was going up the wall. She knew she was a bit of a control freak. OK, a *complete* control freak. She needed to plan ahead. She needed deadlines and dates. She needed to know that everything was where it should be, when it should be. She found it impossible to live or work in chaos. So how the hell was she supposed to live in this limbo? Just waiting and waiting, with no answers, without knowing when or if it would ever end. What if they never found a body? What if this was it for ever? Just a weird numbness, somewhere between crippling grief and blind hope. It was horrible. Francesca wanted to crawl out of her skin and be someone else. She wanted a fast-forward button. Or a rewind button. She wanted to press delete.

The family didn't help. Jade hadn't ventured out of her room since yesterday afternoon, Carlo had gone off somewhere with Christian, William was working on his computer and Angelica was … Well, Angelica was in BIG trouble.

Francesca knocked on her sister's bedroom door and let herself in. Angel was curled up under her pink duvet, groaning, and clutching her stomach.

'Are you feeling any better, Angel?' asked Francesca, trying to sound sympathetic but secretly wanting to give her little sister a good slap.

'No,' whimpered Angelica pathetically. 'I think I'm dying. My tummy … My head …'

'And you only had two glasses of champagne?' asked Francesca sceptically.

'Definitely only two,' she nodded, her eyes looking even more huge and blue than usual in her pale, drawn face. 'I swear, Frankie. I thought that would be OK. I didn't think I would feel like this.'

'Your body obviously can't tolerate any alcohol at all any more,' said Francesca. 'Should I get a doctor?'

'No. No doctors,' said Angelica, shaking her head so fast that her lips wobbled.

'I don't know what you were thinking going out last night, anyway,' said Francesca, opening the shutters and letting the midday light stream into the room. 'You're upset and anxious. The last thing you needed was a late night and a hangover. You've done so well with your rehab this time, darling. I don't understand why you'd jeopardise your recovery like this.'

Angelica squinted her eyes against the daylight and reached out a cold clammy hand to Francesca and squeezed it weakly. 'I'm sorry, Frankie,' she said quietly. 'But I'm in such a mess about Daddy. I wasn't thinking straight.'

'I know, Angel,' said Francesca, forcing every last ounce

of sympathy into her voice. 'It's really difficult to know how to deal with all this. Just try to get some sleep.'

Angelica nodded obediently and snuggled back down, with her head under her duvet, away from the light.

Lying little madam, thought Francesca to herself as she went back downstairs. She didn't believe the two small glasses of champagne story for a minute. Carlo and Angelica had got in at five a.m. Francesca had woken up, heard the dogs barking and the back door being shut. Sneaking in the back door like a couple of teenagers. It was pathetic. Carlo had stuck up for Angelica as always.

'No, Frankie,' he'd lied, straight to her face. 'We got home at two, I swear. And she did only have a couple of glasses of bubbly, I promise. I tried to stop her having those but you know how persuasive she can be.'

Oh well, stuff them all, thought Frankie. They treated her as if she was stupid. She was sick of being taken for granted and clearing up their mess. Maybe it was time for her to be the selfish one. Maybe it was time for Francesca to put what she wanted first. But what was it exactly she wanted? Francesca didn't even know.

Angelica sneaked out of bed and found her Chanel handbag in the pile of clothes on her bedroom floor. She rummaged around inside until she found what she was looking for – a small, blue Tiffany jewellery bag. Inside that was an even smaller sealed plastic bag, containing three paper wraps and five pills. Angelica sighed with relief. She had enough to keep her going for a couple of days.

The Angel on her right shoulder was distraught. Don't do this, Angelica, she pleaded. Last night was just a blip. Flush the drugs down the toilet. You're strong, you can get through this without that rubbish. Remember how good you felt when you were clean? Be brave, Angelica. Remember what your therapist said. 'I am amazing. I am amazing. I am amazing.'

Go on, said the devil on her left shoulder. Have a line. Just the one. A little pick-me-up. What harm can that do? Look at what you're going through, Angelica. You can't honestly be expected to get through this crap without a bit of help from the laughing gear. Bugger what the therapist said. What does she know about being Angelica LaFata? 'I am weak. I am weak. I am weak.'

Angelica sat on the floor and held the bag in her hand. Her head was pounding, her stomach ached and her heart … Well, her heart felt as if it had been smashed into a million pieces. Where was Daddy? Why had he gone? How was she supposed to carry on without him? Who would look after her now? Just one little line and all that pain would go away. Just one little line. What harm could it do?

Jade watched the pathetic little junkie through the crack in the bedroom door. That girl had no backbone. The first sign of trouble and she pushed the self-destruct button. Did it every bloody time. That was the problem with spoilt little rich kids. They'd never had to learn to stand on their own two feet so they needed a crutch. Angelica had her drugs and her drink, Carlo had his cars, his yacht and his women, and even Saint Francesca had her vices. She was a control freak for a start. And a workaholic. She barely spent any time with those lovely little boys of hers. Poor things must think the nanny's their mum. Francesca seemed to think that the whole world would crumble if she didn't run the house and the office. But nobody was indispensable. No one was *that* important. One day Francesca would discover that for herself.

It had made Jade laugh when Francesca had accused Angelica and Carlo of coming home at five a.m. It wasn't them she'd heard! It was Jade, sneaking back in after spending the night with her lover. God, this house was so full of secrets and lies. Fatty had always been lecturing them all about loyalty, trust and the importance of honesty within the family. But look at them now! Creeping around, hiding their dirty little secrets from one another, like squirrels stashing their nuts. Well, Jade supposed, they had learned from the master. Nobody's life was more of a lie than Fatty's. Jade knew that for a fact.

Oh well, not long now. Jade wouldn't have to put up with the poisonous atmosphere in this creepy old house for much longer. A few more days and then she'd be gone. He was almost ready for her. He'd promised. Soon they would run off together and start afresh a very long way from here. Jade couldn't wait.

Carlo was stretched out on his back on a lounger, his hands behind his head, watching the coast bob up and down in the distance. Christian was next to him. The friends lay there in comfortable silence, each lost in his own thoughts, as *Pulling Power* drifted down the coast towards Antibes. Any awkwardness Carlo had felt over the Sasha business had gone. Like she'd said, it was a one-off. It wasn't as if it was going to happen again so there was no point in Christian finding out. Carlo was glad the incident wasn't going to ruin his one real friendship but he was also gutted that he would never lie flat on his back with the luscious Sasha astride him again.

He tried to wipe the image of her out of his head but it lingered. The truth was, that image had been popping in and out of his mind since yesterday morning. The way her thighs had gripped his waist, the way her tongue had thrust its way into his mouth. Oh Jesus, he could feel himself getting hard now … How bad was that? His dad was missing, probably dead, and all Carlo kept thinking about was getting his rocks off with his best mate's girlfriend.

'You thinking about your dad?' asked Christian, his head on one side, full of concern.

Carlo rolled onto his front and felt his cheeks burn with shame.

'Um, yeah, of course,' he lied. 'Can't think about anything else.'

This was true up to a point. Carlo couldn't think about anything else – except Sasha! But of course his dad's disappearance was doing his head in. What was he supposed to think? Do? Say? It wasn't like there was a body to mourn, or a witness to explain what had happened, or concrete evidence. Carlo had decided that the best thing to do was to take his mind off things. That's why he and Christian – and the five-man crew, of course, it wasn't as if Carlo actually knew how to sail a yacht – were taking this little day trip to Antibes and back. Call it therapy. He'd once seen a yacht in the harbour named that – *Therapy* – and suddenly he got it. There really was nothing more soothing for the mind than a sail along the Med on a bright spring day, with a few beers and your best mate.

'Um, stop me if this is a bad question,' said Christian cautiously. 'But if your dad is, um, well, you know …'

'Dead,' said Carlo flatly.

Well, there was no point pussyfooting around, was there? Dad was almost certainly dead. It wasn't as if he could swim!

It was Christian's turn to blush. 'Um, yeah, if Fatty is

dead, what happens now? With LaFata International and the properties and the assets and everything?'

Carlo shrugged, he hadn't really thought about it before. 'I doubt much will change at all,' he mused. 'Francesca and William run most of the business already. Dad bought us all our apartments as presents, so they belong to us. Same with the yachts and cars. I'm not sure what'll happen with my allowance but I guess it'll just carry on until I get my inheritance.'

'And if they never actually find his body?' asked Christian.

'Fuck, I don't know. I'll have to ask Frankie about that. How long does someone have to be missing at sea before they're officially dead?'

Christian shrugged his broad shoulders. 'I dunno,' he said. 'I've never known anyone go overboard before.'

Carlo shuddered. The thought of his dad drowning was a nightmare. And yet … if he was brutally honest with himself, he suspected he wasn't as heartbroken as he should be. He felt almost guilty at the empty, numb feeling he had inside. Shouldn't he be bedridden and on Valium like Jade? Or a stressed-out nervous wreck like Frankie? Or angry and tearful like Angelica? All three women had cried this morning. He'd seen them. But he hadn't managed to shed a tear since the harbour yesterday morning. Maybe it hadn't sunk in yet. How could it sink in when there was no body?

'So, you're not going to have to get a job or anything?' asked Christian.

'God no!' said Carlo, turning back over and sitting up, his hard-on having subsided. 'What the fuck would I do?'

'Oh come on,' said Christian. 'There must be something you'd like to do. I mean, if things were different and you had to work like, you know, ordinary people.'

Carlo scratched his head and readjusted his Ray-Bans. The truth was he hadn't ever thought about it. He'd never had to think about it. The family had always been, well, stonkingly rich, so a work ethic hadn't really been necessary. He didn't understand why Frankie worked so bloody hard. She was always in the office and even when she was at home she was stressed out about work. LaFata International could quite easily have afforded to employ someone else as Fatty's number two on the board of directors. Quite why Frankie didn't spend her time shopping, lunching and beautifying herself like ordinary women in Monaco was beyond him. Angel was different. Being a model wasn't exactly a proper job, was it? Pouting in front of a camera for a couple of hours now and again, and wiggling up and down a catwalk. It was hardly difficult. And anyway, Angel did it for the attention. Angel did everything for attention.

'Nope,' said Carlo, eventually answering Christian's question. 'Can't think of anything. I wanted to be a fireman when I was little, and then I quite fancied myself as a footballer and, briefly, when I first got my licence I thought I'd quite like to be an F1 driver, but other than that ...'

'OK, just imagine, if there was no money, what would you do?' Christian continued.

'But there will always be money,' said Carlo, getting bored with the 'let's pretend' game. 'So there's no need to even think about it.'

'But if you had to ...' Christian was beginning to get on his nerves.

'Well, I wouldn't get a job,' said Carlo. 'I would just pack a backpack and bugger off travelling.'

'Travelling?' Christian raised a surprised eyebrow. 'But you've travelled all over the world.'

'No, not that sort of travelling. Not private jet, helicopter transfers and five-star hotels. I mean the sort of slumming-it travelling blokes our age do after university and before getting a job. I'd like to see some of the world. The *other* world. Africa, Asia, South America ...'

'I thought you'd been to all those places.' Christian was being a bit thick now. He didn't seem to get it.

'I've been to South Africa, Kenya, Thailand, Hong Kong, Mexico, Brazil ...' replied Carlo. 'And they all looked the fucking same. Nice big hotel, gorgeous beach, lovely swimming pool, great food, fabulous service. I might as well have stayed in Monaco. I didn't actually get to see anything different from what I see here every day. Just a load of rich white people sunbathing and drinking cocktails.'

'Yeah, I see your point. And that might be fun for a while,' agreed Christian. 'Living out of a backpack, sleeping in, like, huts and stuff, eating rice and beans. But I couldn't do it. I'd miss my home comforts too much.'

And then Christian's face broke into a grin. 'Like Dom Perignon, and foie gras, and Prada underpants, and my helicopter!'

Carlo couldn't help smiling. 'Well,' he said. 'When you put it like that ... Maybe I'll leave travelling to the plebs.'

And the two men lay back in their loungers. Carlo stared at the perfect blue sky above him. He did quite fancy the idea of backpacking. He'd mentioned it to his dad once a couple of years ago. Fatty had almost fallen over, he was laughing so much.

'Over my dead body will a son of mine go travelling. What would people think? Anyways, you would not last five minutes. You are a soft nancy boy. I cannot imagine you with no maids, no car, no lavatory! You would come home after two days and you would be laughing stock. No. You wanna travel, Giancarlo, you take private jet and you stay at Four Seasons.'

Over his dead body. Now there was a thought …

'D'you ever get bored of your life, Chris?' asked Carlo, sitting back up and taking a swig of his beer. 'D'you ever wonder if there's something better out there?'

Christian shook his head and looked at Carlo as if he was completely nuts. 'What? Better than Monaco? Better than yachts and nightclubs and fast cars and gorgeous girls? No! We're the lucky ones, Carlo. We're living the dream.'

Carlo cast his eye over his luxury yacht, with its designer fittings and state-of-the-art technology. The truth was it didn't make him happy. Even before his dad had gone missing he wasn't happy. For a long time he'd felt a low-lying discontentment simmering in his veins. He'd kept buying faster cars and bigger yachts. He drank increasingly exclusive champagne, bought stupidly expensive clothes and fucked more and more beautiful women. But it still wasn't enough. Maybe he was just greedy. But he didn't want more than he had. He just wanted different.

'Where d'you see yourself in ten years' time?' he asked his best friend, suddenly realising that they'd never had such an in-depth discussion before.

'Here, of course,' said Christian. 'Well, not here on *Pulling Power* exactly, but here in Monaco. With a nice big apartment on the beach and maybe a villa down the road at Villefranche or Beaulieu for the weekends. Somewhere to take the wife and kids …'

'Wife and kids?!' spluttered Carlo.

Christian nodded. 'Oh yeah, I don't want to be a bachelor for ever. That's just sad. I definitely want to be married by the time I'm thirty.'

A horrible thought hit Carlo – what if Christian was

planning to marry Sasha? That would be a disaster. He'd probably ask him to be the best man and how could he do that when he'd screwed the bride?

'So, is Sasha "the one"?' he asked nervously.

To his relief, Christian shook his head. 'No, definitely not. She's gorgeous, and she's fun, and she's great in bed ...'

Carlo felt his muscles tense. He hated the thought of Sasha sleeping with Christian. Which was crazy obviously, she was his girlfriend, but still, it felt all wrong. He'd kind of hoped she was only great in bed with him. That it had been a special chemistry thing between them that had made her so horny.

'... but she's not wife material.' Christian was carrying on, oblivious to the green-eyed monster on the lounger next to him. 'Sasha's like a wild tiger. There's no taming that one.'

Chapter Sixteen

Robbie lay in bed, getting his thoughts together for the day ahead. He was trying to think about leads and contacts but his mind kept wandering back to one person. *Her.* They'd first met six months ago in the bar of the Hotel de Paris, Robbie feeling out of place in his tatty clothes, her in a black pencil skirt, crisp white shirt and black stilettos that showed off the perfect curve of her calves. He'd thought she was the most beautiful, graceful, elegant woman he'd ever seen. He'd thought she was way out of his league.

Nothing had happened between them. They hadn't kissed or anything dramatic like that. It was just one of those chance encounters that could mean something, or could mean nothing at all. But whatever it was, he couldn't stop thinking about it. About her. She'd got under his skin. And now he was back here, in her home town, and he wondered if he should try to make contact.

It had started off innocently enough. They'd got chatting, and he'd bought her a drink, and then they'd carried on chatting right through the afternoon. She'd told him his accent was sexy and then she'd blushed. For such a confident, accomplished woman, there was something still childlike about her.

They'd made each other laugh and then he'd made her cry by asking her about her marriage. And for some reason she'd told him how unhappy she was and then, of course, he'd told her about his divorce and about how much he missed his daughters. And they'd bonded. Two lonely people, getting smashed together in the Hotel de Paris.

The more she talked, the more she fascinated him. Everything she said made perfect sense and he found himself sitting there with this virtual stranger thinking, this is the woman I should have married. This is the one! Och, maybe it had just been the drink, or the surroundings, or the excitement of talking to such a hot woman. But then again, Robbie wasn't daft. He wasn't some silly romantic or a love-struck teenager. There had been a real connection between them. He hadn't imagined it. That's why, when he'd messed it all up, he'd been so gutted. Maybe he should have been more upfront with her, told her he was a journalist straight off. But he hadn't been talking to her as a reporter, he'd been talking to her as a *man*. It had ended in an argument. She'd stormed out so quickly that, as her court shoes clipped away on the marble floor, Robbie had practically seen the sparks fly from her heels.

Robbie tried not to think about her but it was hard. He was in Monaco and he was *that* close to her. But she probably hated him. She'd told him she never wanted to see him again. And she was hardly going to welcome him now, was she? Besides, perhaps she didn't even remember the encounter. Maybe it had only been a big deal to him? He scrolled down the contacts list in his phone, just to check it was still there. Her number. She'd given it to him before they argued. Did he have the nerve to get in touch? Not right this moment, that was for sure.

He threw himself into his work instead, phoning or doorstepping every contact he'd made the last time he'd been in Monaco on the LaFata story. If he'd been doing a profile of the guy, he'd have been fine. Everybody wanted to talk about what a funny, brilliant, charismatic, powerful and generous man Giancarlo LaFata was. And the emphasis was definitely on the *was*. Nobody believed for a minute that the guy was still alive. The mound of flowers being laid on the quayside beside *Vigorosa*'s berth was growing by the hour. Not that the yacht was there any more. The police had taken it off to their maritime dock and had screened it off from the public while it had the fine-tooth comb treatment from the forensic team.

Most people seemed to think it must have been a tragic accident – potent brandy, a morbid obesity problem and the inability to swim. And the body? Well, it would turn up any day now. A few conspiracy theorists were suggesting Mafia connections but that was just daft. Fatty had left Sicily when he was fifteen and he'd never been back. Besides, everybody knew the Italian Mafia were on their knees these days. It was the Russian Mob who ruled Europe now. And it was the Russian connection that Robbie was most interested in. Fatty had been in business with quite a few Russian companies and individuals and not all of them were saints, by all accounts.

'Hi, Simon,' he said, flopping down in a chair beside his friend at a pavement café overlooking the bay. 'How's it going?'

'Slowly,' said Simon with a sigh. 'I'm getting nowhere fast.'

'Same here,' said Robbie. 'I know it's cheeky, Simon, but you couldn't give me any details you've got on LaFata's Russian business associates, could you? And obviously, if I've got anything you need, it's all yours.'

Simon raised a sceptical eyebrow. Robbie knew he'd just broken the journalist's code. Never reveal your sources and never ask a rival hack to do your hard work for you.

'What? I'll scratch your back, if you scratch mine?' asked Simon.

Robbie nodded. He needed help. He needed a story. And desperate times called for desperate measures. He was fully expecting Simon to tell him to bugger off, but instead the older man nodded.

'I'll give you everything I've got on the Russkies if you give me everything you've got on the son-in-law, William Hillier.'

'Deal,' said Robbie gratefully. 'I know quite a lot about him actually but he sounds like a right boring bastard. I doubt you'll get much dirt on him.'

'I'm not so sure,' said Simon mysteriously. 'I've been looking into his hedge-fund portfolio and it makes for quite interesting reading.'

Just at that moment, Dan sauntered into the café with a smug grin on his face.

'Morning, ladies!' he said cheerfully.

'It's afternoon,' stated Simon.

'Is it really?' asked Dan. 'Already? Christ, I've only just got up. Stayed out until two, when the LaFata kids finally decided to stop partying and go home and grieve for their daddy. Then I was up until half four filing my copy. Front-page splash this morning, though. So all worth it!'

'Your job's a piece of piss, really, isn't it, Dan?' teased Robbie. 'Here we are, me and Si, sweating over criminals and economics, and all you have to do is describe what Angelica was wearing and what car Carlo was driving.'

'There is slightly more to it than that, Robbie,' replied Dan, still grinning. 'But not an awful lot more. I also had to list their choice of bars and nightclub and report the shocking fact that Angelica, who's allegedly teetotal after rehab, had two glasses of champagne.'

'Two glasses of champagne, my arse!' scoffed Robbie, remembering her dead eyes. 'Two glasses of champagne and half a ton of narcotics is more like it.'

'Oh God, yeah, definitely,' said Dan. 'But short of following her into the ladies there was no way I could prove it. And the LaFata lawyers are like pit bulls. They'd sue my bollocks off if I printed that. So that's my main objective, to find some low-life dealer who'll fess up to supplying her. If the price is right, of course.'

'I wish I had your budget,' mused Simon, dejectedly. It was a sad fact that tabloids paid more than broadsheets, and that showbiz journalists had the most generous expense accounts of all.

'Celebrities sell the most papers,' replied Dan, with a cheeky wink. 'It's a simple case of economics. Thought you'd be the first to understand that, Si.'

'So that's your week, is it, Dan?' asked Robbie. 'Chasing Angel around?'

Dan's grin grew even bigger. 'Oh, it only gets better, boys. I get to chase Angel, and then I'm going to pop off to Cannes for the Film Festival, then it's back here for the Grand Prix at the weekend. Can you imagine the tan I'm going to have by the time I get back? If I ever go back, that is. I love this place. I think I've found my spiritual home. I wonder if there are any jobs going at the *Monaco Times*?'

'You lucky bugger,' said Robbie enviously.

What he wouldn't give to stay on the Riviera until after next weekend! Not because he wanted to go to Cannes, or see the Grand Prix – actually he would love to see the Grand Prix but that wasn't the main reason. No, the longer he stayed here in Monaco, the more chance he had of meeting up with *her*.

Robbie noticed a man of about Dan's age at the next

table. He was sitting alone reading an Italian magazine and looking unbelievably cool. Robbie found himself studying the guy closely. How did these bastards manage to look so bloody smooth? He wore narrow-legged black trousers with a white shirt, tucked in at the waist, a Hermès belt (even Robbie recognised that logo) and shiny black lace-up shoes, also narrow and slightly pointy. Even his black socks looked as if they'd been ironed. He was remarkably well groomed, no chest hair peeped out of his undone shirt, just smooth tanned skin. He was clean-shaven, without a spot or a pockmark on his face. Although he did have a sharp, inch-long scar on his right cheek, but that only seemed to add to his glamour. His eyebrows were thick but neat, his nails were clean and square. He wore a gold watch and a plain gold wedding band. His teeth were almost as white as the crisp, cotton tablecloth. And Robbie could smell his aftershave from here.

He rubbed his own rough cheeks. He hadn't shaved for a couple of days. With Dan's words ringing in his ears, he looked down at his battered Converse, his trusty Levi's that were almost through at the knees and his ink-stained nails. Maybe he was a disgrace? What was he thinking, fantasising about a woman like *her*? Look at the men she was surrounded by. Why the hell would she be interested in him?

'Are you OK, Jade?' asked Francesca, with that annoying saintly smile of hers. 'I know this must be really tough for you, darling. But please don't shut yourself away. We're your family now and we're here for you.'

Jade forced herself to smile weakly at Francesca and muttered, 'Thanks, but I think I'd rather be alone.'

'Well, if you're sure,' said Francesca. 'You know where I am if you need me.'

Francesca put a cup of tea and a *tarte aux fraises* on Jade's bedside table. It was like living with Mary Bloody Poppins. Nobody could be *this* nice. Not all the time. She bet Francesca had dreams about murdering people in her sleep.

'Sometimes it's better to have company,' added Francesca as she left the room. 'I'll be in the drawing room.'

Jade wondered if it was Francesca who was craving company. She must get lonely. William shut himself away in his room the whole time and the kids were always with the nanny. Not that Jade cared about Francesca's feelings. She'd never let any of the LaFatas in.

In fact, Jade had always found it easy to keep people at a distance. She knew how to be pleasant and keep them sweet without ever actually showing them what went on inside her head. She'd never been one for temper tantrums. She didn't like to raise her voice. She'd learned in the children's home that shouting and screaming got you nowhere but into more trouble. Better to keep your mouth shut, your head down and just get on with things. That way you weren't labelled a troublemaker and you'd have more chance of getting fostered.

Francesca didn't have a clue that Jade had been brought up in care. None of them did, except Fatty. He'd helped her create a false past that she could use whenever anybody asked her about who she was or where she came from. They pretended she was from Kent, the daughter of a mechanic and a beautician. They made up a brother for her, who worked at the garage with their dad. And said Jade had been a croupier. That's where she was supposed to have met Fatty, at a poker game in a casino in London. It all sounded very cosy. In reality, Jade was an orphan and an only child.

She'd lost count of the number of foster homes she'd lived

in over the years. Was it eleven? Or twelve? Some families she'd liked better than others but most were OK. Jade found she could rub along with pretty much anyone if she behaved like the child they wanted her to be. The Smiths were into football, so Jade spent every Saturday in the terraces, cheering on their team. The Robinsons were into board games, so Jade became a whizz at Scrabble and Yahtzee. The Johnsons were outdoorsy types, so Jade pulled on her hiking boots and followed them up mountains in the wind and the rain. The Flannighans were sporty so Jade developed her talent for gymnastics so that they could be proud of the medals she won. She remembered how they'd displayed her trophies on their mantelpiece beside her school photo. They'd had no kids of their own and she'd really thought that was it. She'd thought she'd become a fully-fledged Flannighan. She'd let herself believe in the happy ever after. What a mistake. They'd let her down just as everybody had always let her down. She was a pretty child and well behaved at school. Most of the foster families had wanted to adopt her right up until the moment they'd seen her psychological profile. Then they'd changed their minds. The Flannighans turned out to be no different from the rest.

At the age of seven, Jade had been labelled by the system. 'Withdrawn, emotionally detached, incapable of developing strong bonds with others, lack of empathy.' The list went on. What sort of way was that to talk about a little girl? Oh, they gave their explanations. The report gave a detailed account of her early years. It described the abuse and the neglect, the way her so-called mother had left her alone for days at a time, in soiled nappies, with nothing to eat and no one to look after her while she robbed and prostituted her way around London, desperate for her next fix. Christ, no wonder Jade hated junkies!

Jade's earliest memories were of being alone in a cold, dark flat. Hungry and scared, calling for Mummy. But Mummy never came. It turned out that Mummy had died of a heroin overdose in a squat over in Camberwell. When the social workers had come to take her away Jade had been malnourished, dehydrated and anaemic. She'd been four years old at the time.

And so, despite her best efforts to fit in, she'd never got the chance to be part of a proper family. She'd stay a few months and then it would be back to the children's home until the next family came along and the whole thing would start again. It was her fate. Her destiny. To just keep drifting from one set of people to the next, never really belonging. Nothing was permanent in Jade's life.

She was still doing it now, here with the LaFatas. She acted the part of the silly little trophy wife because that's what they expected her to be. And so she'd pretended to be upset when Fatty hadn't named his yacht after her, and pretended to hang on his every word, and pretended to be devastated when he went missing. But maybe that report had been right. Scratch the surface and Jade had no real feelings. Emotionally detached, incapable of developing strong bonds with others. It was all true. Or at least it had been until recently. Until she'd met *him*.

She'd opened up to him. He'd understood because he was trapped in a pretend marriage too. She began to trust him. Told him her darkest secrets about her distant and not-so-distant past. He'd held her tight and stroked her hair and told her everything was going to be OK, that she had him now and he was going to save her. He was going to change her destiny.

He didn't flinch when she told him about her career as a dominatrix. He just nodded and said he understood, that it wasn't surprising after all those years of neglect and abuse. He told her that it was just an outlet for her pent-up anger and frustration. A way of getting some power back, and of hurting people like they'd hurt her. It was human nature to want to lash out. Jade had just done it more literally than most – with a whip in her hand! He said that he admired her, actually, the way she'd taken control of her life. She'd never done drugs or been in trouble with the police and she'd made good money for herself. He said she was a fighter, a survivor. He called her his warrior princess. It was a bit cheesy, but she kind of liked it.

Jade had never known love. In fact, until recently, she hadn't even believed in it. How could she believe in something she'd never felt? How could she know that it was real? But now, ever so slowly, she was beginning to believe. He loved her. She was sure of it and she was beginning to let herself love him. She'd opened up a little door in her heart and let him sneak in. And now they were leaving together. Just a few more days. And then maybe, just maybe, Jade would get the 'happy ever after' she'd never let herself dream about.

Her thoughts were disturbed by another knock on the door. It was bloody Saint Francesca again.

'Jade, just wanted to let you know that the police are here. They need to have a look around the house. They'll want to come in here, I imagine, this being Fatty's bedroom …'

Jade wasn't panicked. She'd got rid of everything she'd needed to. There was nothing incriminating for the police to find.

'Do you want to come and sit with me while they're here?' asked Francesca.

God, the woman was desperate!

'No thank you, Frankie,' replied Jade in her sweetest voice. 'I think I'll go for a swim. It'll help clear my head.'

'Oh, OK,' said Francesca. 'Whatever helps, darling.'

'Angelica, the police are here,' said Francesca.

Shit! Angelica sat bolt upright in her bed. She hadn't thought about that. Of course the fucking pigs were here, sniffing around. They wanted to know what had happened to Daddy. But they might find more than they'd bargained for in Angelica's room.

'Um, OK,' she said, feeling flustered. 'Give me a minute, Frankie.'

She waited until she heard Frankie's footsteps on the stairs and then she stuffed the Tiffany bag down her bra. Oh fuck, what else did she have hidden around here? She hadn't lived at Le Grand Bleu for years, not officially anyway. And her bedroom was still decorated with the pink Flower Fairy wallpaper she'd chosen when she was nine. Even the white four-poster bed was in the shape of Cinderella's carriage. It was all so sickly sweet! And in sharp contrast to her boho chic apartment in an art deco apartment block downtown.

But she always ended up back here whenever things went wrong. When rehab failed, or the tabloids found out about an affair with a married man, or when she was dropped, in disgrace, as the face of a famous cosmetics brand, this was where she ran. Back to her pink room in Le Grand Bleu. Back to Daddy. The problem was that when things went wrong Angelica always turned to her little bags of sweets for help. She'd always kept a stash here, just in case of emergencies. And so hidden all over this bedroom were uppers, downers, Es, speed, coke and weed. Angelica rummaged through her favourite hiding places – the dolls' house, the musical jewellery box, the kitten-shaped pyjama case, the ballet bag, the clarinet case, under the saddle of the wooden rocking horse – until she'd gathered quite a stash of goodies. Wow! She hadn't expected this much. This would keep her sorted all week!

She checked, and double-checked, every nook and cranny until she felt sure she had it all. Then she took a couple of uppers (because she was still feeling down about Daddy) and topped it off with another line of coke. She felt so much better than she had done this morning.

'See, told you I was right,' said the little devil on her left shoulder with glee.

Chapter Seventeen

Francesca couldn't bear it. They were ransacking the place. Going through neatly filed correspondence and carefully archived family photos and tossing them into messy piles on the floor. They'd moved ornaments off their spots, knocked pictures so that they hung at crooked angles and walked muddy footprints all over the Persian rugs. She knew they were just doing their jobs, and they were trying to find her dad, but she couldn't stand watching her home being torn apart. Only two days ago everything had been in its place and now there was nothing but chaos.

She knocked on William's door.

'Um, erm, hi,' she said, almost nervously. He didn't look up from his computer. 'What are you up to?'

'Working,' he replied flatly, still concentrating on his computer screen.

'Really? Why?' she asked. 'It's Sunday.'

William shrugged. 'These figures aren't going to balance themselves,' he said, sounding slightly impatient.

'William, you're *always* working,' she continued. 'I thought maybe we could spend some time together, you know, under the circumstances.'

William finally looked round but there was no sympathy in his face. 'You're worried about your dad, I know,' he said matter-of-factly, 'but letting the business slide is not going to bring him back. The most useful thing I can do is to keep the cogs of LaFata International turning.'

Francesca sighed and nodded. Maybe he was right. Perhaps that's what she should be doing too, keeping herself busy, making herself useful.

'Perhaps I'll go to the office then,' she said. 'Take my mind off everything. I can't stand being here with the police going through all Dad's stuff.'

'Good idea,' said William turning back to his laptop. 'There are a couple of files on my desk that I could do with you bringing back with you. Don't forget them. Cheerio then.'

He didn't notice the tears sliding down her face. He seemed so disinterested, dismissive. And cheerio? Who said cheerio any more? Sometimes William felt like a total stranger to Francesca. Where was his compassion? Why couldn't he even try to comfort her? OK, so they were going through a rocky patch but her father was missing! It hit Francesca as she stared at the back of her husband's head that she could barely remember how it felt to be close to William. Their conversations were so stilted and awkward these days. They had nothing in common except the business. They never laughed together. Suddenly, Francesca felt painfully lonely again.

It was a trial just getting out of the gates at the bottom of the drive, past all the press. The LaFatas were front-page news. Every paper in Europe was speculating about what had happened to her dad. Accident. Murder. Suicide. It was all complete nonsense. Nobody had any idea what had happened to Fatty. Francesca hadn't read any of the rubbish that they'd written about him but she couldn't live in a bubble. Every time she walked past a TV or radio it was Giancarlo LaFata they were talking about. And worse, the tabloids had pictures of Angelica and Carlo out partying last night. How did that look? God, she was angry with them. But there was no point in having a go at them. They were all suffering in their own ways, she supposed. Francesca wanted to bring the family together in their time of crisis but nobody else seemed to feel the same way. As she drove down the hill towards Monte Carlo, Francesca felt very alone. Well, apart from the three photographers who were following her on their mopeds. She put her foot down on the accelerator and managed to lose them at some traffic lights. Their sort of company she could do without.

She parked the car in the underground car park of the office block in Fontvieille where LaFata International had their HQ. The car park was eerily empty. Nobody worked on Sundays here. Usually the family went to Mass together at the cathedral – Fatty had always insisted. Francesca had taken the boys this morning, determined to keep some sort of normality going for the poor little souls, but no one else in the family had bothered. Angelica and Carlo had still been asleep after their night on the town, Jade had refused to get out of bed and William had mumbled some excuse about having to check the Dubai accounts. It was embarrassing. There had been a huge turnout of Fatty's friends and business associates showing their support and the priest had led special prayers for his safe return but none of the LaFatas, except for Francesca, had been there.

Her heels echoed on the concrete as she made her way to the lift and up to the tenth floor. Francesca didn't even know what she was doing here. What did it matter if she kept on top of the business when her dad was who knows where? It was just an excuse to get out of the house. And a chance to have a look in her dad's private office. Just in case there was anything there that might explain what had happened on

Friday night. Who had he taken on board with him? There were two glasses of brandy but no one had come forward. All his friends had been questioned. It was none of the usual motley crew of ageing billionaires, gamblers and tax exiles. Maybe it was a woman. Dad had only been married to Jade for a few months but he'd always had a short attention span when it came to members of the opposite sex. Had he had a date? Somebody else's wife, maybe? Someone who was too scared or embarrassed to come forward? Perhaps he'd written a name down in his diary, or on a piece of paper or …

She used her swipe key to open the door to the main office. It was just as she'd left it on Friday. She turned on the air con, made herself a coffee and checked the answer machine. She perched on her glass desk, gazing out to sea, and listened sadly to the messages from business contacts, colleagues and friends who'd heard the news.

'This is Tim Solomon, calling from New York,' said one. 'I just heard what's going on there with you guys and I'm so sorry. I don't know what to say except that Fatty is a legend here in the Big Apple and we are all thinking about you guys, and praying for you. Let us know if there's anything we can do here at the bank to help.'

And that from a Wall Street banker! Francesca wiped a stray tear from her cheek and switched on the computer system. She checked her emails next. It was the same thing. Endless messages from people, some she hadn't heard from in years, sending her their love and thoughts.

She fished the key to her dad's office out of the drawer and walked towards his office door. She'd never done this before – snooped in Fatty's office when he wasn't around. She'd never dared! But desperate times called for desperate measures. She turned the key a little nervously but … what the hell? It wouldn't turn. She tried again. It definitely turned clockwise. She was sure of it. She tried again and again. But the key wouldn't budge. And then she tried the door. To her surprise it opened. It wasn't like Fatty to leave his office door unlocked over the weekend. He would never do something so lax. He didn't let any member of staff into his office when he wasn't there, not even Francesca. He was hardly going to leave it open for anyone to walk in. The cleaners would have been yesterday, maybe they forgot to lock up properly after themselves. She would have to have a word with the cleaning company. Yes, that was the only logical explanation.

Still, Francesca's heart was beating faster as she walked into the office. There was always something creepy about being alone in this vast building and today she was especially jumpy. But Fatty's office looked exactly the same as it always had – sweeping panoramic views of the Med, huge mahogany desk, two Apple Mac computers, plasma screen TV, minibar in the corner, Bang and Olufsen sound system, silver-framed photographs of herself, Angelica, Carlo, Jade, the boys. Francesca sighed and caught her breath. She was being stupid; there was nothing to be frightened of here in her dad's office. She spent half her life in this building, it was her home from home.

And then suddenly there was a loud creaking noise and the enormous high-backed swivel chair that had been facing the window swung round to face her. Francesca screamed as she came face to face with a strange man, sitting in her father's chair. She could barely move she was so terrified. They stared at each other for a moment. He was a big man of about forty-five with broad shoulders and a very square jaw. He had cropped blond hair, gold-rimmed glasses and a wide mouth, which was grinning at Francesca as she shook with fear.

'Who the hell are you?' she asked as she managed to find her voice. 'And what are you doing in my dad's chair?'

'Hello, Frankie,' said the man in a friendly tone. 'Do not be alarmed. I am not going to hurt you.'

Francesca could hear her heart beating in her mouth and the three silver bangles she always wore on her right wrist were jangling together as she shook. The man had a distinct Russian accent.

'I am Andrea Dubrovski,' he told her, still smiling at her as if this were a perfectly normal meeting. 'And I am a business associate – and friend, may I add – of your father's.'

Francesca backed slowly towards the door. She wanted to run but her feet felt like lead weights and she tripped over her heels. She fell onto the floor with a thump, her back crashing against the door and slamming it behind her. She was trapped.

'There is no need to be scared, beautiful Francesca. I mean you no harm,' continued Dubrovski.

'Wha-wha-what are you do-doing here?' stammered Francesca. 'How did you get in?'

Dubrovski shrugged. 'Is no big deal. It is easy when you know how.'

'And how did you know I'd be here?'

Francesca had never been so scared in her life. Had this man followed her? But no. He was here already. Waiting for her. What was going on?

'I have a lot of friends. They let me know who will be where and when. Like I said, is no big deal.' He grinned again and flashed a glimpse of gold tooth.

'What do you want from me?' demanded Francesca, sitting up and rubbing her bruised elbows.

'Sit, sit,' said Dubrovski, offering her the chair opposite

him. 'You can't be very comfortable on the floor there and it is no place for a lady ...'

Francesca did as she was told, more out of fear than discomfort. 'What do you want?' she repeated, trying to sound firm.

She realised she'd left her mobile in her handbag in the other office. She was totally alone with this, this, this ... Who the hell was he?

'I have a very leetle problem, Frankie,' he said. 'You see, I have given your father a great deal of money recently but now poor Fatty, he has gone up to the great pizzeria in the sky. This is great tragedy, I know, and I send you and all your family my sincerest condolences, but I'm sure you understand, Frankie, that this leaves me with a problem.'

She hated the way he was calling her Frankie, it was giving her the creeps. No one called her Frankie except her close family. Even William always called her Francesca.

'My husband deals with the finances,' said Francesca as calmly as she could. 'Of course he'll make sure you get your money back. Or maybe we'll still want to go through with whatever business venture you and my father have been involved in ...'

Damn him! Her dad had done it again. Got involved in some dodgy deal behind her back. And now he'd gone and left her in this position. She could kill him. Except, of course, he was probably already dead. Her anger dissolved and the sadness and pain took over again. Oh, Dad, what have you done?

Dubrovski laughed at her. 'I do not think it is something you can help me with, my dear girl. And I suspect your husband will find no record of such a payment being made in his books. This was a, how shall I put it? A private matter between your father and me.'

Francesca wasn't born yesterday. A private business matter? No record of Fatty having given him the money? This guy was nothing but an extortionist.

'Right,' she said, taking a deep breath. 'You're asking me to return your money when you have no proof that you ever gave it to my father?'

'That is correct,' nodded Dubrovski. His smile had suddenly disappeared.

Francesca shook her head. 'No,' she said. 'Until I can see a contract, or a bank statement, or some proof of the transaction, I won't be giving you a penny. Now I suggest we schedule a meeting for a more suitable time for you to discuss this matter with my husband and our lawyers.'

There, that was him told. She was feeling braver now.

'I don't think so, Francesca,' said Dubrovski. 'It was not that sort of deal, if you get my drift.'

Francesca did not get his drift. But she did hear the menace in his voice and her heart started to drift back up towards her mouth. All she could hear was the boom, boom, boom of its beating and the jingle-jangle of the bangles on her wrist.

'How much money are we talking about?' she asked, swallowing hard.

Perhaps it would be worth paying him off, just to make him go away.

'Ten million euros,' said Dubrovski darkly.

'Ten million? Are you joking?' asked Francesca incredulously. How the hell could her father have accepted that amount of money without discussing it with her and William first? 'And what was the money for?'

Dubrovski stared at her coldly. 'Do I look as if I am joking?' he asked.

Francesca shook her head. 'No,' she said. 'But I can't get

hold of that sort of money without a meeting with William and the lawyers, so if we could just reschedule—'

'Five days,' said Dubrovski firmly. 'On Friday you will give me the money.'

'But ...?'

Dubrovski stood up. And up. And up. He was at least six foot eight tall. Francesca gulped. He stretched his arms above his head so that the gun, tucked into the waistband of his trousers, was clearly visible.

'I am glad we had this meeting, Francesca,' he said, tapping the gun with his finger. 'I will be here Friday. Oh, and did I mention I want cash?'

'But I can't get that sort of money in cash,' said Francesca desperately.

'Yes, you can,' said Dubrovski, his face grim. 'Or ...'

'Or what?' asked Francesca shakily.

'Or next time I won't be so friendly,' he said. 'Goodbye, Francesca. I will see you in five days. At midday. I will let myself out. I know the way.'

And then he was gone and Francesca was left in her dad's office with her head spinning and her life in even more chaos than it had been before.

Chapter Eighteen

Carlo lay on his bed and stared at the ceiling. He'd decided to stay in his apartment tonight. Alone. Le Grand Bleu just reminded him of all the crap that was going on. Frankie had told him that the police had been there all day and that the place was a mess. Angel was still feeling rough and Jade, apparently, had gone back into hiding in her bedroom. Frankie herself sounded even more on edge and stressed out than she had earlier and Carlo really wasn't in the mood to deal with anyone else's grief.

Besides, the house was so full of his dad's stuff that it did Carlo's head in. His coats and blazers still hung in the porch, his dog-walking boots were still lying by the back door. Portraits hung above fireplaces and photographs of Fatty's grinning face, posing with politicians, movie stars and F1 drivers lined the mantelpieces and shelves. He was there in every comfy leather armchair and half-read book. His favourite Breton biscuits were in the jar in the kitchen, his collection of opera CDs were on the stand, his cologne was in every bathroom, his cars were in the garage and his voice was on the answer machine. All his stuff was still there but he was gone and it just felt so fucking wrong. Carlo couldn't stand it. The house was too quiet without him and it felt suddenly too big for one broken family. No, Le Grand Bleu only reminded Carlo of what was missing. And tonight he just wanted to forget.

He'd felt bad that he hadn't gone to Mass with Frankie that morning. Dad would have been livid if he'd known. So, after his day's sailing with Christian he'd popped into the cathedral and given confession. It was the first time he'd stepped into the confession box for years and he'd felt claustrophobic as he'd shut the door behind him and made the sign of the cross.

'Bless me, Father, for I have sinned. It's been ...' Carlo had had to pause to think at this point. 'It's been, um, four years since my last confession, and these are my sins.'

'Please, go on, my child ...' the priest had encouraged him.

Carlo's list of sins had been long and embarrassing and, as he'd listened to himself speak, he'd realised what a shallow, selfish, self-centred wanker he'd become. A sense of deep shame settled on his shoulders as he'd confessed to drinking, swearing, masturbating, disrespecting his mother, disrespecting his sisters, disrespecting his father. He'd confessed to lying (to everyone), cheating (on women and at cards), breaking the law (by driving too fast after too much champagne) and gambling (at any given opportunity). And finally he'd had to admit to his worst sin of all.

'And last Friday, Father, I slept with my best friend's girlfriend ... And, if I'm completely honest, I'd really like to do it again. For these and for all the sins of my past I am truly sorry.'

The priest was silent for a long, long time. Carlo could hear the sound of his heavy breathing and guessed he was in shock. It was quite a list of mortal sins that he'd just had to endure. And then the priest simply said, 'Do not be so hard on yourself, my child. You have had a difficult few days. Say six Hail Marys.'

'Oh, my God, I am heartily sorry for having offended

Thee,' the words tripped off Carlo's tongue. How many times had he said them as a boy? Not because he meant them. But because he'd been told to say them. He carried on, 'I detest all my sins because of Thy just punishments, but most of all because they have offended Thee, my God, who art all good and deserving of all my love. I firmly resolve, with the help of Thy grace, to confess my sins, to do penance, and to avoid the near occasion of sin. Amen.'

The priest said the prayer of absolution and then told Carlo, 'I absolve you from your sins in the name of the Father, and of the Son and of the Holy Spirit. Your sins are forgiven, go in peace.'

'Thank you, Father,' said Carlo, desperate to get out of the suffocating little wooden box.

What a pile of crap! Carlo had left the church remembering why he'd stopped going to confession in the first place. It didn't make him feel purged or cleansed. He just felt worse about himself than ever. And now here he was, lying on his bed, feeling so low that he could happily throw himself out of the penthouse window, if only he had the nerve. But that would just be another mortal sin to add to his collection. Carlo was a (very) lapsed Catholic, but he did still kind of believe in the whole heaven and hell thing. Or at least, he sure as hell wasn't going to risk finding out the hard way if it was true. If he died now, there was no doubt about which direction he would be going. Carlo would be going down! And an eternity in hell and damnation was not his idea of a good time. Maybe he should stick around on earth for a bit longer and give himself the chance to redeem himself. Yeah, that was probably the best plan.

Suddenly, the buzzer to the apartment rang. Carlo was in two minds whether to answer it or not. It was probably Christian, worried about him, trying to be a good mate by bringing round a few beers. But Carlo had spent all day with Christian and he really wasn't in the mood for any more male bonding. To be honest, he really wasn't in the mood for anyone tonight. The buzzer rang again. This time, whoever was downstairs left their finger on the buzzer for a really long time.

'All right, all right, I'm coming,' muttered Carlo, as he got up and made his way reluctantly to the intercom.

'Yup?' he answered. 'What d'you want?'

'A piece of your ass,' said a sexy American voice. 'And another look at that itty-bitty cock of yours.'

Jesus, it was Sasha!

'Um, right, well you'd better come in then,' he said, trying to sound casual, but wanting to whoop with joy.

It was Sasha! She'd come back! But Carlo was a state. He hadn't even had a shower this morning, or shaved. And he'd been at sea all day so his skin and hair were covered in salt. He stripped his clothes off and jumped in the shower, frantically scrubbing and shampooing. He only just had time to wrap a towel around his waist before he heard her knock at the door.

She stood there in a navy and white stripy minidress and gold sandals, with a bottle of Jack Daniel's in one hand and a huge packet of crisps in the other.

'Provisions,' she said with an all-American whiter-than-white smile. 'I heard what happened to your old man and it sucks, Carlo baby. So I thought maybe you could do with a little cheering up, Sasha style!'

'Thank you,' said Carlo, still trying to get his head around the fact that she was here, in his apartment. 'You're being very nice to me this evening. Where's the abuse?'

'I figured you've had a hard enough time these last coupla days, so I thought I might go easy on you for an hour or two. Don't worry though, baby, my sympathy'll wear out pretty damn quick. I'm not exactly known for my patience so the old, abusive Sasha you know and love could be back any minute. In the meantime, enjoy Little Miss Nice Sasha, she's a rare treat. Now where's your ice?'

Carlo pointed to the ice-making machine on his fridge, handed her a couple of tumblers and watched as Sasha bent over in her minidress. It rode up, revealing a luscious length of toned, smooth, brown thigh. Her dress stretched over her perfect, round little arse, and Carlo had to catch his breath as he thought about what was waiting for him just a couple of inches above her hemline.

She handed him a JD on the rocks and said, 'Cheers!' clanking her glass hard against his. 'To happier times!'

'Happier times,' agreed Carlo, taking a swig.

Sasha jumped up on to the white Corian worktop and sat there, legs crossed, staring at Carlo, quizzically.

'So, d'ya think Christian's sussed?' she asked. 'Bout you and me?'

Carlo shook his head. He didn't want to think about Christian. He just wanted to enjoy his time with Sasha without worrying about the guilt. Maybe he'd start confessing once a week, maybe that way he could screw Sasha regularly and then absolve himself. Anyway, he felt sure that sex with Sasha was better for his soul than any number of Hail Marys.

'Think I'm done with him anyway,' she said breezily. 'He's a nice guy but he's a bit, well, dull …'

'Really?' Carlo tried not to sound too excited about the prospect of his best mate being dumped but his mind was already racing.

Was that why Sasha was here? Did she want to be his girlfriend now? Surprisingly, the thought made Carlo smile.

Carlo, the world's greatest commitment-phobe. Carlo, who didn't 'do' relationships, or brunettes, or girls under five foot ten, or Americans, come to think of it (too annoying). And yet here he was, desperate to date this short, dark, mouthy American.

'Really,' Sasha nodded. 'Christian's sweet but he's too serious for me. A bit heavy-duty on the relationship front. He's into "exclusivity". I mean, yawn, how boring is that? I don't wanna just sleep with one guy. I'm twenty-two years old. I ain't settling down yet!'

Carlo tried to hide his disappointment. Sasha wanted to sleep around. The thought of those thighs wrapped around any other man made him want to punch the wall. God, she'd got under his skin. What was that all about? He knew it would be hypocritical to judge her. She was only saying what he'd said himself a hundred times. Yup, this time he'd definitely met his match. Being with Sasha was like looking in the mirror. She was a female version of Carlo, except maybe she was the real deal? Carlo was perfectly aware that he only pretended to be the 'Big I Am', as Sasha had put it. But she didn't seem to be pretending at all. This girl seriously didn't seem to give a damn.

She uncrossed her legs slowly, so that her thighs were a few inches apart. 'Why is it, Carlo,' she asked, licking her full, red lips, 'that you're always half naked when I see you?'

But Carlo couldn't talk. Sasha wasn't wearing any knickers and he couldn't drag his eyes away from her perfectly waxed pussy. He had butterflies in his stomach and an ache in his groin as his cock strained against the towel round his waist.

'Not that I'm complaining,' continued Sasha, licking a finger. 'I like your body. It gets me all hot and bothered down here …'

Carlo stared, mesmerised, as Sasha slipped her wet finger between her parted thighs. She rubbed herself slowly, rhythmically. She was moaning slightly now and her breath was getting faster.

'I'm so hot for you, baby,' she told him.

She slid to the edge of the worktop and opened her legs wider so that Carlo could see her in all her glory. She licked her fingers again.

'Oh fuck,' Carlo heard himself say involuntarily. 'You are the sexiest girl I have ever met.' He slammed his glass down on the side and grabbed her soft thighs, pushing them even further apart.

'Take your dress off,' he said desperately. 'Please. I want to see your tits. You have the most perfect tits.'

Sasha slipped her dress over her head. She wasn't wearing a bra and Carlo took in the glorious sight of Sasha naked. He'd never wanted a woman so desperately in his life. He kissed her soft, full mouth, his fingers finding those hard, round nipples and then cupping her full, pert breasts. He kissed her neck and her collarbone and then his tongue was flicking those nipples and she was gasping, saying, 'Lick me, Carlo. Taste me.'

And then he kissed her tight, flat stomach and he could smell her now, he was getting closer and closer to the ultimate prize. He kissed the soft smooth skin of her inner thighs as she groaned in pleasure.

'Now, Carlo,' she told him breathlessly. 'I'm gonna come so quickly, baby. You make me horny as hell.'

And then he was there in heaven, lost in the taste and the smell and the feel of her. His tongue flicking her clit, his fingers probing deeper and deeper.

'Oh Jesus, Carlo, I'm gonna come,' she gasped. 'Fuck

me,' she demanded suddenly. 'Fuck me hard, Carlo. I need you now!'

Who was Carlo to refuse? He stood up, kissed her beautiful, soft mouth and let himself slide into her, deeper and deeper. She threw her head back and thrust her hips against his, until they were riding each other in perfect unison. She was screaming now, with no inhibitions.

'I'm gonna come again, Carlo,' she screamed. 'Make me come again.'

And then Carlo couldn't help himself, her body shuddering in the throes of an orgasm, he couldn't hold on any more. He came so violently, so completely, it felt as if he was giving his whole body to hers. The feeling lasted for ages. They stayed there, in each other's arms, naked and sweating, clinging to each other's damp skin, their breathing fast and their hearts pounding.

Finally, Carlo managed to speak. 'I'm not joking, Sasha,' he said, looking her straight in the eye. 'That was the best ever.'

She winked at him cheekily, pushed him away and jumped off the worktop.

'Course it was, baby. I'm really good at fucking. It's one of my all time favourite hobbies,' she said, opening the packet of crisps and shoving a handful in her mouth. 'Gives me an appetite though, I am starving!'

Sasha confused Carlo. She was the opposite of what girls were supposed to be. She didn't seem to have the slightest emotional attachment to him, she was just using his body, like he'd used all those girls in the past. It made Carlo feel, well, a bit cheap to be honest. And, worse, the less she cared, the more keen he became. God, she was a piece of work. He remembered what she'd said last time, about how girls lied during sex. She'd *seemed* to enjoy their love-making but

Carlo had no idea where he stood with this one. Sasha filled him with self-doubt. He began to worry that she'd been fucking with his head as well as his body.

'Um, Sasha,' he asked, bashfully. 'What you said there, when we were making love ...'

Sasha nearly choked on her crisps.

'Let me stop you right there, Carlo,' she said, hands on naked hips. 'We did not make love. That was sex. Very enjoyable sex, maybe even a seven or an eight out of ten, but it was just sex, OK? You don't have to bullshit me. I'm not one of those soppy Barbie dolls you usually get your rocks off with.'

Carlo blushed. She always made him feel so stupid!

'Well,' he continued bravely, 'what you said when we having sex, did you mean it? Or were you lying? Like you told me girls do.'

Sasha shrugged. 'Dunno,' she said. 'I get a bit carried away when I'm coming. I can't really remember what I said. Have you got a ciggie?'

She pulled on Carlo's favourite pale blue cashmere jumper, which barely covered her naked bum, and padded barefoot out onto the balcony. He threw on his bathrobe and followed her. They shared a cigarette as they leant over the balcony, side by side, staring out to sea.

'Sasha,' he asked her, wanting to know if there was more to this ... what? What was *this*? This *thing*. More to this *thing* than just sex. Did they have anything else in common? Suddenly it was important for Carlo to know what made her tick. 'Do you ever want more than this? Than Monaco?'

It was the same question he'd asked Christian earlier. Sasha nodded her head emphatically.

'Hell yeah,' she replied. 'This isn't real. It's not what life's all about. It's a sham, Carlo, and one day soon I'm going to go out there and find out what else there is on offer.'

Her answer pleased Carlo, but it scared him too. Sasha was just like him, as he'd suspected, and that was dangerous. A girl like Sasha could hurt him. Sasha could break his heart.

She didn't stay long. After another glass of JD, she was pulling her dress back over her head and saying that she had to get off to meet Christian. This time she paused at the door and looked Carlo straight in the eye.

'I wasn't bullshitting, by the way,' she said.

Carlo detected a slight blush in her cheeks and it was the closest he'd ever seen Sasha come to looking coy.

'What I said, about you being hot, and being a good lay. It was all true,' she said. 'But don't let it go to your head.'

Carlo smiled and he felt his heart melt into a gooey mess on the floor.

'So, can I have your number, then?' he asked, pretty sure this time that she would give it to him.

Sasha frowned. 'No, Carlo,' she said. 'Don't be daft. I told you. No numbers. I know where to find you if I want you. Have you gone soft in the head?'

And then she kissed him briefly on the cheek, called, 'See you around, sexy!' And she was gone. He watched her saunter down the hall, like a cowgirl who'd just broken a wild stallion. She was off to meet Christian now, her boyfriend, his best mate. She didn't look back.

Father Romano D'Alessio sat silently on a pew, fingering his rosaries, and considering his day. It had been one of the most difficult of his career and his Christian faith in humanity had been stretched to its absolute limit.

He thought briefly about young Carlo LaFata, who'd

come to confession today for the first time in years. The boy had lost his father and had turned to the church for support. The thought made D'Alessio smile and perhaps even restored his faith a little.

Carlo had a good soul, Father D'Alessio felt sure of that. A priest had a way of sensing these things. He'd heard the deep shame and guilt in his voice and it had taken him by surprise. Father D'Alessio was a man of the Lord but he was also a man of the people. He knew what was going on in the world around him and he was well aware of Carlo's reputation as a playboy. But today, Father D'Alessio had glimpsed a different Carlo LaFata.

The poor boy's sins were so ordinary and mundane. A twenty-three-year-old who'd slept with his best friend's girl? In this day and age? In Monaco? It was hardly the stuff of hell and damnation! And yet the poor boy was so full of self-hatred and self-flagellation that it made D'Alessio want to take him in his arms and console him.

Father D'Alessio wished he could have told the boy about the sins of others. Oh, he never would, and never could, reveal a confession, but sometimes he wished he could tell the good people how bad the real sinners were, just so that they would stop beating themselves up.

When he thought about the other confession he'd heard today it made his blood run cold. Extortion, fraud, violence, theft and murder. It was the stuff of nightmares. The burden of knowledge weighed heavily on Father D'Alessio's soul. He would pray all night now. Never before had he needed the Lord's help so desperately. He would pray for the good people and he would pray for the sinners too.

Chapter Nineteen

Francesca couldn't sleep. Her mind raced with grotesque images – her dad's bloated body, being tossed around by the waves; Dubrovski's menacing grin, the glint of his gold tooth, the glimpse of his gun; Angelica's beautiful face, drawn and wasted, with the life sucked out of it. Angel had gone out again. She'd refused to say where she was going or who with. Francesca had a horrible feeling that her little sister was slipping off the rails once more and, for the first time, Francesca didn't feel strong enough to save her. Her heart pounded in her ears. She was wide awake and she couldn't imagine that sleep would ever come. How the hell did she get here? In the middle of this nightmare, so lost, and scared and alone?

Francesca had always been the responsible one. She'd spent her entire adult life looking after the others, controlling everything, sorting out their problems and cleaning up their mess. But who would look after Francesca? Hot tears poured down her cheeks.

She hadn't told anyone about Dubrovski, yet. Not even William. Not yet. She knew she would have to talk to him about it tomorrow, she had no way of getting the money without William's help, but for now she just wanted to shut the whole terrifying incident away. She closed her eyes and tried to sleep but the images kept haunting her. Francesca felt as if she was going insane. She felt weak and lost. She had no one to turn to.

'I can't cope,' she told herself out loud. 'I can't cope any more.'

And then she curled up into a ball and sobbed, her shoulders heaving, her heart breaking. She had never felt so sad, or lonely, or scared before. All she wanted was for someone to scoop her up and fix everything. She wanted to be the one who was looked after for a change. She wanted to feel protected, cherished, precious, adored. She wanted to feel someone's arms around her. She wanted to give up control …

Angelica felt brilliantly, dazzlingly, amazingly, crazily out of control. She was standing at the front of her yacht, travelling at sixty knots through the Med in the dark, pretending to be Kate Winslet in *Titanic*. Her hot-pink chiffon dress was billowing around her and her hair was being whipped wildly around her face in the wind. She felt alive and free.

'Faster, faster,' she shouted to the skipper, Pat – or Pirate Pat as she liked to call him because it made her laugh and him frown. 'Let's go to Cannes! Let's party.'

'Be careful Angelica,' said her friend, Milly. 'You're off your head, hon, you might fall!'

Actually, Milly wasn't exactly a friend. Well, she was, kind of, if you could count a girl you'd only met two hours ago as a friend. But she was fun. They were all fun! This group of mad Australians she'd met in the bar. They were tourists just passing through Monaco, catching a glimpse of how the other half lived, as they put it.

'I'll show you how the other half *really* live,' Angelica had offered, up for a party with whoever was in the mood.

'Come on, let's take my yacht out. You guys ever been on a yacht?'

There had been a lot of quizzical looks, and mutterings of 'Is this chick for real?' and then the Aussies – a guy and two girls – had decided what the hell, and followed her down to the quay. Pat hadn't looked too impressed about the impromptu party, but tough shit, it was her yacht and he was paid to do whatever she told him to do. So were the rest of the crew.

'We need champagne, lots of champagne, pink champagne!' Angel had ordered the stewardess, whose name she'd forgotten because she was new. The last one had walked out in a huff. Stupid cow!

'*Daddy's Money*.' Connor, the Aussie bloke, had read the yacht's name out loud. 'Is that what this is all about? Your old man's loaded?'

'Disgustingly, filthily, obscenely loaded,' Angelica had giggled. 'Actually, he's missing at the moment but I'm sure he'll turn up.'

'He's what?' Trina, the little redhead had asked, all wide-eyed and confused. 'Your dad is missing? Missing how?'

'Oh, it's no big deal.' Angelica had shrugged. 'He's just messing with us. I mean the police think he's dead but I know he's not so … Come on, climb on board. Let's take *Daddy's Money* for a spin!'

Her new mates had looked a bit freaked out at first, as if they didn't really trust her, but now they were having a ball. They were on to the third bottle of champagne and their cute little Aussie faces were all happy and excited and awestruck.

'Want a line, anyone?' shouted Angelica, jumping down from her perch at the front of the yacht.

The three friends exchanged quizzical glances again, looking to each other for support.

'Um, I don't know,' said Milly eventually. 'D'you mean cocaine?'

'Of course I mean cocaine, silly,' Angelica giggled. 'I didn't mean a washing line, did I?'

'I don't think we should,' said Trina, who was turning out to be a bit of a square. 'We've never done it before.'

'Up to you, babes,' said Angel. 'Connor? Milly? You want some?'

Milly was the most fun. 'Sure,' she said. 'I'll try anything once.'

'OK,' said Connor. 'I'm up for it.'

Trina shook her head huffily and said, 'I don't like this at all, guys. We don't do drugs. You're just trying to impress *her*. This is really fucking wrong.'

Angelica smiled at the little party-pooper sweetly and said, 'How can it be wrong, when it feels sooo right?'

Trina walked off and sat on a chair at the other end of the deck. She looked like she was going to cry. What a loser! The others followed Angel inside and watched her rack up three fat lines. She rolled up a fifty-euro note and showed them what to do. And then they were coke virgins no more.

'So what do you do, Angelica?' asked Milly, her eyes like saucers from the coke and the excitement.

'I'm a model,' replied Angel, a little miffed that they hadn't recognised her. 'You don't know who I am?'

Milly and Connor shook their heads. Oh well, supposed Angel, they were from Australia, it was the other side of the bloody world. Maybe they were from the outback or something and never actually read fashion magazines. Actually, looking at their clothes, she should have known they didn't read fashion magazines.

By the time they'd polished off the fifth bottle of champagne, Milly was looking a bit green.

'We'll be in Cannes soon,' Angelica promised her. 'I'll take you to a really cool club and introduce you to all my friends.'

'I really don't feel very well,' said Milly feebly. 'I think I'm going to be sick.'

'Have an E,' Angel suggested. 'I've just had one. It'll perk you up.'

'She doesn't need any more drugs,' said Connor. 'Are you crazy? She's not well. You need to take us back to Monaco, back to our hostel.'

'I'm not going back yet,' said Angelica defiantly.

God, nobody was any fun any more. Even Carlo had refused to come out with her tonight. And then suddenly Milly was throwing up everywhere.

'Yuk!' said Angel in disgust. 'You just splattered puke on my Jimmy Choos. Be careful, for fuck's sake. They're ponyskin.'

Connor turned on her, looking angry suddenly. 'Look, Daddy's Girl,' he said with a look of disgust on his face. 'I don't care who you are, or how much money you've got, Milly's not well. Just tell your skipper, Pirate Pat, or whatever the hell you call him, to turn this boat round and get us back to our hostel, OK?'

'It's a yacht, not a boat, you ignorant Aussie moron,' said Angel furiously. 'And we're going to Cannes.'

How dare he speak to her like that! After she'd taken him and his stupid little friends on her yacht and plied them with bubbly and Charlie, and offered to take them to Cannes! Christ, how many times would *nobodies* like those guys get a chance to do something like this? She was doing them a favour.

Milly was rolling on the deck now, clutching her stomach and retching violently. Trina looked up from her perch at the far end of the deck, saw that Milly was on the floor and ran over to her. She glared at Angel as she bent down beside her friend.

'I knew something like this would happen,' she said angrily. 'Milly, I told you not to touch that stuff.'

But Milly just whimpered. Turned out the little madam was quite an actress. She was doing a really good job of playing the dying swan, while everybody fussed around her. Everybody except Angel, of course, Angel wasn't falling for it for a second.

'She's in a really bad way,' said Trina tearfully. 'I'm scared. She's never done drugs before. What if she dies?'

'Am I going to die?' murmured Milly from the floor.

'Oh, for fuck's sake,' said Angel impatiently. 'She's had one line of coke. One line of coke never killed anybody. She's seasick, that's all. She'll be fine once we get to dry land.'

'I've had enough of you,' said Connor suddenly. 'I've never met such a spoilt, nasty, unfeeling bitch in my life before. I'm going to talk to the captain.'

Angelica couldn't believe the cheek of these people. Who did they think they were? She was the one who gave the orders round here. Milly was groaning and moaning on the floor, and Trina was rubbing her friend's forehead and crying pitifully, saying, 'It's OK, Milly. Connor's gone to speak to the captain. We'll be back at the hostel soon.'

There was no way Angel was having this. She stormed off after Connor and found him talking to Pirate Pat.

'I demand that you take us to Cannes,' said Angel, stamping her Jimmy Choos.

Pat gave Angelica a withering look and said, 'Angelica, I'm turning the yacht round and going back to Monaco. Your friend over there is feeling really unwell and this is all wrong.'

Angel felt her blood boil. 'You do as I say, Pat!' she yelled. 'Take me to Cannes. I demand you take me to Cannes or I'll sack you.'

'Don't bother,' said Pat. 'I resign. I'm going to take these poor kids back to Port Hercule and then that's it. I quit. You're impossible, Angelica. I know you're going through a tough time but there's no excuse for treating people the way you do.'

Angelica stomped off inside and lit a cigarette. Well, fuck them, fuck them all! She didn't need them anyway. She didn't need anybody. She racked up another line of coke, and then another, and another. She found a half-drunk bottle of pink champagne and swigged it until it was empty and rolling about the floor as the yacht bounced over the waves.

When they finally got back to Monaco, she watched as Pat and Connor carried Milly off the yacht and laid her down on the ground. Pat got her a blanket from the yacht and wrapped it round her. What a bloody drama queen that girl was being. She was just doing it for the attention, that was perfectly clear.

Trina, the little sourpuss redhead, came up to Angelica and said, 'If this is how the other half lives, you can keep it. We might be ordinary, and broke, and not very glamorous, but at least we're decent human beings. I wouldn't treat a stray dog the way you treated Milly tonight. It doesn't matter how much money you've got, if you've got no heart, you're not worth anything!'

'Screw you!' screamed Angelica. She was sick of people lecturing her and telling her what a bad person she was.

Did they think she didn't know what a failure she was as a human being? Did they think she hadn't noticed? 'I am weak. I am weak. I am weak,' said the voice in her head. Connor, Pat and the new stewardess, whose name Angel still couldn't remember, were all staring at her now too. They were looking at her as if she was a piece of dirt.

'And screw you!' she said, pointing at Connor. 'And you!' She pointed at Pat. 'And you!' She pointed at the nameless stewardess. 'And you!' She pointed at Milly, still laid out on the ground in her blanket.

And then Angel stumbled off into the night. The quay-side felt as if it was swaying beneath her feet and her head spun, so that the lights of the bars by the harbour trailed like comets in front of her eyes. She kept bumping into people, and tripping up in her heels, and she didn't know where she was any more, or where she was going. And she'd left her bag somewhere. Where was her phone? And, fuck, she felt strange now, everything was swimming ...

She wasn't sure where Christian came from but suddenly his face appeared, and then his strong arms were picking her up and throwing her over his shoulder, and he was telling her she was going to be OK. And then nothing.

Christian watched Angelica sleeping from the chair in the corner of his bedroom. He'd been sitting there all night, making sure that she was all right, studying her breathing, watching closely as her chest rose and fell. She was lying face down on his bed, with her arms and legs spread out, still in her bright pink dress and her make-up from the night before. Her face was smudged with eyeliner and lipstick and her golden hair was matted and tangled in knots around her head. But to Christian she was still the most beautiful thing he'd ever seen.

He'd been at a bar by the harbour, having a drink with Sasha, when the commotion had started. Sasha had been an hour late for their date and then, when she did eventually turn up, smelling of Jack Daniel's and cigarettes, she'd been really distracted and detached. She didn't seem to be listening to a word he said, she just kept staring off into the distance and when he asked her what she thought about something, she'd say, 'Hmm? What was that? Sorry, baby, I was miles away.'

It was almost a relief when people had started pointing at something that was happening on the quayside.

'Oh God,' he'd heard someone say. 'Look at the state of that. She can barely walk.'

He'd turned to see what they were talking about and seen a girl weaving her way along the quayside on wobbly legs, muttering to herself and pushing people out of the way. She'd tripped up and lost a shoe, but carried on regardless, hobbling on one flat foot and one heel. She had no jacket or bag. She was dressed like a catwalk model but behaving like a tramp.

'I feel sorry for her,' another voice had said. 'She should be locked up for her own safety.'

It had taken a few minutes for Christian to realise that the tramp was actually Angelica. She was standing still now, looking around, obviously confused and disorientated. He'd rushed out of the bar, without explaining what he was doing to Sasha, and run up to her just as her eyes had glazed over; if he hadn't been there to catch her, she would have fallen flat on her face.

Sasha had caught up with him as he'd carried Angel to his car.

'Jesus, what a frigging mess,' she'd said, eyeing Angelica's crumpled body. 'Shall we get Carlo?'

Christian had shaken his head. 'Carlo's got enough to worry about,' he'd said. 'I can deal with Angelica.'

'D'you wanna hand?' Sasha had offered.

But Christian had said no. He'd sent Sasha home in a cab and concentrated on the real love of his life instead. And now he watched her sleeping. Her mouth was open, and every now and then she made a snorting sound like a little piglet, then she'd lick her lips, murmur in her dreams, and be quiet again. It made Christian smile.

Last night he'd thought about calling Francesca, but he'd decided he could cope with Angelica on his own. Best to let her sleep it off, sober up, and then take her home. The poor thing would have been in serious trouble if Francesca had seen her in that state. She'd have been straight on the next plane to Arizona and back to her detox boot camp in the desert. Maybe it was the best place for her, Francesca seemed to think so, but Christian wondered if there was somewhere closer to home that might be able to fix Angelica. For all her hissy fits and foot-stamping, Angelica was a girl who just wanted to be liked. She needed to be near people who loved her.

Christian remembered when Angelica had been a little girl, the way she'd always followed him and Carlo around Le Grand Bleu. Carlo would get annoyed with her as she skipped behind them to the tennis courts or the swimming pool.

'Go away, Angel,' he'd say. 'Shoo! Go and find your own friends to play with.'

But Angelica had never seemed to have any friends round to play. Sandrine LaFata had tried inviting Christian's little sister, Ingrid, over for play dates with Angel but that was a disaster. Ingrid had always been serious and studious and, even at seven or eight, she'd found Angelica's giggling and girliness irritating. She still couldn't stand Angelica now.

It hadn't crossed Christian's mind at the time that the little girl might have been lonely but in hindsight she must have been. She used to do anything she could to get the boys' attention. They'd be halfway through a game of tennis and she'd suddenly appear out of the bushes, naked, and streak across the court. Or when they were in the pool, messing around, dive-bombing each other, she'd jump in and pretend to drown, just so one of them would have to save her. Sometimes she'd hide in the wardrobe in Carlo's room, listening to them. She could be there for hours before they discovered her.

Christian had never minded Angelica hanging around. He'd thought she was funny and cute. He still did. He wished she'd see him as something more than her brother's friend. But that was just wishful thinking. And it was better to be a friend to Angelica than nothing at all.

Chapter Twenty

Sasha's feet pounded the treadmill, harder and harder, and the sweat trickled down her forehead until her mouth tasted salty. She made the machine go faster and faster and changed the incline of her run so that she was practically climbing Mont Blanc. Her heart was pounding, her chest was tight and her muscles ached but still she kept running, through the burn ...

Jeez, she needed an outlet for her frustrations. The bastard had got under her skin and into her head and now she couldn't stop thinking about him. His gorgeous, buff body, those frigging puppy-dog eyes, the way he brushed his hair off his face and ... Oh, God, what had she done? This was not going according to plan. She was not supposed to have feelings for Carlo LaFata. Of all the men she'd flirted with, played with, screwed around with, it had to be that egotistical, self-obsessed, vain son-of-a-bitch that had finally, *finally*, got into Sasha Constantine's heart. A place no man had gone before.

Sasha ran and ran and ran but she couldn't pound away the feeling in her stomach, of butterflies and excitement and anticipation. She knew she'd have to see him again. Soon. She wouldn't be able to help herself. Her body was desperate for him. Oh, she'd made out it was no big deal, that she just liked sex. She wasn't about to let Carlo know that she was hot for him. Hot for him? Christ, that was the understatement of the frigging year! She was on fire! Sasha just had to stand in the same room as the guy and her nipples got hard and she needed him to touch her and kiss her and oh, God, just thinking about him made her horny as hell.

Sleeping with Carlo had blown her mind. She had never, ever, felt so sexy, so alive, so turned on. But then she'd known for months that it would be like that. She'd gone out of her way to be extra rude and argumentative around him, pushing him away, denying the sexual attraction between them because, well, because he was Carlo LaFata, for crying out loud! What a cliché! She was just as bad as the rest of them now, his gaggle of adoring girls, who followed him around, fawning over him, putting up with his bullshit treatment, dropping their panties if he so much as looked at them.

But no, Sasha was not going to be like all those other girls. She was worth more than that. If Carlo wanted her, he would have to play the game her way. It was going to take all her strength and will, but Sasha was going to keep playing it cool. She would not give him her number, however much she wanted him to ring. She would not be sweet and kind to him, even though his dad was missing, and he looked so lost and heartbroken and all she wanted to do was put her arms around him and kiss away his pain. No. No. No. No. No!

Slam, slam, slam. Her feet pounded the treadmill still. Her mind kept racing. Christian? What the hell did she do about Christian? She'd only started seeing the poor guy because he *wasn't* Carlo. If that made any sense. She'd been so hell-bent on convincing herself, and everyone else, that she hated Carlo, that she'd said yes when Christian had first asked her out. And then he'd been so polite and gentlemanly it was kind of difficult to get rid of him. What's more, he was close to Carlo, so she could still hang out with Carlo, and argue with Carlo, and dance with Carlo, without actually becoming just another tick in his little black book. Except now she'd gone and screwed Carlo anyway. Not just once, when she was drunk, that would have been almost forgivable. But, no, Sasha had given in again in the morning when she was completely sober and then again last night. She'd just turned up on his doorstep because she couldn't keep away. Then she'd had to go on a date with Christian. What was she thinking? She'd lost the frigging plot.

Oh God, she would have to finish things with Christian now. Not because of the guilt, that she could live with, but because how could she ever go back to screwing Christian? Sweet, kind, boring, crap-in-the-sack Christian? She couldn't. Wouldn't! It would be like having one mouthful of fillet steak and then having to go back to eating a bowl of corned beef. Sasha just couldn't imagine sleeping with Christian ever again. But that wasn't the scary part. No. The really scary part was that she couldn't imagine sleeping with *any* man other than Carlo ever again. Not that she'd told him that either, of course. Hell no. She'd carried on her act, pretending she wanted to be free, to see lots of guys and sleep around. But it was all so much bullshit. Sasha wanted Carlo completely. Mind, body and soul. It wasn't just the sex that had blown her mind.

Something about the way she felt about Carlo scared the hell out of her. When she was around him she felt completely out of control, not just physically, but mentally and emotionally. Finally, it had happened. Now she knew what all those soppy love songs were about. She got it now. She understood. This was love. It wasn't something Sasha had ever experienced before. She had never needed or wanted anybody. But she wanted Carlo. She wanted him so badly and she wanted him for keeps. Sasha was a smart cookie. She had a psychology degree from Yale. If anyone could get into Carlo's mind and play with it, it would be her. Because Sasha didn't want to play the field. She was a one-man woman, and Carlo was her man. He just didn't know it yet.

She turned the running machine up to the fastest level and felt her blood pump through her veins. No pain, no gain, she told herself. She thrived on a challenge. She was dogged and determined and stubborn as hell but she could be patient too. Sasha would play the long game with Carlo. A guy like Carlo needed the chase. He'd had it too easy, had everything handed to him on a silver platter. But Sasha was not going to tie herself with a ribbon and hand herself to Carlo LaFata on a plate. He was going to have to fight for her. Only then would he truly want her and appreciate her. Only then would she get him for keeps.

'I know I said you needed a makeover but what is this? A midlife crisis?' asked Dan, eyeing Robbie's shopping bags nosily. 'Prada? Gucci? Hugo Bloody Boss? Jesus, Robbie, they must be paying you too much!'

Robbie felt his cheeks burning with embarrassment and slid his bags under the table guiltily. 'I wish,' he mumbled, still blushing. 'Haven't bought myself anything new for years and just thought, after what you said last night, that maybe I needed to smarten up a bit. You know what it's like out here, how flash everyone is, thought I might get taken more seriously if I dressed the part ...' Robbie knew he was rambling but he was trying to justify it to himself more than to Dan. He hid behind the menu and pretended to be thinking about lunch.

'So, how is work going?' asked Dan. 'Not well, I'm

assuming, if you needed to buy a new wardrobe to get any-where.'

'No, it's going OK,' said Robbie truthfully. 'You know they found his car?'

Dan nodded. 'Can you believe it took them three days? And it was only parked two streets back from the harbour.'

'Mental,' agreed Robbie. 'I wonder how they missed it.'

'Who knows, but that's it pretty much confirmed, isn't it? LaFata's a goner,' mused Dan.

Robbie nodded. 'No clothes or belongings were taken from the house, his bank accounts haven't been touched, his passport's in his safe and his car's been gathering dust in La Condamine all weekend. He's dead, all right.'

'His bank accounts haven't been touched?' Dan's eyes widened. 'How d'you know that?'

'Heard it on the radio about five minutes ago,' sighed Robbie. 'Difficult to get a scoop on this story with so many hacks crawling all over the place. How's it going your end? Angel behaving herself?'

'Thankfully not,' grinned Dan. 'She went out again last night. Ended up on her yacht with some Australian back-packers. Long story, but she was absolutely wasted, Robbie. You should have seen her.'

'I'm glad I didn't,' said Robbie. 'Gives me the creeps to see such a lovely young girl in that state. Makes me think of my two, you know. It won't be long before they're into boys and make-up and clothes and God knows what else.'

Dan chuckled. 'You sound like a right old woman. Have some lunch, have a drink, go back to your hotel and try on your midlife crisis gear, that'll make you feel young again.'

'Piss off, Dan,' laughed Robbie.

'I'm pissing off right now,' grinned Dan. 'Going to talk to those Aussie kids about their night with Angel. One of them only just got out of the hospital. Must have been some party!'

He shook his head in wonder and stood up to leave. 'Oh, and Robbie,' he added over his shoulder, 'if you're having a makeover, you might want to do something about your hair. It's a bit ...'

'A bit what?' asked Robbie, touching his mop of sandy blond hair. His hair was his crowning glory. Heather had always said she loved it. Well, she'd said it once, when they first met.

'Well, it's just a bit 1994, isn't it?' said Dan. 'A bit Brit-pop.'

Robbie wondered if he had time to squeeze in a trip to the hairdressers. God, what had got into him? He knew his faults but he had never been vain. And now here he was, in the middle of the biggest story of his career, and he was worrying about his appearance! It was all for her, of course – the clothes, the shoes, the aftershave, the expensive shaving oil. He'd finally found the nerve to text her, telling her he was in town and asking if she wanted to meet up. But she hadn't replied and he wasn't holding his breath. So why was he doing this?

The police were in the office today, checking through all the computers and files. They seemed to think that the business might hold a clue to what had happened to her dad, but Francesca was sure they were wrong. LaFata International might have had a few minor setbacks recently – they'd had to close the odd branch of Fatty's and the Dubai venture had turned out to be a complete fiasco – but who hadn't had problems in the last year? There was a global recession going on. Even in Monaco!

The children had been told to stay away from the office

until further notice. Francesca didn't know what to do with herself. She'd woken up at five a.m., after a couple of hours' broken sleep, and busied herself with tidying the house. There were maids and cleaners to do that sort of thing, of course, but she found it therapeutic. The police had left things in such a mess and she just wanted to get everything back in its place, back to normal. But the house was tidy now and it still felt wrong. Francesca knew that with Fatty gone, Le Grand Bleu would never be the same again. It would never feel like home.

She'd given up hope of ever seeing her father alive again now. She knew Carlo felt the same. It had been too long. There was no logical explanation. Fatty's passport was in the safe in his bedroom and William had checked his personal bank accounts. Her dad hadn't used his bank card since Friday. The last purchase he'd made was for the bottle of Hennessy Beauté de Siècle brandy.

Angel was still in deep denial, going out, meeting her friends and behaving as though nothing untoward had happened. Oh, it was a front, of course. She was just putting off the inevitable, shelving her emotions so that she didn't have to deal with the huge, crushing tidal wave of grief that was to come. All Francesca could do was wait until reality bit Angelica on her perfect little bum. And who knew what would happen then – Francesca certainly wouldn't be able to rescue her sister this time.

Normally Francesca would have sought solace at the office, but that wasn't allowed. And, anyway, after the Russian's visit yesterday, she wasn't so sure she wanted to go there today. The boys were at school, Carlo was at his apartment, Jade was in bed – again! – and Angel had stayed at Christian's last night. Christian had called this morning and said that he'd bumped into her in town last night and invited her to crash at his place. He said she was still asleep but that she was fine. It was a bit odd, him calling like that. Maybe Angel and Christian were seeing each other? That would be nice. Christian was just the sort of solid boy to look after Angel properly and keep her from going off the rails. Yes, if that romance blossomed, it would be a weight off Francesca's mind.

She knocked on William's door with her heart in her mouth. She didn't want to tell him about what had happened in the office the day before, but she knew she had no choice. Despite the gulf between them, she needed his help like she'd never needed it before.

He looked up from his screen when she entered the room, shut his laptop, took off his glasses and laid them carefully on the desk, but he didn't smile. His expression was fixed and gave nothing away, except for a glimmer of something cold in his eyes. What was that? Hate? Resentment? Mistrust? She wasn't sure. And then it was gone. Francesca wondered if she was getting paranoid from all the anxiety and lack of sleep.

'William,' she said, sitting down on the chair next to him, 'something strange happened at the office yesterday. We have a problem.'

'Another problem?' asked William, raising his eyebrows. 'There seem to be a lot of those around at the moment.'

'I'm afraid this one is really serious,' she said. She took a deep breath and explained about Andrea Dubrovski's surprise visit. She told him how scared she'd been, there alone with a threatening Russian giant. About how he'd been waiting for her in Fatty's office, in Fatty's chair. About how he'd somehow known she was going to be there and somehow got into the office without a key. She told him about the gun in his waistband.

'Should we tell the police?' she asked, shaking again from reliving the events of the day before. 'William, I don't know what to do. I don't want to get Dad into any trouble and he's obviously been involved with this man in some way but we can't have people breaking into the office, can we?'

'Of course we can't involve the police. This is a business matter. But we obviously need to do something about the security systems,' replied William matter-of-factly. 'So that this sort of thing can't happen again.'

Francesca was shocked at William's lack of sympathy. OK, so they no longer shared a bed, but they'd been married for eight years, she was the mother of his children and she'd been threatened by a man with a gun!

'Aren't you concerned?' she asked. 'For my safety? *Our* safety?'

'No,' said William coldly. 'Not particularly. The Russians do things differently, that's all.'

'Differently?' Francesca couldn't believe what she was hearing. 'William, the guy broke in. He had a gun!'

'Don't be so naive, Francesca,' said William, almost impatiently now.

His words rang in her ears. '*Si è ancora ingenuo, bambino.*' You are still naive, child. It was the last thing her father had ever said to her. And now William was saying the same thing. What was she missing here?

'Look, you must know that your dad messed around with some fairly colourful characters.' William softened a little now. 'When he was around we didn't talk about it. We pretended it wasn't going on. But you must have known, Francesca. Surely! And now that Fatty's gone we're the ones who are going to have to deal with these people until all of your dad's debts are cleared.'

Francesca's head was spinning. Colourful characters? Debts? What was William talking about?

'I don't understand,' she said, reeling. 'Me and you, we're the ones who've always dealt with running the business.'

'Francesca, are you blind, deaf and dumb?' asked William incredulously. 'I thought you were supposed to be an intelligent woman? We head up the dull, respectable, *official* side of LaFata International. Your dad has always had his own deals on the side. Big deals. The high-risk stuff. And the men he deals with – or dealt with should I say – are not nice, friendly accountants from Fulham, or charming bankers from Wall Street. Now that your dad has gone, we're going to have to clear up the mess he's left behind. I thought you understood that.'

'No,' said Francesca, feeling tears of frustration, disappointment and fear well up in her eyes. 'I don't understand any of this. What debts? I thought we were doing OK.'

'Francesca, we are not doing OK,' said William. 'I've got people crawling out of the woodwork left, right and centre claiming that Fatty owed them money. What do you think I've been doing on my computer all day, every day since he disappeared?'

Francesca shrugged and wiped her tears on her sleeve. 'I didn't know,' she said, quietly. 'I honestly didn't know.'

'So how much does this Dubrovski character want?' asked William, sighing, as if the Russian was just another irritant on a long list of annoyances.

'Ten million,' she said shakily.

William shrugged. 'Well, that's not so bad,' he said, sounding almost relieved. 'That we can do. And when does he want it?'

'Friday,' said Francesca. She suddenly felt exhausted. It

was all too much to take in. She felt as if her brain was shutting down.

'OK, not a problem,' said William, getting his personal organiser out and noting the date.

'William, are we going to be all right?' asked Francesca. 'Financially, I mean?'

William sighed again and looked her straight in the eye. 'Well, things are going to be different, Francesca, that's for sure. Nothing is going to stay the same.'

Chapter Twenty-One

Robbie looked at himself, a little tentatively, in the mirror. He could see he looked OK. Better. More man about town than downtrodden divorcee. But he did feel a little bit daft, like a guinea pig from that reality TV show – How to Look Good and Be Ten Years Younger While Knowing What Not to Wear Naked, or whatever it was called.

Heather had always watched all those shows. Urgh! Heather! He was trying not to think about her. She'd really gone and done it this time. Robbie had called earlier to talk to the girls and Grace had dropped a bombshell.

'I've been looking for you on the news, Dad,' she'd said excitedly. 'There's loads of stuff about that Fatty man but I haven't spotted you yet. Try to wave next time you see a TV camera, OK?'

'OK, sweetheart,' he'd laughed. 'I will.'

'Mummy says she knew him, you know,' Grace had continued, talking as fast as only an eleven-year-old can. 'She used to be at school with his daughter, and they were best friends and they used to go riding together, and she got to drive in his big, green car, that was chauffeur-driven and—'

'What?' Robbie had tried to stop her mid-flow, his head spinning, trying to take in the information. 'Grace, slow down, wait a minute. Mum knew Giancarlo LaFata? She was best friends with—'

'With his daughter, Francesca. Yes,' said Grace. 'I heard her tell Fraser all about it. She was kind of showing off a bit, I think. Cos he's really famous and everything. Or at least he was, wasn't he? I think he might be dead, Dad. What do you think? Cos I know you're the expert and everything and you would know more than me but he must have drowned, mustn't he? We were talking about it at school and Annabel said that her mum said that ... but Chloe thought no, she thought ...'

But Robbie's mind was racing, trying to work out why Heather would have kept this from him. All the years they were together. She knew how important this story was to him. And she could have helped!

'Grace, sweetheart, can I just have a quick word with your mum, please?' he interrupted his daughter.

'Um, yeah, sure, Dad,' said Grace, sounding confused. Robbie *never* asked to speak to Heather.

'What do you want, Robbie?' asked Heather, without even trying to keep the disdain from her voice. 'I thought you'd be far too busy chasing gangsters and ogling topless models on the beach—'

'Do you know Fatty LaFata?' he demanded, cutting her off mid-flow.

Silence.

'Well, do you?' he demanded again. 'And Francesca LaFata?'

'Well, yes, as a matter of fact I do, Robbie, but I really don't see that that's any of your business.'

'None of my business? You knew I was working on the LaFata story. Even when we were together you knew I was interested in the guy. I know we're not married any more but it might have been nice if you'd told me. You could have helped me.'

'Why the hell would I want to help you, Robbie McLean?' she asked, her voice dripping with venom.

'Because I'm the father of your children?' he suggested, trying to keep the hurt out of his voice. 'Because I've never done anything to hurt you? Because I know I'm not perfect but I'm a decent bloke just trying to make a living and if my career takes off then it's our daughters who benefit?'

'Our daughters don't need your money,' replied Heather smugly. 'They have Fraser now.'

'Oh yeah, for how long?' Robbie knew he was being childish but he couldn't help himself. 'Until you get too long in the tooth for him and he trades you in for a younger model. How old's his PA, Heather? Is she pretty? Does he take her on business trips?'

'Oh shut up, Robbie, you're just jealous,' snapped Heather. 'Just because you're still woefully single doesn't mean you have to be so bitter about my healthy relationship. God, is it any wonder I never introduced you to Francesca?'

'What?' Robbie couldn't believe his ears. 'You're still in touch with her?'

'Yes,' said Heather impatiently. 'Sporadically. We exchange Christmas cards, the odd email. We have coffee when she's in Edinburgh, always have done.'

'What? Even when we were together?' asked Robbie.

'Yes.' Heather sounded bored now.

'Why did you never tell me about her? Why did I never meet her?' he asked, almost desperately.

He heard Heather sigh. 'The truth?' she asked, her voice a little softer now.

'The truth.'

'Because I was embarrassed,' replied Heather. 'A little bit ashamed.'

'Of me?' asked Robbie, a lump forming in his throat. Suddenly so many things made sense.

'Yes, of you,' Heather admitted. 'You didn't fit in with my schoolfriends, especially not the likes of Francesca LaFata. You didn't talk properly and you were always so scruffy so I kept you separate ...'

Her words cut him to the bone but the pain was almost cathartic. Robbie felt a strange weight lift off his shoulders. All these years he'd been beating himself up, wondering what he could have done to save his marriage and suddenly it dawned on him that there was nothing he could ever have done. Heather was a shallow, social-climbing snob. A boy from a council estate was never going to be good enough for her, however hard he'd tried. He hung up on her while she was still talking. He didn't need to hear her bullshit any more.

Working class, yes, that he was and proud of it. But scruffy? Not any more. What would Heather say if she could see him now? In his swanky new gear – charcoal-grey Gucci trousers, black Prada shoes, a brand-new white shirt with one of those big collars that all the smooth bastards round here wore. He'd bought some of those dark denim, slim-legged jeans too (also Prada), a grey cashmere V-neck sweater and a new belt, socks and underpants. He added what he'd spent up in his head and realised that it came to more than his car was worth. But for now he pushed that thought to the back of his mind.

Robbie ran his hands through his newly cropped hair and rubbed his smooth, shaved cheeks. Then he put his Ray-Bans on, just to see the finished look. Very Daniel Craig! The boy had done good. Who needed Trinny and Susannah, eh?

Just at that moment there was a knock on the door.

Robbie jumped. And then remembered that he'd asked Simon to come over this evening to discuss work. He took off his sunglasses and opened the door.

'Who the hell are you?' asked Simon sarcastically. 'And what have you done with my friend Robbie? You know, the scruffy one with the mop top and the ripped jeans.'

'I threw him off the balcony,' replied Robbie.

'Fair enough,' said Simon. 'I never really liked the chap much anyway.' And then he grinned and shook his head.

'Dan's right, you are obviously having a midlife crisis, Rob. But I have to admit you look good. You must have met a woman ...'

'Chance would be a fine thing!' laughed Robbie. 'But I live in hope.'

Well, he hadn't met her. Not on this trip. Not yet. But he had left a message on her voicemail. She'd once told him she thought his accent was sexy, so perhaps that would work better than the text she'd ignored. And he'd used Heather as an 'in'.

'Hi, Francesca, Robbie McLean here,' he'd said, trying to sound confident and casual, despite the butterflies in his stomach. 'Just wondered if you fancied catching up while I'm in Monaco. Got a really weird coincidence to share with you too. Thought we might have a laugh about it. You see, you know my ex-wife. Heather McLean, um, I mean Heather Mountstevens. Small world, eh? Anyway, give me a call if you fancy a drink. Hope you're OK, you know, with everything that's going on and ...' He'd known he was rambling and that there was no way she would be 'OK' at the moment with her dad missing, and he'd stalled, mid-message. 'And, erm, and, um, and, so, eh, see you later, maybe? Bye.'

He blushed at the memory. He doubted she'd get in touch. But he hoped.

'Right,' said Simon, interrupting Robbie's thoughts. 'Down to business. May I introduce you to Andrea Dubrovski ...'

He opened a file on the desk containing several documents and photos of a blond man who looked like a cross between a game-show host and an Olympic wrestler.

'A delightful character, Russian, ex-KGB, naturally, aren't they all? Now in "property" and "oil"; again, aren't they all? Citizen of Monaco, collector of art and artefacts, and gambling buddy of LaFata's, and, here's the interesting part, rumoured to have given our dear friend Fatty upwards of ten million euros in the last few weeks.'

'Whoah!' Robbie had to steady himself on the desk. It made his little shopping trip look decidedly modest. 'Any idea what the money was for?'

Simon shrugged. 'Apparently it's a private deal, so I'm guessing it must have been for one of LaFata's paintings. He's got a private collection worth a couple of hundred million stashed somewhere in that mansion of his up the hill there.'

'So, any rumours about credit crunch suicide are way off the mark then?' asked Robbie. 'With all those yachts, properties, businesses, and now you're telling me he's got this art collection, I don't see how the recession could have been hurting him too much.'

'Well, I'm not so sure about that,' continued Simon. 'It seems Francesca LaFata and William Hillier have been winding down some of the smaller ventures. Eleven branches of Fatty's have closed in the UK this year alone, not to mention three hotels, and the Dubai project is a complete shambles. The official line from LaFata International is that the building contractors went bust, which is true. But the contractors themselves are arguing that the reason they went bust was because Fatty never paid them a bean.'

'So, why wouldn't Fatty just sell off some assets?' asked Robbie.

'Because when you are this stonkingly wealthy, the stakes are raised a hundredfold. Yes, his personal assets are worth billions but LaFata's outgoings are mind-blowing. The problem is that for the last couple of years his profit margins have been dwindling at an alarming rate and he's been making a loss on some of his businesses, but his spending habits haven't changed. In fact, if anything, they've got worse. Fatty has been buying up companies as quickly as his daughter and her husband have been selling them off. If you then factor in the drastic cut in interest rates and work out that any income from his savings has effectively disappeared, well, it doesn't take a maths whizz to work out that the guy was in trouble.'

'Hence selling off paintings and artefacts to private buyers?' asked Robbie, pointing at Dubrovski's photo.

'Exactly,' replied Simon. 'And I'll come back to the Russian in a minute. Now, today, shares in LaFata International have bottomed out because of Fatty's disappearance and the company is worth less than a tenth of what it was worth last Friday. Whether he fell, or he jumped, or he was pushed, the bottom line is that he's left his family in a serious financial mess. It's like Maxwell all over again. Those poor LaFata kids are about to get a terrible shock.'

'But shouldn't Hillier have been safeguarding the family against this sort of thing?' asked Robbie, feeling almost angry at the guy. 'He's the financial director.'

'Yes, yes!' Simon was nodding excitedly. 'And that's where I need your help, Robbie. There is something seriously fishy going on with the LaFata investments and hedge-fund portfolios. A guy of Hillier's experience and expertise should never have left the business this financially exposed. Not unless he was doing it on purpose.'

'On purpose?' asked Robbie, the cogs of his brain working overtime. 'What? Are you suggesting that William has been deliberately losing the family money?'

Simon nodded. Robbie noticed that Simon's glasses had become steamed up in his excitement. 'Yes. And what I want to know is why?'

Robbie thought for a moment. Maybe this did kind of make sense. He knew quite a bit about Francesca and William's marriage, he remembered her tears in the Hotel de Paris. It was certainly no match made in heaven.

'All I know for sure is that Francesca and William's marriage is rocky. It's little more than a business arrangement these days. Obviously I can't reveal my source ...'

'Obviously,' agreed Simon. 'Nor can I reveal mine but let me just say that the police are definitely concentrating on the business side of things.'

Robbie nodded, understanding what Simon was telling him. 'Hillier and Fatty weren't close,' continued Robbie. 'Never have been. And by all accounts Hillier must have been feeling pretty undervalued and unappreciated by the LaFatas. He gave up a high-flying City career for the sake of his wife's family and yet, in the end, neither his wife nor his father-in-law appreciated it. At least, that's how he must have seen it. Resentment can be a dangerous emotion.'

'I think we've got something here, Robbie,' said Simon excitedly. 'I really do. I think this is my story. I think William Hillier has been bleeding LaFata International dry.'

'But you don't think he would actually kill Fatty over this? Surely!' said Robbie.

Simon shook his head. 'You're the crime reporter, I'll leave the conspiracy theories up to you. No, I don't think for a minute that Hillier killed his father-in-law, but I do think it must have finally dawned on Fatty how close he was to losing his billions and I guess the stress got to him one way or another. Either he jumped, or his heart gave out with the strain.'

'So, where's my story?' asked Robbie, feeling almost disappointed by Simon's conclusions. 'Where's my crime?'

'Right here,' said Simon, banging his finger on the photograph of Dubrovski's face. 'This guy is a criminal, a gangster, I'm sure of it. And he's not the only low-life scum that Fatty's been involved with over the years. I think your story is the fact that Giancarlo LaFata was not the upstanding, self-made businessman that he portrayed himself as at all. I think if you scratch the surface you'll find all sorts of dodgy dealings going on. If LaFata was prepared to take money from this guy, he must have been prepared to do anything to make his billions.'

Robbie thought about the Giuseppe's fire in Edinburgh, and the rumours of money laundering and fraud that he'd heard from Fatty's early years. He'd been on the right track all along. Now all he had to do was follow his nose and he'd end up with the biggest story of his career. The pressure was on, though. He had to be back at his desk on Friday. He only had three more days in Monaco.

Chapter Twenty-Two

Francesca had chewed her normally immaculate nails down to the quick. No matter how hard she tried she could not put Dubrovski to the back of her mind. His was the last face she saw when she went to sleep at night, he haunted her dreams, and he was still there, leering at her in the morning when she woke up. William had told her not to worry but how could she *not* worry when a Russian giant was threatening her? What if William was wrong? What would happen if they didn't get the money? Where would Dubrovski stop? Would he hurt her? Would he hurt William? And worst of all, what about the children? You heard about kids getting kidnapped all the time. If Dubrovski didn't get what he wanted from Francesca, how far would he go? She thought about Benito and Luca's innocent little faces, their huge, unquestioning brown eyes, full of love and trust. What if she was putting them in danger? If anything ever happened to them she would die. They were her life, and without them … Oh God, she had to wipe that thought from her mind. It was unbearable.

She needed to get William back onside. She needed to talk to him, to tell him her fears and to make him understand how they must pull together this time. Francesca felt horribly vulnerable and alone, she felt helpless. How could she protect the children when she couldn't even help herself? But if she and William were a team, they would be stronger, wouldn't they? Together we stand, divided we fall, and all that. Perhaps this crisis would be the catalyst to save their marriage. Sometimes good things grew out of terrible circumstances. Yes, she would take William out for lunch today and explain to him how she felt. She would tell him she wanted to give their marriage another chance. She would make a real effort, dress up for him, make him feel special. Perhaps it was what she should have done years ago.

She stood in her underwear and surveyed the contents of her walk-in wardrobe sceptically. It was full of austere business suits. A hundred different variations on the same theme – row upon row of black pencil skirts, white shirts, neat little jackets, black court shoes. Yawn. Francesca wanted to look different today, girlie, she didn't want to be the sensible, boring one any more. She wanted to show William that she was more than just a business colleague. She was a woman and she was his wife.

The bedroom door banged open and Angelica walked in without knocking. Francesca was still in a bad mood with her about her behaviour the night before last. It turned out she hadn't been out on a date with the lovely Christian at all, she'd been up to no good with a group of Australian backpackers on her yacht. She'd behaved so outrageously that the captain of her yacht had resigned and one of the Australians had ended up in hospital. Not that Angelica had told Francesca any of this. Of course not! No, Francesca had had to read about her sister's antics in the newspaper.

'What do you want?' she asked Angelica in her best 'I'm still very, very cross with you, young lady' voice.

'Just wanted to say sorry,' said Angelica, all doe-eyed and pouty-lipped.

'Don't bother making those eyes at me, Angel,' warned

Francesca. 'You know it doesn't wash. I've told you, there's no point in being sorry if you won't go back into rehab. Until you agree to do that, I don't want to hear it, OK?'

Angelica climbed onto Francesca's bed and curled up like a cat. 'I can't go anywhere with Daddy still missing,' said Angelica. 'What if he turns up and I'm off in a clinic somewhere? It's not right.'

'Angel,' said Francesca patiently. 'We've been through this a hundred times. Daddy isn't going to turn up. Not the way you want him to. You've got to start accepting it, darling.'

Angel hugged her knees to her chin and shook her head like a petulant toddler who refused to accept it was bedtime.

'I won't,' she said simply. 'I can't, Frankie. If I start believing that Daddy's …'

She trailed off, unable to say the dreaded word. Dead.

Despite herself, Francesca felt her heart melting. How did Angel always manage to do this to her?

'OK, darling,' she said gently. 'Let's not talk about it any more. We'll just wait and see what happens and deal with whatever comes along.'

Angelica nodded.

'But please, Angel, promise me you'll stay clean from now on.'

Angelica nodded again but she couldn't look Francesca in the eye.

'Why do you never wear short skirts?' she asked suddenly, changing the subject, eyeing her sister up and down in her underwear.

'Hmm?'

'Short skirts. You never wear anything above the knee. But you've got great legs. Gorgeous legs. It just seems like an awful waste,' said Angel.

'I'm thirty-five,' replied Francesca. 'It's wrong to wear short skirts if you're over thirty.'

'Why?' asked Angelica. 'Who says?'

'I don't know, it's just the rule, isn't it?' said Francesca.

'I don't like rules,' said Angelica. 'Rules are there to be broken.'

Well, that was no surprise. They all knew that Angelica never did what she was told. But for once, Francesca had to admit that her sister had a point. Why shouldn't she wear a short skirt? Not a miniskirt exactly. Not a tiny little, bum-grazing body-con number like Angel wore. But something above the knee might be nice, for a change. The only problem was, she didn't actually own anything like that.

'Angel?' asked Francesca. 'Have you got many of your clothes here with you? Or are they all at your apartment?'

'I've got the stuff I had in Miami. I came straight from the airport with my suitcase, remember. Why?'

'I was just wondering if I could borrow something,' said Francesca a bit sheepishly.

Asking to borrow clothes from her twenty-one-year-old sister seemed ridiculous at her age but she felt ready for a change, and her wardrobe was as good enough a place as any to start. Angelica loved the idea. She sat up and smiled, properly, genuinely, for the first time all week.

'Oh my God, I would love, love, *love* to style you, Frankie. Can I? Please? I'll make you look totally fabulous, I promise.'

It made Francesca happy to see Angel excited by something other than partying.

'OK,' she agreed. 'Just don't make me look like mutton dressed as lamb.'

'I will turn the muttometer on now,' giggled Angel. 'If it pings, we'll know we've gone too far.'

She jumped off the bed and ran out of the room, returning a few minutes later with armfuls of dresses, shoes, belts and scarves.

'Oh my God, I have wanted to do this for years, Frankie,' she squealed. 'I am going to knock years off you. Years! Just wait until William sees you. You'll look like his daughter.'

Francesca grinned but she didn't want to look like William's daughter. She just wanted to remind him that she was his wife.

An hour later, Francesca found herself standing in front of the mirror, staring at herself in amazement. She looked like ...

'One hot mama!' said Angel, standing back to admire her handiwork.

Even Francesca had to admit she looked good. And the muttometer hadn't pinged once! She was wearing a flowery Luella tea dress that hugged her body, gave a great cleavage, and then floated down to just above her knee. Angel had wanted her to wear cowboy boots with the dress but Francesca had decided that was taking her a bit too far out of her comfort zone. So they'd settled on a pair of cream platform Miu Miu sandals instead. Oh, and a matching clutch bag.

'I'll never get all my stuff in there,' Francesca said, eyeing the little bag sceptically.

'Why not?' asked Angel. 'There's plenty of room for your lippie, your purse and your phone. What else do you need?'

Normally Francesca would have needed her personal organiser, pens, notepads, her diary and the odd file she was working on, but today she didn't really need a thing. So the clutch was perfect.

'Where are you going anyway, Frankie?' asked Angelica suddenly. 'Looking so damn hot!'

'It's a surprise for William,' said Francesca. 'I'm going to take him somewhere nice for lunch.'

Angel looked disappointed.

'Bo-ring!' she pouted. 'Why waste that supreme hotness on William? Like he's even going to notice your legs.'

'Because he's my husband,' replied Francesca.

'Urgh!' grunted Angel. 'I never understood why you married him in the first place. He's sooo dull ...'

'Angelica,' Francesca warned her.

'What? He is! I was hoping you had a secret lover or something. I thought that was why you wanted to get all tarted up.'

'Nope,' replied Francesca. 'I just want a nice lunch with my husband and I want to look pretty for him.'

'I give up on you, Frankie,' sighed Angel. 'You waste yourself. You're too good for him.'

Francesca shrugged. 'What? Like you're too good to throw your life away on drink and drugs? I'm not sure you're one to judge, Angel.'

'Maybe not,' said Angel, sounding very serious suddenly. 'But I'm not a complete airhead, whatever you think of me. And I'm telling you now, William is all wrong for you. You're not happy, Frankie. You two don't love each other. There's no joy there. It's painful to watch. Christ, you're just kidding yourself! Your life isn't any more real than mine.'

And with that she got up off the bed and left the room.

Francesca stared at the woman in the mirror. She barely recognised her reflection. Angel was right, she wasn't happy with her life the way it was. But she was trying to fix that. And building bridges with William was a step in the right direction. It had to be. What was the alternative?

*

William Hillier checked the accounts one last time. It was almost done, months of planning, budgeting and moving funds from one account to the other. Fatty's disappearance had made things far more complicated in one way – the share price of the company had plummeted and investors were suddenly wary, some were even threatening to pull out. But William had managed to keep most of them sweet. He'd convinced them this was just a blip and that things would soon settle down again. But, in another way, Fatty being gone had made things remarkably easy.

He showered, enjoying the feeling of the powerful jet of water on his skin, and then changed into his smartest business suit. It was important he looked the part, gave the right impression, kept playing the game. William had always been very good at playing the game. Then he packed a spare pair of trousers, some clean socks and underpants, a couple of shirts and his wash bag. He was all set to go.

He knocked on Francesca's door, leaving his suitcase on the landing outside. She was wearing a silly summer dress that was far too flouncy and frivolous. He thought it was completely inappropriate for a woman of her age. But now wasn't the time to criticise his wife for her dress sense. What Francesca did, or didn't do, really didn't matter any more. It was no concern of his.

'Francesca, I have to go to an emergency meeting in London,' he told her.

'Oh?' She looked surprised, disappointed. 'I didn't know about that.'

'No,' he said patiently. 'As I said, it's an emergency meeting. It's only just been scheduled. There are a few problems with our share index. The hedge-fund managers want to discuss where we go from here.'

'But I was going to take you out for lunch.' She looked

genuinely upset but William felt nothing. No guilt. No remorse. 'I thought we could talk.'

'I really don't think we have much to talk about, Francesca,' he replied, knowing he sounded callous but not caring any more.

He watched tears well up in her eyes.

'Please, William,' she said, taking a step towards him. 'Can't you get a later flight? I'm sorry I've let things get to this point between us, but I want to fix things. You're my husband. I—'

'Oh, don't be so melodramatic, Francesca,' he interrupted, removing her hand from his arm. Oh, now she wanted him to be her husband, did she? Now when she was feeling scared and out of control? Well, she should have appreciated him years ago, shouldn't she? Not when it was way too late. She was desperately trying to blink back tears. She looked pathetic to him.

'How long will you be gone?' she asked, sounding desperate. 'There's so much going on here, I don't know if I can cope without you.'

But Francesca was going to have to learn to cope without him.

'Just a couple of days,' he replied. 'You'll be fine. We can conference call if anything important crops up.'

A shadow fell over Francesca's face suddenly and the tears started again, thick and fast. 'You will be back before Friday, won't you?' she sobbed. 'We need to get that money to Dubrovski.'

'Yes, yes,' he said impatiently. 'Don't worry about Dubrovski. I told you, I'll only be gone for a couple of days.'

'How are you getting to the airport?' asked Francesca hopefully. 'Can I drive you? Maybe we can talk in the car?'

'No, thank you. That won't be necessary. I'll drive myself,' he replied. 'I'll leave the car there.'

'But you hate driving,' said Francesca.

'I'm a big boy now, Francesca,' replied William. 'I'm sure I'll cope.'

Why was she suddenly showing so much interest in him now?

'I must be off,' he said abruptly. 'Cheerio.'

'Oh, OK, bye.' She gave him a little wave. Her eyes were still damp with tears. He still felt nothing, even though he knew it would be the last time he saw her.

William had said goodbye to Francesca a long time ago, not literally, but in his own quiet way. He had loved her once, very much indeed. But he'd never known quite how to show her how he'd felt. He'd thought that giving up his career and running her father's business would have been enough. But it wasn't. She'd grown increasingly distant, busying herself with the children and the business, pushing him further and further away. He'd always known she didn't enjoy making love to him. It had upset him greatly over the years. And then, one night, he'd seen the look in her eye. It was a look of utter disinterest. For William that was the beginning of the end. He'd moved into his own room the following day.

He would have liked to have said a proper goodbye to the boys, but they were at school now and he couldn't be seen to turn up there and make a fuss. He'd kissed them as they'd left this morning. They'd looked surprised but pleased at his affection. Kissing them was not something he would normally have done.

As he drove down the drive, William glanced at the house one last time in the rear-view mirror. He wouldn't miss Le Grand Bleu. It had never been home. It was a sad, old place, filled with secrets and lies. The LaFatas were welcome to it. It suited them very well.

Francesca sat on her bed and toyed with her phone. Her tears had dried now and her hurt at William's casual dismissal had been replaced by anger. How dare he go off and leave her and the boys at a time like this? They were grieving and they were in danger. And he simply didn't seem to care. It was obvious he didn't love Francesca. And, if she was brutally honest with herself, she knew she didn't love him either. Maybe Angel was right. Maybe she'd been living a lie.

Her finger hovered over the send button for a few moments longer and then she did it. She watched her response slip away into cyberspace and she wondered where it would all end. She'd opened Pandora's box and she didn't know if she was about to do something completely mad or completely sane. All she knew was that the rules she used to live by meant nothing any more, so why keep following them blindly? Where had it got her being the good girl of the family, pleasing everybody, and always doing the right thing? Was she happy? Hell no! But maybe she could be. If she followed a different path ...

Chapter Twenty-Three

Robbie sped away from Monaco along the Grande Corniche in the R8, feeling like Jenson Button – only better! He had the roof down and his new Ray-Bans on and he felt like he was king of the world as he floored the car along the mountain road with the Kings of Leon blasting in his ears.

'Whoah-oh-oh, your sex is on fire!' He sang his heart out and thought about her. The sun blared down on him, the sky was impossibly blue, and every now and then, as he turned a corner, he would get a glimpse of the azure sea. It sure beat the Edinburgh city bypass in the rain! But he couldn't be any further from all that now – the crap weather, the discontentment, the stifled dreams and his ex-wife. No, today he was wild and free. Today he was the man he'd always wanted to be and he was on his way to meet the woman he wanted to be with. She'd replied. Finally. And any doubts he'd had evaporated the minute he'd read her text.

This road wasn't a direct route to his destination, hell, it wasn't a direct route to anywhere, in fact he was doing a huge loop, almost as far as Nice, and then turning back on himself on the lower roads, but the drive had nothing to do with getting from A to B. Robbie was just driving for the sheer, raw enjoyment of it. Besides, he'd been too excited to sleep, or eat, or work this morning. So he'd left the hotel early and gone for a spin. Today was the day. Finally, after all those months of fantasising, he was going to see her in the flesh. He was wearing his new Prada jeans and the pale grey cashmere sweater. And his new shoes of course! A bunch of lilies lay on the passenger seat, waiting for her. Robbie felt like a teenager off on his first date.

He turned the car sharply off the Grande Corniche and wound his way down the N53, a treacherous descent of hairpin bends with mind-blowing views and adrenalin-pumping turns. He passed the place where Princess Grace had died in a car crash and noticed the bunches of flowers at the side of the road. The beautiful Grace Kelly, still remembered and mourned almost thirty years after she'd gone. Robbie wondered if the people of Monaco would still remember Fatty LaFata fondly in time. He doubted it. When the truth came out about that crook, they'd be glad they'd seen the back of him.

And then he was on the Moyenne Corniche, winding down towards the coast, heading west, back towards Monaco. He turned onto the Basse Corniche, passed the postcard perfect port of Villefranche, where the whopping great cruise liners docked, and on through glittering Cap Ferrat, glimpsing gilded billionaires' mansions behind high hedges and tall white walls, crawling with bright pink bougainvillea.

Finally, he drove into the idyllic seaside resort of Beaulieu-sur-Mer and pulled up beside the restaurant. There was no way they could have met in Monaco itself. She was a married woman and she couldn't be seen to be sneaking off for lunch with a British journalist! He reread her text message on his phone, just to make sure he was in the right place, checked his appearance one last time in the wing mirror, and then in he went, carrying his lilies along with his fragile expectations. As he walked through the restaurant, he passed the very same smartly dressed man that he'd seen in the café in Monaco a couple of days before. The impossibly well-groomed man, with the gold watch and the scar. Robbie smiled at him, but the guy just stared right through him. Oh well, he had scrubbed himself up a bit since the other day, the guy obviously hadn't clocked him.

Robbie sat on the terrace in the sun. He was five minutes early. What should he do now? Order champagne and have it waiting for her on ice? Nah, too cheesy. Too James Bond. Wine? But would she want red or white? He really did know very little about her. Instead, he ordered himself a beer, just to take the edge off his nerves.

And then he saw her, weaving her way through the tables, past the impeccably dressed man from Monaco, walking towards him looking nervous in a pretty summer dress that showed off her incredible legs. She took his breath away. She really was the most beautiful woman he'd ever met and she was here, risking it all, for him! It didn't seem real.

He stood up to greet her, his hands shaking a bit with nerves.

'Hello, Robbie,' she said, almost shyly.

He wondered if he should kiss her on her cheek, hesitated too long and then kissed the fresh air above her head as she sat down. He blushed. As she sat down, Robbie couldn't help noticing that her short, floaty dress rode up and exposed a generous flash of firm, tanned thigh. He dragged his eyes reluctantly from her luscious legs and sat down opposite her.

'You look drop-dead gorgeous,' he found himself saying. And then he kicked himself because it was a tacky, stupid thing to say and it didn't even began to describe how beautiful she looked. Besides, they barely knew each other.

'You look ...' She eyed him up and down. 'You look

different, Robbie. Your clothes, your hair. Where are your trainers? What is it you look like? Oh I get it, you look like a native!' She laughed.

'I've been shopping,' he said, blushing even more now.

'Maybe, but a leopard can't change his spots with just a few new designer clothes.' She eyed him a little warily. 'You're still a journalist and I still shouldn't be having anything to do with you. You're dangerous.'

Robbie sighed. Maybe she was just here to have another go at him? The last time, once he'd finally told her what he did for a living, she'd flipped and accused him of taking advantage of her to get to her father. She'd said she felt used and soiled, called him a low-life hack and stormed out.

'I'm not dangerous,' he said, finding his tongue.

'But you're only in Monaco because of my dad's disappearance, aren't you?' she demanded.

Robbie sighed and nodded. They both knew that was the truth. There was no point denying it.

'Yes, I'm in Monaco to investigate what's happened to your dad but I'm not here, in this restaurant, for that. You have to believe me. I'm not here as a journalist. I'm here because I …'

She cocked her head and looked at him quizzically. 'Why?' she asked. 'Why are you here then?'

'I could ask you the same question,' he replied, holding her stare.

It was Francesca's turn to blush and she looked away.

'I don't really know,' she said. 'I shouldn't be. I must be mad.'

'Mad, maybe, but you've forgiven me?' asked Robbie gently. 'You don't still think I'm a low-life hack?'

Francesca shrugged. 'I don't really know you at all, Robbie McLean,' she replied. 'But I'm here, aren't I? So I guess I

must have forgiven you. But I'm not going to talk about …'
She trailed off and a frown fell over her pretty face.

The poor woman must be going through hell, thought Robbie. To him Fatty LaFata was just a good story, but to her, well, the guy was her father!

'How are you coping?' he asked, trying to sound concerned without sounding nosy.

She bit her lip and glanced away from him for a moment, towards the sea. A shadow darkened her lovely face.

'Robbie, I'm not going to talk to you about my dad,' she said, turning back to face him and looking straight into his eyes, almost defiantly. 'I can't. Won't. So, don't …'

He opened his mouth to speak but she held up a finger and said firmly, 'And if that's why you're here, then I'm going now. It took a lot of trust for me to come and meet you today so …' She half stood up, ready to bolt.

Robbie placed his hand gently on her forearm. 'Fran, please, stay. I'm not going to ask about your dad. I'm not here because of him. I'm here because of you …'

He trailed off, because what else could he say? It was simple and it was true. He didn't care who her father was, he just liked being around her. He could see in her wide grey-blue eyes that she wanted to believe him but she was scared. And who could blame her? He was nothing to her. Not yet. But Robbie wouldn't use her to find out about Fatty. This had nothing to do with his job, or who she was, and her father's name would never be mentioned if that was the way she wanted it to be. He held her gaze, imploring her to believe him. Eventually she sat back down.

'OK,' she said, still a little hesitant. 'I'll give you the benefit of the doubt. I mean you used to be married to my friend so you can't be all bad …'

Robbie grinned. 'Yeah, but she divorced me, remember!'

Francesca laughed, seemingly despite herself. 'I suppose Heather was never exactly my best friend.'

'No?' Robbie asked. 'She painted it like you two were bosom buddies.'

'We were,' said Francesca, grinning now at the memory. 'But only if I did exactly as she told me! I think she only hung out with me because it meant she got to be driven by a chauffeur. She terrified me most of the time. You should have seen her with a lacrosse stick in her hands. Bloody terrifying!'

'Sounds like Heather,' nodded Robbie. 'Quite the social climber even as a schoolgirl. Be my friend, rich kid, or I'll deck you!'

'Yeah, something like that. Still, I can't believe she's your ex-wife,' mused Francesca.

'Of all the gin joints …' Robbie grinned.

'I know, another strange coincidence,' said Francesca, but she didn't join in the joke. She still had her guard up.

'When did you last see her?' asked Robbie.

'Oh, we had coffee, it must have been, gosh, four or five years ago now. I was pregnant, I think,' Francesca remembered. 'I thought she told me her husband was a media executive,' she continued, a smile starting to spread across her lips. 'Media executive indeed!'

Robbie guffawed. 'She couldn't possibly have admitted to being married to the likes of me.'

'And what would she say if she could see us here now?' Francesca asked him.

'She would burst a blood vessel,' laughed Robbie, wishing Heather *could* see them now. 'She would wonder what the hell you saw in the likes of me!'

The minute the words were out of his mouth, Robbie wanted to gobble them back up. He didn't even know that she did see anything in him. What an idiot he must have sounded!

'I, uh, erm, I ...' He blushed furiously. 'Not that you do see anything in me, obviously, a woman like you, and you're married and we're only here as ...' He rambled on.

'Friends,' said Francesca firmly. 'I'm here because you made me laugh last time we met and I could do with some cheering up.'

'Of course,' said Robbie, wishing the ground would open up and swallow him. 'Friends.'

Francesca grinned at him. She looked mischievous suddenly. There was a twinkle in her eye. She was flirting with him. Robbie's stomach did a triple somersault at the thought. Maybe, just maybe, she felt the same.

They sat in silence for a moment. It wasn't an uncomfortable silence. It was that feeling you heard about but never expected to experience: the one where a perfect stranger feels like your oldest friend.

'So, are you going to offer me a drink?' she asked suddenly. 'Or am I just going to watch you drink yours?'

'Oh, I can do better than that,' grinned Robbie. 'If you're really good I might even buy you lunch!'

And then they caught each other's eye and smiled. And in that second Robbie knew that she felt it too. The connection. She might not do anything about it, except share a lunch with him, she was still a married woman, but at least he knew that he wasn't imagining it. What he felt was real.

Francesca didn't want to fall for Robbie, but she wondered if she had any choice. It was the same feeling she'd had the day she'd first met him. She could dress it up any way she wanted, but the truth was she couldn't get enough of him.

However dangerous and inappropriate he was, he made her stomach lurch. The sexiest thing about Robbie, Francesca decided as she watched him digging into his steak frites, was that he had absolutely no idea how incredibly sexy he was. Unlike her brother, and all the other strutting peacocks in Monaco who glanced at their reflection in every shop window and fully expected every woman to drop her knickers at their feet, Robbie was blindly, blissfully, shockingly unaware of his own attractiveness. Even in his new gear, he had no idea how heart-stopping he was.

He was so animated, so alive, it made the hairs on her arms stand up in excitement. Every gesture, every word, every movement he made seemed to be charged with energy. When he talked, and he talked with passion about all sorts of things, his eyes flashed and his face would light up, or darken, or frown, or break into a wide, easy smile, depending on the subject. She noticed how his eyes darted around the restaurant, taking everything in. He was, she decided, probably the brightest man she'd ever met. He wore his intelligence in the laughter lines around his eyes and on the smile that often played on his lips as if he was thinking about a joke that only he got. He looked as if he was always one step ahead, as if his mind was already rushing on to the next thing.

He had none of the contrived good looks of the men round here but he was way more attractive than any of them. He wasn't tanned, or waxed, a few stray hairs from his chest poked up out of the top of his T-shirt and even in his smart new clothes, he had an air of relaxed insouciance. His strong thighs strained beneath his tight jeans, flexing as he moved. When he pulled his jumper over his head, he threw it in a crumpled heap on the chair beside him, rather than folding it up neatly as Carlo or William would have done.

His T-shirt was untucked, his sleeves were pushed up and every time he touched his hair it became more messed-up and undone. That was it, he was undone. Relaxed, comfortable in his own skin. Real.

And, oh God, was he handsome too. He had dark blond hair, with the hint of a curl, wide, almost cat-like hazel eyes, with pupils rimmed with distinct black circles as if someone had drawn around them with a pen just to highlight their beauty, and then there were his eyelashes, so full and impossibly long that Francesca thought it must be a struggle for him to blink under their weight. His cheekbones were high and sculpted, his jaw strong and square and his fine, aquiline nose had the slightest bump in the middle, the result of a fight or an accident that he hadn't had time to tell her about yet. He was tall, about six foot two maybe, and broad-shouldered, but his hips were slim and his legs were long. He was in great shape. Francesca doubted that Robbie was the sort of man who worked out at the gym but he was so full of energy that he must have burnt off every calorie he ate. She watched him now, tucking into his fillet with enthusiasm, chatting every time he finished a mouthful, washing it down with great gulps of beer.

'Och, this is excellent steak,' he enthused. 'I know Aberdeen Angus is supposed to be the best but I've been to Aberdeen hundreds of times and I've never had a piece of meat this tasty.'

Francesca loved his accent. Maybe because it reminded her of Edinburgh, and her mum, and the boys she'd had her first crushes on. His smooth Scottish lilt washed over her like a lullaby and she could have listened to it happily for the rest of her life. It was the voice of her childhood. The sound of home.

She remembered the first time she'd seen him, leaning

casually against the bar in the Hotel de Paris, looking totally out of place in the swankiest of bars, wearing ripped jeans, a crumpled shirt and a pair of battered Converse All Stars. She hadn't been able to take her eyes off him. She was waiting for Angelica at the time. They'd been supposed to meet for afternoon cocktails. It turned out that Angel, being Angel, had forgotten all about their date. She never turned up. Not that Francesca minded in the end. In fact, Angelica's absence had been a major bonus that afternoon.

Francesca had kept finding herself drawn to the rugged stranger at the bar. She'd glance up at him, and he'd be looking at her, and then she'd blush and look away again. When it happened for what was probably the twentieth time, he raised his glass in her direction and grinned, a sort of cheeky, friendly grin. There was nothing smooth or lecherous about it.

Eventually, he sauntered over and asked if he could join her. Then Robbie, being Robbie, had said, 'Oh, God, I sound like a right plonker. I promise I'm not hitting on you, it's just you look friendly and everyone else in here looks …'

He'd glanced around the bar at the elegant, well-dressed guests, talking quietly among themselves, and pulled a face. 'Well, they look like they're at a wake, to be honest.'

Francesca had found herself giggling, despite herself, already reeled in by his broad smile and Scottish accent.

'I'm not a mad axe murderer or anything,' he'd continued. 'I'm just a bit of a Billy-no-mates and I could do with a new friend to chat to for a bit.'

'OK,' Francesca had said. 'I'll be your new best friend. My sister seems to have stood me up so it looks like we're in the same boat. You don't sound like you're from round here. Let me guess … Edinburgh?'

Robbie had nodded. 'Right first time.'

'So am I,' Francesca had said, a little excitedly. 'Well, originally anyway. Left when I was fourteen. Isn't that a coincidence?'

'Of all the gin joints, in all the world ...' Robbie had grinned.

'She walks into mine,' Francesca had finished the sentence for him, laughing.

'Right,' he'd said, throwing himself down on the chair beside her. 'If this is going to work out, this new friendship of ours, I'm going to have to come clean from the start. Best friends should be totally honest with each other, don't you think? No lies.'

Francesca had nodded, intrigued.

'I know who you are,' he'd continued breezily. 'You're Francesca LaFata. And before you think I'm a crazed stalker, I'm not. It's just because I'm from Edinburgh, obviously I know who your dad is, which means I also know who you are.'

'Oh,' Francesca had said, taken aback by his boldness. 'Right.'

Maybe she should have been more wary at that point. Alarm bells should have rung. But Frankie couldn't drag herself away. She was mesmerised. Thirty seconds after meeting him, he'd stolen a bit of her heart. The handsome stranger in the Hotel de Paris.

'Robbie McLean,' he'd said, shaking her hand so firmly it hurt.

She'd immediately glanced at his wedding finger and been relieved not to see a ring, guiltily feeling hers. A couple of drinks later and she'd had the nerve to ask him about his marital status.

'So, there's no wife back in Edinburgh?' she'd asked, bold from her cocktails.

Robbie's face had clouded over and his forehead had knotted, as if desperately trying to find the right thing to say. 'Um, no, my wife is … What is she? How can I put it?'

Francesca had tried to second-guess him. It was obvious that she'd struck a raw nerve, that something was wrong, and she'd immediately jumped to the wrong conclusion.

'Oh my God,' she'd stammered. 'She's not dea—'

'Oh, Christ, no!' Robbie had thrown his head back and laughed. 'She's not dead. She's just my *ex*-wife, that's all! She dumped me. Ran off with her boss. Bit of a touchy subject to be honest …'

Francesca had felt the most enormous relief. And then she'd felt incredibly guilty for feeling something so wholly inappropriate about a virtual stranger when she was still very much married herself. The drinks had flowed that afternoon, and the conversation had come easily. Afternoon had turned into evening and they'd carried on, offloading on each other about their failed marriages, their lost hopes and their fragile dreams. They'd kept bumping hands on the table as they gesticulated excitedly, and then, as evening had turned into night, they'd ended up playing footsie under the table like naughty teenagers at Sunday lunch with the parents.

'Fran … can I call you Fran? Francesca's too much of a mouthful after nine beers.'

She'd nodded, even though no one had ever called her Fran before.

'I wish I wasn't going home tomorrow,' Robbie had blurted out, and then he'd blushed, and laughed at himself.

'I wish you weren't going home tomorrow too,' she'd told him and she hadn't felt embarrassed at all. 'Can't you stay a couple of more days? I like having a new best friend.'

''Fraid not. Got deadlines to meet. If I don't get a story to my boss tomorrow morning, he'll have my guts for garters ...'

And then he'd stopped, mouth wide open, with a look of complete horror on his face. 'Did I say that out loud?' he'd asked, trying to make a joke of it.

But it had been too late for Francesca. Her heart had slammed shut again. This man, this handsome stranger who'd seemed so different, was nothing but a snooping reporter.

'Oh. My. God. You're a bloody journalist!' she'd spluttered. 'Oh, God, no! You've just been using me, haven't you? You've been plying me with drinks to get information out of me. So much for new best friends being honest with each other! Huh? You evil, low-life, scumbag hack ...'

She'd known at that moment that she had to walk away. Her dad had always forbidden any of them to talk to journalists at all. Ever. Under any circumstances. As far as Fatty was concerned, journalists were the lowest of the low. Never to be trusted. They were beneath lawyers, estate agents and even the tax man. And now he'd been proved right. This man. This silver-tongued, floppy-haired, twinkly-eyed bastard had just charmed her innermost secrets right out of her. She'd told him things she'd barely admitted to herself before. She'd given him her business card, for Christ's sake. Her private mobile number! What a bloody fool she was. Now her most private thoughts would be splashed over some tabloid. Francesca had never felt so duped in her life. She'd been tempted to throw her drink over him but had somehow managed to control herself. Instead, she'd turned on her heels and practically run out of the Hotel de Paris.

He'd called after her, telling her that he wasn't going to print anything she'd told him, that he'd been chatting to her because he liked her, that their meeting had nothing to do with his job.

'It's just one of those coincidences, Fran,' he'd shouted. 'Of all the gin joints in all the world, remember ...?'

But she'd kept on running until she could hear his voice no more. She didn't believe a word he said. And she'd been trying to forget about him ever since. OK, so he'd kept his word. He hadn't printed a story about her. She'd checked. Googled his byline almost daily for the next few weeks. Nothing. And then, even when she felt sure he wasn't going to publish her secrets, she'd carried on Googling him, just to see what he was up to, and to stare at the grainy little headshot of him on his newspaper's website. God, he was handsome. And he was a talented writer. But he was still a journalist. And a liar. Robbie McLean was dangerous. So what the hell was she doing here now? Being drawn right back in by his charm?

'So how are things with William?' asked Robbie, a little tentatively.

Francesca hesitated before she replied. Could she trust him? She definitely wasn't going to tell him anything about her dad, or the business, or Angel, but William? Did he deserve her loyalty any more? She remembered how cold he'd been with her that morning before he'd left for London and so she replied simply, 'Well, I wouldn't be here with you now if things were good at home, would I?'

Robbie nodded. 'That's all I wanted to know,' he said.

He insisted on paying the bill, which Francesca noted. As a LaFata, she was used to being the one who picked up the tab.

'What now, then, Fran?' he asked her, with a glint in his eye. 'Are you going to run out on me again or have I redeemed myself?'

'Let's just say you're back on the shortlist for the position of my new best friend,' she teased. 'Anyway, I don't want to go home yet. How about a walk on the beach?'

'Well,' he mused, 'as long as you're not going to take advantage of me. I don't want you jumping me the minute we find a secluded cove.'

'The thought hadn't even crossed my mind,' lied Francesca, with faux annoyance.

'Really?' asked Robbie. 'Och, that's a shame ...'

The sexual tension between them hung in the air so heavily that Francesca was surprised the other diners hadn't complained. They'd been eyeing each other with much more ravenous appetites than they'd looked at their plates of delicious food. God, what was she playing at? Francesca just didn't do things like this. She'd never so much as looked at another man since she'd met William all those years ago. And yet here she was on the verge of ... of what? An affair? The thought terrified and thrilled her in equal measures.

'Come on,' she said. 'Let's get out of here.'

They crossed the road and walked briskly along the palm-lined promenade, overtaking glamorous middle-aged women walking ridiculously small dogs.

'I want to hold your hand,' said Robbie.

Francesca shook her head. 'Too risky,' she replied. 'Too many eyes. But I know somewhere private.'

She led him down onto the beach. They took off their shoes, giggling like kids, and hurried through the sand, round a headland and away from the town. Her heart was thumping now and her stomach churned. She knew she was being tempted to cross a line but she didn't know if she could stop now even if she wanted to.

'You'll have to wade,' she told him when they reached

what looked like the end of the beach. 'There's a lovely little secluded cove just round these rocks.'

'So you are just after me for my body,' said Robbie.

The sea was quite calm, but the waves lapped around her bare legs and splashed Angelica's dress with water all the same. Francesca looked behind her and laughed at Robbie with his jeans rolled up to his knees, paddling with a daft grin on his face, gingerly holding above the sea his new shoes and the bunch of lilies he'd bought her, slipping every now and again, getting his jeans wetter and wetter.

'Nearly there,' she said, rounding the corner and glimpsing the perfect empty beach ahead.

Just as they took their last few steps towards the shore, a freak wave came from nowhere and soaked them to their waists.

'It's freezing!' gasped Robbie. 'Where did that come from?'

Francesca turned and saw Robbie, his jeans sodden, and she burst out laughing.

'Oh, it's all right for you,' he teased, laughing too. 'You just look all sexy and provocative, with your dress clinging to your legs like that. I look like a drowned ra—'

But before the word could get out of his mouth, a second, even larger wave, hit them. This time they both fell into the sea, swallowing mouthfuls of water as they laughed, and then, as they tried to catch their breath, they found themselves dumped on the wet sand, in a tangled heap of shoes and flowers, arms and legs.

Robbie threw his new shoes onto the dry sand along with the now rather bedraggled lilies and pulled himself up onto his muscular arms, so that he was lying above Francesca, his face just inches from hers, his body touching hers, his hot breath on her face. He stared at her with a wild, desperate longing, and Francesca felt her body lurch towards his. And then his lips were on hers, and she was pushing her aching, wet body up towards his, wrapping her arms around his neck, her legs around his thighs. Every nerve in her body longed for him as she lost herself completely in his strength and his smell and his desire.

'Oh, Jesus Christ, Fran. You are so beautiful. Too beautiful,' he whispered breathlessly into her ear. 'Too good for me.'

He kissed her cheeks and her eyelids. He kissed her neck and her collarbone. Francesca shivered with the sheer perfection of the feeling. He unbuttoned her wet dress, slowly, his hands shaking slightly, and as he revealed her flesh and the lace of her bra, he looked at her tentatively, asking with his eyes if this was all right.

She nodded at him, God, yes, it was more than all right, it felt like the first 'right' thing she'd done in years. And then his face was buried in her cleavage, kissing her gently but passionately, his hands discovering her body for the first time. He unbuttoned her dress further until her stomach was bare and heaving with excitement and breathlessness, and then his lips were there, tickling her waist, caressing her stomach, down, down …

Francesca was overwhelmed by a surge of passion she'd never felt before. She wanted this man. She needed him. She craved his hands on her body, and his lips on her skin, and parts of her body that had been dead for years were waking up and crying out to be touched by him.

'I need you, Robbie,' she whispered.

He pulled her wet dress over her head, and then he undid her bra. He groaned loudly as her breasts were revealed, and then he kissed her nipples, her stomach, her … Oh, God. It was sheer bliss. He pulled her knickers down until she was lying there on the sand, completely naked, soaking wet, with the waves lapping her and Robbie above her, staring at her, shaking his head, saying, 'Oh. My. God, Fran. You are perfect. Completely perfect. I think I've died and gone to heaven.'

And then he was struggling out of his soaking jeans, his T-shirt, his boxer shorts. The feeling of his naked skin against hers was better than anything she'd imagined. She stroked his smooth back, his powerful, round bum, and pushed him against her. She could feel him rock hard against her. She looked him straight in the eye, opened her legs and let him in, slowly, carefully, gasping as she felt him deeper and deeper inside.

'Robbie,' she almost pleaded. 'I need you now.'

And then his lips were on hers again and he was so deep inside her, and her body was melting into his as the waves lapped their naked skin and the sun shone down. Francesca felt tears roll down her cheeks and merge with the salty sea water. She didn't know why she was crying. Guilt? She knew that would come later but for now they were tears of joy. To be held and desired by a man like Robbie felt so rare and beautiful that it made her weep. It was magical. Francesca had been reborn.

The Italian man watched the lovers from the clifftop path above their private beach. He couldn't help but smile to himself. He was a romantic at heart and could recognise true love when he saw it. He felt it himself every time he looked at his wife, and he'd seen it in the restaurant, as he'd observed the lovers enjoying each other's company so much more than their lunch. But Francesca LaFata was not this man's wife. She shouldn't be in his arms. She belonged elsewhere. And, sadly, their love affair would not last long.

It was doomed. Beautiful, passionate, brief, and doomed.

'*Triste, molto triste,*' he said to himself, as he watched the lovers embrace in the waves, blissfully unaware that they were being watched.

He glanced at his gold watch. It was time to go. He'd got what he'd come for and now he had to deliver the bad news. His boss would probably have wanted him to put an end to this little tryst here and now, but he didn't have the heart. It would be over soon enough. Let them enjoy the magic for a short while, with passion in their loins and hope in their hearts.

He slung his suit jacket over his shoulder and sauntered back to his red Ferrari. As he drove back along the winding coast road to Monaco, he wondered about the lovers. He hoped they were wrapped in each other's arms on the beach now, talking about their plans for the future. A future that would never come. He hoped they were happy, savouring the moment. Because that moment would have to last them a lifetime. In time it would become nothing but a faded memory of how life might have been.

In a way there was something perfect, magical and intensely beautiful about such a brief love affair. It would never be tarnished by real life. She would never have to pick up his dirty socks. He would never have to listen to her nag. He would never have to see her gorgeous body wither and grow old, or have to endure watching her die. And then he glanced at his shiny gold wedding band, and thought of his own, beautiful wife. He wanted her to nag him, he wanted to grow old beside her and he wanted to die first, so that he would never have to live without her.

Did this man feel that way about Francesca LaFata? Did she feel that way about him? Sometimes life could be so cruel.

Chapter Twenty-Four

'I'm going to Cannes,' said Angel, with a petulant pout. 'And there's nothing you can do to stop me, Carlo. Anyway, since when did you start getting all goody two-shoes on me? Who died and made you the moral majority in this family?'

Who died? She asks who damn well died?! Carlo stared at his little sister in disbelief. He wanted to shout, 'Dad! Dad died, you silly little cow!' But, of course, he didn't. Angel was still steadfastly refusing to accept for a moment that their dad might not be coming home, despite the huge weight of evidence to the contrary. She carried an unspoken threat around with her, like one of her designer handbags. It was there in the tilt of her head and the wary look in her eye. It said, 'Don't you dare tell me the truth, Carlo. Protect me. If you tell me the truth I'll crumble and no one will be able to put me back together this time.' And as usual Carlo did as she wanted.

Instead he sighed patiently and tried again to persuade her that a wild party with her old friends on a yacht in Cannes was the last place she needed to be going right now.

'Angel, sweetheart,' he said. 'Look at yourself. You haven't eaten for days. You're getting all skinny again. And you've got bags under your eyes. You look tired. You know I love a party more than anyone but even I can't face Cannes this year. Not right now, with everything that's going on.'

'I can't face Cannes this year,' she mimicked him. 'I'm Carlo and I'm a born-again square.'

He bit his tongue and tried to swallow his anger. She really could be a proper little madam sometimes. He used to find it funny when she behaved like that with their mum, or Francesca – she'd never behaved like that for their dad, of course, she saved angelic Angelica for him. Carlo had always played the part of the naughty sidekick, half encouraging her to misbehave. But he didn't want to be Angel's sidekick any more. Suddenly the joke was wearing very thin.

Christian had told him what a state she'd been in the other night when he'd found her, half-unconscious, on the quayside, and now Carlo was beginning to feel genuinely worried about her. He didn't know why it hadn't hit him years ago. Angelica was properly screwed up. If she carried on like this she was going to die. Maybe it was because he'd never stared death in the face before now. He'd always been protected. He was a LaFata. Untouchable. He thought the rest of his family were too. But Dad was gone and, if things didn't change, Angelica could easily be next.

It wasn't that he'd never experienced death but it had always been in a detached, third-hand kind of way. His grandparents were all gone, but they'd been old and far away, and there had been his dad's third wife, Darcie, who'd killed herself with sleeping tablets and painkillers. But she'd had the good manners to do it on her own in a villa on Lake Como, so it hadn't affected Carlo too badly. Besides, he'd been away at school at the time and missed most of the drama.

But now, with Dad missing, everything felt shaky. The foundations of Carlo's world had crumbled and he found himself questioning everything he'd believed before. Like the money. He'd always assumed the money was there for keeps. He'd been born into it. He wasn't like Francesca, who could remember life in Scotland, in a small house, with barely enough money to pay the bills. He didn't know any other way.

He was well aware that his dad's disappearance had caused the company's share price to plummet. And now the police had told him that they were freezing some of the business accounts. Something to do with an investigation into money laundering. It made no sense to Carlo and there was no one around to explain it to him. William had gone to London for some meeting or other, and Frankie was God knows where. Angel had told him that their sister had sped off in her car that morning looking as if she was 'off on a hot date!'. As if! Yup, Angel was definitely losing it again if she thought for a minute that Francesca would have an affair. She didn't have it in her.

Carlo was beginning to feel a heavy weight on his shoulders that he'd never experienced before. Suddenly, his bubble had burst, and everything he knew had been turned on its head. Dad was gone. The business was obviously in trouble. Even Frankie wasn't being her usual predictable, rock-like self. She was behaving erratically and unreliably, swinging from being nervous, upset and angsty, to being almost, well, excitable and childish. And then there was Sasha – sexy, scary, awesome Sasha. His feelings for her were playing heavily on his mind too. He cared about her. He really cared about her and it scared him. God, it was all too much! Carlo felt … what was it exactly? Worried? Responsible, maybe? Well, that was a first. And he didn't like it. He didn't like it one bit. Maybe this was what they meant when they talked about reality biting. It was biting him on the arse like a hungry Rottweiler and it hurt. It hurt like hell.

He looked at Angel in her tight little minidress and dangerously high heels, legs up to her armpits, all huge blue eyes and tumbling blonde hair. She thought she was all grown up but she was still a kid. What did she know about responsibility or consequences? She thought she could do as she pleased, get wasted, hang out with dangerous people, sleep with other women's husbands, party her way through life and get away with it unscathed. But she couldn't, Carlo realised suddenly. Nobody could. Not even their dad. Maybe Angelica was more like Fatty than any of them had realised. They both thought they could do exactly as they pleased and come up smelling of roses. But life was certainly no bed of roses right now.

'Oh well, bugger you, Carlo,' said Angelica now, flicking her hair over her bony, bare shoulders and turning to the door. 'I'm going anyway, with you or without you. It's the party of the year and I'm missing it for no one.'

'What? Not even for Dad?' Carlo asked gravely. 'Not even out of respect for your own family?'

Angel looked at him as if he was a total stranger. 'Whatever,' she sing-songed with a flick of her hand. 'I have absolutely no idea who you are, you boring, tiresome man, but if you see my brother Carlo anywhere can you tell him there's a shit-hot party going on down the coast, please? I'm sure *he* wouldn't want to miss it for the world.'

And with that, she was gone. He watched her speed out of the drive in her white Mercedes AMG convertible, with the top down. She passed the paparazzi with her huge sunglasses on and gave them a saucy wave. She was heading right back into the lion's den and there was absolutely nothing Carlo could do to stop her.

He sat on the sofa as the light of the day faded into evening, and felt very small, frightened and alone. He wanted to talk to someone. He played with his phone, flicking through his contacts and realised with a heavy heart that there really was no one for him to turn to. There were just endless names of people he knew would be fun to party with. Acquaintances, drinking buddies, girls he'd screwed. There was Christian, of course, but he'd leant heavily on his best friend these last few days, and anyway, Chris was kind and well meaning, but just seeing him made Carlo feel guilty.

Most people would turn to their mums, but Carlo's mum was ... Well, Sandrine was a law unto herself. Almost as flaky as Angel. She would be busy with her toyboy and her poodles in her villa in St Tropez. Or recovering from her latest procedure. When he'd told her about Fatty all she could think about was whether or not there would be any money in it for her.

'Don't be ridiculous, Mum,' Carlo had told her. 'You divorced fifteen years ago. He's had two more wives since you. You got every cent in the divorce settlement.'

'Ah,' she'd said in her breathy French accent. 'But you do not know men like I do, *mon chéri*. I have always had a special place in your father's heart. I do things to men that a boy your age cannot understand. I am expecting he will remember me in his will.'

His mum was totally nuts, not to mention deluded. She'd been a complete babe in her day – that's where Angel got her exquisite blonde good looks from. When she was younger, his mum had looked very much like Brigitte Bardot, but unfortunately was without the acting talent, which was why her career had dried up so disastrously over the past ten years. Now she was a bit of a joke in France. But she was happy enough. Sandrine had never been bothered by criticism. She thought she was the money and no one could tell her any different. She hadn't exactly aged gracefully.

She'd had her boobs done so many times that her chest now entered a room a full five minutes before the rest of her body, her lips were deformed and misshapen with collagen, and she was so heavily Botoxed that Carlo hadn't seen a hint of an expression on her waxy face for years.

His mum wasn't what anyone could call the maternal type either – well, not unless you counted her fondness for much younger boys as sex toys. She'd pretty much given birth to Carlo and Angelica and then handed them straight over to their nanny so she could carry on sipping her champagne, unencumbered by annoying little people with sticky paws and runny noses. No, Carlo had no desire to call his mum and cry on her shoulder. She'd never been there for him before and she certainly wasn't going to be there for him now. Or for Angel. Whenever Sandrine talked about her daughter's wild ways it was with boastful glee.

'Ooh, she is just like her *maman*!' she would chirrup. '*Très, très belle*. She has such *joie de vivre*! I am proud of *ma petite chérie*. She is a great beauty with many, many friends. My Angelica knows how to have a good time. Men will fall in love with her, girls will be jealous of her. It is not her fault. She is a free spirit who needs to fly. Just like me.'

The stupid thing was that Carlo had kind of agreed with his mum. He'd thought Angel could cope. That it was just her character to be wild. But now he wasn't so sure. Maybe Angel behaved the way she did because she needed help. God, he wished he'd had a mum like Francesca's. Maybe that was why Frankie was so sorted, because she'd had a good solid start with a proper mum, who'd cooked and cared and remembered birthdays. It must have been tough for Frankie, losing her mum at such a young age, but at least she'd had one to begin with. Sandrine might have given birth to Carlo but her maternal responsibility had ended there.

So there was nobody for Carlo to call. If he'd had Sasha's number maybe he'd have phoned her. But he didn't have Sasha's number, did he? She'd refused to give it to him. Not once but twice! How humiliating was that? If he had any self-respect he'd have told her to shove it and moved on to one of her friends by now. So why was it that he couldn't stop thinking about her?

Carlo decided to head back to his apartment in town. Le Grand Bleu was deathly silent with Angel gone, Jade in her room, William in London and Francesca ... Where was Frankie anyway? Ah well, she would turn up. She was probably dealing with some important business thing that Carlo wouldn't understand.

He was about to step into his Lamborghini when Frankie's Range Rover Sport roared into the drive. His sister stepped out of the car looking as if she'd just survived Hurricane Katrina. Her dress, which was much shorter than usual, was soaking wet and her hair, normally so sleek and groomed, was matted and covered in sand. She had no lipstick on but a distinct flush in her cheeks. She was smiling and singing to herself cheerfully.

'What the hell happened to you?' asked Carlo, scratching his head.

'Oh, nothing,' replied Frankie breezily. 'I just went for a lovely long walk on the beach and kind of, well, fell in.'

'You went for a walk on the beach?' asked Carlo incredulously. 'On a week day? When you could have been working?'

Frankie shrugged. 'Yup, so what?'

'Oh-kay ...' said Carlo, totally weirded out.

See! Everything had gone completely crazy. Nothing was as it was meant to be. Francesca did not wear little floaty minidresses. She did not disappear all day without telling anyone where she was going. And she certainly did not go for walks on the beach and accidentally fall in! He watched her saunter up the stairs to the house. She seemed strange. Changed somehow. She had a kind of glazed, faraway look in her eyes. Carlo had seen many women leaving his apartment wearing exactly that expression. She looked as if she'd just had sex! Jesus, could Angel have been right? Did Frankie go off on a hot date? Was she seeing someone behind William's back? No! No frigging way. OK, so William was a boring, prematurely aged tosspot and Francesca, who even Carlo had to admit was seriously beautiful, was way too good for her husband but still …

Carlo shook his head hard and tried to lose the idea of his sensible sister screwing around. Right now he needed the real Francesca back.

'Frankie!' he called after her, chasing her up the stairs. 'Frankie, wait!'

It seemed to take a long time for Carlo's voice to penetrate Frankie's brain. But eventually she looked round and said, 'Hmm? Were you calling me, darling?'

'Um, yes I was, very loudly and for quite a long time!' he retorted.

'Sorry, Carlo,' she said, sitting down on the steps and staring up at the sky. 'What a gorgeous night. Isn't it lovely? Look at the stars, darling.'

'Yes, yes, they're very pretty,' said Carlo impatiently. He sat down on the steps beside her. 'Look, Frankie, I'm really worried about Angel. She's gone off to some big party in Cannes and I really don't think it's a good idea.'

Frankie lost her whimsical expression and sighed, suddenly looking like his older sister again.

'Why don't you follow her down?' she suggested. 'Just to keep an eye on her.'

'I don't want to go to a party, Frankie,' said Carlo. 'It's the last thing I want to do with Dad missing and the business in trouble. I want to be here to help and I want to keep a clear head.'

'Wow!' said Francesca, patting his knee. 'I'm proud of you, Carlo. That's a really mature way of looking at things.'

She didn't mean to be patronising but Carlo felt a little hurt by her reaction.

'I am twenty-three, Frankie. I'm not a kid any more. When the shit hits the fan, I do know how to behave,' he told her.

'I realise that now, darling,' said Frankie, smiling at him. 'I'm just a bit surprised, that's all. Pleasantly surprised.'

'But what are we going to do about Angelica?' he asked desperately. 'She's off the rails again, Frankie. I didn't want to tell you this but I'm sure she's back on the drugs. She's been acting really weird, she's not eating, her eyes are glazed and she seems wired the whole time.'

Francesca nodded sadly. 'Well, we've tried rushing in and saving her before. How many times now?'

'Six,' said Carlo. 'She's been in rehab six times.'

'And every time we force her, she just goes back to her old ways the moment she gets out.'

'She lasted nine months this time,' Carlo reminded her. 'I really thought that was it, that she was cured.'

'So did I,' sighed Francesca. 'Well, I hoped at least. But you're right, she's off again. She's pressed that self-destruct button.'

'So, shall we go down to Cannes and get her?' asked Carlo. 'I mean now. Just get in your car, drag her out of the party and take her straight to a clinic? There's a really good place just outside Marseille apparently. I looked it up online.'

Frankie squeezed his knee fondly. 'No,' she said. 'I don't think so. Not this time. That's what we've done before and she's never learned. That's the problem with Angel, someone's always been there to fix things for her. She never has to face any consequences.'

Carlo nodded. He'd thought the same thing himself. 'So?' he asked.

'So we leave her to destruct this time,' said Frankie. 'Wait until she hits rock bottom and asks for help. She won't get better unless she wants to, Carlo. We can't make her stop drinking or doing drugs. She has to do it for herself.'

'But she's so weak,' said Carlo, feeling weak himself. 'Fragile. Doing nothing – what sort of help is that?'

'It's the only thing left to do,' said Francesca. 'I've been through it, over and over in my head. Angel's so deeply in denial about everything. She won't admit she's got a problem, she won't accept responsibility and she definitely won't believe that Dad's gone for good.'

Carlo watched as Frankie bit her bottom lip, trying to stop it from wobbling at the mention of Fatty.

'Carlo, we have to let her go this time. She doesn't want to face reality right now. She's running away as fast as she can. But it will catch up with her, and when it does, she'll ask for help because it will hurt like mad. Then and only then can we step in. When she asks for help we'll be there, we'll get her the best treatment we can. But until then, all we can do is wait.'

Wait? Wait? Carlo wasn't sure he had the patience. He seemed to be doing a lot of that right now – waiting for Dad's body to be washed up, waiting for Angel to implode, and waiting for Sasha to come round again and ease his pain, as only she could.

Chapter Twenty-Five

Jade waited until it was quiet and dark, just like he'd said, and then she picked up her bag and sneaked down the stairs. Carlo had gone now and Francesca was having a bath. She said goodbye to the dogs for the last time, kissing their soft heads and nuzzling their ears. She would miss them. But the rest of them – Saint Francesca, Carlo the International Playboy, Angel the not so angelic – well, they could all go to hell. This time she gave the dogs lamb cutlets for their dinner. She watched them for a moment, tucking into the family's evening meal, and it gave her a warm feeling inside. And then she let herself out, through the garden and over the wall just as she'd done earlier in the week.

The car was waiting in the lay-by, just like he said it would be. She found the keys on the back wheel arch where he'd hidden them and let herself in. Jade could hardly wipe the smile off her face as she drove out of Monaco along the Moyenne Corniche. Finally it was happening. They were running away together. Away from the LaFatas, away from her past, away from the pain.

She left the car at the base of the village of Eze, and walked up the steep lanes towards the castle remains at the summit. The village was quiet now that the day-trippers had gone home, and nobody noticed Jade, hauling her bag up the steep path towards freedom and hope and her future. She would meet him in the Jardin Exotique, where they'd often met before, and kissed and talked and planned their escape. And now those dreams were about to become a reality.

She waited on the cliff's edge, staring out to sea, watching the winking lights of the fishing boats coming in with their evening catch. Soon he'd be here and then they'd walk down the steep mule path, through olive and pine groves, to the Basse Corniche below. And then they'd be on the road again. Heading anywhere. Anywhere but here …

'Jade!' a voice called in the distance. 'Jade! Over here.'

Jade turned round and spotted a figure in the darkness a little further along the cliff. The voice sounded muffled. Was it him? Of course, it was him. Who else could it be? She hurried towards him, smiling, and then suddenly she stopped, her smile frozen on her face.

'It's you?' she said, confused for a moment. 'But … How? Why? I don't understand. I thought …'

But it didn't matter what Jade thought any more. The strong hands grabbed her shoulders and pushed her towards the edge of the cliff. She tried to fight back but he was too strong. She tried with all her might to dig her heels into the ground but the loose stones just slipped under her feet. And as she teetered for a moment on the edge of the world Jade realised that she'd been right all along. It wasn't safe to let anyone in. There was no such thing as love. There was never going to be a happy ever after. And as she fell towards the earth and the wind rushed past her ears, her life flashed before her, just like they said it would. It hadn't been much of a life. She wasn't too sad to be letting it go.

Robbie couldn't wipe the daft grin off his face. Fran had been everything he'd fantasised about and more. What a woman! What a wonderful, sexy, smart, gorgeous, amazing woman! He lay on his hotel bed and relived the afternoon. Bliss. He closed his eyes and imagined being with her now, her smooth, tanned skin against his, her long, long legs wrapped around his thighs, her ...

His phone rang, interrupting his daydreaming just as it was getting interesting. Bollocks! He picked up his mobile and glanced at the illuminated screen. 'Lord and Lady Fuckwit' it said.

'Hello!' answered Robbie, cheerfully, expecting it to be one of the girls.

'Robbie,' barked Heather's voice. His heart sank. She was the last person he wanted to talk to right now.

'We need to talk about Ruby's behaviour,' she said sternly.

'What about Ruby's behaviour?' he asked, genuinely confused. Ruby was a total sweetheart. A little bit cheeky sometimes, maybe, but she was a good girl. Bright. Popular. Sporty. She always got glowing reports from school. Robbie loved his youngest daughter's company. She always made him smile.

'She has become increasingly rude, difficult and obnoxious of late, particularly towards Fraser ...'

Ah, so that was it – Ruby didn't fall for Fraser's charms. She saw right through him. Like he said, she was a bright girl.

'Isn't Fraser big enough and ugly enough to fight his own battles?' asked Robbie, mildly amused by how seriously Heather was taking this. 'She's an eight-year-old, not a prop forward.'

'Hmmph. I might have known you'd be completely unsupportive,' said Heather angrily. 'Fraser is in a very awkward position here. He is a very sensitive man and he is well aware that he has to tread carefully when disciplining his stepchildren but she really is becoming impossible, Robbie.'

'In what way?' he asked, still finding it hard to take Heather seriously.

'She called him …' Heather hesitated and cleared her throat. 'She called him …'

'What?' urged Robbie, getting impatient.

'She called Fraser Fuckwit!' Heather said in disgust. 'I mean, can you believe it? Where on earth does she get such a word?'

Oops. Robbie knew exactly where Ruby had got it from. She must have overheard him on the phone to his mum. 'I'll have a talk to her when I get back,' he said, feeling ever so slightly guilty that Ruby had got into trouble through his childish behaviour.

'Fat lot of good that will do, I'm sure,' snapped Heather.

'Well, what do you suggest?' asked Robbie, exasperated. 'Lock her in the coal shed? Wash her mouth out with soap and water?'

'She has been banned from watching television for two weeks,' stated Heather grandly. 'Fraser thought that was a suitable punishment and I agree. So, when you do get back from your little holiday and you remember your parental responsibilities, you must support our decision to punish Ruby and enforce the rule at your house too.'

'Oh, must I?' muttered Robbie. 'Look, Heather, I'll have a talk to her, I've told you, and I'll make sure she understands that she can't use abusive language like that. I'll tell her she has to give Fu— I mean Fraser a bit of a break, OK? But I'll discipline my daughters my way, OK?'

'You won't win their respect that way, Robbie,' sneered Heather. 'You think that always being the nice guy makes them love you more. You let them stay up late and you feed them junk food but that's not love, that's just being irresponsible.'

Robbie sighed; he was in such a good mood, why did Heather always have to rain on his parade? She was being unfair. He was a good dad. He always made sure the girls did their homework on time, he ironed their uniforms even when he didn't have time to iron his own shirt. He made them spaghetti bolognaise and he took them out for hot chocolate with whipped cream and marshmallows. He read them Burns poetry and let them watch old Billy Connolly videos. He took them to watch Hearts play football and to the zoo, even when it was minus three and Corstorphine Hill was the coldest, windiest place on earth. And, most importantly, he loved them more than life itself. Heather could throw anything at him but she'd never make that accusation stick. But Robbie didn't rise to the bait. Normally he would have but not today. Today he felt as if he had a Ready Brek glow. He had his daughters and now he had Francesca in his life too, nothing else could touch him.

'Well, we'll just have to agree to disagree on that one,' he told Heather calmly. 'I met your old friend Francesca, by the way.'

He couldn't help himself. It was just too deliciously tempting.

'Oh?' He could hear the intrigue in her voice. 'What did she say about me?'

Robbie smiled to himself. Heather didn't ask if her 'friend' was coping with her father's disappearance. Or if she was well. No, Heather asked what Francesca had said about her. It was always all about her. Well, she did ask ...

'She said you only wanted to be her friend so that you could ride in her dad's car. She also said she was scared of you, and most interestingly, she seemed to think that you used to be married to a media executive. Can't think where she would have got that idea, eh, Heather?'

Robbie laughed. Heather had obviously been stunned into silence.

'Are the girls about?' he asked chirpily. 'Can I talk to them?'

'They're at their piano lesson,' snapped Heather, and then the line went dead.

Robbie grinned again. Heather must be feeling very small right now. Ha! Who's the daddy now, eh?! He lay back on his pillows and went back to his daydreams of Francesca.

Chapter Twenty-Six

William Hillier could see Lake Como from his window, the sun rising to the east, the still water sparkling in the bright early morning sunshine, the pine-clad hills rising from its banks, casting ghostly shadows. The view was quite breathtaking and if it hadn't been for the tight ropes tied around his wrists and ankles, and the duct tape stuck fast to his mouth, he might have been quite content, just sitting here taking it all in.

He'd almost got away with it. He'd been so close. For months he'd been scraping off the odd hundred thousand here, the odd half a million there, transferring the monies from one account to the next, investing it, moving it, reinvesting it, until, finally, he'd had enough in his secret offshore account to make his escape.

Francesca had trusted him completely with LaFata International's accounts. She obviously hadn't had much respect for him as a husband but as an investment banker she'd thought he was the bee's knees. And she was right. William was good. He was the best. In financial terms, he could practically turn water into wine. But he hadn't been quite good enough. He hadn't factored in everything. He'd underestimated his father-in-law and only now did he realise what a dreadful mistake that had been.

They'd killed Jade. He'd seen the grainy mobile phone video footage of her falling off the cliff with his own eyes.

He'd tried to turn away, but the suave Italian man with the scar had thrust the phone in front of his face, over and over again, until he'd had to witness the horrific scene. The terrified look on her pretty little face as she'd teetered on the edge and then the final glimpse of those perfect blue eyes. At that final moment there had been a change. She'd seemed to let go of her fear. What was it? Acceptance, perhaps? That it was over? That this was just the way it had to be? Her fate? That the cruel world had beaten her for good this time, just as she'd known it would? But it shouldn't have been that way. They should have been free by now.

It broke William's heart. Because he did have a heart, despite what Francesca thought. He'd never been good at showing his emotions, but they were there, as strong and passionate as the next man's, hidden beneath the layers of respectability and false grandeur he'd developed over the years. And he had loved Jade. He'd wanted to save her. She was Rapunzel, trapped in her ivory tower by that bastard Giancarlo LaFata. And William had so desperately wanted to rescue her, to be her knight in shining armour. He'd got so close.

Jade had made him the man he'd always wanted to be. While Francesca had always made him feel inadequate, Jade needed him, and that made him feel proud and strong, like a real man. Francesca had it all – money, brains, beauty, power. She wouldn't even take his name when they married, for crying out loud! How did that make a man feel? Jade had had nothing but a pretty face, a sweet nature and a thousand secrets to hide.

It had started innocently enough. Jade would bring him in a cup of tea, perch on his desk, ask him questions about what he was doing. She seemed interested in his opinion. She listened to what he said. She made him feel important.

They were both outsiders at Le Grand Bleu, and they were never allowed to forget that. They were not LaFatas. They were just invited guests who could outstay their welcome at any point. William was well aware, now that he and Francesca no longer shared a bed, that his days were numbered.

The pair bonded quickly and before William knew it, Jade had him doing things he'd never imagined he'd do. They escaped together whenever they could. He would pretend to go out to a meeting or a business function and she would scramble over the back wall. He'd pick her up and they'd go driving around the mountain roads, stopping at remote villages for dinner. Sometimes they sneaked out at the dead of night and just went for a spin, happy to be away from that house, their prison.

And then there was the sex. Wow! That had blown William's mind. He'd always been a traditional, missionary-position kind of man, but Jade taught him tricks he hadn't known existed. She made him watch porn, and put on shows for him, wearing sexy underwear, with her vibrator. Francesca had never even pretended to enjoy sex with him but Jade … Jade screwed him with gusto! Finally, at forty-three, William Hillier had woken up and suddenly believed that anything was possible. As long as he had his adoring, adorable Jade by his side.

Oh, God, what had they done? Poor, sweet, misunderstood Jade. She was born one of life's victims and now she'd died the same way. And he hadn't managed to save her. Worse, it was all his fault. It had been his idea and his plan. And now, because of William, Jade was dead. He knew he'd be next. They were only keeping him alive so that they could retrieve all the money he'd stashed away.

His captor would swagger in soon, looking like a film star

with his dark good looks and well-cut clothes, smelling of expensive aftershave, and grinning at William with perfectly straight white teeth. He would burn William's skin with cigarettes, perhaps break another of his fingers by stamping on his hand with those fine Italian leather shoes. He would wrap his powerful arm around William's neck and squeeze until William found himself gasping and blurting out another bank account number. He'd be here any minute now. The sun had risen. It was the start of a new day. Perhaps it would be William's last.

Francesca slept in. It wasn't like her to sleep past six thirty but here she was, languishing in bed at eight o'clock. Her heart was torn. Whenever she thought about her dad, it felt as if a claw was ripping at it, trying to pull it from her chest. When she thought about the business, the police investigation, the crashing share price, the Russian! Oh God, the Russian! The panic that gripped her made her lose her breath. But then, when she thought about Robbie and his loose, easy smile, her breath eased and her stomach felt warm inside. For a moment at least. And then the guilt set in. It ate away at her happiness and made her feel wretched and ashamed. What sort of woman was she? Who was she to have these feelings for a man who wasn't her husband? William was no angel but he didn't deserve this. What would he do if he knew? It would destroy him. And the boys, oh sweet Jesus, those adorable, precious boys. She hadn't just betrayed William, she had betrayed Benito and Luca too. She'd crossed the line and now there was no going back. She couldn't undo the deed. And what's more, she wasn't sure she wanted to.

She checked her phone. There was a message waiting for her from Robbie.

Been dreaming about you all night. Can't think about anything else. Hope you're ok and bearing up. Would love to see you later if you can escape. Thinking about you. R x

She stared at the message for a very long time, unsure how to reply, or whether she should reply at all. Her heart was desperate to see Robbie again, but her head told her to walk away now, before she got in too deep. It could only end in tears. She was still staring at her phone when there was a knock on her door. It was Audrey, the maid, and she looked anxious.

'Madame,' she said in a nervous voice. 'The police are downstairs.'

The panic rose up again in Francesca's chest, worse than ever this time, and as she scrambled out of bed and into her dressing gown, her knees were shaking so much that she thought her legs might give way beneath her. What could the police want? Was it bad news? Had they found something? Why else would they be here at this time in the morning? Somehow she managed to get down the stairs without collapsing. The police stood in the vast hallway, a man and a woman, looking sombre and respectful. They wore plain clothes. This was serious, they'd sent the detectives.

'Madame LaFata?' asked the woman, an attractive redhead of around Francesca's age.

Francesca nodded but couldn't speak.

'I'm afraid we have some bad news,' said the lady detective. 'We've found a body.'

And then Francesca's legs gave way. She knew he was dead. She'd been expecting this visit for days, but now they were here, the messengers, to confirm her worst fears, she couldn't bear it.

She collapsed onto the cold tiled floor and sobbed. 'Daddy!' she cried. 'Please, Daddy, no!'

The lady detective hurried over to her and bent down beside her.

'*Non*, Madame LaFata,' she said, placing her hand on Francesca's arm gently. '*Non. Non. Non.* You misunderstand. It is not your father's body we have found.'

'What?' Francesca looked up, the hall swimming in front of her. 'I don't understand.'

The male detective stood forward now, reached out his hand and helped Francesca back to her feet. He was a stout, moustached gentleman of about fifty, with a kind face.

'Madame LaFata,' he said. 'I am sorry if we have shocked you. It is the body of a young woman we have found. On the cliffs below Eze. We believe it is Jade LaFata. Your father's wife.'

'Jade?' said Francesca, her voice trailing off and her mind racing. 'But it can't be Jade. This must be a terrible mistake. She's in her room. She must be.'

'*Non*, she is not in her room,' said Audrey solemnly. 'When I took her tea this morning she was not there and the bed had not been slept in.'

'Oh, God, no!' said Francesca. 'Poor Jade. How did this happen?'

The male detective gave a Gallic shrug and shook his head. 'We are not sure yet, Madame LaFata. We will not know until we have carried out an autopsy, but Eze is a popular suicide spot and Madame LaFata, she has been distraught over your father's disappearance, *non*?'

Francesca nodded sadly. Poor, poor Jade. She'd been so quiet and reclusive these last few days and Francesca suddenly realised how much she'd neglected the poor girl. She'd lost her husband and none of them had given her feelings much thought; they'd been far too caught up with their own sorrow.

'If I'd known she was feeling suicidal,' said Francesca, desperately feeling the need to explain how this could have happened, 'I would have done something. I didn't know she was in such a bad state. I really didn't know …'

The truth was, Francesca knew very little about Jade at all. She realised, suddenly, that she'd never asked Jade anything about herself – she knew she was from Kent, and that her father was a mechanic, was that right? But that was it. She'd never met any of Jade's family or friends. Her dad and Jade had sneaked off to get married in St Lucia. The witnesses had been two strangers they'd grabbed off the beach. No, Francesca had never really given Jade a second thought. She'd just let the girl get on with things. And now she realised with a shudder that she'd let her get on with ending her own life.

'I feel dreadfully guilty,' said Francesca. 'I should have been there for her. I should have talked to her. I mean, I tried a couple of days ago, but she just kept herself shut away in her bedroom. I thought she wanted to be alone.'

The detectives nodded sympathetically. 'Is not your fault, Madame LaFata,' said the lady detective. 'If a person is suicidal, they will find a way. This was not a cry for help. A person does not jump from the cliffs at Eze if they hope to survive. She had made her decision. You could not have stopped her.'

'But it's such a waste. She is, was, oh God! She was so young. And we don't even know for sure if my father is dead yet …' Francesca knew she sounded like Angelica now, desperately grasping at some non-existent straw.

The male detective shook his head. 'No, we do not know for sure what has happened to your father, Madame LaFata, but you must prepare yourself for the worst. The next time we are here, it will probably be to inform you that we have indeed found your father's body.'

Francesca sighed deeply and felt her shoulders slump. 'I'm not sure how much more of this I can cope with,' she said. 'Have you got any new evidence?'

The male detective nodded. 'A little,' he said. 'I am afraid I cannot give you much detail but we now believe that your father was in some serious trouble with his various businesses.'

'I know things weren't great,' said Francesca, feeling defensive now. 'But I'm heavily involved in all aspects of LaFata International's business empire and we're coping. At least, we were coping before the share price dropped.'

The male detective gave his Gallic shrug again. 'I am sure what you say is true and we are certainly not investigating you, Madame LaFata, or your side of the business. But I think, perhaps, your father did not tell you everything that was going on. I'm sorry but that is all I can say.'

It was what William had said and it was what her father had said before he'd gone. She didn't know everything. She was naive. Francesca felt wretched. She didn't want to hear about the business any more.

'And the second brandy glass?' she asked, fighting back tears of frustration and wounded pride. 'Have you got DNA yet? Fingerprints?'

This time the female detective shook her head. '*Non*,' she said. 'We have only found your father's DNA. We have no idea who he was with. If anybody ...'

'If anybody?' asked Francesca warily. 'But there were two glasses. He obviously had company.'

The shrug again. '*Peut-être*,' said the male detective. 'We do not know anything for sure yet.'

Francesca frowned. There were so many questions and no answers. And now Jade was dead. Why? Why had she felt desperate enough to kill herself?

'Do you think my father committed suicide too?' she asked shakily.

'We do not know that either,' said the male detective. 'We have no answers until a body is found.'

Francesca rubbed her face with her hands and tried to regain her composure. It was Jade she should be feeling sorry for right now, not herself.

'Have you informed Jade's parents?' asked Francesca, hoping that she wouldn't have to call strangers and tell them that their daughter was dead.

'*Non*,' said the lady detective. 'She was an orphan. She had no family. Apart from you, the LaFatas.'

'What? But what about her family in Kent? I thought ...' Francesca's voice trailed off. What the hell did she know about anything any more anyway? *Si è ancora ingenuo, bambino.*

Robbie checked his phone for the umpteenth time. Why hadn't she replied? It had been over an hour since he'd texted. He was desperate to see her later. How was he supposed to get on with his day until he'd heard from her? Until he knew that he was going to see her gorgeous face later he wasn't going to be able to concentrate on anything. Let alone uncovering the biggest story of his career.

He felt like he was walking a tightrope. On the one hand there was Fran, and his feelings for her. On the other hand there was her father – who Robbie was determined to prove was one of the biggest crooks in the Western world. Not to mention a murderer, if the Giuseppe's fire was anything to go by. But how could he have both the woman of his dreams and the scoop of a lifetime when the two were so irreversibly linked? Surely if he wrote the truth about Giancarlo LaFata, Francesca LaFata would never forgive him. Why was life so damned complicated?

He checked his phone one more time and then switched on the TV. He flicked through the channels, past the kids' programmes, the football and the shopping channels, until he found the news. Jade LaFata's face was plastered across the screen. He turned the volume up and listened in shock as the newsreader explained that her broken body had been found in the early hours of the morning, at the foot of the cliffs at Eze Bord de Mer, by a man walking his dog. The police were not looking for anyone else in connection with the death.

Christ almighty! Fatty's wife had topped herself! His thoughts turned immediately to Fran. No wonder she hadn't replied to his text. She must be dealing with the aftermath of this. Christ, how much more crap could that poor family have to deal with? He wished he could call Fran and talk to her, tell her that he was here for her and thinking about her. But of course he couldn't, that was against the rules.

And then Robbie started wondering why. Why had Jade LaFata killed herself before Giancarlo LaFata's death had even been confirmed? He remembered that Fatty's previous wife had also committed suicide. In Italy somewhere, wasn't it? An overdose? Yes, that was right. A young opera singer called Darcie, she'd been six months pregnant at the time, which had made the whole thing doubly tragic. Losing one wife to suicide was unfortunate. But two? That sounded downright careless to Robbie. The lover in him told him to leave well alone, but the journalist in him told him to keep digging.

Chapter Twenty-Seven

William's phone was ringing in his jacket pocket, hung on the back of the door. His captor stopped what he was doing, put down the knife, and looked William square in the eye.

'You will answer it,' he stated flatly.

What? How could William talk to anybody now? His back was sliced up like a joint of pork, his fingers were swollen and broken and his arms were covered in cigarette burns. He wanted to curl up and die. He'd had enough. He was fairly sure his torturer was merely keeping him alive for the fun of it now.

'Is your wife,' said the Italian man. 'Be normal, or ...' He waved the knife in front of William's face.

'William,' it was Francesca. 'Jade's dead.'

William wanted to scream out, 'I know. They killed her. I saw them. Tell the police it was murder.'

But of course he didn't. He tried to keep his voice as unemotional as possible, and tried to mask his pain.

'I'm so very sorry to hear that,' he said. 'Whatever happened? Suicide?' He glanced at his captor who grinned back.

'No, you're right, it's very sad. Very, very sad.'

'Yes, you do that. Keep me informed.'

'No, I don't think there's any need for me to cut short my trip. I'm sure you can cope with the funeral arrangements.'

'London? London is fine,' said William, looking out of

the window at Lake Como in all its sparkling, Italian glory. 'Wet, but what's new, eh?'

'Yes, yes, Francesca, I'll definitely be back by Friday. Send my love to the boys. Give them a kiss from Daddy and tell them that I love them.'

William felt his voice break as he pictured his sons, knowing he would never see them again.

'I have to go now, Francesca,' he said, unable to carry on the façade any longer. 'Take care of yourself. Goodbye.'

The Italian took the phone from William and placed it neatly back in his jacket pocket on the back of the door.

'Right,' he grinned, picking up the knife. 'Now where was I?'

William sounded weird. Francesca wondered if the stress of the situation was finally hitting even him, the most stoic, unemotional man in the world. Or maybe he sensed that something had changed between them. That she was somehow different. It was the first conversation they'd had since she'd slept with Robbie and she felt sure he must somehow have been able to pick up on her guilt. But no, there was definitely something else. Send my love to the boys? Take care of yourself? William never said things like that. She supposed he had been quite close to Jade. It must have been a shock hearing that she was dead. She'd seen them sharing cups of tea and cosy chats in his office now and then. She'd thought it was sweet that they'd struck up this unexpected friendship. William never opened up to Francesca any more, and she doubted that Fatty and Jade had deep and meaningfuls, so Francesca had thought it was nice that the pair felt they could talk to each other. Odd – the banker and the bimbo. But so what? Life was odd. And getting odder by the minute.

267

So Jade was an orphan. Why had she pretended to have family in Kent? Perhaps she'd wanted to invent a nice, cosy imaginary life for herself. Maybe she'd seen her marriage to Fatty as a fresh start and had decided to reinvent her past. Poor kid. She had no one. Now it was up to Francesca, a virtual stranger, to organise her funeral. Francesca didn't even know what religion Jade had been, but she guessed it would be right and proper to have her buried in the family plot in the Cimetière de Monaco, alongside Darcie.

It all felt horribly familiar but at least when Darcie had died, Dad had been around to help. He'd kept reminding them all that Darcie had been unstable, that she'd been on antidepressants all her adult life. He said that she'd stopped taking her tablets because of the pregnancy, she'd been trying to protect her baby, but her attempts had backfired. Without her medication she'd been unable to cope with her nerves. It was such a tragedy, he'd said, and then he'd wept, his huge shoulders shaking, at the loss of his wife and his unborn child. Some cruel people had started rumours that her dad had walked out on Darcie a few days before she died, but that was utter rubbish. He'd just sent her off to his holiday house on Lake Como to give her a break. Fatty had loved Darcie. Of all his wives, Darcie was the one who had had her father's heart. Just as Angelica was undoubtedly his favourite child, Darcie had been his favourite wife. The one true love of his life.

And now Jade was gone too. Francesca's body felt heavy. She was so tired. Tired of coping. She needed a release, a break from all this sadness and loss. Perhaps she was no better than Angel. Angel had her drink and her drugs, and Francesca had her Robbie. She knew it was probably the wrong thing to do, but she needed him now. She picked up her phone.

Things awful here. I guess you've heard about Jade. Poor girl. Feel guilty I didn't notice how low she was. Seems things are going from bad to worse. Except for you, obviously. Would love to see you later. Hotel Negresco, Nice, 8pm? F x

'Except for you, obviously.' She certainly knew how to melt a guy's heart. Robbie read and reread Fran's message. He couldn't help smiling to himself. Well, that would certainly help get him through the day! He went back to his work with new enthusiasm. Right, where was he? Giancarlo LaFata and his alarming propensity to lose people who were close to him.

Simon had been sure that the biggest crime story relating to Giancarlo LaFata had been his link to shady Russian 'businessmen' and, having done some in-depth digging, Robbie had found out that this was indeed true. Andrea Dubrovski was certainly a nasty piece of work and about as legitimate as Bernie Madoff was trustworthy. He had ties to the Russian mob and there were rumours of gunrunning and associations with illegal sex trafficking. And Fatty had definitely been a friend of the guy. They'd played both golf and illegal high-stake poker games together. What's more, money had definitely changed hands. It was a *good* story but Robbie felt sure it wasn't *the* story. Besides, the police were on to LaFata already. The offices of LaFata International were now crawling with serious fraud officers. The word on the grapevine was that they were investigating money laundering, embezzlement and theft charges relating to LaFata's personal business deals. And with the police in-volved, the chances of getting a fresh story, that no other journalist knew about, were slim.

But Robbie had a journalist's nose and he smelled

something bigger. He was sure of it. Somewhere in the tangle of lies that was Giancarlo LaFata's life, he felt sure the truth was lurking like a snake in the grass, and it would be nastier and more shocking than anything Robbie had uncovered before. The waters were muddied, but he was hell-bent on finding out exactly what was going on beneath the surface.

He wrote down the names of all the people connected to LaFata who had died prematurely and then sat back and surveyed his list:

Darcie LaFata, wife – suicide
Jade LaFata, wife – suicide
Giuseppe Romano, restaurant owner – fire

And then the cogs of Robbie's mind started turning faster and he added:

Pete Wallace, journalist – car crash?????

It was a long shot. And he was probably getting carried away with his conspiracy theories, but wasn't it something of a coincidence that Pete had died while investigating Giancarlo LaFata?

Robbie carried on looking through all his background notes on LaFata. There was one more suspicious death, swinging tantalisingly off the LaFata family tree.

Alessandro LaFata, father – cause of death unknown.

It took Robbie two hours to track down a phone number for the LaFata family in Sicily, but eventually he got through.

'*Pronto?*' said a cheerful woman's voice.

Shit, Robbie didn't speak a word of Italian.

'Um, yes, hello,' he started. 'Do you speak English?'

'Not so much,' said the woman warily. 'What you want?'

'I'm a journalist investigating Giancarlo LaFata's disappearance and—' started Robbie.

Click. The line went dead. Damn! He hated it when they did that. But it was part of the job. Phones were hung up, doors were slammed in his face. Robbie had grown a thick skin over the years and he wasn't one to give up easily. He redialled the number. It rang for a very long time.

'*Pronto?*' said the same woman, tentatively this time.

'Please don't hang up,' Robbie pleaded. 'Just listen to what I have to say.'

The woman was silent but she didn't hang up.

'I want to know about Giancarlo's father,' he began. 'Alessandro.'

'My husband's father,' said the woman, finally finding her voice.

'Ah, so you're married to Giancarlo's brother …?'

'*Si,*' confirmed the woman. 'I am Salvatore's wife, Elisabetta.'

'And you were close to Giancarlo?' asked Robbie gently.

'No, *non ho mai incontrato,*' she said. 'Um, I am sorry, no I have not met him. He leave Sicily many, many years ago now. He no come back.'

'Is your husband home?' asked Robbie hopefully.

'No, he is at work,' said Elisabetta LaFata. 'I must go now. I should not talk to you.'

'Wait!' said Robbie desperately. 'Let me give you my number.'

'No, I must go …'

'My name is Robbie McLean,' he said hurriedly. 'And I can be contacted at the Fairmont Monte Carlo—'

The line went silent again. A dead end. Ah well, on

to the next lead. Robbie dialled a local number. Florence Michel, Darcie's best friend. Maybe he would have some more luck with her.

'Mum, what are you doing?' demanded Carlo, scratching his head and watching Sandrine and her entourage march into Le Grand Bleu as if they owned the place.

'I am here to get my painting,' she said breezily, shouldering her son out of the way and walking straight into the drawing room as if this was still her home.

Carlo took a deep breath. His mother had just arrived unannounced, wearing a bright pink Lycra minidress that was at least twenty years too young for her, five-inch gold heels and carrying her most ridiculous, minuscule dog under her arm. Carlo was not in the mood for his mother. He'd come up to the house to help Francesca deal with the aftermath of Jade's suicide. It was awful that his dad's wife had felt so desperate that she'd thrown herself off the cliffs at Eze. Carlo felt gutted and guilty as hell. He realised now that he hadn't known Jade well at all, but she'd been sweet and pretty and she'd made his dad happy. And Carlo had done nothing to make sure she was OK over the last few days.

Carlo was low. Very low. Jade was dead, his dad was still unaccounted for, Frankie was acting strangely and Angel was off in Cannes doing God knows what with God knows who. She hadn't come back to Monaco last night. She'd said she was staying in Cannes all week – too many parties to miss during the film festival to bother with family emergencies, obviously. He'd spoken to her briefly on the phone this morning to tell her about Jade, but she'd seemed horribly unaffected by the news. What had happened to his kid sister? She seemed not to care about anything or anyone except herself these days. It was as if her emotions had been switched off. She'd always been spoilt but once upon a time she'd had some compassion. She'd been such a soft, gooey, sentimental little girl. He remembered her breaking her heart over the death of every family dog, carrying dead birds and mice home to give them 'proper funerals' and weeping every time Carlo was sent back to boarding school. Where had that girl gone? Carlo missed her. Angel was lost, and, as Frankie had said, nobody could find her but herself. He felt useless.

And now his mum was here. Just what he didn't need! Worse, she wasn't alone. Sandrine had arrived with her toyboy, Frank – a twenty-two-year-old hunk of beefcake who was all biceps and no brain – and her agent, Blaine Edwards, an overweight and overbearing Australian idiot, who Carlo could happily punch. And to top it all, she'd brought a film crew with her!

'Mum,' he said, following her into the drawing room and pushing past the hangers-on. 'Who the fuck are all these people? Why is there a cameraman here?'

'Do not swear at me, Giancarlo,' replied his mother, pouting at the camera. 'I did not bring you up to disrespect your mama like that. Tsk. Tsk.'

'Mum!' Carlo hissed, trying his hardest to swallow his anger. He wanted to throttle her but knew that he was on film. 'What the hell is going on?'

'I am doing a reality TV show,' she smiled cheesily at the camera, 'to show the public how wonderful and exciting and fulfilled my life is. Isn't that right, Blaine?'

'Sure is, sugar,' said Blaine Edwards, licking his fat lips and rubbing his hands together. 'We're relaunching your mum's career, Carlo.'

'What? Again?' asked Carlo sarcastically. 'How many attempted comebacks will that be?'

'*Ta gueule*, Carlo!' whispered his mum in his ear. 'Shut up!' And then she smiled up at the camera and simpered, 'Ooh, stop being such a grump, Carlo, *mon petit lapin*.'

'I am not your little bunny, Mum,' he snapped. 'Why have you brought these people? Now of all times? Jade is dead. Dad is missing. This is not appropriate, *Maman*!'

'Now, now, Carlo, be nice to your old mum,' grinned Blaine, obviously loving the fact that the camera was missing none of the action. 'Be a good boy and show us where the painting is.'

'Bugger off,' muttered Carlo. 'Mum, what painting? What are you talking about?'

'My wedding present from your father.' She smiled sweetly. 'My Toulouse-Lautrec. Is with his collection. He said it would be safer in his vault than on my wall but he is gone now so I will take it, *oui*?'

Carlo had alarm bells ringing very loudly in his ears. He had never heard of a painting that had been a wedding present and it wasn't his place to let his mum help herself to his dad's art collection. He had to get Frankie. She'd know what to do.

He ran up the stairs two at a time and found Frankie in her bedroom on her phone. She shrugged at him as he burst in and said, 'That's weird. I can't get hold of William. The police want all the Dubai accounts. They're missing from the office. He must have them with him but he's not answering. Must be in a meeting. I'll try later. What's up? You look stressed.'

'It's my mother,' said Carlo breathlessly. 'She's downstairs with a load of cling-ons ...'

'Cling-ons?' Frankie raised an eyebrow.

'Frank the Wank, Blaine the Pain, a rat masquerading as a dog. Oh, and a film crew.'

'Oh, bloody hell, Carlo.' Francesca flopped onto her bed with a look of despair on her face. 'That's the last thing we need right now. Your mum on one of her publicity stunts.'

'I know, I know,' said Carlo apologetically, always feeling as if he had to make excuses for his mother. 'I couldn't stop her. You know what she's like.'

'What does she want?' asked Francesca.

'A painting. A Toulouse-Lautrec apparently. She said Dad gave it to her as a wedding present and she wants to take it home now.'

'Oh God.' Frankie's shoulders slumped. 'They used to fight about that all the time. You probably don't remember, you were too young, but when they divorced she wanted to take it with her. Dad said it was too precious to be hung on a wall and should stay in the vault and be kept safe as a family heirloom. She used to scream at him and threaten legal action and all sorts. Then I think he gave her some money as a kind of deposit. A promise that he'd keep it safe. That shut her up.'

'Oh, right,' said Carlo. 'Figures. Mum will do pretty much anything for money. Which is why she's downstairs now with a bloody film crew. But she's right this time. The painting is hers.'

'Yes, in theory,' nodded Francesca. 'But it's worth millions, Carlo. Even you must see why Dad was a bit sceptical about letting Sandrine hang it on her wall. You know how many parties she throws. It would get splattered with red wine, or stolen by some male escort she'd hired for the evening.'

Carlo flinched. It was one thing him criticising his mother, which he did constantly, but he still found it difficult to swallow when Frankie had a go at her.

'OK, maybe, but if he gave it to her as a wedding present then it's rightfully hers,' he said.

Frankie was quiet for a moment and then she nodded. 'Yup, you're right,' she said. 'Let's just give her the painting and get rid of her. It doesn't seem very important in the grand scheme of things, does it? I'll get the key to the vault.'

Francesca lifted a mirror off her wall and revealed her safe. She keyed in her code, opened the door and took out a set of keys. Carlo followed her back downstairs.

'Francesca, *ma belle*!' cried Sandrine, when she saw her stepdaughter. 'Let me look at you, *ma chérie*.'

The older woman held Francesca at arm's length, eyed her up and down and then hugged her to her ample bosom before kissing her three times on the cheeks.

'I am so truly, deeply sorry for your pain, Francesca,' she declared, wiping a crocodile tear from her cheek. 'Your poor, poor father. And that child bride of his. Jade? I see it on the news. *C'est une tragédie*!'

Carlo cringed at his mother's melodramatic performance. She never had been much of an actress. It was all for the cameras, of course. She barely gave Frankie the time of day usually.

'Nice to see you, Sandrine,' said Francesca, although Carlo could tell the words were being spoken through gritted teeth. 'Let's get on with this. We have a lot to deal with and we really could do without any press intrusion.'

Francesca glared at the camera. 'In fact,' she continued, 'I think everyone should stay up here while I collect the painting.'

'*Non*,' said Sandrine, suddenly cold. 'I want to come with you, and my friends also. Is important for my artistic integrity that I allow them to film everything.'

'Mum!' Carlo scolded. 'Please. You're getting your painting. Just let Frankie deal with it.'

'*Non*,' she repeated defiantly. 'We will come also.'

She pushed past Carlo and Francesca, calling, 'This way, boys. *Vite*! *Vite*!' She teetered on her high heels along the polished marble floor to the stairs that led down to the basement, with her toyboy, her agent, her film crew and her tiny rat dog scurrying behind her.

'Oh for God's sake,' muttered Carlo under his breath. 'I'm sorry, Frankie.'

'Not your fault,' said Francesca. 'Just be more selective in your next life when you're choosing which womb to be born from.'

She smiled at him and squeezed his arm lovingly. 'Come on, let's go before they raid the wine cellar.'

At the bottom of the stairs, Francesca managed to squeeze to the front of the crowd.

'I have the key,' she explained patiently to Sandrine, who tutted, wanting to be in front, as always.

Carlo hung back and followed the others through the corridors of wine racks. It was dark and cold down there. He shivered. The cellar had always given him the creeps. It reminded him of childhood games of hide and seek when he'd sneak down and hide between the dusty bottles of vintage Château d'Yquem and Petrus. He'd always been competitive by nature but he used to will Francesca or Angel to find him quickly when he was down there. One time, he'd been so freaked out by one of the cats suddenly leaping down from a shelf, that he'd knocked over a bottle of wine and smashed it on the floor.

'That is a bottle of 1978 vintage Romanée Conti!' Fatty had bellowed. 'Is worth more than ten thousand pounds, you idiot boy!'

Urgh, Carlo shuddered at the memory of the beating he'd got that night. He hated this place. Now Francesca was unlocking the heavy metal door of the vault.

'Please turn the camera off,' she was saying. 'For security purposes.'

'*Non*,' said Sandrine abruptly. 'We will edit carefully. You can check the footage if you wish. But I need these shots. I want my fans to see my happy face when I get my beloved painting back.'

Carlo could see his sister rolling her eyes as she pushed open the door and searched for the light switch. The bright strip lighting blinked three or four times before going on properly and illuminating the vast vault.

'What the ...?' Francesca gasped.

Carlo peered over her shoulder and into the room. The last time Carlo had been down there it had been full of paintings, sculptures, gold artefacts, priceless furniture. It had looked like Aladdin's cave. Now it was completely bare except for one large canvas, propped up against the wall.

'Holy shit!' he said. 'What happened here?'

'*Mon dieu!*' cried Sandrine. 'Where is my painting?'

'Where are *all* the paintings?' Carlo asked. 'And the sculptures?'

'I don't understand,' said Francesca in a small voice. 'Where has it all gone?'

'Well, that's a turn up for the books,' said Blaine Edwards, barely hiding his excitement from his voice. 'I thought you said there was a billion euros' worth of art in here, Sandrine, babes? But there's diddly squat! This is going to make great TV!'

'Turn off the cameras,' shouted Francesca.

'Where is my painting?!' screamed Sandrine, with her hands clutching her face.

'Turn off the bloody camera,' repeated Francesca angrily.

'No way,' shouted Blaine gleefully. 'This is gold-plated television.'

'What has that bastard Giancarlo LaFata done with my Toulouse-Lautrec?' demanded Sandrine, turning towards the cameraman so that he could take in the full horror of the situation.

'Turn off the cameras, NOW!' yelled Francesca.

Carlo stared in disbelief as his mother swooned with fake shock, Blaine Edwards rubbed his chubby hands together in excitement, the tiny dog yapped, the cameraman kept rolling and Francesca shouted, 'Stop filming!'

And then he'd had enough. Somebody had to take control and that somebody was going to have to be him. The cameraman was short and slightly built. It was easy for Carlo to grab the small handheld camera from him.

'What are you doing, Carlo?' screamed his mother. 'Put that camera down!'

'OK,' said Carlo calmly. And then he smashed the camera onto the stone floor. He watched, with satisfaction, as the glass and plastic flew across the cellar and scattered beneath the wine racks.

'The show's over,' he said coldly, and then he made his way through the corridors of wine and back up the stairs to the daylight.

Chapter Twenty-Eight

Robbie sat on the beach sweating in his smart trousers and shirt, staring out to sea, watching a yacht sail effortlessly by on the horizon, and contemplating life. It was late afternoon and the sun was beating down on the sand. Behind him, he could hear the barriers being erected for the weekend's Grand Prix. He would be flying out on Friday morning. Maybe he would be able to catch some of the pre-qualifiers on Thursday? No, that was daft, he would be too busy with work. And he'd be gone before Saturday's qualifiers and the Grand Prix proper on Sunday. It was all wrong. Just as Monaco came to life he would be leaving. Worse, he would be leaving Fran. And heading back to his lonely, bachelor existence. Work was going well but his heart felt heavy. A man needed more than a career to get him through life. He would give up a million front-page splashes for the love of a good woman. For the love of Fran.

And yet, what Florence had just told him was going to crush Francesca. How could he publish what he'd found out? Would she forgive him? Would she understand that he was just doing his job? Telling the truth? Or would she shoot the messenger? Was it a risk he was willing to take?

Florence had been Darcie LaFata's best friend. She was a tiny, black-haired, brown-eyed elf of a woman of around Robbie's age, with a heart-shaped face and a gamine crop.

She'd chain-smoked Gauloises as she'd sipped her black coffee and talked frankly about her best friend.

'Now, I can speak,' she'd explained to Robbie. 'Giancarlo LaFata is dead, everyone knows that. And I am sick of biting my tongue. I have been a coward. I have not honoured Darcie's memory. I have been too busy looking after myself.' She'd bitten her bottom lip and Robbie had noticed a bead of bright red blood appear. Then she licked the wound and carried on.

'I was scared of what LaFata would do to me if I spoke out but I'm not scared any more. I have to tell you what I know,' she'd said.

And then she'd told him. Darcie had been twenty-eight when she'd met Giancarlo LaFata, and already a world-class operatic superstar. He had been smitten but she took some persuading.

'He pursued her for months,' Florence had told him. 'Flowers, diamonds, haute couture dresses, even a puppy!'

Finally Darcie had succumbed and within months they were married and living together in Le Grand Bleu. But Darcie's career had taken her all over the world.

'New York, Tokyo, Sydney,' Florence had said. 'I never knew where she was. I don't think she knew which city she was waking up in half the time. Giancarlo didn't like it. He would get angry.'

And so Fatty had tried to convince his new wife to give up her career. He'd wanted to have a baby with her, hoping that that would keep her close.

'Darcie told him she would try to conceive, but it was a lie. She was a workaholic. She lived for her singing. And so she carried on taking the pill behind his back. She wasn't ready to be a mother and settle down. She was so ambitious and still very young, and I think also she had doubts about having a baby with Giancarlo.'

'Did she not love him?' Robbie had asked.

Florence had shrugged her narrow shoulders, held her hands heavenwards and pouted her scarlet lips. 'What is love? How do you measure such an emotion?' she'd asked. 'I think she was certainly very fond of Giancarlo but, no, he was not her big love. Not the love of her life.'

'Opera,' Robbie had mused. 'Opera was the love of her life.'

'*Non,*' Florence had said curtly from behind a veil of cigarette smoke. 'Opera was her passion, the love of her life was Javier Alvorado.'

Robbie had almost choked on his coffee. 'Javier Alvorado?'

'*Oui.*' Florence had nodded her short, shiny black hair vigorously. 'Javier was the one.'

'But …?' Robbie's brain had gone into meltdown. Javier Alvorado was an Argentinian Formula One driver. Or at least he had been until he'd died in a fatal crash during a warm-up for the Malaysian Grand Prix a few years ago.

'They were in love. Darcie with him. Javier with her. It was one of those *très* passionate affairs. Cannot live with, cannot live without. They fought, they broke up, they cried, they made up, and so on. He would not marry Darcie though. He said he was too young and not ready for the commitment. So, she left him, and she married LaFata in defiance, I think. But Javier was Darcie's lover before LaFata, during LaFata and after LaFata.'

'After LaFata?' Robbie had asked, confused. 'But she was still with Fatty when she died.'

'*Non.*' Florence had shaken her head again. 'She left him a few days before she died. The baby, it was not his. It was

Javier's. She could not live the lie. It weighed too heavy on her mind, so she told Giancarlo the truth.'

'How did she know the baby was Javier's, not Giancarlo's? I thought she was on the pill?' probed Robbie.

'She got very sick, six months before she died. It was a bad stomach bug when she was in Hong Kong on tour and you know, sometimes, when a woman is sick her contraceptive it does not work. Giancarlo was not with her but Javier was there in Hong Kong. The dates added up. Besides, Darcie did not enjoy sex with Giancarlo. He was getting old and very overweight even then. She liked his humour and his friendship but physically she was not interested. Javier, however, she was putty in his hands ...'

'And she told Giancarlo everything? Even that the baby was Javier's?'

'*Oui*, she was very honest, Darcie. Too honest for her own good ...'

'Oh my God,' Robbie had spluttered. 'She confessed everything and then she killed herself?'

'*Non.*' Another shake of the head. 'I think Giancarlo killed her. He loved her too much. He could not bear to lose her to another man. He was like that. He needed to possess everything – businesses, yachts, planes, houses, people. Darcie was a free spirit, he could never own her. It drove him mad, I think.'

'But what proof do you have, Florence?' Robbie had asked her.

'Darcie called me from the house at Lake Como. Giancarlo had sent her there to think things over. He hoped she would change her mind and that they would raise the baby as his. You see, he really loved her. But she was not going back to Giancarlo, she was running to Javier. She had her ticket. She called me to say goodbye.'

'She wasn't suicidal?' Robbie had probed.

'*Non*, she was excited.' Florence lit another cigarette. 'She was looking forward to the future. Javier had said he would marry her. He was pleased about the baby. She told Giancarlo it was over for good and the next thing I know she is dead. But she did not kill herself. Darcie got depressed from time to time. She was an artist, she had strong emotions, but she never wanted to die. She loved life, she loved Javier and she loved the baby she was carrying. *Non*. She did not take those pills of her own accord.'

'And you think Giancarlo LaFata made her take them?' Robbie's heart was racing at a thousand beats per minute. This was it. This was the big one!

Florence nodded. 'Not in person, of course. He did not get his hands dirty, that man, but one of his men will have done it. I am sure. They made her take those tablets and they left her to die alone in that lonely house by the lake. *Salop!*'

Florence had stubbed her cigarette out angrily in the ashtray and looked up at Robbie with tear-filled eyes.

'You tell the world this, Robbie McLean,' she'd almost pleaded with him. 'For Darcie. Please do it for Darcie and for me.'

Robbie had nodded. It was his job and his duty to tell the truth. But he was torn. He watched the yacht sail out of sight, eastwards towards Cannes and the glittering film festival that was going on there. How would Fran react when Robbie printed that story about her father? He picked up a handful of sand and watched as it trickled between his fingers onto the beach. He didn't want to hurt Francesca. He loved her. He was sure now. But what about Darcie LaFata? And all the other lives Fatty had destroyed? Robbie let his mind wander to a house on Lake Como and a scared, pregnant young woman being left to die, slowly and pain-fully, on her own. No. He couldn't keep this one to himself. Francesca would understand. If she loved him like he loved her she would understand.

'Sorry,' said Carlo glumly from behind a cigarette. 'I lost my temper. I shouldn't have smashed that camera and I shouldn't have kicked Mum out like that but ...'

Francesca shook her head and sat down beside him on the bench under the gazebo. He looked so handsome in his cream suit with his dark tan and there was something else about him. Had he filled out recently? Or perhaps his features had changed. Suddenly her baby brother didn't look like such an overgrown kid any more. And the truth was she was proud of Carlo for standing up to his mother and taking charge like that.

'I'd have done the same thing if you hadn't got there first.' She smiled at her younger brother, fondly.

'Really?' Carlo looked up at her cautiously. 'You're not pissed off with me?'

'No!' Francesca leant her head on his shoulder. 'Your mum was way out of line bringing that film crew here at a time like this. I'm proud of you, Carlo.'

He smiled weakly back at her.

'But what about the art collection, Frankie?' he asked. 'Where's it gone?'

'I think Dad's the only one who knows that. Knew that ...' Francesca's voice trailed off. She was still not used to talking about her father in the past tense.

'D'you reckon he sold it all?' asked Carlo, blowing smoke rings into the late afternoon sky.

Francesca shrugged. 'Probably. I've learned more about Dad's business deals this last week than I learned in fifteen years of working for him. He was screwed financially. He must have needed the cash. I mean, nobody could have stolen the collection. Only me and Dad had keys and who could have walked out the house unnoticed carrying Monets, Manets and Toulouse-Lautrecs?'

Carlo nodded thoughtfully.

'I've tried ringing William to ask him if he knows anything about it but he's not answering his phone. Anyway, I doubt he knows any more than we do.'

'Are we going to lose everything, Frankie?' asked Carlo, leaning his head against hers.

Francesca thought carefully about her answer. Carlo had been born into great wealth. He didn't know any other way of life. Francesca could remember living in a council flat with no heating. It got so cold that her mum would get into her little single bed beside her and cuddle up to tell bedtime stories. Most nights Francesca had fallen asleep curled up in the safety of her mother's arms. She hadn't needed money when she'd known she was so dearly loved and, in a way, those days had been some of the happiest of her life. She knew there was a world beyond money. But Carlo? Carlo and Angelica knew nothing other than yachts, private jets and servants. At least Angelica had her modelling career to fall back on but Carlo had nothing – no qualifications, no training, no vocation. Would he lose everything if the money was gone? She gazed up at him and noticed the proud slant of his jaw and the determined look in his eye. Carlo had changed and now she saw how. Perhaps losing his father had finally started him on the journey to becoming a man.

'We might lose all this,' said Francesca, eyeing the vast gardens, the tennis courts, the swimming pool, the cars in the drive, the house itself. 'But we'll never lose everything, Carlo. We've got each other.'

Carlo nodded and smiled down at her. 'And that's worth more than anything, isn't it, Frankie? Family. It's all that counts. That's what Dad always said.'

Chapter Twenty-Nine

The Italian is in his Ferrari now heading back to Monaco. He is listening to Vivaldi and thinking about the work he still has to do before he can go home. The journalist, McLean, is proving to be a problem. He is digging too deep, getting in way over his head like his friend Pete Wallace did before him. He must be careful or he will never see Scotland or his darling daughters again. And now he has been talking to Florence Michel. Silly boy. Curiosity killed the cat, doesn't he know that?

And Francesca thinks she is falling in love with him! Ah, she is being a silly, silly girl. He is smart enough maybe, and attractive to women with his good looks and his Scottish charm, but he is not in her league. In some respects Francesca is a very clever woman but she has never had good taste in men. At least William Hillier is not going to cause her any more trouble. He is gone and so is his girlfriend, Jade. Good riddance to them both. He was a thief and she was a whore — a match made in heaven, may they rot together in hell!

The police have found that LaFata International was not quite as successful as it had seemed. The assets have been frozen, bank accounts stopped. Giancarlo LaFata's personal businesses are being scrutinised and soon they will discover the extent of the fraud and the debts. It is Francesca who will suffer. The poor girl thought she was running a legitimate company. She is proud and she has a strong sense of right and wrong. To be so closely linked to these little indiscretions will upset her greatly.

288

She looks at life through her rose-tinted spectacles, seeing only good in people and expecting everyone to live by her own high moral code. But she is naive. Or perhaps she is just a breath of fresh air. Is it her strength or her failing that she has such high morals? Only time will tell.

Of course she will have to deal with the Russian on her own now. William will not be back to help her find the money. She will not be able to get her hands on that sort of cash from any bank account either. It will be a test. It will do her good.

Giancarlo Junior has been a surprise. A pleasant surprise. He has not crumbled as one might expect. The way he stood up to his mother was impressive. She is a stupid woman – the dumbest blonde who ever walked the earth – but her son has never crossed her before today. Perhaps the boy has balls after all. It will be interesting to see what happens next, when he realises that he has nothing to his name but the designer shirt on his back. That will be the real test. Carlo LaFata – man or boy?

Poor Angelica, she is not coping as well as her brother and sister. She will not begin to accept that her daddy has gone for good. But her father cannot protect her any more. It is a tragedy, but it is also a fact, and until she faces the reality of the situation she is living in a dream world. She has turned, as always, to drink and drugs to numb her pain but she is only putting off the inevitable. She will hit rock bottom soon. She is hurtling towards it now, in Cannes. Who will pick her up and fix her this time? Daddy is gone. He cannot help her. Perhaps that is for the best. It is time for the baby of the family to grow up at last.

What is a LaFata without money? Without power? Is there any substance to the name? The father came from nothing. He built his fortune from sand. He did not always take the righteous path but he clawed his way to the top the only way he knew how. And now he has left the next generation of LaFatas to fend for themselves. They are adrift in the middle of the ocean without life rafts to cling on to. It is interesting to watch them, flailing around, out of their depth. But will they sink or swim?

Chapter Thirty

Robbie's mind was racing as he showered. Giuseppe Romano, Darcie LaFata, Javier Alvorado, Pete Wallace, they'd all died after they'd got in Fatty's way. Was it some sort of twisted coincidence? Was Robbie getting carried away with his conspiracy theories? It was all too much to take in.

He was desperate to see Fran this evening but how could he keep this from her? He had so many questions to ask. But they had their rule – he wouldn't ask about her father and she wouldn't tell. And yet … Surely she couldn't know about any of this stuff? Francesca was as straight as a die, Robbie was as sure of that as he'd ever been about anything in his life. Simon had told him that all Francesca's business was legitimate, that she had a brilliant reputation as an honest and trustworthy businesswoman and that she was admired in Wall Street, the City and beyond. It had made Robbie proud when Simon had told him that Francesca was more shocked by Fatty's dodgy dealings than anyone. She was a good girl. His girl.

Robbie dried himself off and got into his new clothes. He glanced at himself in the mirror. He looked smart enough but was he good enough for Francesca LaFata now? Hmm, he doubted it. Scratch the surface and he was nothing but a working-class kid from Wester Hailes. But he did a good job of pretending in his designer gear. He thought about

Ruby's favourite fairy tale – *The Emperor's New Clothes*. Was that him? Masquerading around Monaco in his fancy clobber thinking he was the bee's knees when it was clear to everyone that it was all a sham?

He was almost ready for his date when Dan knocked on his door and came dancing into the room with the widest grin Robbie had ever seen on his face. He looked like he was going to explode with excitement.

'Calm yourself, Dan,' said Robbie. 'You'll give yourself a hernia prancing around like that.'

'I've got it, Rob!' he said, rubbing his hands together and bouncing up and down on his toes. 'The scoop of a lifetime. And it's all mine!'

Robbie eyed Dan warily. Surely he couldn't be on to the suspicious deaths too. He was a showbiz reporter, he wrote about arguments, affairs and addictions, not murder.

'Aye? What's that then?' asked Robbie, straightening his tie in the mirror. He was going the whole hog for Fran tonight – sharp trousers, white shirt, black tie, shiny shoes.

'Och, I can't tell you, Rob,' teased Dan, throwing himself down on the bed with a bounce. 'More than my life's worth.'

Robbie watched his friend in the mirror as he bounced up and down on the bed like a five-year-old. He was obviously gagging to tell Robbie his news.

'What are you doing here then? If you're not going to tell me?' he asked.

'Just wondered if you fancied a trip down to Cannes this evening,' he replied. 'I've got two VIP passes to the party of the year on some Indian prince's yacht, and if you don't come with me, I'll have to take Simon. And much as I like the old codger, he's not exactly going to do my street cred any good, is he? Whereas you, Mr Prada, will help me pull in the laydeez ...'

'Well, thanks for the invite and for the compliment – I think that was a compliment ...' Robbie said.

'It was,' nodded Dan. 'Not quite sure how you do it but the girls always fall at your feet, McLean. The girls in my office fight over the crime stories cos they know you'll be covering them.'

'They do?' asked Robbie, flattered despite himself. 'Really?'

'Yes, really,' said Dan. 'They call you Rob the Throb. But don't get a big head, all right? Anyway, stop preening yourself, Romeo, and tell me – are you coming to Cannes?'

Rob the Throb. He'd had no idea! Maybe the fact that Fran liked him wasn't so incredible after all. Robbie smiled at his reflection in the mirror. There was life in the old dog yet. Pushing forty, as Simon had reminded him, but so what?

'So?' Dan was asking him. 'You coming with me?'

'Sorry, Dan, I'd love to but I've got work to do tonight,' replied Robbie, thinking about Fran and the 'work' they'd be doing together later in their room at Hotel Negresco.

'Work? Dressed like that?' Dan's eyebrow shot up quizzically.

'Yup.'

'Yeah, right. Simon's got you sussed. You do have a woman, don't you, McLean?' grinned Dan.

Robbie shook his head. 'Don't be daft,' he said, maybe a little too quickly. 'I told you, it's work.'

'Bullshit,' laughed Dan. 'Rob the Throb's got himself a hot date.'

'No, I haven't,' said Robbie firmly.

'Och, don't get your knickers in a twist, mate,' said Dan. 'Everyone's at it. You'd be surprised ...'

'Would I?' asked Robbie. 'So is this your big scoop? An affair? Who? Fatty?'

Dan shook his head. 'God, I really shouldn't tell you but it is so exciting. And I've filed my copy. You'll read about it tomorrow anyway.'

'So tell me,' Robbie encouraged him, dying to hear the gossip and change the subject away from his own private life.

'Och, I dunno ...' Dan mused. 'I really shouldn't. I don't know if I can trust you.'

'Look, Dan. Unless it's the crime story of the century, you're in no danger of me nicking your scoop. Anyway, I couldn't beat you to the front page now even if I wanted to, so you're secret's safe with me.'

'OK,' said Dan, bouncing up and down on the bed again. 'Jade LaFata was a dominatrix.'

'A dominatrix? What? On the game? Whips and gimps and all that weird stuff?' asked Robbie. 'Christ, that really is a good story.'

'It gets better,' said Dan, excitedly. 'She was called Madame Jaja and she was into really hardcore stuff. She was in porn films and she had her own website. That's how Fatty found her. The dirty old git got his kicks from all that stuff.'

'No way!' laughed Robbie.

'And there's more.' Dan carried on, his eyes widening now. 'The marriage was more of a business arrangement than anything else. He basically gave her the trophy wife lifestyle and she whipped and kicked his fat old arse whenever he felt the need.'

'That's brilliant,' said Robbie, grinning.

He hated Giancarlo LaFata and everything he stood for, so the thought of the whole world knowing about his warped sexual habits was very appealing. And then Robbie thought about Fran, and how shocked and upset she'd be when she read the papers, and the smile faded from his face. Poor Fran. To have a man like that as your father! Robbie had always thought he'd bottomed out in the dad department but Fatty made his dad look like Mary Bloody Poppins.

'There's even more,' said Dan, getting up and standing behind Robbie at the mirror. 'Jade was having an affair,' he nodded his head vigorously.

'Really?' Now that was interesting.

'With …' Dan teased. 'Wait for it …'

'Who?' demanded Robbie.

'William Hillier!' announced Dan with a flourish. 'Her stepdaughter's husband. Can you believe it? The dominatrix and the bespectacled banker. Who knew?!'

Robbie felt the blood drain from his face as he tried to take in what Dan had just said. Jade, like Darcie before her, had had an affair. The coincidences were getting ridiculous. And with Fran's husband. Oh, Jesus, how the hell was he going to face her tonight knowing that?

'Are you OK, Robbie?' asked Dan, staring at his friend in the mirror. 'You've gone a bit pale.'

Robbie nodded and tried to regain his composure. 'Yeah, yeah, I'm just a bit surprised, that's all. I wonder if Fatty knew.'

'I don't think so,' said Dan. 'I came across the dominatrix stuff on my own when I was digging into Jade's background. She was an orphan, you know? Brought up in care in south London. And obviously Fatty knew about that, but the affair … no. That was top secret. Simon put me on to it.'

'Simon?' asked Robbie. 'How would he know about an affair?'

'He's been researching where all the money's gone, hasn't he? And he was suspicious about the way Hillier was investing. Oh, I dunno, I don't understand all that crap, but anyway, the interesting bit was that he found an offshore bank account that Hillier had set up in Jade's name, and he's been putting large amounts of cash in there every month for the last six months. I reckon it was their getaway fund. I think the star-crossed lovers were going to run off together. Maybe Hillier changed his mind when Fatty died, got cold feet. Maybe that's why Jade topped herself. Nothing to do with Fatty's disappearance at all.'

Robbie's brain felt like it was going to melt it was working so hard.

'And Francesca?' he asked. 'Did she know?'

Dan shook his head. 'She's the only LaFata that comes out of all of this unscathed. Fatty's a perverted fraudster. Jade's a porn star. Hillier's a thief and an adulterer. Angelica's a junkie and Carlo, well he's not a criminal as far as I can tell, but he was screwing his best mate's girlfriend when his dad went missing so he's no saint, that's for sure. But Francesca LaFata …' He shrugged and nodded. 'She seems to be a complete sweetheart. Everyone loves her. Except her husband, obviously, seeing as he's been shagging the mother-in-law!'

'Jeez, what a mess,' was all Robbie could bring himself to say. 'Poor Fran.'

'Fran?' laughed Dan. 'It's Francesca to you. Frankie to the family, so I've heard, but she doesn't like anyone else calling her that. Right, I'm off to Cannes. Sure I can't tempt you?'

'I'm sure,' nodded Robbie.

He'd never been more sure of anything. A party with a bunch of vacuous celebrities, egotistical billionaires and Euro aristocrats? Or a night in a hotel room with Fran? His sweet, beautiful, perfect Fran. It was a no-brainer.

'Well, enjoy your "work", McLean.' Dan winked as he headed to the door. 'And don't you breathe a word of what I've told you or I'll tell Molly Buchan that Rob the Throb's got the hots for her, OK?'

'OK,' Robbie said, forcing a smile. Molly Buchan was the news editor on Dan's paper. She was a fifteen-stone sumo wrestler of a woman who looked like Peter Kay in drag.

'Oh, and before I forget,' called Dan from the door, 'tomorrow night, it's casino night for you, me and Simon. It's all arranged. You and Si are off on Friday so we've decided to gamble with whatever expenses you've got left. See if you can't make a profit out of this trip. A lads' night out. No excuses.'

'I'll be there,' promised Robbie. But tomorrow night seemed a very long way away.

As he drove to Nice, Robbie's head buzzed with everything he'd been told. Facing Fran, knowing that William had been having an affair with Jade, and not being able to tell her. That was going to be difficult. And how was she going to react when this story broke? She was already so wary of journalists, and now she was going to hate them even more. The press were picking over her life like vultures on a corpse. What if she tarred him with the same brush? She was sleeping with the enemy. How long before she kicked him out of bed?

Och, but no, he and Fran were good together, weren't they? They had a way of blocking out the rest of the world and just getting lost in each other's company. She wouldn't write him off because of his job. God, he hoped not. He couldn't bear the thought of losing her when he'd only just found her.

Robbie had other worries too. His biggest was that Jade's demise was so spookily similar to Darcie's. And yet Fatty had disappeared three days before Jade's death. He couldn't possibly have had anything to do with it. Unless one of his 'men', as Florence had put it, had cleared up any unfinished business after Fatty's demise. But why would they? Loyalty? When the boss was dead? It seemed unlikely. Money? But how would any of Fatty's men gain from Jade's death? No. It didn't make any sense. Maybe Jade had killed herself after all. Perhaps Dan had been right and William Hillier had got cold feet and broken her heart. There was no way anyone else could have been involved. No, he was being paranoid, getting carried away with the drama of the whole thing.

Robbie drove into the bustling evening crowds of Nice and along the palm-lined Promenade des Anglais until he spotted the huge, pink-domed roof of Hotel Negresco. Robbie thought the place looked more like a palace than a hotel, with its curves, domes and terraces. The Negresco sat overlooking the Bay of Angels like a beautiful pink pineapple. He pulled up outside and gave his keys to the valet. Glancing at his watch he saw he was five minutes early. He had time to make one quick call.

'Florence?' he asked, when the woman's voice answered the phone.

'*Oui, qui est-ce?*'

'Florence, it's Robbie McLean.' Robbie talked quietly and quickly. 'Look, I'm probably being paranoid and over-cautious but I'm a bit worried about you.'

'Worried about me? In what way, Robbie?' asked Florence nervously.

'I'm worried for your safety, Florence. I don't want to freak you out, and, like I said, I'm probably being paranoid, but I think you should go away for a while.'

'Go away?' Florence sounded confused now. 'But why?'

'Just to be on the safe side. Until things calm down a bit. What you told me about LaFata, it's serious stuff, and I'm worried that somebody might be angry with you for telling me those things.'

'But Giancarlo is dead,' said Florence. 'I do not understand. Who could want to hurt me now?'

'I don't know,' said Robbie. 'But LaFata had friends. It's just a precaution, Florence.' He tried to keep his voice calm. 'Have you been to the police with what you told me?'

'*Non*,' said Florence, her voice sounded small and shaky now. 'I have no proof. It is just an instinct. They will not take me seriously. Not with everything that is going on. They will think I am simply a, how you say it in English? A nutter. They will think I am crazy.'

Robbie thought for a moment. Florence was probably right. The police must have people coming forward all day every day with outlandish tales about Giancarlo LaFata. They wouldn't take Florence's hunch seriously. Besides, they were so busy trying to find LaFata's body and investigating his business that they would probably put suspected past crimes to the back of their very long list.

'Well then, I definitely think you should go, Florence,' repeated Robbie. 'Is there somewhere you can stay? Away from Monaco? The further the better? Just until things calm down here.'

'My sister lives in Australia,' replied Florence. 'I have never been. It is so far away. But I have been meaning to visit for some years. She has a baby I haven't met yet. A little boy ...'

She sounded scared now and Robbie felt bad for having panicked her. But he could be doing her the biggest favour of her life. He could be saving her life.

Chapter Thirty-One

Carlo lay in bed with a sleeping Sasha in his arms. He was coming to terms with the fact that everything had gone – his dad, the money, the art collection, Jade. The foundations of his life had been washed away in less than a week and he was lost. But for now, he was OK. Here, lying in the dark, with Sasha naked beside him, he felt safe and at peace. She'd finished with Christian. Not for him. Carlo knew that. She'd ended things with Christian because she hadn't been happy with him. It had nothing to do with her fling with Carlo. She'd made that clear. There had been no talk of a relationship. She'd made him no promises, given him no false hope. Hell, she still hadn't even given him her phone number. But she was here. And now she was asleep, snuggled up against his chest, and it felt comforting. For now, it was enough.

He watched her full, red, perfect lips quiver as she dreamed. Of what? Him? He hoped so. He was smitten. Totally smitten with the little sex kitten. He'd never felt anything like this for any girl before. He found her brazen sexiness addictive. He wanted her so much it made him ache just to think about her. But it wasn't just the sex. He loved her provocative, ballsy straight talk too. He loved that she teased him and questioned him and never, ever fell for his bullshit the way those other girls did. He loved her sense of humour, her razor-sharp mind and her soaring self-confidence. He even loved that she was making him chase her. It excited him. Made him even more desperate to have her. Carlo just hoped that one day she'd give in and let herself belong to him.

His phone started ringing on the bedside table. There was no bottle of champagne to knock over this time. Sasha didn't like bubbly. She was a no-nonsense hard liquor kind of girl. And Carlo loved that about her too. She opened her eyes sleepily at the sound of the phone.

'Who is that?' she murmured. 'I was having such a nice sleep too.'

Carlo glanced at the phone.

'Oh crap, it's Christian,' he said. 'Shall I leave it?'

Sasha stretched, like a cat, and shook her tangled mane of hair. 'No, you get it, hon,' she yawned. 'I'm gonna jump in a shower and get off. Things to do, people to see. I'm a busy, busy gal ...'

Carlo swallowed and tried to hide his disappointment as she climbed out of bed and stretched again, fully naked with her beautiful back to him. He couldn't drag his eyes away from her. The smooth, tanned skin, the round pert arse, the curvy, toned thighs. God, she was something else. He felt himself go hard again. He tried to reach out to touch her but she patted his hand away.

'No, not now, you young stud,' she laughed. 'Answer the phone. Christian probably wants to tell you all about the heartless American bitch who just dumped him.'

She disappeared into the bathroom and Carlo answered the phone reluctantly.

'Christian,' he said, forcing himself to sound normal, and not guilty as hell. 'What's up?'

'Oh, nothing much,' said Christian. He sounded low. 'Sasha finished with me today.'

'Oh, God, Chris, mate, I'm sorry.' Carlo winced.

'Nah, it's OK,' said Christian. 'It's for the best, I suppose. We weren't really suited. I told you she wasn't wife material, didn't I?'

'You did,' replied Carlo. 'And there are plenty more fish in the sea.'

He cringed at his own lame clichéd response. But what could he say? Sasha was in his bloody shower!

'I know, I know,' sighed Christian despondently. 'But she is very hot and I will miss her. I know you don't like her but she really is quite a lot of fun when you get to know her.'

Carlo thought about how much fun he'd just had with Sasha.

'Yeah, I imagine she could be a lot of fun,' he replied. 'But there are other girls. You're a popular guy. You'll find your marrying kind soon.'

'Hmm, maybe,' mused Christian. 'But for now I just need to have some fun. Which is why I'm calling you. Party tonight? In Cannes? It's Amar's bash, on his yacht. Should be amazing. Lots of celebs in for the film festival. You know what Amar's like. His parties are the best!'

Amar had been at school with Carlo and Christian. His parties were awesome, it was true. The son of an Indian prince, Amar was so rich that his bank balance made Carlo's allowance look like pocket money. He spent more on one party than Carlo spent in a year. And that was going some because Carlo was a BIG spender. Amar also had some very impressive friends. He spent most of his time in his Knightsbridge bachelor bad (a five-storey mansion a stone's throw from Harrods) and he was very chummy with all the Brit celebs. Then, when he wasn't in London, he had his LA beach house, so he was matey with all the Hollywood set too. Yes, Amar was a very useful kind of friend to have. But Carlo was in no mood for a party.

'No, I'm sorry, Chris,' he said firmly. 'But I'm not in a fit state to socialise. I have to keep a clear head with all the stuff that's going on.'

Christian's response was reasonable, as always. 'I thought you'd say that, Carlo,' he said. 'And I do understand. I admire the way you're coping with all this. Your dad would have been proud. I just thought I'd ask in case you felt like escaping for a while.'

'Thanks, mate,' said Carlo, watching Sasha appear from the bathroom in a fluffy white towel. 'But no. You have a good time. Try to forget about Sasha ...'

Sasha stuck her tongue out at him, saucily, and let the towel fall to the ground, revealing her killer curves.

'She's not all that. She does nothing for me,' Carlo carried on, winking at her and pulling back the duvet to show her his erection.

'No, you're right. Maybe Scarlett Johansson will be at this party. Now, she looks like good marrying material,' said Christian stoically.

'Well, have a good time. Give Scarlett my love and we'll catch up tomorrow, yeah? Bye.'

Carlo had barely put the phone down before Sasha was on top of him again, kissing his stomach, teasing him with her tongue. Oh, Christ, she was good. She really was all that. She was all that and then some!

Francesca had stepped over the line again. Hell, she'd leapt over it this time. She was drawn to Robbie, like a moth to the flame, and nothing could keep her away. Not even the crushing guilt that churned in her stomach and tugged at her heart. She knew what she was doing was wrong so why was it, when she was in his arms, that nothing had ever felt so right?

The hotel suite was exquisite, even by LaFata standards. Francesca felt like she was starring in her own film – a love story, of course – as she soaked in the gold bath. They'd had a meal in the room, just the two of them, a feast of scallops and caviar to start, followed by succulent sole stuffed with hazelnuts and chanterelle mushrooms, all washed down with a delicious chilled Chablis. Then they'd made love, slowly, indulgently, exploring each other's bodies, savouring every touch and kiss, lost in the enormous four-poster bed which was swathed in blue satin. And now he'd run her a deep, hot bubble bath and he was fetching her a glass of ice-cold champagne.

She slid down in the tub with a grin and had to stop herself from whooping with joy. She was the cat that got the cream. Outside these four walls, life was a mess, full of heartbreak, worry, guilt and pain, but right here, right now, Francesca was cocooned in a bubble of love. Nothing could touch her tonight. Only Robbie.

He smiled at her, an easy, relaxed smile that spread slowly across his handsome face.

'For you, madam,' he said, handing her a champagne flute. 'Mind if I join you?'

'Oh, a naked waiter? I've never had such thorough service before,' she giggled. 'Please do.'

He stepped into the deep bathtub and slid down behind her, wrapping his strong arms and legs around her and stroking her wet skin softly, kissing her neck gently, so that she felt completely enveloped by him.

'Do you think we stand a chance?' she asked him hopefully.

Robbie sighed in her ear and she felt his body deflate.

Oh no, she'd said the wrong thing, let herself wish for too much. Francesca wished she'd never asked the question. She knew the answer. How could it work? Yes, they were perfect together, here in their bubble. But in the real world? No. It was impossible. How could they have a future together?

'I don't know,' he said, a little sadly. 'I want it to. I would love it to. But you're married, we live in different countries, we both have kids to consider. Maybe one day, Fran. Maybe our time will come, you know? If we're patient ...'

'Who knows the future.' Francesca forced herself to smile, even though her heart ached.

'Who knows the future,' Robbie repeated. 'Let's drink to that.'

Francesca turned round to face him and clinked her glass against his. The future. It was a blank page. It hadn't been written yet and until it had been they still had a chance, Francesca and her Robbie. God, she was falling for him hard. He was her little ray of hope in the middle of a dark world.

She was leaving him again. Just like she always did. On her terms and at her convenience. Carlo didn't want her to go. He wanted her to stay here in his apartment all night. Hell, he wanted her to stay for ever. He knew he was being toyed with but he couldn't help himself. When it came to Sasha Constantine he had no will power to fight back.

'Can I have your—' he started as she opened the apartment door.

Sasha spun round and put her finger on his lips. Her nails were long and painted bright red.

'No, Carlo,' she said. 'You know the score. No ownership, no promises, no future and definitely no phone number.'

'But I thought ...?' Carlo tried to keep the desperation

out of his voice. This was the third time she'd done it now and he didn't understand. Why did she want to screw him but not want anything more?

She got up on her tiptoes and kissed him lightly on the lips. He could smell her perfume. The scent of oranges and vanilla mixed with the pungent aroma of sex. He kissed her back, passionately, hard. He wanted to stay there for ever, lost in her beauty. But she pulled away.

'So, I won't be seeing you for a while,' she said breezily, tossing her hair off her face. 'I'm off straight after the Grand Prix. Back to my folks' place in the Hamptons for the summer. I won't be back in Monaco till the fall, Carlo baby. Try not to miss me too much. *Ciao!*'

And then she sashayed off down the corridor, out of his life again, for months this time, without a backward glance. Carlo's heart lurched after her but his feet stayed firmly on the ground. He wanted to run after her, to stop her. But he knew there was no point. She didn't want him. She'd made that crystal clear. He watched her go and had to fight the urge to cry. A whole summer without Sasha! The thought was unbearable.

Francesca had to leave, like Cinderella, at midnight. She had to get back to the house in case her children woke up and needed her there. Robbie understood. He thought about his girls and wondered if they were missing him like he was missing them.

He watched Fran slip on her shoes and brush her hair. He was intoxicated by her. Everything about her fascinated him. The way she moved, the sound of her voice, the tilt of her head. He wanted her with every molecule in his body, but could he have her? No. It was ridiculous. There were too many barriers in their way. Would she even want to know him in the morning, once the tabloids had landed on her front doormat? Hmm, he was scared. He'd been so wary for years, since Heather had left. He'd wrapped his heart in cotton wool, never letting any woman close, terrified of getting hurt again. But Francesca could hurt him. He knew that already. He was in way fucking deeper than he'd ever thought he would be. Deeper than he had been with Heather. Fran blew his mind. It seemed crazy after such a short time, but he was pretty sure he had fallen in love with her. And didn't love conquer all? So maybe, one day? Who knew the future? It was their mantra now. Their only way of getting their heads round the situation.

Tomorrow Dan's story would be headline news and Fran would have to deal with more scandal surrounding her father's disappearance. Fatty had been front-page news all week. A few ex-lovers and hookers had come forward to the tabloids already, selling their stories about Fatty's sexpertise, and speculation about his dodgy business deals had been spread over columns and columns in the broadsheets. But this time Fran would get dragged in.

The news of William's affair with Jade would be a terrible shock to her. He believed her when she said she didn't love the man, but he was still her husband and the father of her children. She'd be horrified. And then a selfish thought crept into Robbie's mind. Would she leave him now? Francesca could be free of William soon. He found himself wondering if William's affair could be a good thing. Would it be easier for him and Fran to be together? No! He was fantasising again. Keep real, Robbie. There were still four children, two divorces, a gaping social divide and a thousand miles between Edinburgh and Monaco to keep them apart.

Robbie felt disloyal and guilty, sitting there, watching Fran getting dressed, knowing what she didn't know about

William and Jade and her father. Part of him wanted to warn her – about the story, about her dad's shady past. Christ, maybe Fran was in danger too. She was second in command at LaFata International and with Fatty gone, his girl was first in the firing line for anyone who thought the LaFatas owed them money.

'Fran,' he started tentatively. 'If I find out things, you know, about your dad ...'

She lifted her hand. 'No, Robbie,' she said, not angrily, but definitely. 'Don't tell me anything. Ever. It's the only way this can work. I'll never mention Dad in front of you and you never ask me anything about him. I thought we'd agreed that.'

'We did,' Robbie nodded. 'But there are all these stories, rumours and questions. And not just about your dad ... '

But she interrupted him before he could warn her.

'I'm a big girl, Robbie.' She smiled at him now to show him she wasn't cross but she looked determined to make her point. 'I can handle whatever they say about him. I know he was no angel, but he was my dad and I loved him, whatever he did. Please don't worry about me. You don't have to protect me from the truth. I don't need you to save me. Just be there for me, OK? My new best friend, remember.'

'OK,' he agreed. 'Best friend with benefits. I'll sign up for that!'

That bit was easy. Being with Fran took no effort at all. It came as naturally to him as breathing. And saving her? Well, he hoped it would never come to that but, as they said, who knew the future?

Chapter Thirty-Two

Christian's mood lifted the minute he walked onto Amar's gigantic superyacht. Amar was so rich that he could probably have bought up the whole of Cannes and thrown in Antibes and Juan-les-Pins for good measure, even now, during the film festival, stars and all. There was not one but three Rolls-Royce Phantoms parked in a neat row outside, and a very shiny green helicopter sat on the helipad, having just dropped off Beyoncé and Jay-Z. A pretty pink Porsche was wrapped in a huge pink ribbon on the deck.

'Christian, my friend,' shouted Amar, appearing through the crowds like a messiah, in a pristine white tux. He wore enormous, pimp-style shades, even though it was after midnight, and enough bling around his neck, on his wrists and in his ears, to pay off Britain's national debt twice over.

He caught Christian looking at the Porsche and launched straight into one of his monologues. Amar was, and always had been, the most talkative person Christian had ever met. He barely drew breath once he got going.

'I see you've spotted the pink pussy Porsche. My little joke.' He spoke very quickly and excitedly, patting his schoolfriend on the back. 'A prize for the best pole dance tonight. I've had a pole put up on the dance floor just for a laugh. The girls are loving it. And the boys seem to be enjoying it too, if you know what I mean. I think Kate

Moss has probably got it covered, she did such a good job in that White Stripes video, d'you remember? But Angelica LaFata's doing a pretty good job of it too. She's off her face, bless her. Very good value she's being this evening, very good value indeed.'

He pushed Christian through the crowds of Hollywood stars here for the festival, Formula One drivers here for the Grand Prix, handsome young billionaires here for the ride, and leggy young blondes here for the billionaires. And still Amar kept talking.

'And, oh my God, Chris, Angelica's mother, Sandrine! She's been having a go at pole dancing too and it's hilarious. She thinks she's still got it but it is cringeworthy, I'm telling you, absolutely the most hilarious thing you have ever seen. The woman must be like, fifty or something, hard to tell under all that plastic surgery obviously, but she's ancient, and she's got her boyfriend with her. Now, when I say boy, I mean boy! He's younger than us I reckon, but nowhere near as good-looking, of course. Come. Come. This way. Where's Carlo, by the way? Haven't seen him all week. Mind you, I suppose he does have rather a lot on his plate at the moment. God, can you believe it about Fatty? What a shocker! Hasn't stopped Angelica though. On top form to-night, our Angel. Absolutely top, top form! She's a trouper that one, a real trouper.'

So Angelica was here. Christian found himself straightening his shirt and brushing his hands through his hair as he followed Amar, deeper and deeper into the glittering party.

'Scarlett Johansson's here somewhere,' Amar was saying now. 'Looking totally bloody amazing. You've got the hots for her haven't you, Chris? I'll introduce you if you like ...'

But Christian didn't care about Scarlett Johansson any

more. Not now he knew *she* was here. Angel. His Angel. He carried on following Amar, straining his neck to see if he could spot her in the crowd. He squeezed past Lewis Hamilton and Nicole Scherzinger and climbed over Nicholas Cage's outstretched legs. Flavio Briatore was holding court to a gaggle of young models to the left, while Roman Abramovich chatted to three sons of Russian oligarchs on his right, and then, there in the middle of it all was Angel.

Christian's jaw almost hit the deck. She was wrapped around a pole in the middle of the room, surrounded by a crowd of slobbering men of various ages. Her strapless dress had slipped down to her slim waist, so that she slithered, topless, around the pole. Her eye make-up was heavy and black and it had begun to run down her beautiful face in the heat of the party. Her long blonde hair fell in heavy curtains down her skinny shoulders, brushing her naked breasts as she wriggled and gyrated. Christian watched in horror as she licked her lips provocatively, threw her head back and sighed as if she were in the throes of an orgasm. She had a weird, fixed smile on her face, but her eyes had died. The lights had been switched off. There was nothing going on behind those huge baby blues and it made Christian want to cry.

'Excuse me, Amar,' he said, knowing he was being rude but not caring about anyone except Angelica.

He pushed past the leering, jeering men and reached Angel just as she started to unzip her dress.

'Angelica, what the hell are you doing?' he asked, trying to grab her arm. 'Stop this!'

'Christian!' she shouted above the music. 'I'm good, aren't I? Unzip me, Christian. I'm gonna dance naked.'

'No,' said Christian. 'Come down from there, you're behaving like a stripper, Angel.'

'I ain't nobody's angel!' she laughed, manically, wriggling out of her dress without Christian's help, and tossing it into the crowd. 'I'm a bad girl, Christian. D'you know that? A bad, bad girl.'

She was naked now, except for a tiny red thong and a pair of five-inch leopard-print mules. There were times when Christian would have given his entire inheritance to catch a glimpse of Angelica LaFata naked, but not here, not now, not like this.

'Come on, Angel,' he shouted, taking off his jacket and trying to hand it to her. 'Please. Put some clothes on. Get down.'

The men watching Angelica were getting annoyed with Christian now, booing him and telling him to piss off out of the way.

'Yeah, piss off, Christian,' shouted Angel. 'You're just as boring as fucking Carlo these days. What is it? Are you gay? Don't you want to see my body?'

She circled her nipple with her finger and looked at him with her dead eyes. Christian shook his head in disgust and walked away. He found Sandrine in a corner, snogging her toyboy like a teenager at the school disco.

'Sandrine.' Christian tapped her on the shoulder. 'Sandrine!'

Sandrine turned round and pouted at him with her in-flated trout mouth.

'Christian,' she said. 'Christian, darling, I am very busy, can't you see this? Where are your manners? Your mother, she did not bring you up like this.'

'Sandrine, I'm sorry to interrupt you but have you seen Angelica?' demanded Christian.

'*Mais oui, oui!*' replied Sandrine cheerfully. 'She is sexy, *non*? She is very good at entertaining the boys. Just like her mother.'

'Sandrine, she's taken her dress off. Look! She's naked.'

Sandrine craned her neck to see her daughter. 'Oh, how funny,' she simpered. 'Angelica is being a tease. Ah, but she has a beautiful body. Where is the harm?'

Christian couldn't believe his ears. What sort of mother would encourage her daughter to behave like this?

'Sandrine, she's obviously high.' He talked slowly and clearly so that there could be no doubt about what he was saying. 'She doesn't look well. I'm worried about her.'

'Oh, Christian, Christian,' soothed Sandrine, brushing Christian's cheek with her taloned fingers. 'You have always been such a serious boy. Angelica is fine. She is just having fun. Maybe you need to loosen up a bit and have some fun too, *non*?'

And then she turned back to her toyboy and thrust her tongue down his throat again. Christian didn't know what to do. He wished Carlo was here, or Francesca, she would take charge. Angelica was obviously on the edge but he felt helpless to do anything about it. He could hardly drag her off the dance floor kicking and screaming. He grabbed a glass of champagne from a passing waiter, and waited and watched from afar as Angelica's routine got more and more pornographic and the crowd went more and more wild.

Now she was playing with her thong, teasing her audience of lecherous creeps, pinging the tiny string of fabric on her thigh. Christian necked his champagne and fought back tears of anger. How did it come to this? What happened to the cute little girl who used to hide in Carlo's cupboard? Where had Angel gone? Christian didn't even recognise the girl dancing naked in the middle of the room.

And now she was pulling down her thong, stepping out

of it, revealing her Hollywood wax to the world. The crowd went wild but Christian felt sick. She looked so skinny, and young, and vulnerable, like a fawn surrounded by hunters.

'No, Angelica!' he shouted across the room. But she couldn't hear him over the music and the chanting of the crowd. He pushed and shoved his way through the heaving bodies, desperately trying to reach her, but the ogling men had closed in tight and he couldn't even see Angelica now. And then suddenly the cheering stopped and an eerie 'Ohhh ...' echoed around the room. The crowd loosened its grip on the pole and Christian managed to shove his way to the front, just in time to see Angel's body slither down the pole and fall in a crumpled heap on the floor.

'Angel!' Christian yelled. 'Angel!'

He bent down to touch her but her body shuddered suddenly and then convulsed. And then his beautiful Angel started fitting, with her eyes rolled back in their sockets and foam bubbling from the corner of her mouth. A trickle of blood dripped from her nose.

'Oh Jesus Christ!' Christian shouted. 'Is there a doctor here? We need a doctor! Please! Please!'

One of the leggy blondes came forward, in a tight white cocktail dress, and bent down beside Angel.

'I'm a nurse,' she said calmly, taking Christian's jacket from him and placing it under Angelica's shuddering head. 'She's having a seizure. Has this happened before? Is she epileptic?'

'No,' said Christian. 'She's a drug addict. That's what's wrong with her.'

'OK,' said the nurse, still calm. 'Everybody stand back. Give her space.'

The nurse stroked Angel's hair and spoke quietly and soothingly to her. The trickle of blood had turned into a deep, red pool that stained the nurse's white dress. Gradually the fitting stopped, her arms and legs were still, and her eyes rolled back into place. She moaned like an injured animal and stared up at Christian with a terrified look on her face.

'I'm scared, Christian,' she whispered. 'Please help me. Please help me. I don't want to die.'

And then her eyes closed and she was completely still.

'Angel,' said Christian desperately. 'Angel?'

He shook her bony shoulder and tried to rouse her but there was no response.

'What's wrong with her?' he asked the nurse, panic-stricken. 'Why won't she wake up?'

'We've got to get her to hospital. Is she your girlfriend?' she asked.

'No,' Christian shook his head. 'She's an old, old friend. I've known her since she was a little girl. Please God, don't let anything happen to Angel. Tell me she's going to be OK.'

'I can't tell you that,' said the nurse. 'We need to get her to hospital straight away.'

'Take my helicopter,' said Amar, appearing out of the crowds. 'I'll call the hospital, tell them you're on your way.'

'Can we take her back to Monaco?' asked Christian, hopefully. 'She needs to be at home.'

The nurse held Angel's wrists and took her pulse and then she nodded. 'Her pulse is weak but she's breathing. How long will it take to get to Monaco, Amar?' she asked.

'Fifteen minutes,' he replied. 'Shall I call Carlo?'

'Yes please,' said Christian, wiping a stray tear from his cheek. 'Tell him to go straight to the Princess Grace Hospital.'

*

316

Carlo ran through the corridors with his heart pumping in his chest and a lump in his throat. Frankie had said they had to leave Angel to hit rock bottom on her own but she was wrong. They should never have gambled with their sister's life. It was too precious. He should have gone to Cannes, he could have stopped this. He slid round a corner at breakneck speed and bumped straight into Christian, who was pacing the corridor looking wrung-out and grey-faced. Christian's coffee spilled all over both of them, burning their hands and splattering their white shirts with stains, but neither of them flinched.

'Shit, sorry, Chris,' said Carlo. 'Where is she? Is she OK?'

Christian swallowed hard and nodded his head towards a closed door. Carlo could see that Christian had been crying and for a moment he thought the worst.

'She's in there with the doctors now,' Christian replied. 'She's unconscious. They said it's serious but she's stable. We've to wait out here. They'll let us know if there's any change. Oh God, Carlo, I'm so sorry. I tried my best but she was already in a terrible state when I got there.'

So she was alive, at least. Carlo had barely been able to breathe as he'd driven to the hospital, terrified that his kid sister would be dead by the time he got there. All Amar had said on the phone was that Angelica had collapsed and had some sort of fit on the yacht. He said she'd been unconscious when Christian and a nurse, who'd happened to be at the party, had taken her by helicopter to Monaco. Now he peered through the tiny glass window on the door and caught a glimpse of a skinny little body, hooked up to tubes and machines. Then the curtain was drawn abruptly in front of him and Angel disappeared.

'What's wrong with her? An overdose?' asked Carlo desperately, chewing his nails.

Christian nodded. 'Looks that way but they're waiting for the tox results.'

Carlo flopped down on a hard, straight-backed chair and buried his head in his hands. The tears came hard and fast, soaking his face and stinging his eyes. Christian sat down beside him and patted his knee.

'All we can do is wait,' he said.

'I'm sick of waiting,' sobbed Carlo, his shoulders shaking. 'I can't take this any more, Chris. I'm not strong enough.'

'Yes you are,' said Christian. 'You bloody well are, Carlo.'

But he wasn't. He knew he wasn't. It was all too much. Carlo felt like he was going to explode. He heard the brisk, clip-clip of Francesca's heels before she appeared round the corner, looking distraught.

'What's going on?' she asked. 'Where's Angel?'

Carlo stood up and stared at his sister. Saint Francesca, who'd told him he had to leave Angelica to rot. The tears were still streaming down his face and a tight fireball of anger burned in his stomach.

'She's in there, getting emergency medical treatment because she's damn well OD'd, Frankie!' he shouted. 'And it's all your fault. You said we needed to let her go. Well, look what's happened. You've probably killed her!'

He pushed Francesca's shoulder so that she stumbled backwards and banged against the wall opposite. She stared at him in confusion and pain.

'Carlo, stop this,' said Christian, standing up and pulling him back from his sister. 'It's not Francesca's fault.'

'Yes it is!' shouted Carlo. 'I wanted to stop her going to Cannes.'

Francesca rubbed her head where she'd banged it against the wall. She looked so tired and distressed that Carlo felt almost guilty for being angry with her. But she'd said Angelica would be OK. And she wasn't. She wasn't OK at all. She was in there now with tubes coming out of her and machines monitoring her heartbeat.

'No, he's right, Christian,' said Frankie weakly. 'It is my fault. It's all my fault.'

She sat on a chair on the other side of the corridor and stared blankly into space. Christian and Carlo sat opposite in pained silence. Carlo chewed his nails until his fingers bled. Every now and then a doctor or nurse would come out of Angelica's room and hurry past, head down, avoiding eye contact with the family. Nobody spoke. They had nothing to say.

They sat there all night, the three of them. Christian offered coffee and water every now and then, but otherwise none of them spoke. Francesca didn't blame Carlo for being angry with her. She didn't blame him at all. She'd thought that Angelica needed to work things out for herself but the poor kid had been in no fit state for that. She'd gone too far down the road to self-destruction to see anything clearly. She'd needed Francesca's help but Francesca had turned a blind eye. Why? Why, after all those years of being the one to catch her, why had Francesca chosen now to stand back and let her fall? She sat on her chair and silently beat herself up.

It was just getting light when Sandrine arrived with her boyfriend and her film crew in tow. Francesca felt her blood boil as Angel's mother teetered along the corridor towards her, dressed to kill in a scarlet pencil skirt, wiping crocodile tears from her cheeks and throwing devastated looks at the camera.

'Where is my baby?!' she wailed, throwing her arms open wide. 'What has happened to my poor little Angel?'

Francesca could see from the frowns on Christian and Carlo's faces that they were no more impressed by Sandrine's act of despair than she was.

'Oh, now you come, Mum,' said Carlo coldly.

Francesca noticed that he couldn't even look at his mother. He spat his words out, still staring at his feet.

'We've been sitting here for hours, you were there at the party when this happened. So why have you taken so long to arrive?' he demanded.

'Oh, *mon chéri*, Carlo. Do not speak to me like that. I know you are upset but I had things to do. See, I have bought Angel some flowers,' said Sandrine, holding up a bunch of pink roses.

'Yeah, well, they'll be a big help to her now, won't they, Mum?' responded Carlo sharply. 'She's not even conscious. Where have you been anyway?'

'Oh, here and there,' replied Sandrine vaguely.

'She had to go home to change and then she had to wait for her film crew,' muttered Christian.

'*Mon dieu!*' Sandrine threw Christian an affronted glare. 'Carlo, are you going to let him speak to me like that, your mother?'

'Yes,' said Carlo, eyes still fixed to the floor. 'Look, Mum, just bugger off back to St Tropez. No one wants you here. You're not welcome.'

'Giancarlo!' screeched Sandrine. 'You will not talk like that! Did I carry you in my womb for nine months for you to speak to me in this way? *Non!*'

'You might have carried me for nine months but that's the last thing you ever did to help me,' spat Carlo. 'And Angel. What the hell have you ever done for her? Except to encourage her to go off the rails? You were there last night. You saw how she was behaving and you did nothing.

Christian was the one who helped her. Christian, some nurse, a total stranger, and Amar. You? You did fuck all! You're a total waste of space. Now go. Just go and take that film crew with you. You're an embarrassment. I'm ashamed to have you as a mother.'

'I will not have this, Carlo!' screamed Sandrine at the top of her voice. '*Bâtard! Ingrat bâtard!*'

And then she started hitting her son over the head with the roses, over and over again until pink petals flew around the hospital corridor like confetti. Francesca looked on in horror. Poor Carlo. To have a mother like that. Poor Angelica. No wonder they'd always turned to Francesca for love and support. They had no one else. And she'd let them down. She'd been so tied up with Dad and her own life – the business, Robbie – that she'd shoved them both down her list of priorities. Francesca stood up and faced Sandrine. It was time to take back control. She had never been violent before in her life, but now she grabbed the older woman roughly by the shoulders. She was a good four inches taller than Sandrine in stockinged feet, and now, still wearing her highest heels after her date with Robbie, she towered above her. She backed Sandrine up against the wall, adrenalin pumping through her veins, and pinned her there with her hands either side of her.

'Look, Sandrine,' she said coldly, her face barely an inch from Sandrine's. 'Do as Carlo says. Go home. You're an absolute disgrace.'

'Hmph, you do not tell me what to do, Francesca,' Sandrine hissed back. 'I will go nowhere. Angelica is my daughter and I will stay.'

Francesca glanced at Carlo. He sat on his chair in shocked silence, picking rose thorns from his scalp. A trickle of blood meandered down his forehead and into his eyebrow.

Francesca gave Sandrine one last shove and then let her go. She bent down beside Carlo and gently wiped the blood from his eye.

'I'm sorry, Carlo,' she said softly. 'For letting Angel down. I'll never do it again, I promise.'

He stopped picking at his scalp and buried his head in her arms. She held him there for the longest time as he cried.

Eventually a doctor appeared from Angelica's room. They all watched him warily as he took off his glasses and glanced down at his clipboard. Francesca held her breath. He had all their hopes in his hands.

'I am Dr Schneider,' he introduced himself in a clipped German accent, nodding at each of them individually and then stopping and frowning at the cameraman. 'Please turn off the camera immediately.'

The cameraman did as he was told. Dr Schneider did not look like a man to be messed with.

'Angelica is stable now,' said Dr Schneider with a heavy sigh. 'But she has had a difficult night. When she first arrived she had another seizure and stopped breathing. She was clinically dead for almost a minute before we managed to resuscitate her.'

Francesca squeezed Carlo's hand as she listened. He squeezed back, harder.

'The tox reports show that she'd taken a considerable amount of cocaine and ecstasy, mixed with high levels of alcohol. Her blood pressure and heart rate were abnormally high but we have those under control now. She also had severe respiratory problems when she arrived. We are still very concerned about organ failure as neither her kidneys nor her liver are working effectively at present. She will need to stay in hospital for some time. Angelica is a very sick, frail young woman but she is lucky to be alive and so, for that, we must all be grateful.'

'Thank you, doctor,' said Francesca. 'Is she conscious? Can we see her?'

'Your sister is sleeping. She is sedated, Ms LaFata,' explained the doctor. 'It would be best if you all went home and had some rest. You will be informed when she is conscious and ready for visitors. Thank you for your patience. Goodbye.'

And then he hurried off down the corridor with his head buried in his notes and left the family alone.

'Ah, so she is OK,' said Sandrine breezily. 'We can go home. *Allons-y!*'

Carlo stood up and glared at his mother. 'OK? Angelica is OK?' he roared.

Francesca put her hand on his arm to calm him but he carried on.

'She stopped breathing, Mum. How the hell is that OK?' he demanded.

'I have had enough of your behaviour, Giancarlo,' snapped Sandrine. 'I am in no mood for your tantrums. I almost lost my daughter last night. Have you no respect for a mother's grief?'

'Oh my God!' roared Carlo. 'You are unbelievable. Un-bloody-believable!'

He lunged after his mother but Christian and Francesca hauled him back.

'Let her go, Carlo,' said Francesca, watching Sandrine wiggle her way down the corridor followed by her minions. 'She's not worth it.'

They waited five minutes for Carlo to calm down. Francesca knew it was best to give Sandrine time to leave. The mood Carlo was in, he was likely to strangle her if he had to face her again. The doctors let them watch Angelica through the tiny window in the door for a few moments. It broke Francesca's heart to see her baby sister that way, wired up to machines, unconscious, with her mouth gaping open. Her skin was grey and she had black circles round her eyes. She was still breathing but she looked like a corpse. Francesca shuddered at the thought of what might have been.

'Come on,' she said to Carlo and Christian. 'Let's go.'

They walked slowly out of the hospital together, Francesca in the middle, flanked by her two strong boys.

'The bloody press are here,' muttered Christian, as they approached the exit.

'Keep your heads down and ignore whatever they ask,' said Francesca.

Of course the press were here. Angelica's life always made the news and now her near-death experience would surely make the front page.

'She'd like this,' said Carlo, smiling sadly. 'She loves attention.'

And then they were in the throng of the photographers, being jostled and pushed as they tried to make their way through the car park.

'How is Angelica?' demanded the strangers.

'Is she going to pull through?'

'Was it an overdose?'

'Was it a suicide attempt?'

The trio kept their heads down and fought their way through.

'Had she heard about your father's sexual perversions?' shouted a balding man.

'Ignore them,' repeated Francesca, trying to block out the paparazzi.

They'd printed so much rubbish about her father that

week that she was beginning to feel immune to their questions. This must have been what Robbie was trying to warn her about last night. Another ridiculous story from one of her dad's old flames, no doubt.

'What about your husband, Francesca?' shouted a tall red-headed man. 'Did you know about his affair with Jade LaFata?'

The words took a long time to sink into Francesca's brain. What the hell? What were they talking about? William and Jade? It was ridiculous. She glanced at Carlo and he looked back at her blankly, obviously confused. Francesca stared at her feet, willing them to keep moving.

'Where is William Hillier?' demanded a female voice. 'Have you confronted him about the affair?'

Francesca's head spun. When she looked up she could see her car a few metres away but her legs had gone to jelly and she wasn't sure she could make it.

'Did Jade's suicide have something to do with her affair with your husband?' asked a man's voice.

'What's going on?' Francesca whispered to Carlo desperately.

'I don't know,' he replied, clutching her elbow and leading her towards her car.

Christian forged ahead, pushing the paparazzi out of the way and clearing a path.

'Is it true that your husband has disappeared with the LaFata fortune?' asked another journalist.

'My head's spinning,' Francesca whispered to Carlo. 'I think I'm going to faint.'

'No, Frankie,' he said gently. 'You're going to be OK. Ignore them, remember. That's what you told me.'

Christian and Carlo bundled Francesca into the passenger seat and then jumped in themselves.

'I'll drive,' said Carlo. 'I'll leave my car here and collect it later.'

He revved the engine loudly, beeped the horn and raced through the throng of journalists. Francesca stared out of the window at their shouting faces, blinking as the cameras flashed and trying to make sense of this mad, mad world.

'I need to call William,' she said, fishing in her handbag with shaking hands. 'I need to know what's going on.'

There was a text waiting. She checked it first.

Just heard about Angelica. I am so sorry, my darling, I hope she's OK. You may have heard about today's story by now. Call me when you get the chance. I'm thinking about you. R xxx

But Robbie and his kisses would have to wait. She dialled William as Carlo thrashed the car through the streets of Monaco, although she had absolutely no idea what to say to him when he replied. William and Jade? Surely not! What would Jade have seen in him? But, then again, there had been those cosy cups of tea ... And what was that they'd said about him disappearing with the LaFata fortune? He was in London for a meeting. He'd be back tomorrow. What sort of fantasy world did these journalists live in? She waited with bated breath for William's phone to ring. She waited and waited. But the line was dead.

Chapter Thirty-Three

Robbie stared at his computer screen, reading and rereading his notes. He had so much dirt on Giancarlo LaFata that he could write a novel on the guy, let alone a news story. But did he have the nerve? It was open season on the entire LaFata family in the press this week. Fact or fiction, it didn't seem to matter, every newspaper ran at least two LaFata stories each day. Fatty had been accused of everything from extortion to perversion. But Robbie's story was different. Robbie was practically accusing the man of murder. So, what did he do? His head said 'publish and be damned'. But his heart said, 'What about Francesca?'

He glanced at his phone for the fiftieth time that morning. She still hadn't rung, or even texted him back. Robbie knew that Angelica LaFata had overdosed at the party in Cannes. Christ, how could he not know when Dan and Simon had been there to witness the whole thing? Dan had called him earlier and filled him in on all the gory details – the naked pole dance, the convulsions, the blood dripping out of her nose. It sounded horrendous. He wondered if Fran was still at the hospital. He wondered if she'd seen Dan's story yet. He wondered if she was coping. He wondered if she wished he were there to wrap his arms around her.

Robbie called Dan's mobile. He'd been camped outside the Princess Grace Hospital all night, keeping vigil with the rest of the tabloid press.

'Hey, Robster,' Dan answered chirpily. 'How's it going?'

'Fine, fine,' lied Robbie. 'Just wondered what was going on at the hospital. Being nosy really …'

'Och, I'm back in town now. It was a bit of an anticlimax in the end. Angelica's going to pull through apparently. Close call by all accounts though. The family left an hour or so ago. I felt awful for that poor Francesca. She'd been in there all night, obviously worried sick about her sister, and then she walks out and gets bombarded with questions about her husband's affair with her dad's wife!'

'Dan,' replied Robbie patiently. 'You were the one who wrote that story. So you should feel awful!'

Christ, if only Dan knew how close to home this all was. Robbie imagined Fran having to face those questions and his heart broke for her.

'I don't feel guilty,' retorted Dan. 'Not one bit. I was just doing my job. And how was I to know that her sister was going to OD before the story hit the news-stands? Nah, I just felt bad cos her perfect life's been totally screwed up in the matter of a week and she seems like the nice one, that's all.'

'So, no dirt on Fran, um, erm, Francesca, then?' probed Robbie hopefully. He couldn't bear it if Dan started writing lies about her.

'Not a speck of dust,' replied Dan firmly. 'The woman's a saint in a family of sinners.'

'That's what I thought,' said Robbie, smiling to himself. 'Right, I'd better get back to work. See you this evening for our gambling session.'

'I cannot wait, Mr McLean,' said Dan. 'I'm feeling lucky!'

*

Francesca had called every single one of their London business contacts. She'd tried their lawyers, their accountants, their largest shareholders and their bank manager and no one had seen William. Nobody had even heard he was coming to town. There had been no meeting in London this week, emergency or otherwise. He'd lied to her and now she knew why. Her emotions swung from anger to despair and stopped at everything in between. She thought she knew William. Dependable, reliable, boring bloody William! Or not so boring bloody William as it turned out. According to the press, her darling husband had been screwing her dad's wife for months and the pair had been planning to run away together.

Well, at least the guilt about Robbie had gone. What she had done to William was nothing in comparison to what he'd done to her. Especially if the papers were to be believed and he'd run off with what little was left of the money. And William had known about Dubrovski! Francesca's hands began to shake at the thought. She was screwed. She was totally bloody screwed this time. Her husband had effectively left her to die. God, he must have hated her. What the hell did she do to deserve that? And what sort of man leaves his children in such danger? There was no way she could raise the money now.

Carlo leant against the door, watching her and running his hands through his hair anxiously.

'What can I do, Frankie?' he asked. 'Can I call anyone for you?'

Francesca thought for a moment. She was terrified, she was exhausted, she was heartbroken and she was desperate, but she was not going to lie down and die. It was all down to her now. Her children were depending on her and she was not going to let them down. Not without a fight.

'Yes,' she said, throwing her personal organiser at him. 'You call every airline you can think of and see if he took a flight anywhere. I'm going to find the lying bastard and string him up by the balls. But first, I'm calling the police.'

'The police?' said Carlo, his eyebrows shooting up in surprise. 'But having an affair's not a criminal offence, Frankie. I know you're angry and hurt but you can't have William arrested for shagging Jade.'

'No,' she replied, taking a deep breath and trying to stay calm. 'I can't have him arrested for adultery, or for sleeping with his mother-in-law, and to be honest I don't give a damn who he's been sticking it into. The marriage has been over for years.'

'It has?' asked Carlo, clearly surprised.

'It has,' confirmed Francesca. 'But I can have him arrested for theft.'

'Theft?' Carlo looked at her quizzically. 'But that's all nonsense, the stuff about him running off with the family fortune, isn't it?'

Francesca stared at her laptop, trying to make sense of the various accounts and bank balances she'd brought up on screen.

'No, he hasn't taken much in the grand scheme of things. Dad did a much better job of blowing the billions. But William's emptied our joint bank account,' she said solemnly. 'And it looks as if he's helped himself to approximately, let me see …'

She added up the totals quickly in her head.

'About seven million euros in total from the company.' She shook her head in disbelief and disgust. 'From right under my nose, Carlo. He's my husband. He's stolen from me, from all of us! He's had an affair with Dad's wife and now he's run off and left us to stew. He's got two little boys here. He's just upped and left them. What sort of man would do that?'

'I don't know, Frankie,' said Carlo despondently. 'It feels like nobody's who they seemed to be.'

Francesca smiled at her little brother weakly. 'Well, I haven't changed, sweetheart,' she said. 'I'm still your bossy cow of a big sister, so go off and make those calls for me, please. I need peace to get on here. Give me an hour and then we'll go back to the hospital and check on Angel.'

Carlo nodded and left the room. Francesca closed the door behind him and dialled Robbie's number.

'Fran!' He picked up after one ring.

She wondered if he'd been waiting for her call. She hoped so. She'd been dying to speak to him all morning.

'Are you OK? Oh God, stupid question, of course you're not. What's going on? Have you spoken to William? How's Angelica?' He fired questions at her.

'Whoah,' she said. 'One thing at a time, Robbie.'

'Sorry,' he said. 'But I've been worrying about you all night and I felt helpless because I couldn't do anything.'

'You do help,' she replied honestly. 'Just having you in my life helps.'

'Thank you, but I doubt that's true right this minute. So, first things first. Angelica – how is she?'

'Well, we could have lost her,' sighed Francesca, 'but we didn't. And she's in the right place. In fact she's much safer in hospital than she was on her own in Cannes, so we're just keeping our fingers crossed and hoping for a speedy recovery.'

'That's good,' said Robbie. 'And you? How are you bearing up with all this business about William?'

'Honestly?' she asked. 'If I could get my hands on the

lying, cheating, thieving bastard, I would wring his bloody neck. But I have no idea where he is ...'

And then she stopped mid-sentence. Robbie was a journalist. He was her lover and her best friend, but he was still a journalist – the enemy.

'I can't talk to you about this, Robbie,' she explained. 'You can be there for me but you can't ask any details, OK? You're a journalist.'

'I wasn't asking as a journalist.' Robbie sounded offended. 'I was asking because ...'

The line went quiet for a few seconds.

'I was asking because I love you, Fran,' he said finally. 'That's all.'

Her heart melted and she found herself smiling despite the desperate situation she found herself in. For years she'd had everything she wanted – money, power, a career, status. Everything except love. Now she had nothing. It had all been washed away. But finally, out of the blue, she'd found that one elusive missing ingredient. Love.

'I love you too, Robbie,' she said softly.

Frankie was busy with the police, telling them everything she knew about William's movements. She seemed determined to find her husband and make him pay. Carlo didn't blame her. He'd never been a big fan of William. It wasn't that he hated the guy. No. It was more like indifference. He'd never really given William a second thought. He was just always there, in the background, never making much of an impact on Carlo's life. Oh, but he'd made an impact now. Seven million euros' worth of impact! And none of them had seen it coming. Not even Frankie. They said it was always the quiet ones ...

Carlo decided to go back to the hospital on his own.

He'd called every airline he could think of and got precisely nowhere. They wouldn't give out passenger information over the phone. Carlo guessed Francesca would just have to leave it to the police to catch William. He popped his head round the door and told Frankie he was going to see Angel. She nodded and said she'd meet him there as soon as she was free.

He helped himself to his dad's old Aston Martin. Well, it wasn't as if Dad needed it any more, and he'd left the Lamborghini at the hospital that morning. It took almost an hour to travel the couple of miles to the Princess Grace Hospital. Monaco was bursting at the seams with crowds pouring in for the Grand Prix. The pre-qualifiers started today and many roads were blocked, ready for the race. Usually Carlo loved the Grand Prix weekend. It was the biggest event in the Monte Carlo social calendar and he looked forward to it like a child looks forward to Christmas. But this year he couldn't even begin to get excited. He doubted he ever would again. How could he ever enjoy it now, when it would always remind him of the worst time in his life?

The crowd of press at the hospital had shrunk to a small gaggle and Carlo found it easy to push them out of the way at the entrance. Fuck them! They were scum, all of them. And they had the nerve to judge his family! Journalists made him sick. They were nothing but parasites, feeding off other people's misery.

Angelica was still sleeping off the sedatives when Carlo arrived, but the doctors let him sit with her quietly, just holding her limp hand and stroking her tangled hair. He watched the gentle rise and fall of her chest and listened to the rhythmic beeping of the heart monitor, reassured that she was still alive, at least; broken but not destroyed. She was so much more precious than anything else he'd lost. His sister. His flesh and blood. Carlo would happily have given away his yacht, his car and his apartment for just five minutes in her company. He willed her to wake up and be his Angel again. Not the selfish junkie she'd become, but the sweet, funny little girl who'd followed him around when they were kids. He missed that Angel and he wanted her back.

He squeezed her hand and nearly jumped out of his skin as he felt her squeeze back. It was just the slightest hint of pressure, but it was definitely there.

'Angelica?' he said hopefully. 'Angelica?'

Her tongue moved in her open mouth, as if searching for her dry lips and then her head turned ever so slightly towards him.

'Angel? Baby?' he said. 'It's me, Carlo. I'm here.'

Her eyelids flickered but didn't open and her mouth moved but didn't make a sound. Carlo squeezed her hand again, more firmly this time, and again he felt the faintest squeeze back. He stroked her forehead and her cheeks, kissed her soft hair and whispered, 'Wake up, Angel. Wake up, darling.'

And then he heard her, very quietly, in a tiny, croaky voice.

'Carlo,' she murmured. 'Carlo.'

Her eyelids flickered again and her head turned sharply from left to right and then suddenly her enormous blue eyes were open wide. Carlo stared in wonder as his little sister came back to life. She looked half-dead, pale and far too thin, but she was awake and there was life in her eyes. He passed her a glass of water and held it to her cracked lips as she sipped, struggling to lift her head a millimetre off the pillow.

She looked straight at him and said 'Carlo,' in a tiny,

weak voice. 'I've been listening to my shoulders. I've decided the angel is right. I've told the devil to go to hell.'

She was rambling, making no sense, but she was conscious, at least.

'Ssh, Angel,' said Carlo softly. 'You rest, darling. Everything's going to be all right.'

And then he pushed the emergency button for the doctor to come.

James Sanderson was drunk. It was barely lunchtime, but the man who'd spent his entire life following strict routines and behaving admirably was bombed, blasted, plastered, pickled, gone. Man, his legs were so fried that he wasn't sure he'd be able to make it to the washroom and he had a horrible feeling that he might be about to throw up. But what the hell, another Scotch wouldn't hurt. It wasn't as if he had anything else to do …

Port Hercule was packed full of yachts and superyachts here for the Grand Prix. It was the busiest weekend of the year. He watched the crews busy themselves on their boats in the harbour and felt the anger and frustration burn in his stomach. They had a purpose, those guys, they were getting on with their work, with their lives and their routines. Man, he was jealous! James had no purpose any more. He knocked back his Scotch and ordered another. Why the hell not? What was a skipper without a yacht, eh? *Vigorosa III* had been seized by the police and it didn't look like the LaFata family would be getting her back any time soon, not if the stories in the press were to be believed. His boss was dead, drowned, he'd wash up soon somewhere down the coast, no doubt. And Fatty's kids had been left broke, or so the papers said. He felt for them, he really did, but what about James? He was completely redundant and what's more, he hadn't been paid this week. There was no frigging money to pay him, by all accounts.

He paid for the drinks, somehow, although he could no longer tell the difference between a fifty-euro note and a five-euro note. The barmaid swam in front of his eyes and the ground rocked beneath his feet and then he somehow managed to stumble to the loo before he threw up, violently, into a urinal. Urgh. James felt like death. He stared at his reflection in the mirror – he looked like shit and he looked old. What the fuck had he done with his life? Forty-nine years old and nothing to show for it. Well, screw that. He'd played it all safe, everything by the book, never missing a day's work, never calling in sick, never letting anyone down. And where had it got him? Precisely nowhere! Nah, it wasn't the good guys like James who won at the game of life, it was the chancers and the players. How could he have lived in Monaco for so long and not have noticed that before now? He should have learned from Fatty. That man had never played anything safe. He'd gambled and won, time and time again. OK, so maybe his good luck had finally run out, but, jeez, what a life the guy had led. He bet when Giancarlo LaFata was going down beneath those waves, with his whole life flashing before his eyes, he didn't regret a moment of it. Well, James was going to take a leaf out of his boss's book. Call it a tribute. Today, he would honour Fatty LaFata in fitting style.

The bank teller didn't look too impressed when he staggered up to the counter, but what the hell. It was his money, he was entitled to it, even if he was bombed out of his mind. He staggered up the hill towards the casino with his entire life savings stuffed into the back pocket of his jeans. Twenty-thousand euros; it wasn't much to show for a lifetime.

Chapter Thirty-Four

Robbie rushed back to the hotel to get ready for his lads' night out. He hadn't had time to watch the pre-qualifiers but he had had a very productive last day in Monaco, tying up loose ends and finding more evidence to back up his claims. He'd been speaking to a former detective who'd gone to Italy to investigate Darcie's death. The guy had found the whole thing very suspicious from the start – there had been bruising around Darcie's mouth and also on her wrists and arms. But he'd been warned to back off by 'friends' of Giancarlo LaFata and when the LaFata family had insisted on a private autopsy being done, the detective's superiors had allowed it to go ahead. The death was ruled as suicide and that was the end of the investigation. Not long afterwards, the detective claimed he'd been framed for tampering with evidence during an investigation into gambling irregularities, and he'd been sacked from the force. The guy was obviously bitter and had an axe to grind, but Robbie believed him when he said that Fatty LaFata had destroyed his career.

When Patterson phoned Robbie and grilled him about how it was going, he'd promised his boss that he'd be back at his desk tomorrow afternoon with the most scandalous, sensational crime story the paper had ever printed. And he'd meant it. He'd made up his mind now. He had to run with this story. It was too big to ignore, whatever the consequences. Publish and be damned. But Fran would understand, he felt sure of it.

Ah, Fran. Luscious, lovely Fran. He'd told her he loved her. It had just popped out, earlier, when he'd been talking to her on the phone. But he meant it. He really did. Maybe he was crazy. He could imagine what his friends would say if they knew. 'Have you gone soft in the head, Robbie?' But he wasn't mad. He was totally, completely and certainly sane. They told each other everything – well, *almost* everything – and he felt as if she understood him better than anybody. So of course she'd forgive him for doing his job. Wouldn't she?

He was desperate to see her before his flight home in the morning but life was conspiring against them. She'd been busy with the police all morning and busy at the hospital with her sister all afternoon. And now, tonight, he had this stupid casino night with the boys. Robbie would have blown them out in an instant but Fran had told him he should go.

No, you go, darling. I'm not great company tonight anyway. A is improving physically, but mentally she's in a state. And then there's W … But we can't discuss him. Maybe 1 day, when all this is over, I can ask you questions about your job and you can ask me questions about my family. I'll look forward to it! Have a good evening, don't lose all your money. Maybe we can meet for breakfast before your flight tomorrow? xxx

Breakfast was better than nothing, Robbie supposed. But an hour together was never going to be enough. The truth was he was dreading going home, back to Heather and the rain. He was dying to see the girls and give them a hug, but

338

seeing them meant leaving Fran, and that broke his heart. Robbie enjoyed his job, but there were other papers. He could learn French or work for an ex-pat newspaper. Maybe he could become the Riviera stringer for a paper back home. If it wasn't for those kids he'd jack it all in and stay here in the sunshine with Fran. But that was never going to happen. He did have kids, and he loved them to bits, so he was tied to Edinburgh for ever. A thousand miles from his soulmate. Robbie felt suddenly very low. A quick croissant together tomorrow and then when would he see her again?

He was running late for Dan and Simon now. He'd been supposed to meet them for dinner at seven thirty and it was already ten to eight. He half ran into the hotel lobby and was just dashing towards the open lift when the receptionist called after him.

'Monsieur McLean! I have a message for you!' she called.

He skidded to a halt and grabbed the piece of paper from her. He read it in the lift.

Bernie Ferguson had called from Edinburgh regarding a man named Enzo LaFata Junior. Well, that was a turn up for the books. When he got to his room, Robbie texted Dan quickly, telling him he'd be ten minutes and then he dialled Bernie's number with shaking hands.

Francesca paced her bedroom over and over again, muttering to herself and trying to stay calm. William. There was very little she could do about William. The police had told her that they'd alerted Interpol and there was now an international manhunt under way. He couldn't fly anywhere or take a ferry or cross a border by train without being caught. But he'd had two days to make his getaway before any of them had realised he was gone. His mobile phone records showed that he'd been in Italy early yesterday morning. Italy?! Why was he in Italy? He'd only been a few hundred kilometres away. But the phone had been turned off and nobody knew his movements since then. He could be anywhere by now. Francesca imagined him in the Caribbean, wearing a Hawaiian shirt and sipping a cocktail in a beach bar. He'd always enjoyed their holidays to the West Indies. No one would find him there. If she could get her hands on him now, she'd wring his neck.

And then there was Angelica, poor messed-up Angelica. Francesca was beside herself with worry about her little sister. The doctor had explained that she had severe liver damage and that she must never drink alcohol or do drugs again. Her heart had also been weakened by years of drug abuse and her kidneys were in a pretty poor state as well. Thankfully, she was young enough that her body should do a pretty good job of repairing itself in time, as long as she stayed clean. But the worrying part was what the psychologist had said.

'Angelica is deeply unstable. Her grasp on reality is limited and she is showing signs of delusional, paranoid, narcissistic and, I would go so far as to say, schizophrenic behaviour. Obviously, once she's physically stronger we need to do more assessments before we can come to a diagnosis, but I believe that the long-term effects of her alcohol and drug dependency are more likely to be mental than physical.'

Schizophrenic! Francesca kept saying the word over and over to herself. Delusional? Yes, that was Angelica. Paranoid? Hmm, perhaps. Narcissistic? Yes, definitely. But schizophrenic? It sounded so serious. Schizophrenia was the stuff of nightmares – padded cells and straightjackets.

'She is hearing voices,' Carlo had told her, chewing his

non-existent nails. 'She keeps going on about talking to her shoulders!'

'She's been heavily sedated.' Francesca had made excuses for Angel's behaviour. 'And she took enough drugs to floor an elephant according to the tox reports, so she's bound to be a bit confused.'

'I don't know,' Carlo had said. 'She's woken up, but she's not all there, Frankie. I'm telling you, that girl in there is not the Angel she used to be.'

When Francesca had gone into Angel's room she'd been out of bed, sitting in an armchair by the window. At first Francesca had thought this was a good thing. The last time she'd seen her little sister she'd been unconscious but now here she was, off the heart monitor and sitting up. OK, so she still looked like a ghost – deathly pale, with huge black circles under her eyes and so painfully thin under her hospital gown that Francesca was scared she'd snap if she hugged her – but she was alive at least.

'Hi, Frankie,' Angel had said, in a strange, breathy, far-away kind of voice. She'd glanced up at her sister briefly and then gone back to staring out of the window.

'I'm talking to these guys,' she'd said, pointing out of the window.

Francesca had walked over to Angel and stood beside her chair with her arm resting gently on her sister's bony shoulder.

'Who are you talking to, darling?' she'd asked, confused.

All Francesca could see when she stared out of the hospital window was the Cimetière de Monaco, and then the clear blue sea beyond.

'Strange place to build a hospital,' Francesca had mused. 'Right beside the cemetery. Bit depressing to look at a load of graves from your window.'

'No, it's not,' Angel had replied whimsically. 'It makes perfect sense.'

'What do you mean, darling?' Francesca had asked. 'There but for the grace of God go I?'

Angel had nodded. 'Yes, in a way. I nearly died last night, Frankie. I chose not to. I swear. I saw it all. I was watching myself like I was in a movie and then I was given the choice: to stay or leave. I chose to stay.'

Francesca had bitten her lip hard and squeezed Angel's shoulder. She was beginning to see what Carlo had meant. Angel was certainly a bit detached from reality. An out-of-body experience? Oh dear …

'And now, because I was one of them,' she'd carried on, 'you know, a dead person for a bit, well, now they talk to me too. So, it's a perfect place for a hospital really, because the living dead can chat to the properly dead, and no one gets lonely, you see.'

'That's nice, darling,' Francesca had said, smiling patiently but wanting to weep with despair. Angel was talking to ghosts!

This was not good. Not good at all. Francesca continued pacing. Carlo had been at the hospital all day and had the chance to speak to the consultant psychologist. They'd talked about the possibility of long-term psychiatric care for Angelica. Carlo seemed to think this was a good idea, a positive step forward, but Francesca wasn't so sure. Angelica wasn't mad. Was she? A little bit fragile and self-obsessed, perhaps. And she obviously had an addictive personality but that meant rehab again, didn't it? Not a mental hospital. Anyway, since when did Carlo get to make these decisions? Carlo had always been this flaky, wild, chaotic kid, who crashed his cars, forgot birthdays and screwed around. He didn't have a responsible bone in his body. And yet, suddenly, here he was talking to consultants and having opinions on what should happen to Angelica. Francesca had been telling him to grow up for years but now he was finally doing it, she wasn't so sure she liked it.

But Angelica was in good hands for now. The important thing was to get her better and then they could think about what should happen next. Right now, Francesca had more imminent problems. She had to explain to the boys that their father had left and that they may never see him again and she had absolutely no idea how she was going to break the news to them. She'd only just told them about their grandpa. She'd explained that he'd fallen off the yacht and that he'd drowned. She'd thought it was best to be blunt with them and to give them no false hope that Grandpa might turn up again one day. Francesca didn't believe for a moment she would ever see her dad again, and that was something they all had to come to terms with. But William … Oh God, how did she explain to them about William?

Francesca didn't know she could feel this angry. When she thought about what he'd done to her and the boys she wanted to punch walls, kick doors, scream the whole house down! She'd always been quite a calm and rational woman, but if William walked in the door now she would happily smash his head in with anything that came to hand.

But William wasn't about to walk through the door. The bastard had gone and Francesca was left to pick up the pieces. She thought about Dubrovski and shuddered. How the hell was she going to get her hands on ten million euros by tomorrow? The fraud squad had put a hold on all the business accounts and William had run off with what little they'd had left. Oh, yes, she was standing in a mansion worth millions, with a triple garage and a driveway full of ridiculously expensive cars. She had a yacht in the harbour and a country house near Valbonne. She had diamonds in her safe, a wine cellar full of rare vintages and priceless works of art hanging on the walls, but she couldn't sell any of it for cash before tomorrow. It just wasn't possible.

She was finding it hard to breathe. The panic rose in her chest like a swarm of angry bees. Her head buzzed with them and she couldn't think clearly. The room was too hot and airless. She pushed open the balcony doors, stumbled out and steadied herself on the wrought-iron railings.

'Breathe,' she told herself. 'Just breathe.'

She stared down over the rooftops, like she'd done a thousand times before, to glittering Monte Carlo where life carried on regardless of her own tragedies. She thought about the crowds of excited tourists flooding in for the Grand Prix, happy and excited, glammed up to the nines, ready to hit the town. She thought about Robbie, having dinner with his friends, blissfully unaware of the trouble she was in. What would he do if he knew about the Russian? Would he help her? Could he help her? He didn't have any money, he certainly couldn't help in that way. But would he save her if he could? She knew the answer but it was too much to ask. She was in this on her own.

Francesca gazed up at the stars in the clear black sky and watched them twinkle, as they'd done for countless years. What did it matter to them if one little family was destroyed? What did it matter to anyone or anything in the grand scheme of things? Nothing would change if they all disappeared. The world would keep spinning, the stars would still shine in the sky, and the tourists would still flock to Monte Carlo for the Grand Prix.

She felt her own insignificance more acutely than ever before. She was just one little creature on this planet. Just a bundle of cells, no more or less important than any other animal. She remembered being in the bank a few weeks earlier, before anything went wrong. She'd been queuing and thinking about how trapped she felt with William, when suddenly a woman had screamed and Francesca had become aware of a flapping noise above her head. A pigeon had flown into the bank and was flying, panicked, around the room. Suddenly it flew straight into the glazed window with a sickening thud and fell to the ground stunned. Some customers laughed. One woman said, 'Oh, that's disgusting. Get it out!' But Francesca had looked on in horror as the poor bird got to its feet, flew up to the ceiling again and then smashed straight back into the glass. In that instant, Francesca had known exactly how the bird felt. Trapped. Able to see the outside world, and freedom beyond, but unable to get to it. It was destroying itself in the process, but it was absolutely determined to break free.

While everyone else looked on, Francesca had walked over to the bird and scooped it up in her hands. It had still been warm but she'd had no idea if it was still breathing.

'Don't touch it, madam,' an elderly gentleman had advised her. 'Pigeons are vermin. They carry disease.'

But Francesca had ignored him. She'd carried the bird gently outside and sat on a bench, stroking its feathers, willing it to wake up. Slowly the bird had begun to move. Francesca looked straight into its beady black eyes and said, 'Have your freedom, little bird. It's your right.' And then she'd thrown the pigeon into the air and watched in wonder as it had taken flight. The pigeon flew around her head in a circle twice before flying off, over the roof of the next building and disappearing for ever.

Francesca wished somebody would scoop her up in their hands and save her now. She'd been smashing herself against that glass for years and she'd ended up here – frightened and alone. Her father had always made her feel invincible. He'd made her believe that because she was a LaFata, nothing could touch her. But he'd been wrong. All he'd done was build a glass barrier between his family and the rest of the world. And now the glass was cracking and falling down around their ears. The LaFatas were nothing special. They weren't any more important than any other family. They had been lucky, that was all. And now their luck had changed.

Chapter Thirty-Five

'You're on a roll tonight, Rob!' yelled Dan across the roulette table.

'I'm feeling lucky!' he shouted back.

This was indeed his lucky day. The phone call to Bernie had been awesome. Bernie, bless him, had taken it upon himself to follow up Robbie's leads in Edinburgh while he was busy in Monaco. That's how he'd tracked down Enzo LaFata Junior, Fatty's arch enemy. He was the cousin who had lost out on the family pizza business when his father had left it to Fatty instead. Bernie found him on the streets of Glasgow, just outside Glasgow Central station in fact, stinking of Special Brew, begging in the gutter.

All it had taken to get the dirt was a fish supper, a six-pack of Tennent's lager and a week in a homeless shelter paid for upfront. Bernie had happily obliged. And then Enzo had told him the whole story; he vented years of pent-up anger and he was happy to be taking his cousin down. Robbie felt bad for ever doubting Bernie's journalistic abilities. The guy was a legend. He'd got Robbie the scoop of a lifetime. Robbie felt on top of the world. He was at the peak of his career. Fuck it. He would leave Edinburgh. He would fight Heather tooth and nail for the girls but he wasn't going to live a little life any more. He'd found Francesca now and somehow he was going to make it work. She would have to divorce William, after what he'd done. It would

347

be complicated, and it would take time, years maybe, but they'd be moving forward and working towards the future. Anything was possible. Dreams could come true. Robbie could see it all now.

Being in the Casino de Monte-Carlo was like walking onto a James Bond set and Robbie was beginning to feel that maybe he actually was Sean Connery. They'd each hired a black dinner suit for the evening. It had been Dan's idea and Robbie had thought it was daft at the time but now, surrounded by such opulence and elegance, he felt glad he'd made the effort. He might have been brought up in a West Lothian sink estate but he'd found his spiritual home! God, this place was something else – the vast, domed ceiling, the elaborate paintings on the walls, the glass chandeliers, the groomed, suited men, the beautiful women in cocktail dresses and jewels. Robbie just wished he had Francesca by his side. His very own Bond girl. Now that would have been perfect. Next time he would come with Fran.

'Sixteen!' he called to the croupier. 'Red.'

Sixteen. It was Fran's birthday.

'Whoah!' the crowd around the table gasped. 'Sixteen!'

Simon clapped excitedly.

'What's that now, Robbie?' he asked. His glasses had steamed up again. 'Five grand?'

'Six and half!' whooped Robbie.

He couldn't believe his luck. He'd got the story, he'd got the girl, and now he was reclaiming all those expenses too. A couple of thousand more and he'd have paid for Florence's plane ticket to Perth, along with the hire car and the hotel. Patterson was going to love him when he got back. He could practically smell the pay rise.

'Twenty-one,' he called this time. 'Black.'

Grace's birthday. Robbie knew, even before the wheel

was spun, that he would win. It was just one of those days when everything was going right.

'I don't fucking believe this,' yelled Dan from the other side of the table as the ball teetered on the brink of black twenty-one and then fell neatly into place. 'You must have God on your side tonight!'

'Halle-bloody-lujah! Praise the Lord!' laughed Robbie.

'Don't you think you should stop now?' asked Simon, getting jittery again.

'Si, you told him to stop at five hundred and he's got eight grand now,' scoffed Dan. 'One more, Robbie. Just one more, then you've got ten. Ten grand!'

'Three,' called Robbie. 'Red.'

Ruby's birthday. Ruby red. It couldn't go wrong.

The ball sped around the wheel, so fast that Robbie could barely see it, and then it began to slow down and bounce around; it fell into black seven but leapt out again, hovered on the brink of red eleven but changed its mind and then it bounced one more time before coming to rest in red three. Just as Robbie knew it would.

'You fucking beauty!' shouted Dan so loudly that even the croupier giggled and half the casino turned round to have a look.

'Right, I'm done,' said Robbie, rubbing his hand together in glee. 'Ten grand. That'll do nicely, thank you.'

He scooped up his chips and grinned at the others.

'Drinks are on me, boys,' he said. 'More champagne?'

'Rude not to,' grinned Dan.

'The thing is,' said Robbie, passing the guys their drinks at the bar, 'what I just won is small change around here. It's very uncool that we just got excited about ten grand, you know that, don't you?'

'I know, but ten thousand euros is a lot of money,' said Simon, sensibly. 'To most people.'

'But these aren't most people,' Dan reminded him. 'This lot have watches that cost more than that.'

'You're not wrong there, sir,' interrupted a large American man in a white jacket and red bow tie, sitting next to them at the bar. 'Ain't this place something else? And talking of breaking the bank … There's a guy over there. You see? At the other end of the bar. He just won eleven million euros!'

He pointed at a middle-aged blond man, sitting slumped in his stool a few feet away.

'No way!' exclaimed Dan, who was pretty pissed.

'Yes way,' nodded the American emphatically. 'Apparently he's had a bad week. Lost his job. He took out his entire life savings, spent the afternoon and evening in here and now he's a multi-frigging-millionaire. You see, dreams come true in Monte Carlo. Cheers!'

He raised his glass to Robbie, Dan and Simon. They raised theirs back.

'He doesn't look very happy about it,' Simon noted, staring at the big blond millionaire.

'Oh, he's totally wasted,' laughed the American. 'He can barely talk. But I guess waking up tomorrow and realising he's a very rich man will take the edge off his hangover.'

The champagne was going straight to Robbie's head. He was more of a lager drinker normally but he'd lost count of the number of glasses of bubbly he'd had tonight. He wanted to text Fran. He wanted to tell her all about the money he'd won and about the decision he'd made about the future. He wanted to tell her he was going to make it work. Suddenly, he needed to do it right now.

'Excuse me, boys,' he slid off his stool. 'I'll be back in a minute. Call of nature …'

And then he left Dan and Simon with their new friend. He went off to find somewhere quiet to text Fran and found himself on a terrace, overlooking the sea.

Just won ten grand! Meant what I said before. I love you, Fran. I know our situation is v difficult but I am determined for it to work. Hope you are too xxxxxxxxxxxx

He pressed send and felt very pleased with himself. When did it all start going so right? The terrace overlooked a sheer drop down the cliffs to the sea below. It was breathtaking.

'Is a wonderful view, no?' came a man's voice from behind him.

Robbie turned round and saw the pristinely groomed Italian man from the café and the restaurant. The man with the scar.

'Oh, hi,' said Robbie, a bit pissed and quite happy to see a familiar face. 'We keep bumping into each other.'

The Italian walked over and stood right next to Robbie on the terrace.

'You know what they call this place?' asked the Italian.

Robbie shook his head.

'Suicide Terrace,' replied the Italian, taking out a Cuban cigar from his pocket and lighting it with a gold lighter. 'Many men have jumped from here after losing the family fortune at the roulette table downstairs.'

'Really?' asked Robbie, peering over the balcony to the rocks below. 'That's a bit extreme. It's only money.'

'Only money?' The Italian raised one perfectly plucked eyebrow quizzically and sucked on his cigar. 'You do not have much respect for money, Robbie McLean?'

'Well, it's not that, it's just ...' Robbie stopped, forgetting what he was saying. 'How do you know my name?'

'It is my business to know a man's name, if he is sniffing around my business,' replied the man.

He smiled at Robbie, but his eyes were cold. He blew cigar smoke into Robbie's face and grinned.

'I am confusing you, Robbie McLean. You are not as clever as you thought, huh? Perhaps you do not know the whole story, after all?'

Robbie wished he could clear the champagne fog that was clouding his head. He was trying to think but the cogs in his brain were clanking too slowly. What the hell was going on here?

'Look, mate,' he said, trying to keep the fear out of his voice, 'I don't know who you are or what your problem is but ...'

The Italian threw his cigar over the terrace and gripped the lapels of Robbie's jacket.

'I am not the one with the problem, Mr McLean,' he said menacingly, his face an inch from Robbie's. 'You are.'

He lifted Robbie up by the scruff of the neck and threw him against the terrace.

'You have been making yourself very unpopular around here. Asking too many questions. Talking to the wrong sorts of people,' he spat.

The Italian was about the same height as Robbie and although he was lean he was incredibly strong. Robbie could feel the guy's muscles flexing under his suit. Holy shit, he seemed to be made of steel. He twisted Robbie's collar and tie until they started to choke him. He could feel the Italian's fist pushing into his Adam's apple, harder and harder. He was gasping for air. His eyes felt as if they were bulging out of their sockets and his head, starved of oxygen, felt so light that it might float off his shoulders.

'You go home to Scotland,' warned the Italian, lifting Robbie up by the scruff of the neck and holding his back against the terrace. 'You will not print one word about Giancarlo LaFata.'

Of course, this was about Fatty. Who else? Robbie remembered suddenly how weird it had been that Jade had died after Giancarlo's disappearance. He'd suspected that Fatty's influence stretched from beyond his watery grave, and now he knew for sure. The Italian lifted Robbie higher and higher and then threw him back, so that he was hanging backwards over the terrace with nothing but fresh air between him and the cliffs below. His back felt as if it was going to snap under his weight and he could barely breathe, with his suit twisted so tightly around his throat and his head dangling backwards over the abyss. He tried to speak but no words came out of his mouth, only gargled, choking sounds. I'm going to die, he thought. This is how I'm going to die.

'You have two very beautiful daughters, Robbie,' said the Italian. 'Grace and Ruby. Such blonde, blue-eyed beauties. I have seen them go to school. I have watched them. Your ex-wife, she is always on time but you, you are always late to pick them up. They wait at the gate for you, for half an hour sometimes, every Tuesday. All alone. It would be such a shame if something were to happen to two such lovely little girls, no?'

Robbie felt a sudden surge of adrenalin pump through his veins. They could do what they liked to him but they would never touch his girls. Not one precious, blonde hair on their heads! He summoned all the strength he could find and attempted to lash out at the Italian. He tried to kick his feet and punch his arms, all the time straining against the hand that was strangling him, making him gargle and

353

gag. His head dangled below his body and his back cracked under his weight. He wanted to fight. Needed to fight. But he was as powerless as a mouse in the jaws of a lion.

'It is sweet,' laughed the Italian. ' A father's love for his children. And you love a woman too, huh, Robbie? Or are you just screwing Francesca LaFata, for fun, huh?'

Robbie continued to fight but it was no good. The Italian wasn't even breaking a sweat. His face was as calm and handsome as ever as he hoisted Robbie further over the terrace. He let go of his grip on Robbie's neck ever so slightly, which helped Robbie breathe, but also left him dangling even more precariously and heavily above the rocks. Robbie heard the fabric of his suit start to tear and give way under his weight. All that was saving him from plummeting to his death was the seams of his jacket. Thread. He was hanging by a thread. His heart pounded in his chest like a drum. It was all he could hear – his heart beating and the waves crashing on the rocks below.

'I will make you a deal, Robbie McLean,' said the Italian. 'You make me two promises and I will leave you and your daughters alone. For now at least.'

Robbie nodded. He couldn't speak but he would agree to anything if it meant saving Ruby and Grace.

'*Numero uno*: you never write one word about Giancarlo LaFata in your life. *Numero due*: you never see, speak to, or get in contact with Francesca LaFata again. *Capito?*'

Robbie nodded. He heard the sickening sound of the fabric ripping further as he felt his weight strain against his suit. The Italian grinned at him with perfectly white straight teeth and let him dangle there for a few moments longer. All the blood had rushed to Robbie's head now and he felt as if he was about to pass out.

'You send Francesca a text. One text. That is all. You tell

her it is over. You are going back to Scotland and it is the end of the affair. Tell her you do not love her. *Capito?*'

Robbie glared at the man. He'd never felt such hatred in his life. He wanted to rip his heart out. Because that's what he was doing to Robbie. What sort of choice was this? His daughters' lives or Francesca's love? There was no choice. Nobody could ever compete with Ruby and Grace. Not even Fran.

Finally, Robbie nodded through gritted teeth.

'Good,' said the Italian cheerfully. 'We have a deal.'

He pulled Robbie back up on the terrace slowly and threw him to the ground. He lay there gasping, trying to catch his breath.

'One last thing,' said the Italian. 'The money you have just won, give it to me.'

'What?!' Robbie rubbed his bruised neck and his aching back. 'No!'

His lucky day had turned into the worst day of his entire life. This was a ticket to hell and there was no return flight.

'No?' The Italian laughed. 'But it is only money, Robbie McLean. Is that not what you have said to me just ten minutes ago? And what is money, compared to, say, the life of a child?'

Robbie was beaten. He had no will left to fight. He'd tried to play with the big boys and he'd lost. This was a world he didn't understand. A world he hadn't known existed and he was so far out of his depth that he was drowning faster than Fatty himself.

'Take it,' he said, grabbing handfuls of chips out of his pockets and throwing them at the Italian. 'Take the fucking lot. If this is what money does to you, I don't want a penny of the stuff.'

The Italian picked up the chips casually and put them in his suit pocket. Then he held his hand out to Robbie, offering to help him up.

'Fuck off,' spat Robbie, trying to fight back tears. 'I hope you rot in hell with that bastard Giancarlo LaFata.'

The Italian laughed, at some joke with a punchline only he understood, and said, 'Oh, I do not think Mr LaFata is in hell. I believe he is in heaven by now. Goodbye, Mr McLean, I trust we will not have to do business again.'

Robbie watched the Italian's shiny black leather shoes walk away. They were shoes he'd admired. The shoes that had walked all over him and trampled on his dreams. And then he cried. He curled up in a tight little ball on the cold stone floor and sobbed for the dreams he'd had, that he'd had to throw away. He felt them disappear into the warm Riviera breeze, down they fell, over the terrace, out of his reach, and then they smashed into a million pieces on the rocks below.

Chapter Thirty-Six

Francesca lay in bed with tears streaming down her face. She'd woken early after a broken night, filled with nightmares and cold sweats. She'd reached for her phone and found two messages waiting for her from Robbie. They were going to meet for breakfast and she couldn't wait. He was flying home today but she didn't want to think about that. All she'd wanted to focus on was seeing him one last time.

She'd read the first text and her troubled mind had felt soothed. He'd said he loved her. He wanted to make it work. It hadn't hit Francesca that she was free of William until that moment. She'd been so caught up in her anger and despair that she'd missed the one positive note in the sorry affair – William was gone, he'd slept with Jade, he'd stolen their money, he'd broken their wedding vows. Now, surely she could divorce him and be free. She had felt a weight lift off her shoulders. She would get through this. She could deal with the Russian, and with Angelica. She could come to terms with her father's death and the loss of the family fortune. And then when this horrible mess was all cleared up, she could have Robbie.

She'd smiled as she'd opened his next message. It had been sent at two a.m. Oh, bless. He must have been a bit tipsy by then ... She'd lain back in her pillows to read what she'd expected to be a slushy, drunken message.

My darling Fran, I won't be able to make breakfast this morning. I'm sorry. We can't see each other again. I have children to go home to. You are a wonderful woman, and in another life I know it could have worked, but it's a fantasy and it could never have been real. I meant it when I said I loved you. I do. Very much. But I have to do this. Please understand, I have no choice. I am so sorry to leave you when your life is in such turmoil. Just know that I'll always be thinking about you, and wishing things could have been different. Be careful and be happy. R xxx

And then she'd thrown the phone across the room and wailed like an injured animal. He was her one last glimmer of hope and he'd gone. Now, three hours later, the tears were still flowing down her cheeks and soaking her pillow. A tap had been turned on and she couldn't turn it off again. She punched her fist against her wet pillow and cried, 'Why, Robbie? Why?' She couldn't make sense of it. Had she meant nothing to him? Was it just a fling? Had he been using her for sex? No. It had been more than that. How could she have misjudged him, like that? She'd been sure it was real. Their special connection, the way her body lurched towards his whenever they were in the same room. The way they could talk for hours without catching breath, or just lie together in comfortable silence, lost in each other's arms. She knew it was real. So why was he treating her like a holiday romance? It all felt so horribly wrong. It hurt. It ached so badly that Francesca wanted to crawl out of her body and leave it there on the bed, while her spirit escaped to a happy place, far away from all this heartbreak and pain.

She'd retrieved her phone from where she'd thrown it on

the floor and texted him back, asking why. She'd demanded an explanation and pleaded with him to call her before he caught his flight home. But he hadn't returned her texts and he hadn't called. She'd tried him, over and over again, but it rang and rang and he refused to answer. She looked at her watch and realised that his plane was taking off now. He was leaving her and he obviously had no intention of ever coming back.

And now, when all she wanted was to curl up and hide from the world, Francesca only had four hours before she had to meet the Russian. Four hours to find ten million euros. But she didn't care. What would happen if she didn't get her hands on the money? At worst, he would kill her. And what did that matter now?

She could hear the sound of children's laughter coming from somewhere far away. Francesca dragged her aching body out of bed and walked out onto the balcony. She could see Luca and Benito on the drive below with their nanny, all dressed up in their school uniforms, their faces grinning, hitting each other with their caps and chasing each other round the car while the nanny scolded them half-heartedly. Francesca watched them and her heart lurched out of her chest. Oh God, how could she be so selfish? To think, even for a fleeting moment, that she had nothing to live for? Benito looked up and saw Mummy on the balcony.

'Hi, Mummy,' he called, waving his little hands enthusiastically. 'Love you, Mummy!'

'Love you, Mummy,' Benito joined in. 'Mwah! Mwah!'

They both blew her kisses.

'Love you too, boys,' she shouted back, forcing a smile. 'Have a good day at school and I'll see you when you get back. Now quick, into the car. You'll be late.'

She watched them clamber into the back of the 4x4 and

drive off, still waving out of the window. She would see them when they got back from school. They were all she had and she was all they had now William was gone. She would find the money for Dubrovski. She had no choice. Francesca had given up on her own life but she couldn't give up on her children. From now on she would live for them, and them alone.

Carlo sat beside Angelica's bed and held her hand.

'How are you feeling today, sweetheart?' he asked her anxiously. She looked even more pale than she had done the day before and her face was so drawn that she was all eye sockets and cheekbones, no flesh. Like a cartoon of a ghost, he thought.

'I'm OK,' she said, weakly. 'My head hurts and I feel sick all the time. They're having to feed me through this ...' she indicated the feeding tube, 'because I've got no appetite at all.'

'That'll come back,' Carlo reassured her. 'It's the medication. The doctor explained, remember? It'll make you feel nauseous.'

Angelica nodded. 'I know I'm going to be OK,' she said, trying to smile.

'That's good, hon,' said Carlo. 'That's half the battle. Tell yourself you're on the mend and you will be.'

'Well, it was Daddy who told me I'd be OK,' she replied seriously. 'He came to see me last night.'

Carlo's heart sank. He'd hoped the hallucinations and voices had been a symptom of the sedatives she'd been on, but she was off those now.

'Angelica, you do know that Dad's dead, don't you?' he asked, trying to keep his frustration out of his voice.

Angelica laughed. 'Don't be silly, Carlo,' she scoffed.

'Daddy's not dead. He was here last night. I told you, he came to visit me. He told me not to tell anyone because he'd get into trouble but I can tell you. You're not going to get Daddy into trouble, are you?'

'No,' said Carlo. 'I won't get him into trouble.'

Oh God, she was in a worse state than he'd thought.

'Daddy said that he's proud of the way you're handling things, Carlo.' She squeezed his hand. 'He's still there for us, you know?'

Now he knew she was definitely hallucinating. As if their dad would ever say he was proud of Carlo!

'That's good,' said Carlo patiently. 'You get some rest now, darling. I'm just going to talk to the doctors.'

Angelica nodded and closed her eyes. He watched her slipping off back to sleep and felt a wave of love wash over him. Their father wasn't there to look out for her. That was a fantasy. But Carlo was there for her and he would do everything in his power to save her.

'I want her put in psychiatric care as soon as she's strong enough,' he told the consultant.

The doctor nodded and said, 'I'm glad you think that way, Mr LaFata. I think a psychiatric hospital is the best place for her. But she won't go of her own free will, you know that, don't you?'

Carlo nodded. 'She doesn't think there's anything wrong with her.'

'No, unfortunately, patients are usually the last ones to accept they have a mental illness,' agreed the doctor. 'But you will have to have her sectioned. Who is her next of kin?'

Carlo almost said, 'Our father,' but managed to stop himself.

'Mum, I guess,' said Carlo. Oh shit, he was going to

have to speak to Sandrine. 'But what if she refuses to give permission?' he asked, worried that Sandrine would do her usual thing of refusing to believe that anything was wrong with Angelica.

'Talk to her,' encouraged the doctor. 'Explain the situation. Perhaps she will surprise you.'

Sandrine did surprise Carlo. The woman never failed to surprise him with her lack of maternal instinct.

'Oh, I am not your nest of king,' she said breezily on the phone.

'Next of kin,' Carlo corrected her.

'Yes, that is what I said. I am not your nest, or next, of whatever it is. I signed all that over to your father when we divorced. He was such a control freak, Giancarlo, he would never let me make any decisions about you children.'

'So, who is Angelica's next of kin, now that Dad's gone?' Carlo had asked, trying to keep the exasperation out of his voice.

'I suppose that must be you, Carlo. You and Francesca. Now I must go, I have friends coming for lunch and my hair is still wet. *Ciao*, baby.'

Unbelievable! Carlo sighed. And then he called Francesca.

'We need to sign some forms so that Angelica can get the treatment she needs,' he explained.

'Of course,' Francesca replied. She sounded strange, distant, detached. 'Whatever will make her better.'

'Frankie, these forms, they're giving permission to transfer her to a psychiatric hospital.'

There was silence on the other end of the line.

'It's for the best,' he added, knowing that Frankie hated the thought of Angel being put into psychiatric care. He hated the thought too but what was the alternative? Angel was sick and it was up to them to deal with it.

He heard Francesca sigh heavily, and then she said, 'OK, Carlo. I'll sign the forms. If you think it's the right thing then I'll trust your judgement.'

'You will?' Carlo was surprised. Frankie had never let him make a decision before, not without a fight. 'Can you come here now and do it? The sooner the better ...'

'No, Carlo,' she said. 'Not now, darling. I have some business to deal with and then I'll come to the hospital. It can wait until this evening, can't it?'

'I guess so,' replied Carlo. 'She won't be strong enough to be transferred for a couple of days yet anyway.'

'Right, well give her my love and tell her I'll be in later, OK?' said Frankie.

'OK.'

Carlo went back into Angelica's room and found Christian sitting by the bed, gazing anxiously at her.

'You don't mind, do you?' asked Christian, looking up. 'I just wanted to see her.'

Carlo shook his head. 'Of course I don't mind, Chris. You're part of the family. You're the one who saved her the other night. She'll be pleased to see you when she wakes up.'

'Are you OK, Carlo?' asked Christian. 'You look tired, mate.'

Carlo shrugged. He was tired. He'd barely slept for the past two nights but so what? Angelica was the important one.

'Oh God, this'll cheer you up,' said Christian. 'You'll never guess what happened to James Sanderson.'

'What? Dad's skipper?' asked Carlo disinterestedly. James was a nice enough guy but he wasn't exactly foremost in Carlo's mind.

'Yup,' nodded Christian. 'He practically broke the bank at the casino last night. Won eleven million euros apparently.'

'No fucking way!' Carlo shook his head in disbelief. 'Lucky bastard!'

Christian laughed. 'And I heard he was so pissed he fell asleep at the bar afterwards too.'

'Well, I'm glad someone's on a roll,' said Carlo. 'Cos there's not much good luck going on around here at the moment.'

'Things will get better,' said Christian. 'You wait and see.'

He turned back to gaze at Angel. The look on his face was so tender and loving that Carlo suddenly felt like an intruder. At that moment it dawned on him that his best friend was in love with his sister. And what's more, it felt right.

Francesca looked at the bottles of wine and made a mental note of their worth. Five thousand here, a few hundred there, the odd bottle of vintage worth ten grand or more ... But no, the collection was extensive and worth a small fortune, but it was never going to pay off the Russian. She unlocked the vault and waited for the light to flicker on. There was just the one painting left, a large canvas, wrapped in cloth and propped up against the wall. She unwrapped it gently and stood back to have a look. Ah, it was the Cézanne. An exquisite post-Impressionist landscape in yellows, greens and blues that her father had bought the year they'd moved here to the Riviera. Cézanne had been a local artist, born in Provence, and Fatty had thought it was only fitting that he bought a slice of local history.

Like most of his art, though, it had been too valuable

to keep on display, so it had ended up here in the vault. Francesca looked at the masterpiece and thought how sad it was that such a beautiful painting should be hidden from view. What a tragic irony that the art was too good to be displayed. It made no sense. God, money, it was such a destructive thing, she thought, wrapping the painting back up carefully and carrying it with difficulty out of the vault. Money warped and corrupted everything. Maybe she was glad to be free of it. Maybe life would be better for her, and the boys, now it had all gone.

Francesca had to walk to the office. The Grand Prix weekend was under way and the whole of Monaco was heaving. She struggled down the hill and through the crowds, carrying a priceless work of art. She could smell burned rubber and petrol fumes in the air. The streets may have been like a carnival but the office was deathly quiet when she arrived. The police had gone and taken every computer and file with them. All that was left were empty desks and abandoned chairs. Francesca didn't bother with the key this time. It was two minutes to twelve, he would be here, sitting in Dad's chair waiting for her. She swung open the door boldly and said, 'Hello, Mr Dubrovski.' She wasn't scared. She'd lost everything already. Nothing could touch her now.

The Russian grinned at her like a long-lost friend.

'Francesca, my beautiful girl, you are here,' he said. 'And you have my money, yes?'

'No,' said Francesca, flatly. 'But I have your painting. This is what you paid my father for. The ten million. You were buying the Cézanne.'

Dubrovski sucked the air in sharply between his teeth and shook his head.

'No,' he replied. 'I do not want your painting. I asked for cash.'

'Mr Dubrovski,' replied Francesca calmly, 'I've checked with three independent experts. This painting is valued at ten million euros. It is the one work of art remaining in my father's collection and it was wrapped, ready for sale. You gave my father exactly that sum of money. It doesn't take a genius to work out that you were buying the Cézanne. So here it is.'

She laid the painting on the desk in front of him.

'Well, perhaps I have changed my mind,' said Dubrovski, almost petulantly. He seemed annoyed that Francesca had worked out what the money had been for.

'I don't believe that great works of art are purchased on a try before you buy basis,' she replied. 'You don't get your money back because you've decided you don't like the colour. It's not a cardigan!'

'There you are wrong. Mrs Dubrovski has had the drawing room painted again. She tells me that the Cézanne will clash.' He folded his arms across his chest stubbornly. 'I do not want the painting. I want my money back.'

Francesca was in no mood for Dubrovski's petulance. She stood her ground firmly.

'You bought the painting. My father took the money in good faith,' she said.

'Hmph,' Dubrovski huffed. 'Your father never did anything in good faith. He cheated at cards and he cheated at business. I do not want this painting now. It is tarnished. The police will probably repossess it. And knowing Fatty, it might even be a fake. Give me my money, Francesca, or you will regret it.'

He pulled the gun from his waistband and laid it on the desk beside the painting.

'So, what is it to be, Frankie?' he sneered. 'Your money or your life?'

Francesca swallowed hard. This was not going according to plan. She'd thought he would be happy to get the painting he'd paid for. She'd thought she'd sorted this problem. But here she was in an empty office with an angry Russian and a loaded gun.

'I don't have any money, Mr Dubrovski,' she replied, her voice shaking now. 'You must know that. All I have is this painting.'

'I do not want the painting.'

'Or my yacht,' she said, thinking on her feet. 'You can have my yacht. It's worth at least that ...'

'I have a perfectly fine yacht, thank you very much, Francesca. Besides I have seen your *Conqueror*, she is ugly. I do not like her. I would not pay ten cents for her, never mind ten million.'

Francesca had to agree with him. The yacht had been William's choice, and she'd always thought it was ugly too.

'I have a country estate near Valbonne.' She was getting desperate now.

'Worth maybe five million, only,' shrugged Dubrovski. 'I have seen it. It is nice enough but nothing special.'

'Well, what do you suggest?' Francesca eyed the gun warily. 'You can kill me if you want but you won't get your money back that way.'

'Frankie, I do not wish to kill you,' said the Russian. 'You seem like a perfectly nice young woman. I know you have children and I do not wish to deprive them of their mother. But I need my money.'

They'd reached stalemate. Dubrovski picked up the gun and handled it, almost fondly.

'I did not think I would have to use this today,' he said, a

367

little sadly. 'You have let me down, Frankie. I thought you were the one LaFata I could perhaps trust.'

Francesca heard the safety catch click. It made her jump. Was he really going to do it? What was in it for him? He seemed to read her mind.

'It is a matter of pride I am afraid, Francesca,' he told her. 'I cannot let you walk out of here owing me such a vast sum of money. We had a deal and you have not kept your side of the bargain, so regrettably, I must keep mine.'

He lifted the gun and pointed it at her head. The air seemed to disappear from the room and Francesca found it hard to breathe. She wasn't scared for herself but as she pictured Luca and Benito's faces her knees buckled beneath her. She fell to her knees and found herself pleading with the Russian.

'Please, don't do this,' she begged. 'My boys. Think about my boys. They've lost their grandfather and their father. Don't take away their mother too. Please, Mr Dubrovski. I'll do anything. Anything.'

'I have told you, Frankie, I don't want anything except your money.' He sighed as he put the safety catch back on and laid the gun down on the desk. He scratched his head and looked thoughtful. It dawned on Francesca that he really didn't want to kill her at all. That he felt obliged to carry out his threat but that he'd really rather not if there was any sort of alternative.

'Call your brother,' said the Russian, tossing her the office phone. 'Tell him he has one hour to find the money.'

What sort of reprieve was that? Francesca knew that Carlo didn't have that sort of money at his disposal. He lived off an allowance of five hundred thousand euros a month. It was a lot, but nowhere near enough to save her.

'He doesn't have it,' she replied. 'What's the point?'

'If he loves you, he will find a way,' said Dubrovski, sitting back down on her dad's chair. 'Call him.'

Francesca dialled the number nervously. How the hell did she ask Carlo to find her that sort of money in an hour?

'Frankie,' Carlo sounded tired. 'How's it going?'

His vigil at Angel's bedside was taking its toll. She felt dreadful to be asking him such an impossible favour when he already had so much stress.

'Right, Carlo,' she said, trying to keep her voice calm so as not to panic him. 'I've got myself into a bit of a situation.'

'A situation?' Carlo sounded nervous already.

'No questions and whatever you do, don't panic,' Francesca continued. 'Just listen to me and do as I ask. I'm at the office with a man called Andrea Dubrovski. Dad owes him ten million euros. He has a gun, Carlo, and he says if you don't get the money here in an hour he will kill me.'

'What the fuck!' Francesca had to hold the phone away from her ear, Carlo shouted so loudly.

'I said don't panic,' she repeated. 'One hour, Carlo. The office. Ten million euros in cash.'

'Bu … bu … but …' Carlo stammered.

'Just try your best, darling,' said Francesca and then she hung up.

'Good girl,' said Dubrovski. 'Sit down, sit down. Would you like to borrow my paper while we wait? There's a rather interesting story about your father in there …'

Chapter Thirty-Seven

Carlo elbowed his way through the crowds of Grand Prix fans – overweight Americans proudly sporting matching Ferrari T-shirts and caps, tanned young men in white shirts and gold Ray-Bans with giggling girlfriends on their arms, pretty young girls in denim miniskirts and white vests wearing their VIP passes with pride. The whole of Monaco echoed with the sound of engines roaring and crowds chattering, but Carlo could hear nothing but the sound of his own voice, egging him on, willing him to save Frankie. He walked purposefully, looking straight ahead, barging past people, stepping on toes and never turning back to apologise. He was on a mission to save his sister's life. This was no time for pleasantries.

He searched in four harbourside bars before he found James Sanderson slumped in a chair at the back near the kitchen, nursing a glass of whisky. It was a glorious, sunny day outside but James was sitting in near darkness.

'James,' he said, pulling out a chair beside the skipper. 'I hear you got lucky yesterday.'

'I sure did, Carlo,' grinned the drunk Canadian. 'I'm still celebrating now. Join me for a drink, son.'

But Carlo had no time for a drink. He shook his head and got straight down to business.

'James, do you want to buy my yacht?' he asked bluntly.

James Sanderson looked up in surprise. 'Carlo, I won eleven million, *Pulling Power* is worth five times that.'

'I know,' said Carlo. 'But the offer stands. Give me ten for her now, in cash, and she's yours to keep.'

James stared at Carlo in silence for a very long time. Carlo could practically hear his drunken brain turning over the idea.

'You'll sell me *Pulling Power* for a fraction of her value?' James asked eventually, as if he still didn't believe the proposition.

'Yes.' Carlo nodded with certainty. 'That leaves you a million. You'll be set for life. You can charter her, make a living from her. You won't have to work for anyone else. You'll be free, James. Your own man, your own boss.'

'D'you think I could do that?' asked James, his eyes widening.

'I know you could,' replied Carlo. 'You're the best skipper in the Med, now come on, this offer is only open for another ...'

He checked his watch. 'Another thirty-five minutes and then it expires. Deal?'

James grinned and raised his glass. 'Deal,' he said.

The Russian sighed and put down his newspaper. He glanced at the clock on the office wall and then his gaze settled on Francesca.

'Five more minutes,' he said darkly. 'That is all Carlo has. Is he a punctual boy?'

Francesca thought about the family dinners he'd arrived at three hours late, the weddings he'd turned up to, halfway through the reception, and the birthdays he'd missed altogether. She shook her head.

'No, Carlo is always late,' she replied.

'Is a shame,' muttered Dubrovski, picking up his paper again. 'Is really great shame.'

Francesca eyed the gun on the desk. She wondered if she could grab it somehow and run away. Or shoot Dubrovski instead. And then she eyed the Russian. She took in his gigantic frame, his huge hands, his shifty blue eyes that were only half reading the newspaper. They kept darting over to her, just checking she was still there. He appeared to be relaxed, leaning back in his chair with his enormous feet plonked on the desk between the gun and the Cézanne, but it was an act, Francesca could tell. He was poised, like a tiger in the savannah, ready to pounce. His muscles were taut under his thin summer shirt and his fist clenched and unclenched on his lap. He would be on her in an instant if she tried to make a move.

She thought about the boys. She'd promised them she'd see them after school. But now she found herself wondering if she would ever see them again. It had been too much to ask of Carlo. It had been too much to ask of anyone. Ten million euros in an hour. It was a ridiculous request. Impossible. Francesca sighed. She hadn't thought that death would come like this. The atmosphere was polite and respectful. The threat of what was to come hung heavily over the room. Dubrovski didn't want to kill her and she didn't want to die. But it would be done if Carlo didn't turn up in the next ...

'Two minutes,' said the Russian, without looking up from his paper.

Francesca's heart was beating faster now. She could feel the sweat on her forehead, dripping into her eyebrows and stinging her eyes. She didn't want to die. She'd lost Robbie and her father, she'd lost her fortune and her career, but she realised now that she really, really didn't want to die. She yearned for her boys. The thought of never feeling their sticky kisses or hearing their giggling voices again made the tears prickle in her eyes. But she didn't say a word. She just stood there, in the middle of the room, with tears streaming down her face and a gaping, aching hole where her heart should have been.

'Do not cry, my beautiful Frankie,' said Dubrovski, as he folded his newspaper neatly and placed it on the desk. 'You will not feel a thing. I do not wish to hurt you. It will be over very soon.'

He picked up the gun and walked round the desk. He stood behind her and held the gun to the back of her head. Francesca could feel the cold steel on the nape of her neck.

'No,' she whimpered. 'Please, Andrea, don't do this. My boys. I beg you. My boys ...'

The gun shook against her skin but Francesca didn't know if it was her body shaking or Dubrovski's hands. She couldn't see his face but she could swear she could hear him sobbing gently.

'I am truly sorry, Francesca,' he sniffed as he pushed the barrel harder into her neck.

Francesca heard the sickening sound of the safety catch unlocking and then a loud bang, and a thud, and she was on the floor.

Robbie sat outside his house in the car. It was empty and dark. He had no desire to go in. It wasn't a home these days. He remembered how it used to be. He could still picture the girls in the living room, just back from school, switching CBBC on, bouncing on the sofa, asking their mum for crisps and biscuits and drinks, no doubt. Life used to be normal. So ordinary and suburban. So safe. He thought about the week he'd just had, the people he'd met and the stories he'd been told and it all seemed unreal – a million miles from this ordinary little life of his in Edinburgh. But the two worlds had clashed now. The Italian had watched Robbie's girls at school, he knew where Robbie lived. Robbie had put Ruby and Grace in danger and for what? Nothing! A big fat blank page.

'What do you mean you've got no story!' Patterson had yelled, thumping his fist on his desk, sending papers flying across the room. 'You've spent more than eight thousand fucking pounds. You've sent some French opera singer to Australia. You hired an Audi fucking R8 and stayed at the ponciest hotel in Monte Carlo. You come back wearing new clothes, looking like a bloody Reservoir Dog and you tell me you've no ruddy story, McLean!'

Robbie had seen the boss's face turn purple and the veins pulsing in his forehead. He'd known what was coming next.

'I've had enough, Robbie,' Patterson had said. 'I've put up with your Giancarlo LaFata obsession for years. I let you go to Monaco before, I paid your expenses and I accepted that your story wasn't ready, but now? Now every paper in the country's running Fatty stories on a daily basis and we have nothing. You're a great writer, Robbie, and a top-rate journalist. You've always been a wee bit too big for your boots but you're talented, so I let you get away with it. But not this time. You're taking the piss, son. You're fired! Clear your desk and get out of my sight. You're a disgrace, McLean. A waste of space.'

And so now he sat outside his empty house, with an empty heart. He wanted to see Ruby and Grace, to feel their warm little bodies in his arms. But Heather wouldn't allow it. It wasn't Robbie's day. He wished he could call Fran and check that she was OK. He wanted to tell her that he'd had no choice but to end things. He imagined his daughters through the window. Ruby doing somersaults on the sofa, while Grace danced to some song that Robbie couldn't hear. They weren't there, of course, they were in Morningside, practising their piano, learning how to be nice middle-class girls. But at least they were still safe in their suburban bubble and Robbie had to keep them there. Fran was the sacrifice he'd had to make. Fran and his career. Those girls really were all he had left in the world now. Oh, screw Heather. He didn't give a toss if it wasn't his day. He wasn't going into an empty house. He needed to see his girls. Robbie drove like a maniac all the way to Morningside.

'Dad!' screamed Grace and Ruby in unison as they opened the front door. 'You're home!'

They threw their arms around his waist and hugged him so hard that he almost tripped over.

'Ooh, I like your hair,' said Grace. 'You look very cool.'

'And you've got new clothes,' added Ruby excitedly. 'Did you get us anything new? Did you? Did you?'

'There are presents in my suitcase in the car. You'll get them tomorrow,' he said, squeezing them tight, losing himself in the warmth of their bodies.

Heather appeared from the hall, frowning. 'What the hell are you doing here?' she demanded. 'You don't have the girls until tomorrow.'

'I just wanted to see them, Heather,' he said. It was the truth. There was no ulterior motive.

Heather stared at him suspiciously.

'Is something wrong?' she demanded.

'Grace, Ruby,' said Robbie. 'Let me talk to Mum in private for a minute, yeah?'

They nodded and ran back inside. He might as well tell her now. She was going to find out soon enough anyway when he missed the next maintenance payment.

'Something's happened.' Heather frowned at him. 'It's written all over your face. You look shifty.'

'I've lost my job,' he muttered.

'What?' Heather screeched. 'What do you mean? How? Why? What have you done, Robbie?'

'I didn't get the story I was chasing.' He downplayed events. 'I ran into some pretty shady characters and the long and the short of it is, I have no story. So Patterson sacked me.'

'What? Just like that, he sacked you?' she demanded.

'Yes,' replied Robbie. 'Just like that. It's a cut-throat world, journalism.'

Heather looked as if she couldn't quite make up her mind how to react. She was caught between smugness that he had finally proved himself to be utterly useless, and annoyance that her poor daughters were going to lumbered with the stigma of an unemployed father. Oh yes, and then there was the maintenance ...

'Well, what the hell were you playing at, Robbie? You have two children to support! You have a mortgage to pay! And now you're unemployed!'

'I am.' Robbie nodded, letting her get on with it. What could he say in his defence? It was all true.

'You're so bloody useless, Robbie,' she half laughed, shaking her head. 'How are you going to pay anything towards the girls now? How are you going to keep a roof over their heads when they're with you? Oh, poor Fraser. You mess up and he'll have to pay for it, won't he? But I tell you this, Robbie, if you lose that house, you are not seeing the girls overnight, OK? I will not have them staying in some dodgy flat, you hear me? God, how am I supposed to tell the girls this? Fraser and I are trying to instil a decent work ethic into them and you go and lose your job. What does that teach them?'

Robbie sighed. 'I'll try to sort out this mess as quickly as possible,' he said. 'I just wanted to let you know because obviously I'll have problems with paying any maintenance for a bit.'

Heather sucked in her breath. 'Fine,' she said. 'No maintenance, no access. It's as simple as that. If you don't pay, you don't see the girls. Full stop.'

'You can't do this!' shouted Robbie, losing his cool. 'They're my daughters too.'

'Well, maybe you should have thought about that before you lost your bloody job, Robbie!' Heather had lost her cool now too and they were glaring at each other with utter contempt.

'Mum, what's going on?' asked Grace, appearing from the living room. 'Why are you shouting at Dad?'

'I lost my job, sweetheart,' said Robbie gently. 'Mum's just a wee bit cross with me.'

'Your father,' said Heather, trying to control herself but still shaking with anger, 'has let you down, girls. But he's going now so if you could just say goodbye to him, he'll be on his way. Won't you, Robbie.'

It wasn't a question. It was an order.

Ruby appeared next to Grace in the doorway.

Robbie ruffled her hair affectionately. 'It's all right, girls,' he said. 'Everything will be all right.'

Heather tried to pull the girls back from him, but Ruby screamed. 'I want Daddy!' she shouted. 'Let me see my daddy!'

Grace stood there, sobbing, gazing from one parent to the other in confusion.

Just then Fraser appeared at the door.

'What the hell is going on here?' he demanded. 'I think you should go, Robbie. I'm not sure what this is about but this is very unhealthy for the children.'

Ruby was hysterical now, arms flying, legs kicking, screaming that she wanted her dad. Grace looked on in horror with tears slipping down her cheeks. Robbie couldn't take it any more. He loved those girls more than life itself and he couldn't put them through this pain.

'I'll go,' he said, through the lump in his throat. 'Girls, I love you to pieces. Don't worry about anything. I'll see you both soon.'

Heather slammed the door in his face and he stood there for a moment, listening to his youngest daughter's screams, unable to hold her, or comfort her. It was torture. Worse than anything the Italian had put him through. Maybe he was useless and worthless and all those things Heather said he was. But he wasn't selfish. For those girls he would happily sacrifice his life. Hell, wasn't that what he'd just done! If only Heather knew what he'd given up for those kids.

Chapter Thirty-Eight

Three months later ...

Francesca watched the boys play in the neat little garden of her rented house in Antibes. Their Uncle Carlo was dressed as an oversized cowboy and was chasing the two little Indians around a palm tree with a plastic water pistol. Angelica was out of hospital for the afternoon and was perched happily on Christian's knee, eating chocolate eclairs and sipping tea. She was so much better than before; she'd put on a few pounds and the colour had returned to her cheeks, but there was still a long way to go. The poor girl still swore that her dad came to visit her in the dead of night.

Fatty was gone. His body still hadn't turned up but the police investigation seemed to have ground to a halt. The money had all gone too, of course. The serious fraud squad had had a field day on Fatty's books and pretty much everything had been seized now. Carlo had come up trumps. Not only had he sold *Pulling Power* to James Sanderson and saved Francesca's life, but he'd sold his apartment, his car and even his Rolex on eBay! She was so proud of her little brother. She smiled to herself as she remembered him bursting through the door of Dad's office, sending herself and Dubrovski flying as he did so, clutching a suitcase full of cash. She wasn't sure who'd been more relieved – Francesca, Carlo or Andrea Dubrovski, the world's most reluctant assassin. The only bullet fired had ended up in the ceiling.

Francesca had had to sell the estate in Valbonne, of course. And the yacht. She'd got rid of the nanny and when the school holidays were over, she'd be doing the school run herself. The boys were going to go to the local school. She couldn't afford private education any more. She'd been pleasantly surprised at how resilient the children had been to all the changes. They seemed happy enough. Sometimes they asked if Daddy was coming home but Francesca always told them, no, and they seemed to accept it. William had never been a very hands-on father, so there was little for his sons to miss.

William had vanished into thin air. Francesca felt sure he was still sunning himself on some Caribbean island, living off stolen LaFata funds, while she and the children sold everything they owned just to make ends meet. But he was welcome to the money. He had spent his entire adult life dealing with the stuff, but she doubted he would find happiness in a fat wad of cash. If Francesca had learned anything this year, it was that money meant nothing in the grand scheme of things. Love was what mattered. She watched her family enjoying the hot August afternoon and smiled to herself. She was almost content. If it wasn't for Robbie ...

Oh God, she wished she could stop thinking about him. Every time her phone beeped with a text message, her heart skipped a beat, and she'd wonder, for a split second, if it was him, finally getting in touch. It never was, but she still hadn't quite given up hope. She hadn't had the heart to delete all his texts. She lay in bed some nights and just read and reread them until the tears streamed down her cheeks and her heart ached with longing. Even three months later it still felt so raw – and so wrong! It had been the beginning of something special, not the end. What had happened to him? Why did he desert her like that? Francesca wondered if she'd ever know.

Robbie stared at the nicotine-stained wallpaper peeling off the wall above the TV. It was shiny and textured, with brown and orange swirls on it, and it had been peeling since he'd sat on the exact same settee, twenty-five years ago, watching *Grange Hill*. His mum sat in her favourite chair, stuffing her face with custard creams, glued to *Deal or No Deal*. She was seriously overweight these days and her emphysema was awful. Robbie had found himself being more of a home help than a lodger since he'd moved back in, always doing the dishes and nipping out to buy her more fags. It was a miserable existence.

He'd had to rent out the house. He couldn't afford the mortgage now he was jobless and there was no point in trying to sell it with the property market being so weak. A new family had moved in. Husband, wife, two cute little kids. He hoped they'd be happy there. Happier than he had been.

His lawyer told him he would get better access once he had a place of his own for them to stay. There was no room in his mum's tiny flat and that hovel was no place for the girls anyway. Heather had grudgingly agreed to let him see them after school every Tuesday and every second Sunday. But he had to have them home by six. The absence of their presence was killing him.

Robbie still paid as much maintenance as he could from the odd pieces of freelance writing he was doing, but it wasn't much. His heart wasn't in the job any more. He'd turned down a job on a London tabloid last week. How could he move down south? He missed the girls like crazy as it was and he was only on the other side of town.

He missed Fran too. He missed her so much that he had imaginary conversations with her in his head. She sneaked into his dreams every night. He spent hours on the internet just looking at pictures of her and remembering how it had felt to have her lying in his arms. He'd been so close to texting her a thousand times but he'd always stopped himself. He couldn't put his kids in danger for anything. Even Francesca.

Francesca dropped Angelica back at the hospital with Christian and then drove up the hill to Le Grand Blue with a heavy heart. The faded blue paint that she'd always loved so much suddenly looked very old and worn. The house was a sad, lonely place these days. Its vast rooms were empty, the antiques and furniture all gone, the servants paid off and the cars sold, all except for the Aston Martin, Dad's favourite. That was staying with the house for the new owners to enjoy. The garden was overgrown and neglected. The grass had died during the hot Riviera summer and brambles had started to overrun the rhododendrons.

Fatty had been declared bankrupt in his absence and the house had been repossessed. Tomorrow the new owners would move in. Francesca had no desire to go back to her old home. She hadn't been for weeks, since she'd packed the last of the children's toys and relocated to Antibes. Le Grand Bleu was full of bad memories now. But she had no choice. There were a few bits and pieces she needed to collect before she closed the heavy front door for the last time.

The rooms echoed in their emptiness, floorboards creaked and doors squeaked. Francesca had never realised how huge the place was until now, as she stood alone in the hall of the empty mansion, listening to the house groan. She shuddered. It was boiling outside but the house was deathly cold and devoid of any sign of life.

Right, she would do this as quickly and painlessly as possible. She picked up the cardboard box she'd brought with her and walked into the drawing room. She started wrapping old photographs in newspaper and packing them carefully away. There was a creak above her head. She shivered. God, this house was creepy. Why had she never noticed it before? She carried on wrapping china ornaments and gold carriage clocks. Suddenly, there was a bang from upstairs. Francesca jumped and almost dropped the clock.

She was getting paranoid. Freaking herself out. Stop being so stupid, she told herself. Le Grand Bleu is not haunted. Then she heard a shutter crash against a window and another bang. And yes, those were footsteps, heavy footsteps on the stairs. Francesca's heart was thumping in her chest now. She grabbed the iron poker from the fireplace and tiptoed to the door. The footsteps had descended the stairs and the noises seemed to be coming from the kitchen now, at the back of the house.

She walked silently through the hall towards the kitchen. She stood behind the closed door for a moment, taking deep breaths, trying to summon up her courage, and then she threw the door open and shouted, 'What do you want? This is private property!'

He stood frozen to the spot, with the back door knob in his hand, poised to make his escape, but caught in the act. He looked shocked at first, but then his face broke into a warm grin and he held out his hands and said, 'Frankie, my *bambino*. You look so well. Have you missed me?'

'Dad,' murmured Francesca, dropping the poker on the floor. 'You're alive.'

Francesca had considered every possibility – she'd imagined suicide, an accident and even murder – but she had never, for one moment, expected her dad to turn up alive, and larger than life, in the kitchen. She stared at him, open-mouthed, in silence for a few moments. He looked exactly the same as he had the last time she'd seen him, a little more dishevelled than normal, maybe, but otherwise he was just the same old Fatty in his beige chinos and smart white shirt, huge beer gut hanging over his waistband, radiant smile on his rubbery face.

She didn't know what to do or how to behave. Christ, she didn't even know what to feel. She was shocked. Shocked to her very core. And she was shivering and trembling now in her thin summer dress. Francesca had never known the true meaning of 'torn' before. Half of her was so relieved to see him alive that she wanted to run to him, hug him tight and never let go, but the other half wanted to pick up the poker from the floor and smash him over the head with it, she was so angry that he'd put them all through this. Three months of heartache and misery, police investigations, press intrusion, not to mention bankruptcy, Jade's death and Angelica's breakdown.

Her dad took the decision out of her hands. He waddled over to her, smiling lopsidedly, shrugging his big shoulders and saying, 'Frankie, I am so sorry I didn't say goodbye.' And then his huge arms were enveloping her and he was holding her tight and she was sobbing into his vast chest, breathing in the familiar smell of his cologne, mixed with brandy and the faintest whiff of Cuban cigars. She stayed there, safe in his arms, for a long, long time, letting go of all those weeks of grief, letting him kiss her hair and whisper apologies in her ear.

'Daddy,' she sobbed. 'Where have you been? We thought you were dead.'

Fatty shrugged again.

'I have been watching over you, Frankie. Do not worry. I was not going to let anything bad happen to my *bambino*.'

Nothing bad happen?! The events of the past few months flashed through Francesca's mind like a movie on fast-forward. The day he'd gone missing, Dubrovski, William's disappearance, Angelica's overdose, Robbie ... And the anger rose and the unanswered questions thundered in her head. She pushed him away with all her might and started pummelling his chest with her fists, still sobbing hysterically.

'Why, Dad?' she demanded over and over again. 'Why? Why? Why?'

He took hold of her hands firmly and held her until her anger subsided and all she was left with was the question.

'Why, Daddy?' she sobbed.

'I will tell you the story, *bambino*,' he said. 'Just like I did when you was a little girl, yes? A friend of mine, he collected me from *Vigorosa* in a little dinghy. It was very easy.' He shrugged as if it was no big deal. 'I untied her from her mooring, waited for her to drift out into the harbour a little, and then called him to pick me up. Then I toss my phone in the water, leave two glasses by the brandy and, *voilà*! A mystery!'

'But why did you do this to us? How could you?' Francesca implored.

'Sit down, *bambino*,' he said gently, pulling out a kitchen chair. She collapsed onto it and he sat down heavily beside her with his enormous backside spilling over the seat.

'As I explained to Angel ...' he began.

'Oh Jesus Christ! So you have been visiting her?'

Francesca raged. 'We had her sectioned because we thought she was delusional! Have you any idea of the damage you've caused?'

'Shhh,' he soothed her. 'I know it is hard for you to understand but I had no choice, Frankie.'

'You always have choices, Dad,' she snapped. 'What were you avoiding? Jail?'

Fatty shrugged again. 'Jail, certainly, some of my business deals had been a bit, how you say it? Um, colourful.'

'Colourful?' Francesca scoffed. 'Well, that's one way of describing fraud, embezzlement, money laundering and theft, I suppose …'

'Tsk, tsk, Frankie, I am not a thief. I just do not always play by the rules,' he replied. 'But it was not the police I was running from.'

'Who? Dubrovski?' Francesca asked. 'Nice friends you keep. I've met him. He held a gun to my head and would have shot me if Carlo hadn't arrived.'

'I know, I know,' said her father patiently. 'I have been keeping the, erm, tabs on you *bambinos*. But Dubrovski is a pussycat, underneath. He would never have had the nerve to kill you. He has a soft spot for the beautiful women, you know. Ha, ha, ha. It is his weakness. So, no. I did not run from Andrea Dubrovski.'

'Then who?' Francesca demanded. 'What was so serious that you had to abandon your family?'

Fatty gave her the same condescending look he'd given her in the office that day back in May. 'Frankie, my beautiful Frankie,' he began. '*Si è ancora ingenuo …*'

'Yeah, yeah.' Francesca rolled her eyes. 'I'm still naive. Well, maybe I was a few months ago but I'm certainly not any more. I know exactly what you've been up to, Dad. You're just a crook. A two-bit crook.'

Her father laughed at some private joke she wasn't in on and shook his head. 'No, Frankie. I am not just a two-bit crook. I am better, and I am worse, than you could ever imagine.'

'I don't doubt it,' she said despondently. 'So who? Why?'

'Everyone and no one.' He continued to talk in riddles. 'I ran away and ran to.'

'Ran to what?' Frankie was in no mood for his silly word games.

He shrugged again. 'The future, the past. Things had gone wrong. Our world was not good, Frankie. It had been built on sand and it was slipping into the sea. It was time for you and your sister and brother to stand on your own two feet. You are better off now without the money. You do it for yourselves now. You do it without me.'

'Without you …?' Francesca echoed his words. 'So you're going away again.'

She stared at his face. It was so familiar to her and yet she did not understand this man at all. How could he claim to have loved them and yet have been so cruel? And now he would leave her again. Francesca didn't know whether to feel relieved or bereaved. Did she hate him or love him? The answer was simple. Both. He might as well have taken a kitchen knife and sliced her heart in two. He was the angel and the devil that Angelica always talked about. He was both rolled into one very dangerous man.

Her dad clasped her hand in his huge palm. She sat there, frozen to the spot, wanting to pull her hand from his but unable to move. 'I should never have come back. I wanted to say goodbye to this house. I have watched you, my angels, and I have been proud. But this time I will go for good.'

Francesca nodded solemnly.

'Of course you will,' she said, finally finding the will to

pull away her hand. 'You're a coward, Dad. Nothing but a big, fat, lying, cheating coward. You do all this …' She swept her hand around the empty house. 'You destroy everything. You almost destroy your own children and then you run away, too scared to face the music.'

'I am not scared,' chortled Fatty. 'Nothing scares me.'

She wanted to wipe the smug grin off his face. Underneath it all he was scared. Not of the police, or Dubrovski, or any of the other low-lifes he'd done 'business' with. But he was scared of getting close to people. Even his own children. Especially his own children. He was scared of love. Francesca almost felt pity for him. What the hell would he have now? His life, yes. But what was a life without love? What was the bloody point? Maybe it was for the best if he left again. She knew he was alive and that was enough. The relationship was too damaged to survive but the knowledge that her father was living and breathing, somewhere, was still a comfort to her. He obviously didn't give a damn about her but Francesca still cared about him. Despite herself. He was still her father, whatever sins he'd committed. And now he would ask for her help.

'You need me to lie for you, don't you?' she asked.

He nodded and stared straight into her eyes, imploring her to do as he asked.

'Tell no one you have seen me. Not even Carlo,' he said. There was a trace of menace in his voice.

'Carlo has been brilliant.' Francesca defended her brother. 'You can trust him.'

'I know this,' Fatty sighed. 'I am proud of how my boy has grown to be a man but he must not know I am alive. No one must. You must convince Angelica she was imagining things. She is stronger now but she will believe you, Frankie, in time.'

Frankie shook her head. 'I don't like this, Dad,' she said. 'There have been too many lies. You, the business, Jade and William ...'

'Hmph.' Fatty banged his fist angrily on the table top. 'Well, they were scum. We not need to worry about them any more.'

Francesca eyed her father warily. There was something in the angry tilt of his head and the defiant glint in his eye that made her skin crawl.

'Did you kill Jade?' she asked him, dreading the answer, but needing to know the truth.

'Perhaps a friend of mine may have helped her to make the decision to jump,' he said dispassionately.

Francesca nodded. Suddenly all her worst nightmares were coming true. She felt as if she might be sick. Bile filled her mouth. Her father repulsed her.

'And Darcie?' she asked, her voice beginning to break. Francesca had adored Darcie. They'd been close.

Fatty banged his fist harder this time. 'I will not talk about Darcie!' he boomed. 'It is too painful. The woman broke my heart. She had to pay.'

'What? With her life?' Francesca had begun to cry now. Who was this monster sitting next to her? He wasn't the father she'd always loved and admired. He was a criminal, a murderer.

'It is the ultimate price for us all,' said her father, quietly now.

'I hate you, Daddy!' screamed Francesca, standing up. She picked up her chair and held it, legs towards her father, half protecting herself, half threatening him. She didn't know what to do or where to turn. Fight or flight. Part of her wanted to run out of the kitchen door, out into the light, away from this dark-hearted monster. But Francesca needed more answers. She couldn't leave now.

'Put the chair down, you silly girl,' said Fatty impatiently, as if scolding a petulant toddler.

'No!' she shouted. 'I don't trust you. You killed Darcie. She was my friend.'

'She was a whore,' scoffed Fatty. 'I told you. She had to pay.'

'And what about William?' demanded Francesca. 'Did you make him pay too, Dad?'

Fatty's face broke into a satisfied smile. 'William,' he said. 'William is sleeping with fishes now.'

Francesca's heart fell with a thud into the pit of her stomach. She hated William for what he had done but he should have gone to jail, not to a watery grave.

'He was your grandchildren's father!' Francesca wailed. 'Dad, what have you done? Who are you? I don't know you at all!'

She thrust the chair towards him again, so that the legs jabbed him in the chest. She wanted to hurt him, to make him feel the pain she was going through. But that was what he did. Resorted to violence. And she was better than that. Francesca threw the chair across the room. Her whole body shook. He tried to catch her hand but she snatched it away.

'I wish you were dead, Dad,' she told him and she meant it with a passion. 'You don't deserve to be alive.'

'Oh, you think I am a bad father?' he asked, arrogantly. 'I do not think so. I have given you children everything.'

'Yes, and now you've taken it all away,' she screamed at him. 'Left us with nothing.'

'Oh, poor *bambinos*,' he scoffed sarcastically. 'Poor little rich kids, not so rich any more. Do you think I had any money as a child? Do you think my useless father gave me one cent?'

'I'm sure he didn't mess you up as much as ours has!' she yelled. 'I bet your dad didn't play with people's lives, destroy them, I bet he didn't kill anyone who got in the way.'

'No,' said Fatty defiantly. 'I killed him when he got in my way. It was the best thing I ever did.'

Francesca stood gawping at her father. Had she heard him right? He killed his own father?

The words washed over her like acid, burning and eating away at her very soul. She crumpled to the floor.

'Just go, Dad,' she whimpered, broken now. 'Just go. Disappear. For good this time. You are dead to me anyway. You might as well be drowned.'

'OK, Frankie,' he sighed, gazing down at her and shaking his head sadly. 'I do love you. I love all of you. But you must stand on your own feet now.'

Francesca couldn't speak, she couldn't get up, she couldn't move, so she just nodded her head and pointed to the back door. Her dad took a step forward with his arms outstretched, offering to help her to her feet, but she shook her head. She didn't want his help any more.

'Don't touch me, Dad,' she said.

He patted her head fondly and turned to go. He paused at the back door and said, 'One last thing, Frankie, my *bambino*. Do not do as I do, do as I say, OK? Honour your father. Keep our secrets to the grave. Stay true to me, despite what I have done. That is all I ask.'

She stared at him with love, hatred, pity, anger, bitterness and shame. But she did not agree to his request. Francesca had no idea yet what she would do.

'Where are you going?' she asked him.

'That is my business, Frankie. You will not see me again but I will think of you all, often.'

'That's big of you,' she muttered as she watched her father disappear out of the back door.

Francesca lay on the kitchen floor, hugging her knees to her chest, and tried to make sense of what he'd told her. Jade, Darcie, William, his own father for Christ's sake! How many others? She could have lived with the knowledge that her father was a crook, but a murderer? No. She heard the engine of the Aston Martin start to purr and then it roared off down the drive. She thought about Darcie, pregnant and scared, being forced to take tablets that would kill her. What sort of monster would do that? But he was her father ...

Her mind raced, backwards and forwards. What should she do? He'd been gone how long? A minute? Two? There was no time to waste. He'd be on his way to Italy, soon he would cross the border with friends to help on the other side. Why the hell should he run from this mess scot-free? She thought about the chaos Fatty had left in his wake. Do not do as I do, do as I say. Francesca mulled over her dad's catchphrase until suddenly it hit her. She would defy him. Finally, she would stand up to him. She would do exactly as he had done. She would destroy her own father, as he had destroyed his. But Francesca would do it her way.

She stood up on wobbling legs, took her phone out of her bag with shaking hands and dialled the number. As she made the call, she ran to her car.

'Stay where you are,' ordered the voice on the end of the line. But Francesca was in no mood to take orders.

There was a gardener trimming a hedge on the road outside.

'Which way did the Aston Martin go?' she shouted out of the window.

The man pointed to his right, towards town. So not towards Italy then, mused Francesca. She floored her car down the hill, swerving past tourists and pensioners and hell, even children! As she flew down towards the harbour, she caught a glimpse of him, already climbing the hill on his way out of town. Francesca's hands gripped the steering wheel so tightly that her knuckles had turned white. She was gaining on him now. He was stuck behind a bus bound for Nice, heavily laden with tourists, crawling slowly up the hill. She could see the Aston Martin, bobbing and weaving, pulling out, trying to overtake, having to pull back in behind the bus every time a car came the other way. With every car she overtook, Francesca was a few metres closer. He must have clocked her in his rear-view mirror by now. She wondered what he was thinking. She had defied him. He would be angry. But she suspected he would also be proud.

Francesca got to within three cars of her father before he managed to overtake the bus. And then he was gone, in a cloud of dust and a roar of powerful engine. But Francesca wasn't about to give up. She knew her father and she knew his favourite route. Hadn't she driven it with him a hundred times? As she sped past the bus towards the exit for the Grand Corniche, Francesca heard sirens behind her. She wondered if she was being chased for speeding or whether the police were after her father. It didn't matter. She wouldn't stop for them. Francesca had to see this scene through to the end. She couldn't just let him disappear out of her life for a second time. Not without a fight. This time she wanted to watch him go.

But her Range Rover was no match for the Aston Martin and as she sped up the Grand Corniche, winding her way out of Monaco, she lost sight of him completely. Damn him! Damn him to hell and back again. Her phone kept ringing, over and over, but she ignored it. It would be the police telling her to stop. They had ordered her to stay at the house and they would not be happy at her decision to chase Fatty herself. But Francesca didn't care. All she could see was the road ahead, all she could feel was the adrenalin pumping through her veins. She didn't even know why she was chasing him, or what she hoped to achieve if she did manage to catch him up and stop him somehow. All she knew was that she wouldn't be her father's victim any more. She was in charge of her own destiny. Doing something was always better than doing nothing. She knew that now.

It was early evening and Francesca was driving straight into the lowering sun. Every time she turned a sharp corner, she was blinded by the light, and several times she scared herself by almost losing control. She hadn't seen the Aston Martin for kilometres now. What if Fatty had second-guessed her and taken a different route? Francesca turned sharply down the road that would lead her towards the Moyenne Corniche, hoping that she might catch sight of her father's car as she did so. But all she could see was open road, blue sky, and a black cloud rising from below.

Francesca was so hell-bent on catching her father that she didn't think anything of the black cloud at first. It was just there in the distance, perhaps a kilometre or two ahead of her, and it was rising and spreading, higher and higher, dirtying the brilliant blue sky. But as she got closer she began to smell the burning and the blood drained from her face. Oh no, please no, not now, not like this, no …

The black tyre marks were so clear on the road that they looked as if they'd been painted on. Francesca pulled the Range Rover to the side and parked up, her hands shaking, her breath shallow in her chest. She followed the tracks on foot until they reached the edge of the road. She stroked the crumpled metal of the crash barrier where it had been broken in two, and she breathed in the toxic fumes of the fire below. And then she stood on the edge of the cliff, took a deep breath and looked down.

There was nothing left of the Aston Martin. All she could see were broken cypress trees, smashed by the falling car, deep scars in the cliff face where the vehicle must have hit, one stray tyre was caught in a gorse bush, and there, at the bottom, in the middle of a raging orange fire, was a tangled mess of metal that had once been her father's pride and joy.

Francesca's hands covered her mouth in horror. This time he had really gone. She could hear the police cars' sirens getting close and they eclipsed the sound of her screams. 'Daddy! Daddy! Daddy!' But Francesca knew that Fatty was never coming back this time.

Countdown was on. His mum was glued to the box but Robbie was bored, he couldn't get comfy and he couldn't concentrate.

'Och, for goodness sake, Robbie, will ye stop that fidgeting. Yer putting me off ma programme, son. If you want something to do, make me a cuppa tea, ma mooth's drier than a popcorn fart.'

His mum had always been queen of the crude simile. Maybe that's where he'd got his love of words from.

Robbie got up from his sofa prison. He'd seen enough daytime TV to last him a lifetime so even making his mum a cuppa was something of a reprieve. He waited for the kettle to boil, standing in the tatty little kitchenette, staring out of the seventh-floor window, over the car park, to the rundown shopping centre beyond. Rain trickled down the windows and the sky was the colour of mushroom soup. It was August but it had been a poor excuse for a summer. He remembered his favourite Billy Connolly quote: 'There are two seasons in Scotland – June and winter.' It made him smile, briefly. But then he imagined the colour of the sky in Monaco, where *she* was. He thought about Fran under that brilliant azure sky.

When his phone rang it was the biggest excitement of his day. Dan Donovan. Robbie hadn't heard from his friend in weeks. Well, he couldn't blame Dan. Robbie wasn't exactly on the scene any more and he wasn't very good company anyway. Even Robbie wouldn't want to meet Robbie for a drink these days. The doctor had suggested antidepressants, but Robbie wasn't depressed. He was heartbroken. And there was only one cure for that.

'Rob the Throb,' said Dan. His voice brimmed with excitement. 'Have I got news for you!'

'Good to hear from you, Dan,' said Robbie. And he meant it. He'd been detached from the outside world for way too long. 'What's going on?'

'Fatty LaFata's dead,' said Dan.

Robbie was confused.

'Um, yeah, we know that, Dan. He drowned three months ago.'

'Nope,' said Dan triumphantly. 'He died a couple of hours ago in a car crash.'

'What?' Robbie scratched his head. 'What are you going on about, Dan?'

'The sneaky bastard never drowned at all. He staged his own disappearance. Then he turned up at that mansion of his this afternoon and got caught by Francesca LaFata ...'

Robbie had to catch his breath at the mention of her name. He said it to himself in his head all the time but hearing it spoken, out loud by someone else, suddenly made her very real again.

'You're kidding me!' said Robbie.

'No, I swear, it's true. I just had it confirmed by my contact out there. Francesca turned her old man in, called the cops. Then she chased him herself. She was first on the scene.'

'Is she OK?' asked Robbie a little desperately.

But Dan didn't seem to notice his panic.

'Aye, she's fine. She must be getting used to her dad dying by now, eh?' Dan chortled to himself.

'Brave girl,' said Robbie.

'Anyway, Fatty was in a vintage Aston Martin, Francesca and the police were on his tail, he led them on a wild goose chase all over the fucking Riviera. I mean, can you imagine? It's proper James Bond stuff this. The chase went on for over an hour and they ended up on that stretch between the Grande Corniche and Moyenne Corniche, you know, where Grace Kelly died?'

Robbie remembered driving down the exact same road as he'd gone to meet Fran for their first date. He'd been doing his wannabe Formula One driver thing. The road was steep and winding and full of treacherous hairpin bends and Robbie had had a few hairy moments on it. He imagined Fatty in his Aston Martin with Fran and the cops on his tail and he knew what was coming next.

'And then Fatty misjudged a corner and went straight over the edge,' announced Dan with a flourish. 'The car fell three hundred metres, bouncing off cliffs, breaking up, and then finally ended up on fire in an olive grove. By the time the police got to the wreckage it was burned to a crisp. Nothing left of the Aston Martin but a gnarled lump of tin and nothing left of Fatty but a smouldering pile of bones.'

'Jesus!' Robbie couldn't think of anything to say. He could barely take in what he'd heard. 'So he's definitely dead this time?'

'Och, don't be daft, Robbie,' scoffed Dan. 'You don't fall three hundred metres in a burning car and walk out alive, do you?'

Chapter Thirty-Nine

It had taken a month for the police to finally release the body, but today they'd got rid of the old bastard at last. They'd buried Fatty. Or at least they'd buried the handful of bones and ashes that Fatty had become after the car wreck. Well, goodbye to bad rubbish. Carlo swigged his Jack Daniel's and watched the mourners make polite chit-chat in this opulent lounge of the Hotel de Paris. They were a bunch of fakers, the lot of them. Most of them barely knew his dad, they were just here for the excitement. They wanted to be part of the LaFata scandal so that they could tell their grandkids that they'd been there when Giancarlo LaFata finally went to ground. It gave them a buzz. And they wanted to get their faces in the papers tomorrow too. Well, let them have their five minutes of fame. Carlo didn't care. He just wanted it all to be over.

He walked outside to the terrace, sat down facing the ocean, and turned his back on the wake inside. It was a farce, he wanted nothing more to do with it. He lit a cigarette and glared at the perfect turquoise sea on the horizon. He was sick of Monte Carlo. It glittered but it sure as hell wasn't gold. Fool's gold, more like. It was a pathetic sham of a place and he wanted out.

Somebody slammed a matching tumbler of Jack Daniel's down beside his own.

'Mind if I join you?' she asked.

He recognised her voice. He hadn't heard it in months but he heard it all the time in his dreams.

'Sasha Constantine, what the hell are you doing here?' he grinned at the sexy brunette straddling the chair beside him.

'Oh, I dunno, Carlo baby,' she drawled. 'Thought maybe you might wanna see a friendly face today.'

'You look good,' he said, taking in her tanned, toned curves. 'The Hamptons obviously suit you.'

'Well, you look miserable,' she replied. 'But I guess you just need to get laid.'

Carlo grinned. It was the first time he'd felt genuinely happy for months.

'Is that an offer?' he asked.

'That's a demand,' she confirmed, holding up her glass.

'Cheers,' said Carlo, as he clinked her glass against his. 'What are we toasting?'

Sasha shrugged. 'Multiple orgasms?' she suggested.

'To multiple orgasms,' laughed Carlo.

She grinned at him and her green eyes twinkled. 'I missed you, Carlo baby,' she said.

And then she blushed. Sasha Constantine, the Queen of Cool, actually blushed!

'And I missed you too, you rude, obnoxious little—'

But he didn't get to finish his sentence; she had climbed onto his lap and now her soft lips were on his and her hands were on his chest and he was lost in the smell of oranges and vanilla.

She pulled away suddenly and said, 'Wait! I almost forgot. I've got something for you.'

She began rummaging in her clutch bag.

'What? A present?' asked Carlo, stroking her back and

gazing at her beautiful face as she concentrated on her search.

'Kind of,' she said. 'Ah ha! Found it.'

She brought out a tiny green card with hummingbirds printed on it.

'My card,' she announced. 'I think you'll find my phone number on the bottom right-hand corner.'

'You're giving me your number?' asked Carlo. 'Finally, you're giving me your number!'

'Carlo, baby,' she smiled. 'You had my number from the start.'

She kissed him, tenderly this time, with her green eyes open. She stared so hard that Carlo felt her bore into his very soul. She was all the woman he needed. He couldn't wait to wake up next to her in the morning, and the morning after that, and the morning after that ... Suddenly 'for ever' wasn't so scary.

Robbie's stomach churned as he watched the Mediterranean whizz by to his right. The cab sped along the coast road towards Monaco, towards her. Christ, he was nervous. They were both free now but would she still want him? They'd been through so much this summer. The world had changed for ever for both of them. The ground had shifted under their feet like an earthquake and they'd been left standing in the ruins of their lives. And they'd ended up a thousand miles apart.

The invitation had been sent to the office.

Only Fatty LaFata would have a funeral with official gold-embossed invitations. It looked more like a wedding invite. But then, Robbie supposed, the family probably felt more like celebrating than mourning, given the circumstances. He'd fingered the invitation, over and over, hoping, praying that it had been sent by Fran. Had she held out an olive branch? If she had, Robbie had grabbed it with both hands. But what if it wasn't from Fran? What if the Italian had sent it to lure him back and finish the job? Robbie knew he might be putting his life on the line. But even the faintest glimmer of hope that Fran still wanted him was enough. He needed her back in his life. And he wanted to be at her side. He couldn't imagine how hard this day would be for her. But with Fatty finally gone, it felt like a fresh start. If there was any chance of a future, he'd do anything to make it work – for his girls, for Frankie's kids, for him – and for Fran.

At least Patterson had given him his job back. After Fatty died – properly this time – Robbie had decided it was safe to publish his story. The big story. The one he'd nearly died for. He'd told his boss the whole gruesome tale and then he'd passed his findings on to the police in Monaco, Italy and Scotland. Giancarlo LaFata had been responsible for crimes all over the place. And then, finally, the whole world knew. All he'd been able to think about on the day it finally hit the front pages was whether Fran was reading it. And if she was, what did she think? And then the envelope had arrived at the office, addressed to him.

Patterson had agreed, grudgingly, to this last final trip to the Riviera, so that Robbie could write a follow-up article about the aftermath of LaFata's death. But he'd given him a measly expense account this time – hence the taxi from the airport and the budget hotel he was booked into in the seediest district of Nice. But he wasn't going to Monaco for work this afternoon. No. He was heading there with only one thing on his mind. Life or death? He wasn't sure.

The taxi dropped him off outside the Hotel de Paris – the place where it all began. Robbie smoothed down his suit and straightened his tie. The pavement outside the hotel was teeming with press but Robbie barged his way through and got to the front. A burly security guard put up his hand, but Robbie reached into his back pocket and took out the invitation. Who would be here to meet him? Robbie could barely catch his breath.

'I'm a guest,' he told the security guard.

The man nodded curtly and let him past. Robbie spotted Carlo LaFata first, sprawled on a chair on the terrace with a foxy little brunette on his lap. He had his tongue down the girl's throat and his hands up her skirt. Robbie smiled. Some people never changed. Even at his dad's funeral the international playboy was getting his rocks off. You had to give the guy credit. He had a great talent!

But Robbie wasn't jealous. He didn't want a string of women. He only wanted one. He took a deep breath and pushed open the door to the lounge. It was full of familiar faces – F1 drivers, actors, models, but thankfully no Italian! Robbie's eyes slid over the sea of celebrities and searched desperately for the one face he craved.

And then, suddenly, there she was, standing chatting to another woman, oblivious to his arrival. Was she even expecting him? He watched her tuck her hair behind her ear, chatting animatedly, her hands waving. The other woman was listening intently. Everyone wanted a piece of Francesca. She glanced mid-sentence in his direction. And then she did a double-take. She stood with her mouth still open, staring at him, while her friend looked on, confused. And then the loveliest smile broke over her face and she was waving at him, pushing her way through the crowds, half running in her high heels, with a grin on her face and a glint in those beautiful grey-blue eyes. She seemed oblivious to everyone else in the room as she ran right up to him and threw her arms round his neck. Robbie felt the warmth of her body, and her lips on his, and his head spun and his heart sang. He held her so tight that her feet lifted off the ground. He had no intention of ever letting those feet touch the ground again.

'Of all the gin joints in all the towns in all the world …' he said, when they finally stopped kissing.

'He has to walk into mine,' grinned Fran.

Epilogue

1st January 2010, Acapulco, Mexico

The two old men sit on the hillside overlooking the sea and watch the fireworks exploding over the city below.

'Happy New Year, my brother,' *says the taller, silver-haired man, holding up his glass of neat tequila.*

'Happy New Year, my dear brother,' *responds his cousin jovially, downing his shot in one and slamming his glass onto the table.*

The two are not really brothers, of course, but they are blood brothers. That bond was formed many years ago, many miles from Mexico.

'I still cannot get used to you without your dog collar,' *laughs the older cousin.*

'And I cannot get used to you so skinny!' *the younger cousin replies.* 'I did not recognise you at the airport. You look good, my brother. The Latino lovelies will be knocking down your door.'

'It is so good to be here at last,' *says the younger cousin, Gabriele Fontana.* 'I can't quite believe we've pulled it off.'

'You got a lot of money for the cross of Saint Nicasius. You did us proud, my brother. We can enjoy our retirement here now. We will grow old disgracefully together.'

The older cousin had done as he had promised all those years before. He had kept the relic safe until the right time arrived, and then he had returned it to Gabriele in Sicily. And Gabriele had known exactly where to take it, of course.

'*If you want to get money out of the church, it helps if one is a priest,*' grins Gabriele. '*They were very happy to see it in Rome.*'

'*You are an ex-priest now,*' his cousin reminds him. '*No oaths of celibacy required in Acapulco!*'

'*I never paid much attention to that particular oath anyway,*' laughs Gabriele. '*So, my friend, are you missing your family?*'

His cousin shrugs. '*Of course, a little, but I have my spies and I know that they are doing fine without me. It is for the best.*'

'*Your son?*' *asks Gabriele.*

'*He went travelling with his American girlfriend. They are working at an orphanage in Vietnam now. It will not make him rich but perhaps it will make him happy.*'

'*And your youngest?*'

'*Much better these days. She has a boyfriend. A nice, solid man.*'

'*And the eldest?*'

The older cousin smiles. He is most proud of his eldest child. She was always the good girl, but in the end she was the one who stood her ground. The strongest. She did not do as he said.

'*She has taken her own path. She is writing a book with the help of the journalist she is living with these days.*'

'*A book about you?*' *asks Gabriele.*

His cousin nods and grins. He likes the idea of being immortalised in a book.

The fireworks display below is coming to a spectacular crescendo. The sky is alight with a huge arc of multicoloured stars.

'*So a very Happy New Year to you, Gabriele!*' *the older cousin shouts over the bangs. He picks up two more shot glasses of tequila and hands one to his companion.*

'And a very Happy New Year to you too, Giancarlo,' he replies.

They clink their glasses together and knock back their drinks. They have stopped running now. Finally, after all these years. They have stopped running but they will have to hide for ever.

'I have one final question, Giancarlo,' muses Gabriele. 'Who did they bury at your funeral? Whose bones were in the coffin? I did so wonder as I watched them lay you to rest.'

Giancarlo chuckles, and pours his cousin another drink. 'It was Stephano.'

'Stephano?' Gabriele asks. 'I do not remember a Stephano.'

'The boy with the scar,' Giancarlo replies. 'The good-looking one. He had got too big for his boots. He knew too much and he was becoming boastful.'

'And as we know, my friend,' Gabriele muses, 'pride comes before a fall.'

'A three-hundred-metre fall, in this case,' laughs Giancarlo. 'Ah, but he was a good boy, loyal to the end.'

'Well then, let us toast to Stephano,' says Gabriele, still in excellent spirits.

'Stephano,' says Giancarlo LaFata jovially, raising his glass once more. 'May he rest in peace.'